JULIAN STOCKWIN is a bestselling author of historical action-adventure. He has written eighteen books to date in the Kydd series, as well as his non-fiction title, *Stockwin's Maritime Miscellany*. At the age of fourteen Julian was sent to *Indefatigable*, a tough sea-training school and a year later he joined the Royal Navy. He now writes full-time and lives in Plymouth with his wife Kathy.

julianstockwin.com
@julianstockwin

By Julian Stockwin

The Silk Tree
The Powder of Death

THE POWDER OF DEATH

JULIAN STOCKWIN

Allison & Busby Limited
12 Fitzroy Mews
London W1T 6DW
allisonandbusby.com

First published in Great Britain by Allison & Busby in 2016.
This paperback edition published by Allison & Busby in 2017.

All characters and events in this publication, other than those clearly in the public domain, are fictitious and any resemblance to actual persons, living or dead, is purely coincidental.

A CIP catalogue record for this book is available from the British Library.

10 9 8 7 6 5 4 3 2 1

ISBN 978-0-7490-2084-2

Typeset in 10.5/15.5 pt Adobe Garamond Pro by Allison & Busby Ltd.

The paper used for this Allison & Busby publication has been produced from trees that have been legally sourced from well-managed and credibly certified forests.

Printed and bound by
CPI Group (UK) Ltd, Croydon, CR0 4YY

In memory of my father
Austin E. Stockwin
Officer of the Royal Regiment of Artillery

And alsua wondyr for to se
. . . Crakys war, off wer
That thai befor herd neuir er
– *The Bruce, Booke XIX*

(*And also wondrous for to see
Crakys of war, off Wear
They'd never heard before*)

DRAMATIS PERSONAE

Aylward, Thomas	lawyer
Bacon, Roger	Franciscan friar and scholar
Baldovino of Pisa	smith
Barnwell, Rosamunde	widow, later married to Jared
Beavis, Aldith	Jared's wife
Beppe	manservant
Blacktooth, Sweyn	baker
Blundel, Margery	wife of miller's gristman
Braccio	signore of Perugia
Bury, John	King's treasurer
Capuletti, Giacomo	representative of merchants and guilds
Cesarino	translator
Comber, Hugh	freeman
Corso Ezzelino	Italian nobleman
D'Amory, Everard	baron of Castle Ravenstock

D'Amory, Gervaise	baron's son
David aka Daw	Jared's son
De Beaujeu, Guillaume	Templar Grand Master
De Clermont, Matthew	marshal
De Grandison, Otho	knight
De Villiers, Jean	Grand Master, Hospitallers
Despenser	English baron
Di Campaldino, Umberto	captain, podesta
Di Ferrara, Giannina (Nina)	housekeeper
Dickin of Shrewsbury	pilgrim
Dunning, Will	miller's son
Edward II	English king
Edward III	English king
Edward of Lincoln	church official
Farnese, Bartolomeo	early member of Guild of St Barbara
Father Bertrand	priest
Fivepot, Jankin and Reginald	friends of Perkyn
Frauncey, John	bailiff's clerk
Gayne, Nicholas	knight
Godefroy, Hugh	seneschal armourer
Godswein	friend of Perkyn
Gosse, John	smith

Harpe	Master of the Horse
Hilmi, Köse	quartermaster
Hugh Gamel of York	blacksmith
Jared of Hurnwych	blacksmith
Kadrİye	Jared's concubine
Kettle, William	quartermaster and armourer
Le Warde, Robert	lord of the manor
Longface, Wagge	pedlar
Malatesta, Guido	signore, Arezzo
Marco of Florence	early member of Guild of St Barbara
Maud	Jared's mother
Old Turvey	franklin of Hurnwych
Old Yarwell	franklin
Oliver aka Nolly	carpenter
Osbert	partner in smithy
Peppin, Edward	mercenary
Perkyn	villein
Rawlin, William	agent of House of Barnwell
Sforza, Domenico	agent
Sharpeye, Watkyn	archer, veteran crusader
Streuvel	early member of Guild of St Barbara
Subsey, Hubert	reeve

Van Vullaere, Peter	early member of Guild of St Barbara
Villani, Lucia	Italian noblewoman
Villani, Ruggieri	Italian nobleman
Wang, Chu-li	Chinese gunner
Wilkie	friend of Perkyn
Will	butcher
William of Cafran	ambassador
William of Rubruck	Franciscan monk

CHAPTER 1

Oxford, England. Yuletide, AD 1261,
the forty-sixth year of the reign of King Henry III

The low fire sputtered, its warmth contracting even further in the gloom of the sparsely furnished room. The friar working by a single candle at his high desk looked up in vexation at the sounds of unrestrained revelry floating across the river. He could do nothing – creation at the nib of the pen was won only as the mind soared free of the dross of worldly existence and the common folk could not be expected to realise that their merrymaking was clawing it back to earth.

Roger Bacon's writings had brought him respect and repute from across Christendom as well as criticism and dangerous enemies. His questing intellect had taken him down strange paths, leading him to the unshakeable belief that the mind of God could be revealed in his works of nature rather than the opinions of man. As a university schoolman he taught that the pursuit of philosophical knowledge was the high road to understanding; his sturdy principle, to accept only that which had been amply demonstrated before proceeding further.

A protracted burst of jollity cut through his thoughts again.

Outside, a virginal carpet of snow lay over all, softening the outlines of town squalor. In charity he'd sent his serving boy away to join the merriment, but not before a stern homily on the temptations of the flesh. He was alone, in the upper floor of his eyrie with a dying fire for company.

Drawing his homespun robe closer Bacon got up to attend to the embers, so much poorer than the crackling splendour of the yule log on the opposite bank. The last mummers had finished their show and with Gog and Magog justly slain they were claiming their due in raucous style, careless shrieks of women mingling with jovial roars and laughter. He hesitated – was this not a thing of exemplary wonder, that as a portion of brightness and life against the blackness and unknowns of an evil world, it stood for God's grace infilling the impure darkness of one's soul? Perhaps.

He poked at the fire and was rewarded with a momentary blaze. He added a small log then went back to his desk.

But as he lifted his quill there was a sudden knocking at the door below.

There was no one else now in this little building straddling the roadway over a bridge. Who could it be? He had no fear of robbers for the Franciscan mendicant order abjured wealth and display, but his books and instruments were worth far more to him than tawdry adornments.

Should he answer the door? The sound had been too robust for a drunken well-wisher and seemed to indicate that this was a visitor who knew he was in.

He took the candle, descended the stairs and stood at the closed door.

'Who is there?' he called.

There was no reply. The peephole showed only a vague shape against the white luminosity of the snow.

He slid the bar up and the door creaked loudly as he opened

it to reveal the figure of a large man in a cloak with a curiously pointed hood hiding his face.

'What is your business, my son?'

'Then you do not know me, holy brother.'

Bacon recognised the deep voice. 'Why, by God's sweet passion – it's Brother William!'

The hood was flung back and there was his friend, the high-placed Flemish Franciscan, William of Rubruck.

'Do I see you well, dear Roger?'

'You do! Yes, upon my soul, and the better for seeing you! Do come in, this cold would perish even the warmest heart.'

He closed the door as Rubruck shook the snow off and declared mysteriously, 'Which compared to where I've been fated to go is the merest breath of chill.'

'Oh? Well, you shall tell me of it – but only after I offer you a fine posset.' He found a pan in the deserted buttery along with milk, ale and nutmeg and they mounted the stairs to his study.

While Bacon busied himself heating the milk his visitor took off his cloak – dark and fur-lined, it was well worn and oddly fashioned with its pointed hood all one with it.

'It's been too long, my sage and worthy friend. Let me see, the last time – was it not Paris and the ever-rational Peter Peregrinus, or was it—?'

'Dear Brother, tonight I've come to you alone, to tell of my journeying.'

Something in his voice told Bacon that this was to be no mere recounting of a tale and his interest quickened. The travels of a wise man were always to be valued as a source of true knowledge of the world but he suspected there was more to it than that.

'I'm to be honoured, William. Please go on.'

Rubruck stared at the fire for long moments before he began. 'Know that His Grace King Louis of France has been much troubled by the grievous losses among the holy Crusaders at the hands of the Saracens and thought to take measures as would remedy this. In the year twenty-seven of his reign he dispatched an envoy to the very court of the chief of the Mongols beseeching an alliance against the Mohammedan.'

'Yes?'

'Brother Roger, I was the one who led this mission.'

'Ah. So you must travel into Asia, past Constantinople to the very lands of the Tartars.'

'An immense journey, years in the making.' With a distant look he went on, 'To the capital of the Great Khan Möngke, which is Karakorum, on the far side of the world. Across a vastness unimaginable, a grass desert without end – all summer, a bitter winter and the great heat again for leagues beyond counting.'

'Then you were granted sights of amazing wonder, which you know I'm with child to hear!'

'In good time I shall write at length of these, but for now you must be content with—'

'The monsters who inhabit the boreal realm, the sciapods of one foot – the anthropophagi feasting on human flesh. I've given little credence to such tales but . . . ?'

'None did I see, neither they nor the kingdom of Prester John, my curious friend. Yet I stood at the mount of the Ark of Noah and the Iron Gate of Alexander the Macedonian, but never a great city, for they are a restless people and think not to plant a village, still less a town.'

'May it be said that the Tartar in his home and hearth is nonetheless tutored, gentle in his manners?'

'They ceaselessly travel in a horde, eat millet and meat all but raw for lack of fuel, consuming the fermented milk of mares, to which they add blood. They live in transportable houses of felt, which they call "yurts", and their manners are . . . singular – they drink pot liquor and think nothing of doing their filthiness while talking together. And to revere their parents, they consume their dead flesh and drink from their very skull – in truth, a benighted folk.'

'I weep for your travails, dear William.'

'Do not, I pray you Brother, for is it not written in Ecclesiasticus, "He shall go through the land of foreign peoples, and shall try the good and evil in all things." A deep saying and one I held close to my heart as I progressed through these odious lands.'

'Then I must ask it – were you received at the court of the captain of the Tartars?'

'Which is the Khagan Möngke, who was most obliging. Be aware, Brother, that this is the chief of the peoples who have spread across the face of the earth like no other, whose word may set a host of ten thousand times ten thousand horsemen against any who challenge his will.'

Bacon blinked in wonder. 'This capital will therefore be rich and splendid beyond all conceiving.'

'Excepting stone turtles past counting and a wondrous tree crafted of lustrous silver I found it not much out of the ordinary.'

'Yet you did enter in upon the palace of the chief of the Mongols.'

Rubruck paused a moment in reflection, then answered, 'I did so, Brother.'

'And your mission – may it be said to have succeeded?'

'I laid before him a letter from King Louis, translated by my man Homo Dei. His answer – that if such a one together with

His Holiness the Pope should travel to do homage to himself, he promises good welcome. Naught else.'

'There can be no reasoning with those who are blind to the wider world, I'm persuaded. Yet you will have a higher work – the bringing of the knowledge of Christ's mercy to this horde!'

'As you say. But they are a strange and perturbing race of men. They worship Tengri, the sky god, and are never without their sorceries and idolatries. Superstition rules their lives – even the Great Khan does not eat until the soothsayers read the charred bones of sheep.'

'No heathen is entirely lost to God's grace.'

'You will be astonished to learn that I discovered Christians already in attendance at his court.'

'How can this be?'

'They are none but Nestorians with their vile heresies. Together with a species of shameless idol-worshippers and a coven of sly Saracens. It passed that Khagan Möngke professed himself curious at the claims of the different faiths and set us all to debating their merits with each other together before him.'

'Aha! A foolish pagan priest it is who wrangles with the Master of Rhetoric!'

'Would that it were so. My interpreter was a contemptible creature who I doubt gave true meaning to my words, and besides which I was constrained to ally with the Nestorians against the infidels.'

He sighed. 'The result you may conjecture when I tell you that on taking my leave I perceived my precious gold cross of St Francis, which I had guarded so jealously over such vast a distance to present to him, was there on a wall – but side by side with every other abomination of heathen effigy.'

'A dolorous conclusion to a journey of spirit and hardship,' Bacon murmured in sympathy.

Rubruck looked up with a suddenly sombre expression. 'As you must guess, my tale of far wandering is not the reason for my presence.'

'You wish to discuss a great matter that troubles you.'

'Just so, learned one.'

'Then say on, dear Brother.'

Rubruck rose and went to the window, opening the shutters and peering out cautiously.

'There is no one below us?'

'None. The knaves have deserted me for their merrymaking.'

'That is good. For what I am about to divulge is for your ears alone, my good Brother.'

'Do sit and share with me your perplexity then, William,' Bacon said.

'It is no simple concern, you must believe. It touches on the future of Christendom itself.'

He paused as if collecting his thoughts. 'In Karakorum oft-times the Great Khan was occupied by the affairs of state, leaving we envoys in idleness. You will know me as incurably desirous of knowledge, to promiscuously enquire and learn, and I could not abide that condition. Thus it was that I sought permission to make visit to the privy districts of his capital.'

'You must have seen—'

'It is one revelation alone that astonished and daunted me, my dear friend. One that shook my understanding of the workings of God in nature, the boundary of magic and sorcery – to feel the very trespass of the Devil on our world!'

Chilled by his words, Bacon tensed.

'For what I am about to do, I ask forgiveness, for there is no other way to bring to you the sensations I felt as I first beheld this that I now share with you.'

He rose and went to the window again, and satisfied of their privacy, closed the shutters. Feeling around in his leather pouch he drew out a small object, which he inspected, then went to the candle and offered one end to the flame. It sputtered and fell to a red glow. He threw it to the floor and moved away quickly.

Astonished at his behaviour, Bacon could only watch from his chair.

A livid flash and clap of thunder stunned his senses and the room filled with acrid smoke and the fearful stink of brimstone.

Terrified, Bacon gripped his chair and stared into the gloom with a pounding heart, expecting to be confronted with the diabolical form of Beelzebub himself arising from the nether regions – but he saw only the silent figure of his friend through the slowly dissipating smoke.

'Wh-what is this you're conjuring before me, Brother Rubruck?' he croaked, crossing himself.

'No deviltry, Roger, I swear to you.' He bent to pick up some ashy fragments and placed them in Bacon's uncomprehending hands.

'The work of man.'

'Then how . . . ?'

Rubruck turned over a plate on the serving table. 'See here, Brother, the essence of the phenomenon.'

He brought out another pouch and carefully shook a small pile of grains as grey as his friar's habit on the back of the plate, and leant back to allow Bacon to see.

'Now I bring fire.'

Bacon recoiled fearfully as a lighted taper touched one edge, but it only flared and spat merrily without violence.

'Yet if I . . .' Rubruck poured a similar sized amount but this time led a small trail out to one side. He placed a cup over the plate, brought the flame to it and stood back.

There was an instant's fizz and a sharp *pop*. The cup flew into the air then fell to the ground to smash in pieces.

'At the touch of fire the substance grows angry, and if confined in its rage, it calls upon all the powers of a demon to free itself.'

'This is marvellous in my sight,' Bacon said shakily. 'A deep mystery beyond imagining. Yet you say it's the work of man . . . How is it that . . . ?'

'In his capital, the Great Khan maintains quarters for foreigners, artisans and craftsmen from far parts of his empire engaged in works to add splendour and lustre to his realm. Those of the Cathayans he particularly indulges, furnishing them with all they ask, for they are adepts in the greatest mystery of them all.'

'This . . . this terrible dust.'

'That they call *huo yao*. They make it from unspeakable ingredients by a long process that ends with what you see before you. Roger, hear me – I've seen them call forth torrid leaps of flame as from a dragon's mouth, to send messengers on wings of fire to soar across the heavens and as you've seen, to bring thunder and lightning down to earth at their bidding, a hideous and miraculous sight.'

'A terrible experience, William.'

'Only because I felt it my duty to make investigation, as a scholar and philosopher must.'

'Just so.'

'And now to my dilemma, dear friend.'

'I hear you with respect and admiration, Brother.'

'I thank you, and know also that you are the one out of all Christendom that I can think to bring my troubled mind.'

Bacon murmured a respectful acknowledgement.

'So far as I can know it, the people of Cathay delight only in its ardent properties in spectacle and display, the capacity to affright and awe.'

'This is understandable.'

'Since that day I've struggled with my conscience before God. For want of curiosity in my companions, I, of all in my party, have been made witness to these terrors and portents. And only I, for whatever divine purpose, have been vouchsafed the secret of this infidel magic.'

Bacon caught his breath. 'You learnt of the spells to bring it into mortal existence?'

'I questioned many artisans severally, all of whom gave the same answers. Yes, Brother, I have the secret.'

'Then . . .'

'My dilemma is plain – do I reveal it or no? In the Europe of this dark century of war and hatred, when armies perpetually contend on the battlefield in slaughter and cruelty, how can I be sure that this dangerous knowledge will not be perverted to produce instruments of war more terrible by far than any seen to this day? There are many who would conceive it to be a mortal sin, I believe.'

Bacon leant forward, intensity in his voice. 'I, too, would regard it so, Brother. The secret must remain locked in your breast all your mortal days – it must never escape into this wicked world!'

'As I at first concluded. Yet . . . yet as a philosopher and devoted to the arts of learning I'm sorely distracted by the observation that should I be called to my rest this hour, there will be none in this kingdom to know of its existence, to perhaps pursue its properties unobserved and discover its vitality and significance. Brother Roger, I beg you will allow me to share this dread knowledge with you as a natural philosopher and relieve me of this heinous burden.'

Into the stillness came from the outside the same dull roar of revelry, but within the austere scholar's study the fading reek of sulphur was a token of the frightful things that had passed.

'Very well, Brother Rubruck, I shall accede to your request. But only on the condition that we do kneel and swear together the most sacred oath that this secret shall remain inviolate between us, never to be divulged to the profane and ignorant of this world.'

'I am content at that.'

CHAPTER 2

The village of Hurnwych Green, Warwickshire, England
Hocktide eve. AD 1287, the fifteenth year of the reign of King Edward I

The rain had eased off but still threatened as Perkyn Slewfoot trudged along the well-worn path towards the tithe-barn by the manor house. It was cold and bitter this early in the morning and being a lowly villein he wore just a coarse grey wool jerkin, loose leggings and the old felt hat he'd inherited from his father. His toes showed through his shoes, which were soon caked in mud.

He scratched absent-mindedly; the fleas had been merciless during the night.

Perkyn quickened his pace. He knew the reeve was waiting for him, the hard-faced Hubert Subsey, whose job it was to exact every working hour from those who owed service to their lord of the manor, Sir Robert le Warde.

Sometimes it was two or three days a week he must labour thus under the ancient and inviolable covenant between noble and bound: in return for service in his fields the lord would graciously extend his protection over him.

One morning two winters ago, still in his bed, Perkyn's father had turned his face to the wall in silent despair and died. His eldest son had gone to be a mercenary and hadn't been heard of again and his daughter had been hastily married off at fourteen.

It had left only Perkyn to look after his careworn mother in their humble wattle-and-daub home.

He'd always known he'd never marry for he'd been born with a gnarled ankle that had earned him the name 'Slewfoot'. No girl would look upon such a poor risk as a provider but he didn't pine, for was this not God's way of caring for his mother?

Perkyn just got along with life. With no allowances in their pitiless world for half-work he'd learnt the hard way how to keep up with the others – a hand to the plough; the hoe and harrow; and at harvest time, the sickle.

But provided he laboured on the lord's stipulated days, including the extra boon-work, he was free to work for himself. He had several strips planted in barley and peas. There were three geese fattening nicely and a goat for milk, but he'd had to sell the pig after the wet and bleak winter just endured.

The reeve shouted at the line of serfs bringing the straw baskets of seed. Perkyn filled his pouch then went off with his friend Godswein, the man's gap-toothed smile always cheering.

They set to with their dibbers, each to a strip and within hailing distance. A jab down and twist in the freshly turned soil, a single bean dropped in and on to the next in a time-worn rhythm. The strips were a chain wide and a furlong in length; it was hours before they completed their task, their backs burning with fatigue.

The two sat companionably together on the turfed edge of the field and took out their bread and cheese, trimmed with onions. Godswein shared a costrel of ale with Perkyn.

'God's teeth! On your feet, you fool-born oafs!' The reeve's snarl cut through their rest.

'And we've done it all, the lord's sowing, Master Subsey!'

Godswein said nervously. If the reeve had a mind to, they could be brought before the bailiff and fined for default of their obligation to service.

'That's as well, you low-arsed pair o' drabble-tails. I wants to see you behind a plough this afternoon. Sir Robert needs his winter wheat in the ground afore May Day.'

They hurriedly finished their repast as two scraggy beasts were brought up, the plough with a sadly blunted iron share and coulter.

As they faced up to the strip the first drops of rain spattered down and with it a gusty, spiteful blow.

The oxen were baulky, wanting their byre, the soil sticky and resisting, but in the driving rain they pushed forward, Perkyn at the plough, Godswein with the ox-goad, both silent in the shared misery of hard labour in the shuddering wet and cold.

It was some consolation that for this crop furrows were shallower, but it was heavy going, endless hours of flogging both man and beast until their portion was complete.

Perkyn bid Godswein farewell and tramped home to blessed surcease.

His mother set aside the bundle of rushes she was working on. They would later be dipped into the rancid sheep fat simmering at the hearth in the centre of the room to supply their only light after dark.

'Set you down, m' son!' she fussed as she tended to the other pot on the fire.

Waves of weariness came over Perkyn but the suffocating damp, smoky smell, with its overtones of ancient living and animals, was token of home, with all its memories and solace. His mother had been out rush-cutting and the beaten earth floor was covered with fresh grasses sprinkled with sprays of herbs and wild buds and from the upper beams hung three new cheeses.

'Take off your togs then, my sweeting.' She found his old smock. Obediently he stripped off his soaked clothing, which she threw over the wattle partition to the animals' end of the house. She went to the window, a slat with a hide hinge at the top and took down the stick that held it open. This trapped the smoke from the fire but helped keep away the flies as well as retaining a cosy warmth.

He felt a twinge of guilt – his mother was worn out; bent and shrivelled with age, she showed all of her thirty-some winters and found moving about difficult.

'Have you done with the lord's portion?'

'Aye, I have, Ma.'

But now he had to find the strength to drive the plough again for a freeman in return for the use of the same for himself later. It was hard to take, so much of his strength going into others' land, but this was the life the good Lord had decreed for him, just as he'd given others the grace to rise above it all. It was no use fretting about what could not be, and didn't Father Bertrand make much of accepting one's lot on earth?

She brought him his supper bowl. It was watery pease pottage with a few limp vegetables floating on top. He supped it quickly, the gnawing hunger pangs barely touched.

'I wish and all that I had some meat to give you,' she said wistfully. 'Perhaps when I sell my cheeses – they're very tasty, even should I say it myself.'

'Yes, Ma,' he said mechanically. There'd been no takers for the last, why should it be different now?

The night was drawing in so there was nothing for it but to

turn in to his leaves and straw bed by the goat. His foot hurt and it would be another day of work on the morrow.

As he finished the last of his black bread there were voices outside.

'Perkyn? You sleeping?' It was Godswein. 'Wilkie Bate says if you'd fancy a sup of ale . . .'

CHAPTER 3

'This's right kind in you, Wilkie,' Perkyn said greeting the jolly man whose income from five strips and a goodly number of sheep had enabled him to build a large, three-bay wattle-and-daub house near the river.

The fire crackled and spat in cheerful unruliness and Jankin and Reginald Fivepot with leather jacks and drinking horns a-fill with ale roared a welcome. No less than three tallow candles touched them with gold.

Bate's wife brought in another stout flagon of ale and set it on the trestle table.

'Ah. This'n is for you, Perkyn. You're looking poorly – here's a drink as will set you up, lad.'

'Why, thank you, Wilkie,' he said.

The others paused as he lifted the black leather tankard and drank deeply. It tasted foul and made him retch but he downed it to the end.

There was something in the murky bottom of the vessel. Apprehensively he fetched it out – it was a bloated mouse carcase.

The room erupted in mirth and Perkyn looked around uncertainly, then a broad smile spread and he joined in the merriment.

At the noise, Bate's wife came back and saw what had happened. She scolded her husband and brought Perkyn a fresh drink and a morsel of cake to take away the taste.

An ungenerous soul would have noticed the small ale was no longer quite fresh, but no one was about to complain and it went down quickly.

'A rare drop,' acknowledged Reginald, wiping his mouth.

His good-natured red face creased in merriment. 'As I've brought a splash o' something else, which I returns the friendliness of our Wilkie!'

He reached beneath the table and pulled up a wicker-clad pottery jar. 'Get your cups, goodwife, this is your metheglin – bold rose-hip metheglin, to warm your hearts on a night like this!'

It was a rare treat. A Welsh potation of fermented honey, it was considerably stronger than ale.

'It's Hocktide eve, friends. Don't let's waste this!'

Perkyn felt its crude potency take hold and his cares began to fall away.

Tomorrow was a feast day and all were released from service on the lord's demesne. He was free to work on his own small plot of land, which sadly needed attention – or not! The fine feeling spread and when the dice came out for a game of Hazard he was glowing in the company of his friends.

'Your good mother in humour, Perkyn?' Jankin asked, feeling in his ragged brown hood for his flute.

'Aye, but since we had to sell our pig we've had barely a bite o' meat and she's getting mortal frail.'

Wilkie snorted. 'A fine thing it is when a good woman must pray for a morsel so.'

'Aye!' Jankin mumbled. 'Agin nature, it is.'

'God rot it, but I've a notion to do something about it!' Reginald blustered.

'Oh? And what's that?'

'Why, over yonder there's enough meat to fill us each a pot for a month!'

'Are you saying you're going . . . a-poaching?'

'Well, I . . .'

The swagger fell away quickly at the reality of the words. To enter the woods of the lord's demesne and take a deer was against the dread Laws of the Forest. It would be a dire offence against the callous Baron Everard D'Amory.

His ancestral home Castle Ravenstock loured down on the village from the face of an escarpment several miles away, monstrous and dominating. Within it were lords and ladies, men-at-arms, chambers of torture and a great hall for feasting of unimaginable splendour. The unreachable pinnacle of this earthly world, beings whose existence and movements were inscrutable and not for their knowing.

There was no crossing of their lives. The manor under its lord Sir Robert le Warde directed the affairs of Hurnwych: from rent collections to common grazing rights to the manorial courts. Village met authority in the form of the bailiff in the great hall of the manor, or more often the foul-mouthed reeve, Hubert Subsey.

More metheglin restored the mood but there were thoughtful looks about the table.

'One stag o' size that never would be missed . . .'

'I once saw a haunch of venison. Christ's wounds, it was big!'

'She'd bless you for ever, just for the taste of a collop or two of meat.'

Godswein broke in. 'Enough o' this talk, it's making me

famished to hear it. There's nobody going to take a deer – you down it, there's no way to get it back here! Besides which, someone sees you, the Verderer hears about it and is going after you with a rope.'

'Ah! There is a way!' Wilkie sat back with a superior smile.

'How?'

He leant forward, his face serious. 'It'll take all of us, no hanging back.' Seeing he had their attention he continued. 'The trick is, we want to get it out quick, and as well, that no one notices, right?'

'Yes, Wilkie.'

'So here it is. We've got our rights of pannage and firewood. Anyone sees us with a bag stuffed full, it's our usual load. But it's not – it's a nice fat joint of venison each!'

'So we—'

'Yes! As soon as we drop the beast we sets to on the spot and all together we butchers it quick smart. Won't take long and no one will see us carry any deer out of the woods. Right?'

This far into the evening it was sounding altogether very possible.

'Who's our best shot?'

They all turned to Perkyn.

'Oh, you mean . . .'

'You're youngest, and I've seen you plant an arrow in a magpie at thirty paces.'

'But I've never—'

'You take him, we'll cut him up. Besides, your arrow – you get first choice!'

Perkyn grinned broadly. They trusted him – his friends. He couldn't let them down. 'I'll do it.'

'Stout fellow.'

'When's it to be?'

'What better time than when all right-minded foresters have their feet under a table and their beaks in an ale – Hocktide!'

'Tomorrow morning! Why not?'

CHAPTER 4

Where the river wound through, the woods were dense with thickets and undergrowth on one side. Coppicing and level country had thinned out the other side to more open woodland, rich grazing for deer.

Wilkie was certain what had to be done. 'They go in groups. We sit young Perkyn behind a handy bush downwind from 'em and drive a likely beast past him. He lets fly and we all get to work right there. Easy!'

But it wasn't. With no staghounds and bleary-eyed in the early-morning light they looked about in vain for the herd. And on foot how were they going to cover the distance?

By a fluke they stumbled on a covey that rose from where they'd chosen to lay up during the night. In a frightened body they fled along the edge of the woods where they would pass on either side of the bush where Perkyn was waiting with his bow.

With a rush of anxiety he raised and sighted, desperate to do well. The deer came on in a frantic, close-packed throng but he had the wit to settle on one only and loosed his arrow. As they raced past he saw it, the arrow plain in its shoulder, blood streaking bright as it ran.

The rest disappeared into the brush followed by his wounded target, now stumbling. In a fever of excitement he crashed after it, hearing Wilkie and the others coming up behind. They passed him quickly, for with his withered ankle he could only limp along, but he caught up just as Wilkie put the knife to the creature's throat.

They began hacking and cleaving in a frenzy of fear and exhilaration. A haunch was drawn clear and stuffed into a bag, Wilkie had the head detached and threw it into the low undergrowth. A saddle portion came away. They were going to do it!

Then, out of the morning like a trump of judgement, came the sound of a horn. Another much closer replied.

'The foresters! They're on to us – run!'

They dropped everything and fled. Heart in his mouth Perkyn went after them, desperate to reach the edge of the woodland, off the baron's land.

He saw his friends get there one by one and make off across the common to the anonymity of the village, but sobbing with the realisation, he knew that with his ankle he couldn't move any faster.

With yards to go he heard the thunder of hoofs and in despair found his escape cut off as a horse wheeled in front of him and crashed to a stop. Its dark-featured rider, in forest green and Norman helmet with the arms of the puissant Baron D'Amory on his chest, looked down in evil triumph.

CHAPTER 5

The stone was cold and damp and the cell stank of fear and vomit. Nearly witless with terror Perkyn trembled uncontrollably.

He'd been bound and taken on horseback in front of everyone to the castle, the great edifice that had dominated the village from time out of mind, a feared and mysterious presence.

He'd been dragged into its maw. The reality was terrifying: colossal stone walls towering high, with men-at-arms, traders, brightly costumed servants and serving maids mingling in a constant babel of noise and so many great doors that crashed shut with a finality behind him.

A hard-faced official questioned him, seated at a table strewn with objects – he had no idea what they were. The man spoke in thick-accented English and made asides to others in a foreign language he couldn't understand.

They'd demanded he name his accomplices but he'd stoutly refused.

He was stood roughly against a wall and beaten then asked again. Through the pain he vowed that he would not condemn his friends.

Finally he was taken away and thrown into the cell.

* * *

Outside a moon-faced turnkey in stained leather tunic sat on a stool, bored.

'Wh-what's going to happen to me?' Perkyn ventured through the peephole of the door.

'Shurrup!' ordered the man absently.

'Please! I'm frightened.'

'What you done, then?'

'We took a deer.'

'Oh, so it's poaching, is it? Well, they takes you up before the bailiff and you answers for it. If His Nobbs has had a good dinner he'll just cut off your hands, else you'll swing on the end of a rope. Any more fool questions?'

In a stew of fear Perkyn shrank back hopelessly.

Some time later he heard voices. The lock rattled and the turnkey stood impassive in the doorway.

'On your feet, m' little rascal. You've done bad by having a go at the baron's game – he's making a big noise that he wants a trial quick smart, make an example, and the bailiff don't disagree.'

Two men-at-arms entered and seized Perkyn.

The Great Hall of Castle Ravenstock was vast and gloomy – and to one who'd only known the village, terrifying.

Seated on an imposing chair on a dais at the far end was a richly dressed man who could only be the baron. To one side was a table with officials and clerks and on the other a small pen where Perkyn was led.

The hall fell to a stillness and a hard-featured man at the table stood and glanced at the baron, who nodded irritably.

The man rang a bell and droned on from a book in Norman French, then looked up and rapped a command.

A forester in green marched up to the table.

'Upon your evidence the prisoner Perkyn, yclept Slewfoot, stands accused of the taking of a deer, contrary to the Forest Law. Is this then the man?'

'It is, My Lord.'

The cold eyes turned to Perkyn. 'Do you dispute this?'

What could he say? He'd been seen running from the carcase and had been caught on the baron's land.

'Christ's bones, you ill-faced lackwit. You did it, didn't you?' roared the baron.

In a small, shaking voice Perkyn answered miserably, 'Yes, My Lord.'

The bailiff intoned importantly, 'In confessing to your misdeed you have been—'

'Get on with it, my man! You know what to do.'

The bailiff drew himself up. 'Therefore I find you guilty. The felony having no mitigating circumstances requires I pass sentence on you to suffer the full rigour of the law. You shall hang.'

For a moment Perkyn couldn't believe it – then with a roaring in his ears the full force of the words hit him. He was going to die.

Back at the cell the turnkey shook his head as he pushed him in. 'Told you, didn't I? No good to come of taking down one o' Baron Hooknose's very own.'

They came for him in the late afternoon.

Stumbling and uncertain he was led out into the daylight, his hands bound and his knees weak and trembling.

Would it hurt? He felt tears pricking – he was leaving the only world he knew, harsh and unforgiving as it was, and it would condemn his mother to . . . to . . .

Outside the castle walls was the gallows, a simple raised platform. Stark above it a rope hung down.

A crowd was gathering. Chattering, laughing, staring, they were held back as he was brought near.

Perkyn was prodded up the short ladder to where the hangman waited with heavy patience. Next to him stood Father Bertrand, his long face pale and worried.

At the top Perkyn was rotated to face the crowd. His shaking was now uncontrollable; he was holding on to reason by a thread.

A herald stepped forward.

'As Perkyn of Hurnwych did foully trespass upon the good grace of our liege lord, Baron Everard D'Amory, in that he did slay a hart contrary to the dread Law of the Forest, he is adjudged worthy of death, for which this is your warrant.'

The sea of faces before him held no meaning any more – the world had contracted to his tiny space in it and the sudden shock of the rough and hairy touch of the rope as it was draped over his neck.

Father Bertrand came up to stand before him, mumbling interminably from a book he held. He made the sign of the cross then withdrew.

Taking up the slack of the rope the hangman muttered, 'Ready, friend?'

In the last split second between life and death Perkyn shut his eyes while his soul screamed soundlessly in agony – and then as if from far, far away came a voice. 'Hold!'

Perkyn opened his eyes: Baron D'Amory was on the drawbridge, mounted atop his horse with one hand raised.

No one moved. He spurred forward and came to a halt beside the gallows. He glanced once at Perkyn, a cold, despising look, then addressed the crowd, few of whom had ever set eyes on their liege lord. Several bowed down; others stood gape-mouthed.

'One of my deer was slain. This varlet did not act alone!' His gaze swept the throng, grim and ruthless.

'By the custom of frankpledge you are all and every one accountable for the actions of the villains you harbour. You have not yielded up their persons, therefore this mewling youth is paying the full price for all.'

He drew a deep breath and bellowed, 'I will have justice!'

Apart from the stirring of wind there was absolute stillness.

'Yet in mercy, I give to you a choosing. I will respite this hanging . . . if I get my just recompense. A fine levied upon all Hurnwych Green in the sum of one pound weight of silver!'

An astonished murmur went about the crowd. The life of a villein for a stiff amercement on themselves?

Then the cynical reason for it broke in. The baron was making a show of mercy, a calculated ploy to lessen the harshness of his act. If they were soft-hearted enough to pay, he'd have his silver. If not, he'd then feel free to take his revenge on the lad.

'So what will it be? Who will be the first to pledge their coin?'

Perkyn felt a piteous hope but it died quickly. These were freemen and would care nothing about a worthless bondman, not one of themselves.

'Very well! Let the—'

'I do so pledge, My Lord!'

'Who says this?'

'I, My Lord. Jared the blacksmith. Five groats!'

The kindly smith who always had a good word for the lowly serfs and peasants as they brought their work to him at his forge over the river. Whose skills were legendary, attracting a partner and apprentice even in such a small village. But why . . . ? Perkyn's heart thumped.

'Come along, Hurnwych!' the blacksmith called loudly. 'I've laid out my piece. What say we all give and throw off that rope around his neck!'

There was a stirring and a shout rang out. 'Will the butcher – twelve silver pennies!'

A reedy voice carried over the babble. 'Old Yarwell, franklin. Ten groats!'

'Sweyn Blacktooth, baker. Four groats.'

More pledges came – then more.

Jared held up his hand. 'Enough! One pound o' silver, My Lord. As shall be delivered up before sundown. We beg now for the life of yon Perkyn Slewfoot.'

The jaw hardened but the baron wheeled his horse around and snapped, 'Let him go!'

The rope was thrown off Perkyn's neck and with a sawing at his wrists his hand bindings fell away.

'Well, go on then, m' little lamb,' the hangman grunted peevishly. 'You're free, aren't you?'

Hardly aware of the noise and clamour around him he had eyes only for one: Jared the blacksmith who had given him back his life!

'Sire, Master Jared – how can I thank you?' he babbled, his hands writhing. 'I can't repay, but I – I'll do anything for you, anything! Just tell me, I'll do it! Anything!'

'Calm yourself, Perkyn. Isn't it you with an old mother on her own to look after? She'll be worried where you've been – best you get off home and set her heart at rest.'

In floods of tears Perkyn hobbled off, leaving Jared in the centre of a throng of villagers.

'It was a rare good turn you did today,' declared one. 'Why did you do it?'

He gave a twisted smile. 'As I loathe to see the castle every time have its way with we common folk.'

CHAPTER 6

May Day eve

Jared reached into the blazing forge with his tongs. In a practised whirl he extracted the long billet of iron and placed it on the anvil. He hammered at it with strong, decisive pounding, sending outwards a flying spray of sparks, listening for when his hits returned the hard ring of cooling metal.

His father had taught him everything he knew. The family forge had prospered in the village, producing everything from door latches to ploughshares, and took in work from miles around. He had lost him to an ague some two years previously but a partner, Osbert, had been found, a steady older man now outside shaping a clay mould.

'Give us a good wind, younker!' Jared told the young apprentice at the bellows and plunged his work back into the heart of the fire. He watched the incandescence pulsate to white heat and drew out his iron again. It was hard but rewarding work, bringing a creation of value for man out of the implacable inertness of rock-torn iron, and he revelled in the sheer physicality of forcing his will upon it.

The ghost of what would be lay within the glowing mass and he directed his blows to bring the crude billet ever closer to its outline. Already he'd drawn out the workpiece to length and now was concentrating on producing a sweet curve and at the same time a descending edge. This was going to be a scythe with the blade a full five feet long. He worked steadily, broadening and deepening the blade along the long chine, leaving the mounting tang until later.

'You'll never be done by the morrow, young cub!' Osbert chided him, bringing in his mould to set.

'I will, old man,' Jared retorted with the confidence of twenty years. Tomorrow was a feast day, May Day!

Jared fell to it, hammering with redoubled speed and the unmistakeable shape of the scythe blade began emerging. Two more heatings and he had a wicked pointed end drawn out and the run of the blade sighted and trued.

A deft working with mandrel and punch and the mounting point for the sinuous long wooden handle was ready.

'I'll give you a hand,' Osbert offered.

The piece was formed but now it had to be worked to a hardness along its edge, and that could only be done by peening, cold beating the metal with smaller hammers in a painstaking progression down the blade. They set to together, one manipulating the work on the anvil while the other kept up a rapid tattoo with the hammer.

At last it was done. A workmanlike tool whose hard edge only needed occasional touching with a whetstone to see many years of yeoman duty on grain or grass.

'Fetch us a muzzler, young 'un.'

While the apprentice scurried off for a jug of ale Jared wiped his forehead and sat on the floor against the anvil.

Osbert joined him. 'You'll be going a-maying, then.'

'I might.'

'Maypole ready?'

'Aye, it's up. Me and Nolly did it.'

There was a small pause, then Osbert said, 'She's May Queen, I hear.'

'Who's that?' Jared said casually, fiddling with his belt.

'You don't fool me, lad – young Aldith Beavis, I mean.'

Jared said nothing, staring obstinately ahead.

'Look, none o' my business, but I seen how she looks at you with them deer's eyes as you passes.'

'So?'

'And I seen your sheep's eyes looking back. Now she's of an age, like to be married even before harvest's in.'

'Leave it alone, Osbert,' Jared flared. 'I happen to know old Beavis went to talk with Master Frauncey and stayed a-while, must have had a good hearing. And can you blame him – a blacksmith agin a bailiff's clerk?' he added bitterly.

'Ha! You don't know Beavis as well as I do. He's ruled by Hetty, his wife – won't refuse her anything. Now, here's my advice, take it or leave it. You get out there, open your heart to the damsel, let her know how the wind blows. She takes a fancy, goes back to her mother and they has women's talk as will soon have Beavis ploughing a different furrow. See?'

'I'm to thank you for your help with the scythe, Osbert,' Jared said stiffly.

The ale arrived and they drank thirstily.

'Just you remember what I said. Tomorrow you has your chance – and none other after it,' Osbert said, wiping his mouth on his sleeve.

CHAPTER 7

Jared was awake before first light began stealing into the smithy house, where he lay on an oat-stuffed mattress in the family bedplace in the upper level. Maud, his mother, slept behind a curtain and two servants snored below in the smoky darkness.

He'd thought about what Osbert had said and felt resentful that he'd caused him to hope. Perhaps he was right that the shy maiden did hold him in thrall but he'd never allowed himself to dream. Marriages were settled by parents on the basis of family advantage, social standing or the acquiring of property, even at his level. The base villein, a field labourer, was more fortunate. He had only to gain the assent of a disinterested lord of the manor, more concerned with increasing his workforce.

John Frauncey, the haughty bailiff's clerk who gave himself such airs on account of his learning, would probably rise in the course of time to the position of steward in the manor house. What could he put up against this? His father's careful husbandry had bequeathed him a fine forge and impressive array of tools and skills – but he would always be a blacksmith, earning his daily bread with the sweat of his brow.

He could now make out the pattern of his bedspread: morning

was breaking. Easing himself up he reached up the wall to where his belongings hung from hooks in linen bags. He'd laid out good silver for a new outfit – a doublet in brown and slender green hose under a flaring red jacket; pointed leather shoes and a jaunty felt hat narrowed to a peak over the nose, finished off by a soft leather purse hung from a belt.

'Is that you, Jared?' came a voice from the other side of the bay. The growing chorus of roosters, barking dogs and the like made sleep impossible now.

'Yes, Mother.'

She sat up and drew back the curtain. 'So you'll be off into the woods a-bringing in the May.'

'Aye, I am, Mother.'

'Just you mind what goes on in there, Jared. A goings-on as will have Father Bertrand a-worrying over souls for a sennight, I shouldn't wonder.'

'Yes, Mother.' As if he was going to miss the fun!

Outside, the village was coming to life.

There was a gathering throng at the well, geese were being noisily driven to the common and from afar came the shrill voice of Margery Blundel berating her meek husband, the miller's gristman.

And a quick glance heavenward showed that the day promised fair!

'Good day to you, Nolly!' Jared called to the tousle-haired young man emerging from the carpenter's house next to his.

'And a right merry May morn to you, m' friend,' he laughed, finishing fastening his jacket, clearly as new as Jared's own.

They were soon joined by others heading in the same direction – across the Coventry to Banbury highway to the common, and then to the woods that lay to the north.

'They's about, then!' Nolly chortled.

On the common dozens of girls were kneeling, splashing their faces in the early morning May dew, a sure way to win a beautiful complexion for the whole year. Others were already in the adjacent woods, gathering wild flowers and greenery, their laughter and song lifting hearts now that a hard winter was past.

Wolfscote Forest behind the woods was thick and ancient. Trackways meandered deep inside the lair of outlaws and vagabonds, and within living memory, home to the wolves that gave it the name. Somewhere in its dark heart was a deserted priory that many claimed was haunted by ghosts of the nuns who had been struck down by a deadly plague.

The villagers grazed their pigs and collected firewood in accordance with their ancient rights but none ventured far into the forest – in the cleared areas of the woods was all they needed.

'Good morn to you, Meggy m' love!' Nolly threw at a young girl in a green kirtle, her striking red hair falling around her shoulders. She was plucking bluebells with her sister; they giggled and ran on.

Jared found a particularly fine wood anemone and fastened it to his hat, looking for others to complement it but Nolly had seen something through the trees.

'Pageant wagon's here.'

'Well, let's be at it, sluggard!'

Age-old traditions had the girls gathering flowers and rushes for weaving crowns while the menfolk sought hawthorn boughs and greenery to load the wagon.

A cow-horn sounded an imperious summons. Folk hurried to the pageant wagon from all parts of the woods, a sizeable ox-drawn conveyance more to be seen as the stage for wandering mystery players but now set with a wooden throne. It was gaily decorated with garlands of flowers, draped with greenery and hawthorn and was attended by the Master of the Procession, as usual the well-respected Old Turvey, a Hurnwych franklin of thirty acres.

'I'll thank 'ee to form up, one and all!'

There was a scramble for precedence but the old man was having none of it. Girls first behind the wagon, then at a decent remove the men, to be joined by the approaching cavorting figures of a hobby horse ridden by a youth with an extravagant cap threaded through with May blossoms and attended by two tumblers in green. A shawm and tabor took position in the lead and the procession moved off – bringing in the May!

It was exhilarating and joyful, a release after the bleak winter, and with the slow pace of the oxen Jared joined others in darting out to seize a girl and whirl her around in a frenzied dance.

They crossed the common and entered the village, lined with onlookers, laughing and admiring. Leather mugs of ale were thrust at them and as more joined in the procession the noise grew to an outpouring of merriment.

Jared however began to quail.

There was only one small road through the village and it was going to stop at the house of Beavis – where the May Queen lived. Aldith.

The noise died away as Old Turvey brought the procession to a standstill.

'Oyez! Oyez! Does the May Queen of Hurnwych Green lie within? Your Grace, know your liege subjects await!'

A vision appeared at the door before Jared. In a long white gown, her dark tresses flowing loose, Aldith glanced demurely about her. Supported by Turvey she mounted her throne to sit in regal majesty, bestowing a bashful wave at the throng, who immediately fell to their knees.

Jareth's heart was in his mouth. Had she noticed him in his new red jacket?

The jubilant procession moved off, down to the last little hut and back again, this time turning on to the Banbury road and the bridge over the River Dene. On the other side was the manor with its hall and tithe barns to the right and the village green and church to the left.

Already the green was alive with activity, booths for entertainments set out, trestle tables readying for the feasting and a fast gathering crowd eager for the coming festivities. Over at the maypole several figures stood waiting, the notables of the village.

The Queen of May progressed around the green for a full circuit before the admiring crowd, stopping at last at the maypole.

A wistful girl wearing an elaborate circlet of flowers was handed up, the old May Queen who had the honour of crowning the new, before official witnesses.

The lord of the manor was not present; he possessed several other more substantial villages, and this year apparently was not inclined to spend his time in lowly Hurnwych. However, the bailiff and his underlings were there and to his annoyance Jared saw the condescending figure of Frauncey, looking above it all.

Aldith stood and in a quiet but determined voice intoned, 'This morn it is the month of May. Let all know it by the Maying of Hurnwych, and I proclaim the revels begun!'

With gleeful cries the load of flowers and greenery was plucked from the wagon by the womenfolk to decorate every doorway and entrance and the new May Queen nobly led those chosen to adorn the rood screen of the church away.

'Hoy, now, and we're commanded to go a-rollicking,' Nolly cackled. 'And by all the saints I'll not disobey!'

They headed to an ale booth and claimed a tankard each.

'That John Frauncey!' Jared glowered. 'May he choke on his airs this very day, the bastard!' He drank deeply.

'Him? All the world knows he's an arse-licking churl. Pay no mind to the prat,' Nolly said dismissively, speedily doing justice to the ale.

On the other side there was a burst of delighted laughter. The Jack-in-the-Green had arrived, a figure dressed from head to toe in foliage with a pair of antlers atop, urged on by drum and pipe and a whirl of male dancers with tambourines and tiny bells sewn to their leggings.

'Let's go!' Nolly urged. 'I've a mind to kick up a storm.'

'Not yet. I want to see the games.'

And wait for Aldith to return. Just how did Osbert figure that he had a chance if he was bold enough?

Nolly left to join the crowd about the increasingly uproarious Jack-in-the-Green.

A dwarf jongleur in gaudy motley appeared from nowhere. Tumbling and leaping around Jared he sang a bawdy song, bringing others to laugh at him.

Jared moved away, his mind on what he'd say if she appeared before him.

Osbert beckoned him from an ale booth. 'How now, Jared, and here's one for you, lad.'

He took the tankard but just sipped the drink.

'You think she'll hear me?' he murmured.

'Young Aldith? You won't know until you tries. Here, let's watch the milkmaids dance, always a sight!'

'Not now. You go, Osbert.'

Putting down his ale Jared looked up to see the May Queen returning, surrounded by dancing maidens.

At the edge of the green she was met by lively acclaim, which she graciously acknowledged, then with her following turned to advance to the maypole – toward him!

He swallowed. This was the moment he knew was now or never – she had but to doff her crown at the base of the maypole and be released to join the revelry. And then would be free to . . .

Others had noticed her arrive and were gathering to hail their queen but he was determined to be out in front. He advanced, twitching his jacket and rehearsing what he would say, heart bumping. Aldith was laughing with one of her maids of May and happened to turn his way just as he pushed through the throng to the front.

He felt himself blush and all his words fled.

She smiled encouragingly but with all the village looking on Jared remained tongue-tied.

'Why, Mistress Aldith!' Frauncey executed a perfect genuflection. 'May Queen and none of quality to pledge true allegiance? For shame!'

He took her arm, adding silkily, 'The ox-roast is announced, my dear, and I shall see to it the choice cuts are yours!'

Left standing, Jared felt a wash of humiliation. It was replaced by despair then realisation. Whether it was Frauncey or some other, she was too fine a catch for a mere blacksmith and the sooner he accepted this the sooner he could get on with life.

Suddenly everything went quiet. On the highway from Coventry a tight column of helmeted men-at-arms on horseback was approaching, a great banner aloft. Soon it became clear that this was a progress, a long tail of wagons and grand conveyances, signifying that a noble was on the road.

Nolly came up beside Jared. 'It's Baron Everard, I'd swear it!'

The first column drew abreast, the clopping of many hoofs and jingling of harness loud in the stillness. The men were haughty, grim-faced; their steel bright and polished. The brazen colour of tabards and heraldry spoke of a world of nobility and puissance.

Villagers began dropping to one knee, their heads bowed in submission.

Jared did likewise, but dared an upward glance.

Following the men-at-arms a single figure rode a jet-black horse. Baron Everard D'Amory in a magnificent suit of robes in rich shades of purple and scarlet.

The same stern face, hard lines and powerful authority that he'd seen when Perkyn had been spared radiated out with daunting force, a terrifying presence. Close behind him was his lady, her extravagant mantle woven with striking vermilion and blue patterns. She wore an expression of disdain, looking neither to the right nor left and making play with her pomander to ward off village smells.

Then followed a richly dressed young man on horseback. He looked about with an expression of boredom. Was he the baron's son?

A long line of baggage carts followed and the rear was brought up by another troop of men-at-arms.

The procession came to a stop and Jared heard voices at the head. The bailiff, on his knee, was addressing the baron. As they spoke in the Norman tongue the villagers could not know what passed but with a lordly gesture an attendant threw a spray of coins on to the green and the progress resumed.

Jared followed it with his eyes as it wound past the manor and eventually out of sight.

His gaze flicked up to the castle on the hill.

CHAPTER 8

The merrymaking resumed.

'They're setting up for the bowman's ram,' Nolly said. 'And it's our Watkyn Sharpeye standing agin who may come.'

Jared brightened. An archery contest! An ordinary shot himself, to behold a natural marksman like Watkyn, a veteran of the crusades and pitted against all comers would be entertainment indeed.

He made his way to the gathering crowd – and then saw Aldith and Frauncey together, admiring the ram for prize.

Bitterly he turned on his heel.

How long would it be before she could have no effect on him?

Will Dunning, the miller's eldest, thrust across his path and rubbed his manhood suggestively.

Jared saw red and in a single mighty heave hoisted the youth over his shoulder and to roars of appreciation catapulted him into the pond.

'Let the ale do the talking, you jug-bitten simkin, and count on this!' he yelled at the floundering figure.

Then someone leapt on his back, sending him staggering, but with hard muscles won at the forge and anvil he bent and hefted him forward to join Dunning.

It was the signal for general mayhem. With shouts of glee more joined in, and set upon by at least four Jared was overcome and found himself in the pond as well.

Soaked and muddy he staggered out.

There was nothing for it but to trudge back to the house to strip off his fine clothes, now ruined.

Hauling on his workaday attire he decided to return to the green and find Nolly. There was none to impress now, and he might as well join his friend for a jug or three.

Nolly was over by a booth convulsed in mirth at a drunken juggler desperately trying to succeed with three live rats.

Jared found himself an ale and tried to throw off his melancholy. Another tankard went down quickly.

Feeling suddenly weary, he found a bench and sat, staring at his drink, his thoughts a jumble.

'Why, Jared! What happened to your lovely red jacket?'

As if from a dream he looked up to see Aldith standing over him with a beautiful smile.

Scrambling to his feet he stuttered, 'Oh, er, it got, um, wet. Where's Frauncey?'

'Oh, he's to attend on the bailiff as he speaks with the bishop. Jared, why don't we walk together for a while? It's been so long since we talked.'

Head swimming he strove to grapple with what was happening. One thought burst into his consciousness above all others. This was Aldith and he had her to himself for a short time and . . . and if he didn't lay his heart before her right now he . . .

They walked slowly along.

'Aldith – I . . . I . . .'

'I always enjoy May Day, don't you? So wonderful and joyful, and to see everyone frolic so lifts the heart.'

'I have to talk to you!'

'You are, Jared.'

'I mean . . .'

They reached the edge of the green but Aldith was directing them across the bridge and on to the common.

'You're promised to Frauncey, I know that, but—'

She stopped suddenly and swung him to face her. 'I am not promised to that . . . that drab.'

'But . . . but . . .'

'I will never marry that fool even if it means I shall remain a maid all my life. If the one who I desire so sweetly hasn't the courage to make conquest of me . . .'

He gulped in sudden realisation. Hesitantly he put out his hand – she took it and purposefully stepped off once more, leading them across the common towards the woods.

Heart bumping, her hand in his all fire and flowers, he was quite unable to take in what seemed to be developing. 'Wh-where are we going?' he whispered.

'It's May Day, my fauntkin! Where do you think lovers go on this day?'

Nearly overcome with a river of joy, he fell in with her step as they scampered off into the woods.

CHAPTER 9

Three summers later

'How's this? My mistress wife set fair to turn many a coin more than her goodman?' Jared planted a wet kiss on Aldith's forehead as she worked at the mash tun, bringing on yet another fine ale of the kind that was attracting customers even from the next village.

'Should I return then to my spinning, Husband?' she said archly, wiping her forehead, but there was laughter in her eyes.

She had become an alewife to help with the household upkeep, as was the custom, but had found a gift for the craft. Some said it was the fennel she added, others the quality of the malt or the purity of the river water in Hurnwych, but whatever the reason, on the strength of it they had been able to open a small tavern at the opposite end of the house adjacent to the smithy.

The green bushel over the doorway was sign that a fresh brewing was on offer. There were already thirsty customers in the tavern, and when he returned he was met by a chorus of orders that had the tap-boy scurrying.

Jared nodded to one of their regular patrons. 'And tell me, William, has your black sow brought you increase, yet?'

'By St Frideswilde, she's taking her time,' grumbled the old man tetchily, but brightened at the arrival of his ale.

Nothing could touch Jared's contentment, his happiness at what God had gifted him. Aldith's father had been stubborn but her threat to go to a nunnery and cheat him of grandsons had tipped the balance and they had wedded immediately. The forge was making money and there was every reason to take on a journeyman blacksmith, such was the load of work at hand. As well there was—

'Isn't that your bantling and all?' a customer chuckled, pointing.

Young David toddled in uncertainly, looking to find his father.

'Daw, m' little lambkin, what are you about, lad?'

He bent to pick up his son and his face creased into a cherubic smile.

In the house it wasn't hard to discover what had happened. David's grandmother had nodded off next to the fire as the child played, forgetting that the little fellow could walk now.

Kissing his child he plumped him down into Maud's lap to wake her and wagged his finger in admonishment before returning to the tavern.

A scraggy villein was waiting for him. 'Master says, can you come, it's a pressing matter.'

'Who's this, then?'

'Hugh Comber, and he's at a stand, plough's broke and the horses idle. Just a bit of work on the trace ring and he'll be much beholden.'

A straightforward job, and for a well-to-do freeman with land to the south of the manor, who'd no doubt be generous if he was prompt.

Taking affectionate leave of his wife, Jared left with the villein.

The tavern fell to a contented hum, its customers delaying their return to work while a passing shower played out.

* * *

Not long after there was the sound of horses, several of them. Travellers?

Footsteps, then a handsome man in rich garb and sword stood scowling in the doorway. Apparently the tavern passed muster for he signalled to others behind and stalked in.

'Get out!' he ordered the bewildered drinkers.

Some showed signs of reluctance. Enraged he knocked the nearest from his stool. 'When Sir Gervaise D'Amory commands it, you'll obey or I'll see you kicking at the end of a rope!'

The baron's son! The little room cleared quickly.

'An ale, My Lord?' one of his followers ventured after they'd discarded their wet cloaks.

They were all of an age, riding companions sprawling about indolently. Rakish and with a wicked curl to their mouths the young knights were spoiling for trouble.

'Ale!' D'Amory roared impatiently.

The potboy had fled with the rest but the noise brought both Aldith and Maud, who pulled back in dismay at the sight.

'Sir Gervaise D'Amory and I'll have a flagon of your best brew, and if it isn't fit for a gentleman I swear you'll rue it!'

The women hurriedly left.

With a nervous potboy in her wake, Maud shortly returned with a foaming tankard, which she carefully placed on the table in front of him.

D'Amory looked up sharply. 'Where's the maid? I'm not to be served by an ill-faced old hag!'

Tight-faced, Maud left and returned with more ale, protectively in front of Aldith.

'That's better!' he said with a lewd grin, eyeing the young woman as she set down the ale.

When she made to leave he called loudly, 'And what's your name, maid?'

'Aldith, wife of Jared,' she said quietly, stepping back.

'Is there anything else, My Lord?' Maud asked, taking her place.

'Nothing you can serve me with, old woman,' D'Amory said lazily, his eyes still on Aldith. 'You can leave. Off you go, then.'

Seeing Aldith about to depart as well he rapped, 'Stay! I bid you stay, woman.'

White-faced, she stood against the wall.

Slowly, D'Amory took a pull at his ale. 'God's teeth, and this is good,' he said in pleased surprise. 'Your brewing, maid?'

'Sir, I'm no maid but well married to my husband. And I own the ale is mine, My Lord.'

One of the knights leant forward. 'A pretty enough cuntkin, sire,' he whispered with a cynical sneer.

'As is wasted on these clay-brained villeins,' D'Amory acknowledged.

Aldith bit her lip. 'Is that all, My Lord?'

'No, it is not.'

He leant forward to the others with a wolfish grin. 'I've a mind to have a piece o' the culver myself,' he hissed.

'What, here, My Lord?'

'No, you fool, the place stinks of the farmyard. I've another notion.'

'Sire?'

D'Amory ignored him, finished his ale and planked the tankard down with finality.

Loudly he declared, 'I rather fancy this ale's better than the swill they make in Ravenstock.'

'It is, My Lord,' they all agreed quickly.

'What say I remedy the situation?'

They hastily murmured encouragement.

'Mistress Aldith, my friends do all agree,' he said innocently, 'that you should come with me to the castle to tell the brewer his business. You shall be well rewarded, of course.'

Maud suddenly appeared at the door. 'No!' she cried. 'She's a house and husband to keep and—'

'Get that hag out of here,' D'Amory snapped.

Two knights roughly ejected her.

'Now, fairest flower mine, we leave for the castle.'

He took Aldith's arm and forced her to the door. Outside sullen-faced villagers watched silently as they emerged.

'My lord, and that there's Jared's wife,' begged Osbert, drawn by the noise from the forge and still in his leather apron.

'It is, and she's to perform a service for me.' The knights tittered at the sally.

His palfrey was brought up, a showy black and richly appointed with accoutrements.

'Sire, he needs her—'

A gloved fist caught Osbert squarely, knocking him down. 'And now I do.'

D'Amory twisted round and glared. 'Well . . . ?'

Hastily one of the knights made a stirrup cup with his hands and D'Amory swung into the saddle.

'Send the maid up.'

'Sire, I beg you, no!' Aldith pleaded. It brought restless murmurs, which were quickly countered with the drawing of swords.

'Make haste, you oaf!' D'Amory threw down to the knight

making a back for Aldith to mount the horse. Two others hoisted her up.

'Ride on, then!' he snarled.

The horses clattered off, Aldith looking back piteously, the villagers standing speechless.

CHAPTER 10

'What, not done yet?' Jared said breezily as he returned to the smithy. Seeing Osbert's wounded head and set expression he added, 'M' friend – you've met with a mischance?' The man didn't answer, looking at him with profound pity.

Then Jared noticed a knot of people arriving outside, their faces etched with grief.

No one spoke.

'Something's happened, hasn't it? You're not telling me! Aldith – where is she?'

Maud appeared, her face like stone. 'She's not here, son. Gone with the baron's whelp, Sir Gervaise.'

'Gone? God's bones, what are you saying?'

'He came by, took a fancy and . . .'

In the heavy silence his mind whirled and he clutched at a wooden upright until he steadied.

'He came here and . . .' he began huskily but couldn't finish.

'Took her away for himself. She's with him now.'

The reality slammed in. Jared tore himself away and stormed outside, and choking with tears of helpless rage stared at the grim walls that loured above the village.

'She's . . . she's . . .'

'Calm yourself, son. It happens. She'll be back when . . .'

'No! No! Noooooo!' he howled, unhinged by the emotion that flooded his soul, falling to his knees in anguish.

Maud went to him and held him. 'Steady, my boy, your Aldith will come back to you, I promise.'

He broke down and wept pitifully.

She looked up at the others. 'Please leave us, he's taking it hard, poor lamb.'

Stroking his hair she murmured, 'These things do happen to folk such as we. There's nothing we can do, it's our place in nature. We take grievous hurt if we can't get over it betimes, dear son.'

Jared seemed to pull himself together and she sighed. 'I'll allow as it's a hard thing for a man . . .'

But when he got to his feet she saw on his face such a terrible expression, a bleak fury barely held back, and she went cold.

Throwing off her beseeching arms Jared fixed his gaze on the castle in a long agony of hatred, never wavering in his intensity.

'Come with me, m' dearling. You'll get over it in time.'

He didn't respond.

Osbert came and tried to say something but there was nothing that could reach the iron soul.

He was still there when night fell and others came to share his soundless torment, but late into the night they left him to his anguish.

In the morning they found the huddled figure and carried him to his bed, all the while weeping softly for Aldith who had not returned to him.

The day was still young when a frightened youngster hurried up and whispered something to Maud.

She turned white and sat down quickly. Her features contorted for a moment before she buried her face in her hands.

'Go bring Osbert to me,' she told the child.

He came at once.

'Osbert, I want you to tell Jared. For the love of Christ and all the saints, I can not.'

'They found her in the weir, floating – dead. Like an angel, but quite gone from this world.'

Jared's crazed disbelief turned by degrees into stupefaction; his eyes bulged and he bit on his fists bringing runnels of blood.

Then quite suddenly he threw back his head and howled in a hideous desolation that went on and on, echoing out over the village in an unbearable rage against fate.

No one dared approach him as he swayed to his feet, tears flooding down his cheeks, his features a rictus of heartbreak. He staggered unseeingly outside, the others keeping their distance while he found his way to the woods.

'Leave him be,' Maud muttered. 'Leave him to his grief, Lord save his soul.'

They watched the hunched figure lurch away and disappear into the forest.

He did not return that day nor the next.

No one wanted to thrash about in the depths of the dark, evil forest looking for him and it was a relief when on the third day he appeared at the edge of the common.

'Jared! We've been worried of you, m' friend,' Osbert cried, racing up.

What he saw was not his friend. It was a ragged, staring, pitiful shadow of him.

'Come, lad, we'll have you better in a . . .' He tailed off as Jared pushed past with stark, unseeing eyes, making for his house. Osbert followed behind, his heart going out to the tormented soul.

'Food!' Jared croaked. But he didn't sit nor did he show any sign of recognition. His mother quickly found some maslin and blood pudding and pushed them wordlessly into his hands.

They watched his broken-spirited form return to where he'd come from.

'He's a strong boy, he'll get over it but I grieve he missed her burying,' Maud said with a catch in her throat.

'Aye, but in all kindness it's as well he wasn't at the inquest.'

'That cankered Devil's spawn!' she swore. 'The day of judgement will serve him for his evil, and only then will we see true justice!'

As from Saxon times an inquest into a suspicious death had been set in train by the lord of the manor as soon as possible.

Being the last to have dealings with the deceased, Sir Gervaise D'Amory had been called but the man had lightly brushed aside inconvenient questions by swearing that he'd paid the woman good silver for her advice to his brewer, and if she'd been set upon by robbers on the way back with her money, that was hardly his fault.

He'd offered to summon the servants involved who would swear to it but the court ruled that this would not be necessary and returned a verdict accordingly.

Now there was nothing more to do than let the age-old rhythms of the village go forward – but without Aldith's bright presence in their world. After all, in their hard lives was not death a constant visitor?

CHAPTER 11

The pounding in his head would not go away. Jared plucked a celandine, smelt the flower then brutally crushed it. There was no relief, no lifting of the intolerable pain that had turned his waking hours to a living nightmare. In their daily lives the villagers of Hurnwych saw visitations of God and the Devil in the plagues, ruinous harvests and other doleful events, and knew better than to waste time questioning their fate.

But this! This . . . monstrous thing – it was not the work of God, it was the work of man. One man who had ripped out his heart and soul. A dissolute fiend with all the power of a feudal overlord.

For that there could be no forgiveness, no charity.

Tears welled again – but these were tears of impotent rage; his grief was giving way to a lust for vengeance.

He stared up yet again at the grim turrets and shadowed flanks of the castle – why did God allow the existence of such? Why did he not send down titanic thunderbolts from the heavens in just retribution, to tumble those proud stones to dust?

He knew his soul was distorted in agony. Others had lost their sweethearts and had healed, why not he?

With an insane roaring in his ears the answer came back – this was not anybody's sweetling – this was the saintly Aldith that was lost!

A wave of grief threatened to engulf him, and his mind, flailing to escape its hurt, found release in a spreading, alluring and terrible apparition.

Under his hands was the shrieking form of D'Amory, at his mercy and about to pay for his deed. Here, deep in the forest and far from the sight of man he could visit whatever lingering torments he desired on the white, helpless flesh until the final deadly thrust that would send him at last to a waiting Hell.

Jared's fingers writhed together as if they held the evil neck in them.

Nearby was the sombre ruin he now slept in, the old priory, long decayed and overrun by creepers and shunned by all devout passers-by. The few thieves and vagrants in it had gone, terrified by his moods and sudden rages. He had it for himself. And he'd found below the crumbling ruin of the hall a large cellar down a creaking old wooden hatch. Anything that went on there, however evil, would never be heard by a living soul.

His heart leapt – to exterminate under his own hands, with the most extreme suffering, the cause of his anguish would be joy indeed.

For long minutes he feverishly reviewed the means. Above all it must not be quick – no, it had to be long drawn out and the vermin must know why he was paying, and as well that during that time his death was assured. Yes, if he—

The let-down was cruel. It was just a fantasy. He was here, a cold, wretched, broken creature and the baron's son up there warm and snug in his castle, never even knowing of his tragic existence of endless heartbreak.

It wouldn't happen.

His eyes stung and he heaved himself to his feet in the darkening shadows of evening. Another night, to be racked yet again with guilt and remorse, to shiver and suffer on the cold stone, listening to the night sounds of the forest, the scream of a rabbit taken by a stoat, the hoarse roar of a stag – and the haunting beauty of the nightingale.

Yet he couldn't go back home. Not to where he and Aldith had begun their life together and brought forth young David and . . . and . . .

He howled into the darkness, a long and terrible cry that rose up into the uncaring stillness and at its end left everything unchanged.

At some point in his fitful sleep a thought rose up suddenly like a sceptre and wrenched him to full consciousness. A frightful, wonderful thought that brought back in a flood the ferocious gratification he'd felt in his fantasy.

The fantasy was not impossible – it could come true, by God!

Not quite as he'd like it, but the end result was what counted.

Wolfscote Forest was a D'Amory demesne. The baron used it infrequently for hunting but his son was known to ride the forest paths with his followers and thunder along the trackways in breakneck races.

Therefore the cur would come to him. As they rode along, little would the fiend know that his end was nearing with every hoofbeat. As he passed beneath a tree a figure would drop on him, sending him sprawling to the ground and a wickedly gleaming knife would tear out his throat. He would be in hell long before others could come to his aid, and then it would be far too late, justice would have come to Gervaise D'Amory.

Jared knew that he himself would go down, but then what did this life hold for him now?

For the first time for a very long time a deep sleep came to claim him.

The reality of a cold, wet dawn did nothing to daunt him. He had a mission now, a holy vengeance that would be sacrilege not to follow through.

He vowed he would not speak another word until the stinking corpse lay under his knife.

CHAPTER 12

A first task: he needed a weapon. Behind the door of the forge was a seax, the wounding knife that was the mark of a Saxon, made by his father for a friend who'd clung to the old ways but had passed away before claiming it. Now it would attain its consummation in the blood of a Norman.

The second was not so readily achieved. Where was he to lie in wait? The only way was to hide and watch, learn D'Amory's movements and habits – and then lay his plans.

He knew the forest paths and swiftly made his way to the eastern edge of Wolfscote to a broad track that led into the interior where it was closest to Castle Ravenstock. Jared found a likely hiding place among the undergrowth and settled to wait.

With a terrible patience he let the hours pass, ignoring the occasional villager foraging for firewood, a swineherd exercising his right to pannage, the browsing of his pigs on acorns and the like.

It was late afternoon when he was jerked to a full alert by the subliminal thudding of hoofs through the ground.

It was a group of knights led by D'Amory, restless and ready for their sport.

With a fierce hunger Jared's eyes took in his prey: caparisoned like a prince and on a magnificent beast worth many years of his own earnings; a spiteful leer on his face and an air of careless arrogance – this was the evil whoreson who . . .

He crushed the rising emotion with an inhuman strength. Patience! In a very short time that baron's spawn would have the life torn from him by a Saxon knife and it would be enough.

At the edge of the deeper forest the horses came together, whinnying in impatience as their riders laughed and jested. He could hear them but couldn't understand their French; it didn't matter, it was plain they were debating a race and laying wagers.

He watched intently: a massive-thewed oak was in a fine position as the horses impatiently gyrated below it, well suited for his bloody task.

He had to get closer – around this bush and a crouched run to the next copse and—

A shout from one of them had all heads turning his way. Jared shrank back but with a joyous whoop first one then another drew their swords and urged their mounts to a mad gallop straight towards him.

He took to his heels, plunging further into the dense undergrowth, ignoring the sharp whipping stems and thorns. But it slowed him and the deeper he got, the nearer sounded the pursuit – it would have been madness to have fled down the open forest path.

A clearing and another coppice. The first horses reached the thicket with a crash and he heard the rider cursing and swinging his sword but coming up fast – and his thicket was thinning rapidly.

He had minutes to live unless . . . this copse converged on the previous one over to the left – it was a chance!

Hunched, he ran along the outside and doubled back to where he'd been. He dived to the ground, wiggled into the core of the brush and lay still, hardly daring to breathe.

He could hear them crashing about in the undergrowth and through to the far side and then their baffled shouts, their quarry gone to ground.

After some minutes there was an impatient hail and they trotted back, passing so close he could smell them.

More desultory discussion, a pause and then eager shouts and the wild drumming of hoofs fading into the distance. It was another mad race, and he'd been forgotten.

Jaried cautiously peered out. No one.

He crawled out and took a ragged breath.

One thing was certain. This was their usual trail to and from the castle. They'd be coming back this way and he'd been given a second chance.

Carefully choosing a thicket near the big oak tree he squatted down and waited.

After some time the easy cantering of horses and carefree banter floated towards him on the summer air, but unaccountably the horses stopped, even as the distant cries rose and faded.

Then he had it: this was where the River Dene entered the forest and no doubt they'd stopped to quench their thirst after the hard riding.

He waited but they did not resume. An occasional faint cry could still be heard but that was all. What was going on?

Cautiously he made his way toward the sounds.

The briskly flowing river had widened into a broad stretch

before disappearing around a bend. And the riders were swimming there, naked.

About to withdraw he saw a fallen tree, dark and rotten, that lay near submerged and at an angle from the bank. Edging towards it he felt that he'd been granted a miracle.

Preparations would be simple and he had only to be in position for the next time and he stood fair to snatching back the reality of his fantasy.

Jared crouched in the undergrowth the following day and the one after that, the seax in its scabbard strapped to his back and gleaming sharp after hours of attention.

Then on the next day the horses came panting up. He peered out and there, in blazing reality, was the vile cur who this very day would meet justice by his own hand.

With deadly concentration he watched them strip off and plunge in.

He slipped soundlessly into the water by the dead tree and made his way to the snug little pool that lay hidden in its lee. There he remained and watched.

Hoots and mock screams came from all over the wide expanse as the youths frolicked and splashed in the deeper water, but he had eyes for only one, upstream a little and lazily paddling down in the shallows – past him.

With infinite care Jared took note of the positions of the others and their heedless sporting. In savage elation he knew that he was going to succeed.

D'Amory drew nearer and nearer; Jared tensed, a loop of rough cordage gripped tightly in his hands.

For the baron's son the next instant was violent and incomprehensible as a rope suddenly clamped about his neck and wrenched him underwater. Dragged sideways helplessly he surfaced again, choking and heaving in the little pool and into a nightmare – the figure of a tattered, hairy demon with eyes of a hideous intensity . . . who held both the rope and a knife pricking at his throat.

'A sound, and you're spitted!'

The scream died in his throat and he began trembling in terror. 'What do you want with me?'

'Shut your mouth!'

Beyond them the gleeful shouts continued, but after a time they fell away and cries of alarm rang out. There was aimless splashing about before one had the wit to realise that if D'Amory was in difficulties it were better to go downstream to find him.

The sounds faded as they left but Jared didn't stir, keeping a merciless grip on the rope and the point of the blade unwavering at the soft white throat.

The cries returned, a note of panic in them and the nervous whickering of horses – then Jared heard them riding off in a body to get help.

At last!

'Out, you foul monster. Face down – over there!'

Quickly he sat across the naked body and bound the hands securely, as with a trussed pig to market.

'Up!'

For the captive it was a brutal march, stumbling through undergrowth that whipped and tore at his nakedness under the burden of the terror of the unknown, but Jared knew only the surging of a fierce resolution.

At the ruin he threw back the cellar hatch and prodded the whimpering D'Amory down, careful to keep his rope tether taut.

It was a Stygian darkness below but he'd laid his plans well. A steel against flint, and the punkwood tinder took flame. Two candles were lit, which turned the vast space into an evilly illuminated echoing hell, catching the terror-stricken eyes and rendering perfect the stage for what he was about to do.

CHAPTER 13

Jerking the man forward Jared positioned him in front of a pillar, using the rope to fasten his hands behind it. The final scene was set.

This miserable reptile was the rankest kind of craven vermin, who'd swaggered through life at the cost of those beneath him and hadn't the guts to face a situation without the cloak of noble privilege.

'Wh-who are y-you? What do you want with me?'

Jared said nothing, hefting the seax. It was a long-bladed weapon with a blood guide down its middle and coming to a slender point of exquisite sharpness.

Suddenly he lunged, the point stopping at the throat but bringing the first bright pinprick of blood.

'No!' D'Amory gobbled, his eyes hypnotised by the blade. 'Mercy, I beg!'

Jared relaxed the knife but now it pointed down to the fear-shrunken genitals, causing a contortion, a writhing in an extremity of fear.

'I . . . I'll give you a h-hundred marks – no, a thousand!' he sobbed.

'The baron's cub is only worth a thousand?'

'Ten! Thirty thousand – whatever you ask!' There was hope in his voice, a way out by familiar means, anything but the pitiless death he could see in those eyes.

'You'd go to a hundred thousand?'

'Yes! Of course! I'll borrow from my father the baron and my uncle and—'

The knife whipped up again, and leaning close Jared hissed, 'Not enough. There's not enough riches in the kingdom to set against what you did!'

'What did I do?' D'Amory shrieked, seeing his hopes fade and disappear.

'I'll tell you. You defiled a poor dear innocent . . .' he gulped, his eyes misting '. . . and cast her in the river . . .'

The tears were blinding now and the knife trembled in his hand.

'I couldn't help it!' he howled, 'She bit me!'

It was the wrong thing to say.

In a blaze of unbearable emotion Jared stabbed forward wildly, only at the last split-second thinking to deflect the blade to avoid a killing stroke. It sank deep into the shoulder, bringing an inhuman screech from D'Amory that echoed about the old cellar.

Curiously, it steadied him. In a detached way Jared pondered at how the blow felt just like sinking a knife into a tender cut of beef. The wound gaped and pulsed with blood, the dark-red stringy fibres of muscle tissue working each side of it.

'For the love of Christ!' D'Amory screamed from the edge of madness. 'Mary the mother of God and all the saints, have mercy!'

Still in an unnatural calm Jared lifted the blade and with the utmost deliberation traced a line, drawing beads of blood directly across the hairless chest.

The shrieks were now deafening: he frowned in annoyance.

Another line: this time down to the stomach.

'Jesus! Sweet Jesus, save me!'

It made him indignant. To call upon one who'd never once raised a hand to a soul on this earth.

This time the line went across, deeper, and when he'd finished the screams were utterly unhinged, for flopping out of the belly were coils of slimy grey-green veined innards.

Jared drew back in distaste, the wretched thrashing about of the body making the rupture worse. The man was now unreachable in his torment – was there any point in going on?

Perhaps not.

Closing his eyes for a brief moment Jared breathed, 'I do this for you, my best beloved,' and thrust out hard. The blade impaled the throat entirely through to grate against the backbone, the shrieks cut off in the same instant in a bubbling spray of blood.

He turned the knife once in the wound and stepped back, watching unemotionally as the man's life departed, leaving only a corpse to twitch spasmodically.

It was over.

A wave of trembling reaction seized him. After a moment it subsided.

The contorted and blood-smeared remains hung down from the pillar and Jared gazed at it for a long time. It didn't move.

The roaring fire of vengeance that had so consumed him had now left.

Dully, he left the scene for the outer world, now with shadows lengthening in a fine summer evening. He went to the lichen-covered anonymous tomb he'd selected and levered aside the lid. Inside were desiccated bones and fragments of a shroud.

The corpse was heavier than he thought and he was panting

fast by the time he dragged it there and tumbled it in, sliding the lid back across.

Gervaise D'Amory no longer had an existence.

In a last, almost cleansing act, Jared scattered earth over the pools of blood, rubbing out the stains. The seax he wiped clean – it would be returned to its place behind the forge door, no one the wiser.

It was done.

There was nothing to connect him to the disappearance of the baron's son and he made his way home.

CHAPTER 14

'J-Jared! Son – where . . . ?' His mother tailed off when she saw his condition. Ragged, torn, his features ravaged and eyes bloodshot, he walked unsteadily towards her.

She looked at him searchingly: had a corner been turned? She would not press him to speak of what he'd been through, but praise be, he now seemed to be in his right mind. Whatever had happened in the forest was over.

Later, Osbert awkwardly tried to say something. Nolly stood behind him but could find no words to reach out to his friend in his distress and they both withdrew.

Then Perkyn Slewfoot arrived with a small sweetmeat, which he pressed on Jared. He took it dully: Perkyn stared into his face and left, tears streaming.

At the evening meal Maud tried to read her son's features.

Even the news that Gervaise D'Amory had been carried away to a just death by the very river that had borne his Aldith had not broken the brittle mask.

He said little other than that he would not return to the bed he'd shared with Aldith but would sleep in the smithy – and made her promise that no mention must ever be made of what was past and now gone.

That night Jared made up a sleeping area in the smithy outhouse. In the dark stillness around him the rows of pincers, hammers, swages and all the familiar pieces of the blacksmith's art, still odorous of metal, cinders and burnt oil, were comforting and he let sleep steal up on him.

Then the nightmares began. Through the tortured face of D'Amory came the distant image of a body, floating, untouchably poignant.

D'Amory's face changed to a cunning leer. He'd torn himself away, his naked body acquiring clothes as he ran; rich, noble costumes for he was fleeing towards the louring ramparts of the castle, high on the hill. Once there he could not be touched and would look down on him and mock.

Jared woke up in a sweat, disoriented. Burning memories and a meaningless panic tore at him.

The rest of the night passed in a half-sleep of torments and phantasm.

Osbert cautiously welcomed him back to the forge but at Jared's moodiness and set face he kept his silence. They worked together on a barn door hinge, striking alternately on the brightly glowing metal, but what he saw was frightening. Jared's measured blows turned by degrees into smashing, violent hits with hatred in them and when he flipped the piece into the quenching tub it was with an animal snarl.

There was no easing in the days that followed – nights of delirium racking his brain, days of sullen enduring.

It couldn't go on; for Aldith's sake – for little Daw – he had to break out of this whirlpool of madness.

Was it the price for what he'd done? A stricken conscience that would not rest until he'd been sent mad – or were the nightmares a divine retribution? No! He would never accept that what he'd done was other than a quickening of God's justice on a vile creature whose guilt was absolute.

But now he was being tortured by dreams the hardest to bear – his dearest Aldith coming with outstretched arms to comfort him, the utmost concern and love wreathing the image but overtaken with a hopelessness as it fragmented and dissolved.

He had to get away. The heartbreak when he reached a corner of the house and expected her to be around it, the sudden stabs of feeling when little things unbearably reminded him of her – was more than he could endure.

To where? To roam the countryside like a vagabond, take his chances in some town – it didn't make sense, it had no purpose or object. Yet his overwhelming desire was to be gone from a place with so many hurts.

It came to him: he'd go on pilgrimage.

Some went on penance for the absolving of sin, others to see and touch some sacred relic but his reason would be to lay his ghosts.

The announcement was applauded with relief: that it was in suffrage for the soul of Aldith in Purgatory was quite understood and he stood before his parish priest, Father Bertrand with the calm of certainty.

Delighted at the piety of one of the more tepid of his flock the cleric spoke to him at length about his journey. Was it to be St Winefride's Well in the west or St Cuthbert's in the north? Or for the utmost grace, Thomas Becket at Canterbury? Or even going so far as to commit himself to the arduous and laboured trail that led to Santiago de Compostela?

Jared knew what he wanted. Not weeks or even months of absence but a year or more until the remembrances had finally quite faded.

The Holy Land – Jerusalem.

The worthy Father was taken aback. Was Jared aware how expensive the journey was? Yes, he had money put by, and was it not an obligation for the pilgrim to beg alms along the way?

And, there was the matter of the route. It was a perilous and frightful passage across a Europe in turmoil, bands of thieves and brigands at large in great numbers and godliness nowhere to be found. If he was considering joining a group of pilgrims, he could not choose his companions and if they proved to be robbers in disguise he would be hung along with them.

Jared told him he would go by sea. As a boy he had met a pilgrim who had; he vaguely remembered his tales of boredom and filthy conditions at sea for weeks at a time, but he was young and strong and could endure that.

He heard objections about pirates and Devil-conjured storms but his mind was made up.

Jerusalem it would be.

The village gathered round. Nolly fashioned a fine ash staff, which Osbert finished with a forged tip calculated to give pause to wolves and robbers both. His mother sewed his sclavein, the distinctive robe that set him apart as a pilgrim, and a broad-brimmed hat with bleached palm emblems arrived anonymously.

A final touch was the scrip, a pouch that would carry all his worldly means. This he made himself from leather.

Suddenly, it was time to depart.

The last rite was to have his raiment blessed at the altar with what seemed to be the entire village in respectful attendance, and after a tearful farewell from his mother and a backward wave at his friends, Jared set forth on his pilgrimage.

CHAPTER 15

In only a short while a bend in the road would hide the villagers from sight and he would be alone. He was stepping out on a journey that could bring him back a tranquil soul, or leave his bones in some faraway grave.

He'd given Daw into his mother's care; by the time he returned in a year or so how would his little son have changed? Would he be remembered?

The smithy he'd left with Osbert, a capable pair of hands who'd promised to put by his share of its increase for his return. If he didn't come back – well, Daw would be an orphan and the parish church would be richer by that amount.

Jared gripped his staff tighter, the swing of his loose sclavein quite different to the close-fitting tunic he usually wore and the broad-brimmed hat a strange weight. No doubt he'd get used to it – this was only the first few yards of the unknowable miles that lay ahead.

A figure abruptly emerged from the hedge ahead and began moving toward him with a familiar hobble, Perkyn Slewfoot.

'Jared – Master!' he blurted. 'I'm here!'

'A merry meet, good Perkyn,' he said drily. 'And so you're here.'

'Aye, Master.'

'I've business in a far place, I've no time for talk.'

'Take me with you, I beg! You're on a pilgrimage, you'll need a servant and I shall be—'

'What are you saying! You're a villein, you owe service to Sir Robert and are not free to leave as you will. And besides which, I'm a poor pilgrim, I've got no means to pay a wage.'

'Master, if you take me, your man for a year, it'll settle my conscience of what I'm in debt to you!'

'I thank you, Perkyn, you're a good soul but you've a mother to care for.'

'She's gone. Died o' shame when she heard I was to be . . . so I've no one left, Master.'

Jared had a surge of feeling for the man – they were both running from memories.

'And now you're wanting to be a vagabond, fleeing from your lord.'

'If you'll take me, Master, I go with you.'

It was tempting – a companion and helper through a year or more of hard travel. He glanced at the earnest, beseeching face, the pale-blue eyes framed by fair-haired Saxon curls, and weakened.

'Your foot? It's more miles than you can count. Won't you—?'

'Master, I've followed the plough for many a league. Will this be so different?'

'You'll beg your way, pray for alms?'

'As your true servant, Master.'

'And when we come back, what then?'

A lord's punishment over an absconding bondsman would be dire.

Perkyn's face fell, but he replied obstinately, 'Master, I still go.'

'You've just earned yourself your place, then. And you've forgotten something.'

'Thank you! Thank you, Master! Er . . . forgot?'

'That any villein as can stay abroad for a year and a day, the law says gains release from his lord. When you get back you'll be a free man!'

CHAPTER 16

The sun was out, the smells of the open country pungent on the air, the song of birds carefree and sweet – and every step put a distance between Jared and his hurts. It was going to work!

'Master, where are we headed to?'

'Why, the Holy Land of our Lord Jesus.'

'I mean, are you sure and all, that this is the way?' Perkyn asked nervously.

Jared gave a small smile. A villein never saw anything but his village so Perkyn's ignorance was understandable, but he had once travelled with his father nearly all the way to Tamworth and therefore was a man of the world. He'd spoken to Father Bertrand and a friar from the next village who knew pilgrim matters and they had set him straight. To Banbury and then on to Woodstock near Oxford where he'd no doubt find others on their way south on the Pilgrim's Way to Rye, avoiding London. At that busy port he would take ship for Venice and from there direct to the Holy Land itself.

'Yes, the high road to Banbury, next—'

'Is this it?' Perkyn asked, wide-eyed.

'It must be,' Jared said irritably. Hadn't it always been pointed out to him as such?

But this was nothing more than a cart track in a grassy way, winding along the side of a slight rise, and since leaving Hurnwych they'd crossed a stream and seen several cattle trails wind away on their own. But didn't drovers go direct to market, to Banbury? If so, they were going the wrong way and would have to spend the night in a ditch.

They stumped on but as the sun lowered Jared stopped and sat on the side of the road. To be lost on the very first day! If only—

On the air came a faint jingle and a string of four packhorses and a driver came into view. It drew closer and the sun-reddened man doffed his hat to the pilgrims.

'Saint Christopher's blessing on you both,' he said respectfully.

'God's favour on you, good driver. Are you bound for Banbury, by chance?'

'I am that. Salt and wool, has to be there by sundown.'

Relief flooded Jared. 'Then we'll walk together.'

The spire of St Mary's was a welcome sight above the hills and the little party wound down into the town.

The driver pointed. 'Yonder is Banbury Cross and over there your inn, The Blue Goose.'

A wave of fatigue and reaction washed over Jared and the thought of a good meal was irresistible.

'Let's get ourselves a bed, then,' he told Perkyn.

It was a market day and the inn seethed with humanity.

'Yo, the innkeeper!' he called against the noise.

A short, surly man appeared.

'Two o' your best ales, and we'll sup and have a bed for the night.'

'A bed? That'll be a penny from each o' you.'

'We're pilgrims, Master Innkeeper. Can you not—?'

'A penny, pilgrim or saint, all the same to me.'

This was steep – a free ploughman might toil half the day for a silver penny.

'A penny for both?'

'Each. It's market, I can fill a bed without trying. Take it or leave it.'

The ale was good, and they found a place at the end of a table and readily quaffed it with their stewed mutton.

There were one or two curious glances but Jared was too footsore to join in conversation and demanded his bed.

It was in an open space on the upper gallery around a central well and one of a tight-packed row of cloth-covered straw mattresses in a rope-strung wooden frame.

There were already several occupied with sleepers snoring drunkenly but Jared was too tired to care.

'Hey, you share!' growled the innkeeper when Perkyn made to take another.

Jared shrugged. Finding refuge in his wrapped sclavein he felt Perkyn ease in beside him and with a whiff of musty straw he composed himself for sleep.

The night was not pleasant: so much humanity, coughs, muttering, the barking of dogs, late arrivals – it was something to be endured.

The morning brought grey skies and threatening rain but impelled by the far-distant calling they tramped off down the road, which they were assured would lead to Woodstock.

Some miles further they reached a river, broad and rush-fringed. The muddy road led into the water but there were stepping stones to the other side and they hopped and leapt across, laughing like children.

The going was better – gently rolling pastures and fields, woodland and the occasional village.

At one Jared decided to beg for alms. He sat cross-legged by the stone cross at the centre of the common. With his bowl before him he self-consciously assumed an expression of saintly resolve. Many village folk passed but none so much as threw him a glance.

He took to loudly blessing the passers-by and then began to sing psalms but as he didn't know many he tailed off and simply held up his bowl. By the afternoon he'd acquired two farthings and a foreign coin.

Perkyn had taken a position on the other side of the common and was now surrounded by a knot of people. Jared got to his feet and went to see what the attraction was.

He heard a heart-rending tale of woe, and the piteous sight of the crippled pilgrim Perkyn supporting himself on his staff would have moved the hardest of hearts.

And it did – five groats, thirteen pennies and two loaves of bread.

'For all love, Perkyn! We eat well tonight by your good grace.'

It was not to be. Some miles further on, the rain spattered then sheeted down and a fast run to a field barn saved them a soaking. It didn't ease off until evening and there was little for it but to stretch out in the hayloft, making the best of their loaves and a little hoarded cheese before settling down for the night.

They were discovered in the morning and sent off after a fine mess of pottage and with apples for the road.

'We must be close to Woodstock,' Jared grumbled after some hours of trudging along a windswept ridgeway.

The trail descended into a valley and a gently wreathing fog. Its cold, clammy embrace enveloped them and the meandering trail was hard to follow without being able to see ahead. They stumbled on, not even the sun's direction to aid them, but then came the sound of church bells right ahead.

It was the church of St Mary Magdalene, Woodstock.

Jared and Perkyn were weary and their feet ached but they had arrived. They had but to find the hospice to join the main route for pilgrims to the south.

Woodstock was a pretty town, the highway and square clean and well found.

A friendly passer-by told them that their hospice was further down the road. It was a substantial, stone-built churchly structure. They pulled the bell rope and were met by a lay brother and welcomed in. A milestone on the road to Jerusalem had been reached.

Inside there were fellow pilgrims – men and women, old and young, and from the evening meal tables they called a welcome.

Now part of a pilgrim band they would never be alone again, nor be lost or fear for robbers.

They were on their way!

CHAPTER 17

Rye, south coast of England

The pilgrims reached the outskirts of Rye with mounting excitement. This was where they would take ship to foreign parts and adventures unknown – two souls from the deep countryside whose acquaintance with great waters was no more than the village pond. As they topped the last rise into the town the sea spread out before them, sparkling and immense, stretching completely across their vision from one side to another and out to a fearful empty horizon.

The little band paused to take in the sight before heading down the hill to look for the Mermayde Inn where the shipmen were to be found.

Jared kept close to his new friend Dickin of Shrewsbury who'd been in a ship before, on pilgrimage to Santiago of Compostela. His advice was to closely question the hard-eyed seamen, so different to the land folk, with their muscled upper bodies and hands like claws.

There was indeed a ship about to sail – *Winchelsea*, a cog loading for Lisbon in wool and pewter. There would be no lack of traders from there to Venice.

An alternative was the hulc *Judith of Romney*, larger and

travelling direct to Venice, but this would not arrive here for a week, days in idleness that would cost them dear.

Down at the wharf the ship looked huge; a single mast nearly as high as a church steeple and a fat hull that was fast filling with square packs of wool and wooden cases, which was then planked over. A raised deck aft formed a wide cabin beneath, the whole ship giving an impression of stout but plain utility.

'When can we get on it?' Jared asked, excited at the impossible thought that this entire little world would move across the ocean and then appear in a foreign place just as it looked before him now.

'We'd not be welcome yet. And we've things to do – you'll be needing a few items for a sea journey as they won't give you on board,' Dickin said.

When they struggled back later each carried a mattress, a thick wool coat and a supply of foodstuffs.

Eventually they were let aboard.

Jostled by sailors and dockhands they were shown to the side of the vessel and sternly cautioned to stay there until told otherwise.

From the raised deck a torrent of foul-mouthed abuse had the seamen clap on to lines and heave ropes in a confusing pell-mell of rushing feet and curses. With a bumping and lurch felt through the decking a giant mainsail suddenly blew free, banging and thundering as it was brought under control and the ship took up a definite lean to one side.

The swish of water past the hull told Jared that against all reason the entire structure must be moving. He dared a quick look above the bulwark and with a fearful thrill saw that the waterfront was separated from them by fifty feet of dark water and houses were sliding past, already faster than a man could walk.

The distance widened, the buildings diminished and by degrees the world of land grew less real as their wooden one became their only existence on the widening waste of water. The mouth of the river took a sharp turn to the south – and there was the open sea.

The great bulk of the ship that had seemed so secure and solid alongside the wharf was now jibbing and bucketing with a liveliness that had them hanging on for dear life. Perkyn slid down the deck, eyes bulging with fear. Jared yanked him up again.

The pilgrims looked back at the line of the shore as the familiar trees and fields slipped away. Some mumbled prayers and petitions, for this was an experience unimaginable to honest countrymen. They could only seize a rope and stare hopelessly at the immensity of water – now as far as the eye could see in every direction except the receding shore.

Sailors came around and showed them how to tie their mattress rolls and bag of possessions to the side. They were also at pains to explain what to do if a sea serpent appeared and threatened to swallow the ship and gave many other useful tips.

Further out to sea the winds blew flat and hard. Stinging spray was driven back at every plunge of the bow but Jared was getting used to the roll and heave and determined that he'd tour the ship. Passing from handhold to handhold he found that the only enclosed space was the cabin at the after end of the ship, which was barred to travellers. Above it was an open deck with a rail, which he wasn't about to try to reach.

He lurched forward under the huge straining sail and reached the sharp prow with its ropes soaring up, then returned to where Perkyn was hunched miserably.

'Not as if there's much to see,' he muttered while *Winchelsea* continued its wild dance with Neptune.

In all there were five pilgrims and a chapman trying to make themselves comfortable against the hard side of the ship, out of the wind, blankly enduring.

Jared pulled his coarse greatcoat around him – how could they exist like this for the weeks to Lisbon?

Evening approached. The crew brought up buckets, effortlessly coping with the heaving deck. Their evening meal: sausage and hard biscuit. It was fusty, plain and little enough but he was hungry and devoured his, and was ready with his pot when the ale came around. It was only half-filled but he soon found out why, it sloshed about maddeningly as he tried to drink.

Night drew in and the travellers could do nothing other than to take to their tiny beds under what covering they could find and wait for the dawn.

Stiff and cold, Jared sensed a lightening and saw the sea slowly take form and shape, a sullen grey emptiness without limit until he made out a vague rumpling of coast far off to the left. It didn't register at first that something was wrong – it was on the other side of the ship.

Dickin explained he was now looking at France and that after they turned the corner to the left then he'd see some seas that would make this look like a duck pond.

Hollow-eyed, Perkyn lolled listlessly against the bulwark.

The size of the seas increased by the hour, long murderous rollers came on with a malice that was almost personal, and when they shaped course south they took these at an angle, producing an awkward screwing motion.

With the jerking swoops and lifts Jared lost his grip on what was up and what was down and joined the others in helpless retching, watched by a mocking crew.

They suffered for four more long days until they raised a headland. In its lee was a town and ships similar to their own, but nearer dead than alive they took little interest in hearing that this was Corunna in the Spanish kingdom of Galicia.

The flint-hearted captain would not listen to their pleas to be allowed ashore to die on dry land. To avoid landing taxes he took on their water by boat and put to sea again without delay.

Thankfully, three days later it was Lisbon and *Winchelsea* was squared away for the run upriver to the city. Even more wonderful was their release from a watery hell to the delirious feeling of solid ground under their feet, and a kindly innkeeper who would take in voyagers unwashed for many days and weak with privation.

Perkyn begged that they continue their pilgrimage on foot, as nature intended, but was persuaded by the sight of another ship.

A much larger cog, this had a splendid castle with battlements standing proud above the afterdeck and another, smaller, set right out over the prow. From its lofty single mast fluttered pennons of some noble order of chivalry and well-dressed people strolled her deck. And yes, there was room for worthy pilgrims on their way to the Holy Land.

Guglielmo di Venezia was returning merchants to Venice along with a contingent of knights to Malta, and was victualling for a comfortable journey. As they watched, wine, poultry, barrels of seafood and fruit were loaded aboard. An altogether different experience promised.

They sailed with the tide. However, the lavish cabins aft were provided for the knights and merchants; theirs were little more than stalls and bare timbers, even if these were below, sheltered from wind and sea.

On deck they were ordered to remain right forward, out of

the way of the higher class of passenger and when the fragrant odours of cooking drifted down, for them it was only cheese and salted meats.

At night, packed in below in stifling darkness, there was nothing to do but lie awake with the sound of great creaks and grinding, the sea swashing past in thumps and gurgles and the droning of sleepless conversations.

The stench of the confined space was hard to take. Bilge, stale urine, rat droppings. The lurching movement of the ship in the airless and oppressive dimness brought on seasickness in several and the fetor of vomit had its inevitable effect on the others, transforming it to a hell of misery.

Jared felt the light scutter of rats running over him and gloomily questioned why he'd undertaken this nightmare of a journey. A cooler voice told him that the ship was moving along as fast as he could run, day and night, and these were all miles that he did not have to walk.

Later they passed a massive lion-shaped rock and then the nature of the sea changed. No longer the long swells and hard westerlies, the waves were shorter and steeper and the glittering expanse of water was agreeably sun-drenched.

They had left the cold northern lands behind and now – some weeks directly ahead in the direction of the rising dawn – was the Promised Land, the birthplace of the Christ-child. Against this tawdry reality it seemed too fantastical to be true.

CHAPTER 18

Time passed slowly. They touched at ports for resupply of fresh victuals and wines but if he wanted any variation in the repulsive ship's food on issue Jared found it was yet another demand on his fast diminishing store of coins.

Then, quite unexpectedly, the ship slewed out of its track and sailors raced to bring down the big sail. In a few minutes the vessel had come to a standstill and was drifting aimlessly.

It made no sense, and looking aft Jared could see figures peering down over the stern-quarters and shouting.

'Wonder what happened,' he muttered to Perkyn.

The sail was half-raised again and this time there was a long oar tied to one side, which was used to turn the vessel so it fell before the wind and headed toward a distant hazy coastline.

The mystery deepened.

Just before the evening meal Perkyn returned with news. 'I've a friend, Master, and he's page to a knight and hears it all. He says the rudder's broken and they need to get into a port to repair it, and that's where we're going.'

Later, Perkyn heard that the captain was much worried. If they couldn't get the rudder back in working order the voyage would be at an end. No longer could they sail in the right direction, and worse, if it came on to blow there was every prospect that they would be driven on the rocks, unable to steer away from them.

In the morning the land was much closer and they crabbed along the coast.

A little village of white and terracotta buildings with a single jetty nestled at the foot of a scrubby hillside, encircled by a bay. *Guglielmo di Venezia* came to anchor offshore, too big to come in further, and the captain and others took to the boat.

It would seem that after all they were to be saved.

However, the party returned quickly, clearly in an ill temper.

Perkyn sought out his friend, and came back with bad tidings. The local folk had seen the big ship enter the bay and assumed it was on a raid of sack and plunder. All had fled. There was no one left to do the repair and nobody on board who could. The job was too skilled, there were no tools, no forge in the ship.

Perkyn let his words hang as Jared took in that they needed a blacksmith, then gave a slow wink.

The pageboy was sent to his master with a message and before long Jared was summarily called aft.

'You're a smith?' snapped the captain.

'Aye. Jared of Hurnwych.'

'Take a look and tell me what you think.'

Jared was led to the side and shown the problem under the gaze of curious knights and ladies.

The rudder was suspended by iron pins pivoting through a corresponding socket on the ship, two of them. The top socket had failed and the rudder hung perilously from the lower.

He looked closer. It was an iron fitting, and simple – a flat bar turned back on itself and shaped to take the pin. It had split, releasing the pin to hang free.

Jared turned back with a deep frown. 'It can't be repaired.'

'Why not?' blustered the captain.

'You could try a fire-weld, but it's split once and is weakened. It's like to break again and at the wrong time.'

'Then we're lost!'

'I didn't say that. A new one is not impossible, but where's my forge and anvil?'

A tall, shaven-headed man stepped forward. 'If I take you to one, can you make it?'

Jared nodded; he was their only chance.

'Captain, I'm to take this man to the port smithy where he'll make use of the tools.'

'Yes, sire.'

'And be guarded by my men. Good Jared, I'm Sir Nicholas Gayne. If you're able to rescue us from this calamity you'll be well rewarded.'

Jared inspected the fitting closely, noting its measurements and how it was secured to the hull by through bolts. The heads would have to be filed away and the bolts punched clear to remove the old, and the new would require holes in the right place and a full set of bolts.

'I can do it, but only if the smithy is well found, Sir Nicholas.'

It was gratifying to note the numbers of anxious faces looking at him, waiting for his verdict.

The boat set out for the shore, filled by knights and squires, armed and mailed. Jared of Hurnwych – his bodyguard!

It was not a big village but it took a little while to find the smithy on the road out into the country.

With a quick glance Jared was satisfied. It was a homely, well-kept place, tools and pincers in neat rows on the walls, a full-sized anvil in pride of place, and best of all, a charcoal fire still alight where the smith had abandoned it to run for the hills.

'It will do. Send for my assistant, Perkyn,' he commanded. He'd make sure that his friend would be involved in order to be rewarded as well.

Rummaging around he found bar iron of approximately the right width and by the time a wide-eyed Perkyn arrived he had assembled his gear.

'Wear that,' he said, throwing him a leather apron. 'You're a smith's apprentice for today!'

Jared set him to the bellows, a big goatskin apparatus, and soon the fire was roaring with violet and blue-white at its core.

First the bolt holes. There was a steel hole punch that made short work of producing matching holes in the white-hot iron. Then it was a swage to form the socket eye as the bar was brought around. After some deft persuasion with the hammer he had it trued and set up to full satisfaction.

A final quenching for hardness and he had his new fitting.

'Then we can sail?'

'Yes, Sir Nicholas,' Jared said with confidence.

The knight fished about in his scrip and found silver, which he placed on the anvil with all respect and gratitude to the saviour blacksmith.

CHAPTER 19

Malta, AD 1291

Malta was alive with activity. In its great harbour were scores of ships loading and discharging and many boats criss-crossing the sparkling sea. And ashore – tented camps under every standard known to the Christian world.

Guglielmo di Venezia remained aloof, for its merchants had their business elsewhere: in Venice, where also some of its travellers would take pilgrim ships to the Holy Land. The knights, however, came on deck with their baggage and servants; they had reached their destination and left to join the great concourse ashore.

There would be no delaying. *Guglielmo* would sail when they'd watered, north up the entire length of Italy to fabled Venice, the most prosperous city in the world.

With the vessel still, Jared set to with needle and thread to repair his sclavein while he had the chance. He'd only been at work a short time when he was called aft.

Sir Nicholas Gayne had returned on board and beckoned him over. 'A word with you, Master Jared.'

'Sire?'

'I have an offer for you, to your considerable advantage.

'You are making pilgrimage to Jerusalem, a most worthy and sacred purpose. I know not your means, still less your reasons, but have you considered the cost in dues and tolls? For instance, the Venetians ask a hard price for their passage – fifty ducats, I shouldn't wonder. The Mussulmen will demand their bribes, and where is your gold piece for entry to the Holy Sepulchre?'

Jared inwardly flinched. Nobody had mentioned anything about this to him and if it was true there was no way he could raise this sort of money.

'Offer, sire?'

'Yes, a most handsome one, and won by your own skill. It is within my power to grant you a passage direct to the Holy Land from here, and not only that but a daily fee to relieve your needs. How say you?'

'Er . . .'

'Let me explain. I go to join the Knights Hospitallers sent by our liege lord, King Edward, on the holy crusade lately proclaimed by His Holiness. We sail tomorrow for the kingdom of Jerusalem at Acre but have been much embarrassed by the untimely passing of our armourer and smith. I have seen your valiant work, and should you agree to perform service for us in this office, we should be much beholden to you. I'm sure I needn't make mention that this does not require you to take up arms . . .'

'My pilgrimage—'

'Nazareth is but eight leagues to the south and Jerusalem a little further. You will find time for the visit, I'm persuaded. And in the character of a Crusader and, of course, therefore spared taxes and vexations,' he added smoothly.

All for taking hammer to anvil once more. And in the greatest cause – when he returned to Hurnwych he would have such a tale to tell!

'I shall have need of my apprentice.'

'Of course.'

'Then, My Lord, I'll do it.'

CHAPTER 20

Acre, the Holy Land

The Crusader warship was quite a different craft: strong, well armed and capacious, it had twin lateen masts and could carry horses and much war materiel. Built for one purpose it had no refinements or comforts but Jared was grateful for their snug space near the bow where they were not disturbed.

They made Acre without incident in a convoy of eight ships, the largest with the unmistakeable three golden lions on red of the King of England, and they joined the many others lying off the small quay.

The city was the biggest Jared had ever seen. Well sited on a north–south triangular peninsula and extending inland, it was protected on all three sides by formidable walls along its length with towers at strategic intervals. Its harbour, tucked well in on the eastern side, was out of range and untouchable. This Crusader stronghold would never be starved out in siege.

Ashore, following the baggage train, he took in the most bizarre, curious and exciting place it was possible to imagine. He wended his way through narrow streets packed with humanity, donkeys and street-sellers; exotic smells and human stink heavy on the air along with the babble of strange tongues.

After all his trials he was at last in the Holy Land.

Quarters were in a compound below the north wall next to the grand Hospitaller Fortress, a stone building of such size it made him stare. The wood-framed canvas beds in the dormitory were clean and comfortable and lofty ceilings promised a cool summer's night.

He was given chance to visit his workplace before supper, a building nearby surrounding a quadrangle. Along each side were forges and workshops, at least a dozen in number with a central administration.

'William Kettle, quartermaster armourer of the Order.' A grey-haired veteran looked up from his books at the introduction.

'Jared of Hurnwych'.

'Arms, escutcheons, mail . . . ?' the man grated.

'Wha . . . ?'

'Right,' Kettle said heavily. 'You're general smithing until you see your way clear to do a man's work. Tell Baldovino, someone.' He returned to his books.

Baldovino of Pisa was the head smith and sized him up quickly. 'With Gamel. Until I says so.'

It was the end forge and the smallest. Jared was greeted by a large, red-cheeked man packing away some tools whose face split to a huge gap-toothed grin on seeing him.

'All hail, fellow!' he chortled, clapping Jared on the shoulder. 'As you look a likely sword striker!'

They met again for supper at the refectory.

'A pilgrim paying his way? Where from, brother?'

It did not take long to exchange particulars. Hugh Gamel of York, a child at the last crusade and left fatherless here. He recalled little of the country of his birth and had been in the service of the

Knights Hospitallers since he could remember. Jared's tale was less colourful and he was eager to know what was going on in this so much vaster canvas.

Shrewd and knowledgeable, Hugh explained how over the years the Crusaders had lost ground to the Saracens; Jerusalem and the holy places of Christianity going piece by piece until, with the fall of Tripoli, the only significant holding left from the days of Richard the Lionheart was Acre itself.

There had been a peace treaty in existence that allowed foreigners the right of pilgrimage to Jerusalem and this had worked well, with much trade and prosperity resulting. But recently there'd been an incident in Acre that had seen Mohammedan blood shed and the Sultan in Cairo had taken the opportunity to declare he would seize the city to punish the offenders. Fortunately he had died soon after and the alarm had subsided.

As to the Ninth Crusade, the Kingdom of Jerusalem had shrunk to not much more than Acre. King Henry II prudently shifted offshore to Cyprus when the response to the pope's proclamation had been niggardly in the face of squabbling among the major powers resulting from some kind of dynastic uproar in Sicily he didn't understand. It was just as well the threat had died down for if not they'd be in for a hard time.

'We'd be safe here, surely?' Jared said, remembering the lofty walls.

'You'd think so,' Gamel agreed. 'Inner and outer walls, twenty towers, our own water, can never be starved out.'

He looked around furtively. 'And I hold it to my heart that if we look like being overcome by the Saracens, the likes of we can hop in a boat and be gone, they can't stop us!'

CHAPTER 21

The next day Jared began in the forge. It was straightforward enough: a repair to a massive gate hinge, horseshoes, a wheel rim, endless wire for chain mail. He set to with a will for this was what he did, and he knew his craft.

Perkyn was put to work as well – moving from bellows duty to snatching pieces from the fire with pincers and handing them to Jared, clearly enjoying the sensation.

In three days Gamel pronounced Jared worthy of more warlike employment. This turned out to be pike heads, a trivial task for one of his skills but requiring care at the tip-hardening.

Other pieces came his way: the glaive, a blade on a pole for stabbing and with a wicked hook to bring down a rider, war hammers and many kinds of daggers. These were plain but lethal and intended for nothing more than crude battle hackery by the common soldier.

An armourer's craft was quite different to that of a blacksmith, however. To tackle the elegant and powerful weapons of the knight he must wait for his skills to develop.

Jared saw around him some who specialised in helmets, with their beautifully finished curves and fitments, and others at the hauberk, the universal mail shirt. It was plain that those who tended to the knight's accoutrements were at the pinnacle of the art and looked down on all others.

He worked hard and learnt: the straightforward heat treating of a ploughshare was nothing compared to the delicate tempering required of a blade weapon and the forming of the awkward shapes of body armour at the anvil.

And it was having an effect: no more bursts of hatred, and the tormenting dreams had virtually ceased, retreating into a dull glow of hurt at his core.

After they'd taken their morning meal, Hugh muttered, 'Has you heard, Jared? There's a new sultan in Cairo – Khalil, I think his name is – and he's saying as he's going to see through what the old one wanted.'

'You mean, have a go at Acre?'

'A siege. He's called a holy war and is marching against us. I've a feeling in my bones that very soon we're going to be working all the hours God gives us.'

'We've won before! Richard the Lionheart—'

'Those days are old and gone, m' friend. The Mohammedan is a brave and crafty enemy and there's more of them than us. A lot more.'

'We've got the Lord on our side.'

'If that's so, how is it we're down to this one city? We've got some fine men in knight's hall but are they enough?'

'Who?'

'Why, there's your own Otho de Grandison sent by Edward Longshanks himself with a goodly number. Quite a few Teutonic Knights and of course our Grand Master of Hospitallers, Jean de

Villiers – he's a famous sword and he's got Matthew de Clermont as marshal, a mighty fighter and . . . well, others.'

Jared sensed defensiveness.

'And men?'

'Not so many, don't know for sure. But we've plenty of French crossbows and so many Italians it took twenty-five galleys to bring 'em here. And not forgetting another five from Aragon, and . . .'

'And?'

'Enough of this gab,' Hugh finished testily, 'We've got work to do.'

CHAPTER 22

Rumour turned to reality in less than two weeks. Away to the south a faint dust cloud across a wide front became visible and as the hours passed it grew broader and more ominous.

The Saracens were coming.

Some in the city left. Merchants, the shiftless, the wealthy. It was an easy enough departure for the ones who could afford to as the Genoese and Venetian shippers were laying on immediate transport. For most, however, their life's work and fortune was rooted in the city and to flee would mean its abandoning.

Jared viewed these developments with trepidation. This was not his quarrel – he was a pilgrim, not a Crusader. There was every reason to make his retreat while he could.

'What's to do, Perkyn?' he asked his loyal travelling companion.

'Master, this you must say. For both of us.'

Jared didn't owe the Hospitallers service in the same way as a feudal lord, he was a paid servant and could quit at any time. But then again, was it right to deprive them of a valued artisan at their time of greatest need?

He'd stay. Guiltily, he knew that the decision hung more on the fact that as Hugh had said, if it got sticky they could always get away by boat.

The horde came into plain view – a confusing mass of soldiery on horseback and in columns along with hundreds of carts and followers in the rear. Sunlight glinted on weapons and armour in a stomach-tightening display – Jared's first sight of the dread panoply of war.

As they neared, the gates of Acre were closed and barred. No one could enter or leave save by sea – a formal state of siege was now in effect.

Silent figures in their thousands watched the great army approach and divide as it lay up against the landward walls of the city.

It took shape: to the centre away on a rise was the blood-red tent of Sultan Khalil. The wings of the encirclement met the sea on each side, and beyond it making camp and preparing – out of range of archer and crossbows but in full sight – faces, movements; alien and terrifying.

'We got a lot o' work on,' rumbled Kettle. 'You all know what a siege means. First up, I'll have a thousand crossbow bolts put by, before they start coming to us with their busted weapons. Then we'll hear what the Grand Master wants.'

They set to and laboured into the night, spurred on by what lay outside the walls. The heads of the bolt were socketed, requiring skilled work at the mandrel, while the square-sectioned tip had to be precisely matched on its sides, or the bolt would not fly true. Jared found it was harder than it looked and his first three attempts were scornfully rejected by Kettle.

To his great satisfaction Perkyn was taught how to bring along bar iron to shape while idle youngsters were put to the bellows.

In a rest break Jared went up on to the walls to see for himself.

The siege line was established in depth, with hundreds of figures moving purposefully to and fro. A sea of tents, brazen pennants and banners everywhere and a ceaseless murmur of sound.

The battlements were manned with sentinels standing silently. He saw that the rearing outer walls were matched by an equally sized inner wall. If the enemy scaled the outer they could be assailed from the safety of the inner, a near hopeless mission for even the bravest.

He returned to work reassured.

CHAPTER 23

Four days later there were developments.

The Saracens began massing in lines up and down the siege works. Behind them several engines of some kind were dragged up and men stood by them, as if waiting for a signal.

'Don't like it,' Hugh muttered. 'Looks like Khalil is pressing to close in and start the fun.'

As they watched a single trumpet bayed. It was taken up and along the line, then as one each soldier raised a wicker shield.

Urgent warning shouts passed along the walls and men hustled up from below. In the towers soldiers readied with stands of arms – and the Saracens moved forward.

The reason for the protection became apparent: to shield the men hauling the engines forward. As they came into range a cloud of arrows fell on them from the walls and towers. Men dropped, the first blood of the siege, but the advance went on at a steady and ominous pace.

'What are they doing?' Jared asked anxiously.

'Them's mangonels. Throws stones and fire but they need to get in close enough. We've got ours and we'll give 'em a pounding while they're at it but they're nasty brutes and I'm not staying about to say hello. Come on – all them arrows means we've got more work on our plate.'

The first mangonels fired. In an ungainly swing each hurled an object in a lazy parabola that descended from up in the sky to meet the wall with a splintering crash and a force enough to be felt through the feet. Others, aimed higher, came down in the city streets in a crazy rampage of destruction, stones half as big as a man.

The distant sounds made Jared freeze. Perkyn's eyes met his in terror.

'Don't be a-feared, lads,' Hugh rumbled. 'They can't reach in more than a hundred yards or so. We'll be safe.'

Jared tried not to think of the ordeal of those whose duties kept them at the wall.

There was now a tense, brittle atmosphere. In the refectory men spoke little, keeping their thoughts to themselves.

A strange implement was brought in to the forge with instructions that it be restored and returned with all haste. With a crooked handle and spiked and splayed blade it looked like nothing Jared had seen before but the repair was obvious and a strong fire-welding had the unusually stout haft reattached.

'All speed – you'd better get it to 'em yourself,' Hugh threw at him.

He was told where to find the unit but wasn't prepared for what he came to – a square hole with a pulley arrangement set in the ground some yards in from a tower.

'Get in, then!' he was urged.

Jared was lowered down near twenty feet to a chamber. Leading off it was a passage, the darkness relieved only by occasional dim lights at the far end. A tunnel hacked through raw earth, it reeked of damp and foul effluvia. As he went forward the confined space pressed in on him. From the direction it seemed they were going under the wall, an immense weight of stone above that could collapse on him at any moment.

Gulping, he finally made it to the end where men were working by the light of rush dips, stark jerking shadows flung on the jagged surface of the tunnel. They were hacking at the face at a furious speed and he saw what his implement was for: as one wielded a pick the other would reach through his legs and with a stab and twist bring out the debris with the tool.

The repair was snatched from his hand and put into immediate use by the sweating crew without a word in the fetid, breathless air.

Jared lost no time in reaching sunlight, then finding Hugh.

'Not good,' he muttered. 'They're countermining, m' friend. Means that Khalil is getting serious – he's mining under the towers, wants to bring 'em down.'

He went on: the mangonels were terrifying but not the menace they seemed. On their own the fortifications could withstand the battering as the plunging missiles always hit at an angle. The real threat was invisible and deadly.

The Saracens had started shafts from the safety of their lines headed underground directly towards the walls of Acre. The impregnable twenty-feet-thick walls and high towers were helpless against their insidious creeping and when they had undermined the massive stonework, without any kind of warning the walls and towers both would collapse into rubble, leaving a gaping breach.

Those Jared had seen when he'd delivered the repair were frantically working against time to intercept the advancing menace. At any moment they could break through the earth into an enemy tunnel and then it would be the horror of brutal combat in the cramped darkness.

How could the Saracen miners doggedly drive their shaft ever closer in the certain knowledge that when the moment of consummation came it would mean their instant crushing or suffocation under tons of collapsing earth and stone?

That night sleep was denied Jared. As he lay in the warm darkness it was impossible to keep at bay the thought of the thousands out there dedicated to tearing down their defences and slaying them all without mercy.

The next day it was crossbow bolts again but this time repairing the many score of retrieved quarrels that had been shot by the Saracens at the men on the walls as they fought to fell the hundreds working the giant mangonels.

It was unsettling to hold in his hands instruments of malice that the enemy had sent against them: blunted and bent by their impact on stone, some with blood smears still on them. They were much as their own bolts, individual hammer marks where they'd been rushed to a finish but with a crudeness that could have done nothing for their accuracy. But with thousands a day fired it was vital to keep up stocks. He bent to with renewed purpose.

CHAPTER 24

Jared's uneasy slumber was broken by sounds; not the cry of sentinels nor the snoring of those about him – irregular, sinister muffled movements and the murmur of many voices. He jerked to consciousness. Others did too, looking around for explanation.

'Something's afoot,' grunted Hugh and threw back his blanket. 'I'm off to see what it is.'

Jared joined him.

By flickering torchlight men were assembling in front of the Hospitaller Fortress. The knights in full war array wore the red cross on white mantle over chain mail and plumed helmets. They were led by a gonfanier bearing the standard of the Knights Templar. More knights were in the honours of the Knights Hospitallers. A number of sections of foot soldiers stood behind. In all, a force of some hundreds.

'I told you!' Hugh hissed. 'You know who that is? It's the Templar Grand Master, that's who! Knew it was serious, if he's leading 'em!'

Guillaume de Beaujeu was imposing, his strong features now gentle and devout as he sought blessing for their enterprise.

'They're making a sortie against the Saracens,' Hugh continued. 'I'm guessing against the mangonels. Can't do anything themselves about the mining so they're trying to do what they can. Hard to see what, the poor bastards.'

There were no martial drums or trumpets when they moved off as surprise was vital. Followed by a stream of silent well-wishers the cavalcade made for the St Lazarus Gate. The Grand Master held up his hand and the great gates in the shadow of the wall were eased open as the portcullis was raised and the drawbridge lowered.

Straining to see beyond the distant moon-bleached siege lines Jared took in endless tents, barricades, impedimenta. All was still, quiet as the grave.

Cloths were spread over the road to soften the hoofbeats and without a word the mass of men quickly passed through and into the open ground.

The foot soldiers parted left and right, and picking up speed, the knights broke into a canter and disappeared into the heart of the encampment.

The night was suddenly broken by far-off screams and hoarse shouting. It was impossible to make out what was happening. Jared shifted his gaze to the foot soldiers who were heading for the gaunt structure that had to be one of the giant mangonels.

They reached its base – figures were only now emerging from the Saracen lines and there was vicious fighting but it was too late. A tiny flicker of flame suddenly burst into a furious blaze and the scene was flung into a wild illumination. Black, jerking figures clashed and fell.

The pandemonium in the Saracen camp then seemed to coalesce and focus on one part, the enraged enemy converging on it in hordes with shrieks and cries. The knights were in there somewhere – killing or being killed?

* * *

A small group of knights burst out of the lines, hoofs thudding as they raced for the gate, another group followed soon after. The foot soldiers ran stumbling after them. Several were hacked down from behind by maddened Saracens who in turn were cut down by crossbowmen sent to cover the retreat.

At the gate Jared hastily pulled aside as foaming horses thundered in, spurred by riders with blood-streaked armour and torn mantlets. Wild-eyed men on foot pressed in with them.

The drawbridge went up and the gates were swung to and barred. The sortie was over.

The knights cantered away to their hall while the rest trudged off wearily or sat hunched by the side of the road. Several were wounded and women came to bathe their wounds, surrounded by those who needed to know what the night held for them.

'A right disaster, mates,' one muttered. 'The fool with the Greek fire got leery, scared of what was in front, didn't see where he was going. Tripped and sent the whole lot into the ground instead of at the engine.'

So the objective had not been achieved.

'What about the knights – they slay a few, then?' Jared asked.

The man looked up, a wry grin quickly disappearing. 'What I could see – and I was one o' them sent in to aid 'em – they got into bother just as soon as they gets among the tents. In the dark, their horses gets tangled in the ropes. I saw with m' own eyes three go down, and let me tell you, once on their arse they're easy meat.'

Groaning as his livid slash wound was dressed he went on, 'Stirred 'em up like a wasps' nest. Came at us from everywhere, screeching and howling, we never stood a chance.'

Later as the news spread Jared heard that it was even worse – eighteen knights did not return, a fearful toll.

In the light of day a grisly scene was played out. Captured horses were paraded up and down the Saracen lines in full sight of the battlements of Acre, from each suspended the head of a noble Christian knight who had not survived the night.

CHAPTER 25

Some days later, without warning, the Tower of Blois crashed down into ruins – a terrible death for defenders and miners alike. There was no breach, for the mighty Accursed Tower lay intact beyond, but it was clear that Khalil was throwing all he had into the siege.

The King's Tower barbican went soon after but the tangle of collapsed masonry was unusable as a breach. Where was the mining going on now? Soldiers atop the wall between the two towers carried on doggedly, aware that at any moment the mighty stone fortifications could suddenly give way under them in a killing avalanche.

In the smithy there was little conversation as a pall descended.

'Did I say I lost heart?' Hugh said in a forced voice. 'Stands to reason, they've sent for reinforcement, haven't they? We've just got to hold until they come for us.'

'And when will that be?' Jared came back.

'I don't know, do I?' the big man exploded. 'When they does, Christ save us!'

'So if they gets a breach in the walls, they come in after us?'

'God's wounds, Jared, use your noggin! We've still a fair force of knights – it's their job to stop the breach and I wish 'em well, but it'll be the sure sign to me to find a boat and be away from here. Until then I stays and does my service to the Order as pays me. And you?'

'The same, brother,' he said uneasily.

CHAPTER 26

In a wild swing Acre's fortunes changed.

First one then several sail were spotted on the western horizon, then dozens, until the sea was crowded by ships. Crusader ships!

Word flew about and before the first had rounded the point by the Templar Castle the walls were covered by an hysterical multitude welcoming their saviours.

Safe from attack in the enfolding harbour, forty ships landed their freight: two thousand infantry and a hundred knights, commanded by King Henry II of the kingdom of Jerusalem and ruler of Acre, come to personally safeguard his realm.

Received by heralds, trumpets and knights in full pageantry the young King acknowledged his reception.

'A welcome in the Castle of the Templars awaits you, Sire.'

'I thank you, Grand Master,' the King replied gravely. 'And we have no time to waste, I believe.' They rode in procession together to the massive fortress.

Within, the Great Hall was set out in splendid pomp but Henry had no time for ceremony.

'I bid you and the chiefs of all the Orders of Christ to attend on me privily, none other.'

In an inner chamber he took his place at the head of the table and demanded of the Templar Grand Master, 'You have called for reinforcements. Do tell me why.'

'Your coming is most opportune, Sire. The situation is indeed grave and dolorous.'

'How so?'

'The Saracens are dedicated to the capture of Acre. To this end Sultan Khalil spares neither expense nor lives. There are four great and seventy minor engines of war, their mangonels which ceaselessly play on our walls and city to the great terror of the inhabitants. At the same time they're investing our towers and walls with mining and excavation to effect a breach, which cannot be far delayed.'

'What has been your response?'

'We have attempted sorties but have been driven back at grievous loss, Sire.'

'And else?'

'Nothing that has proved effective, My Liege.'

Henry took a deep breath. 'Then pray tell, Grand Master,' he said heavily, 'what you expect me to do with my reinforcements? Fall upon the unbelievers, make challenge of combat – drive them into the sea?'

At their silence he gave a look of contempt. 'No suggestions? Then I have one.'

'Sire?'

'If we're unable to sortie and it is a matter of time only until our walls are breached then . . . we must treat with Sultan Khalil for a peace.'

There was instant pandemonium.

'A peace? We will be forced to a withdrawal!'

'To abandon Acre to the Saracens? Sire, this is sacrilege!'

'The last city left of the conquering Holy Crusades – the very final soil to fly the banner of the faithful! Sire, it's—'

'Silence!'

He waited for the murmurs to die.

'Did I say an abdication of territory? The Sultan is here to avenge an injury – it may cost us dear, but if we offer to compensate in the matter of a large sum he will listen.'

'Large sum?' The Grand Master of Templars was instantly on guard. Of all the military orders his was the most wealthy and its treasures were stored here, in the Templar Castle.

'Can you think of a better outcome, My Lord? For a payment in restitution now, Acre continues to prosper under our flag and some thousands of rich Venetian and Genoan merchants will have cause to bless you.'

Guillaume de Beaujeu nodded reluctantly: the eventual sack of the city would not outweigh the gains of an immediate end to lives lost and, more importantly, the daily cost of maintaining an army of many thousands indefinitely. The calculating Sultan would negotiate.

'Who is your wisest knight, Grand Master?'

'In these matters? I believe it must be William of Cafran, Sire.'

'Then he is appointed my ambassador. Do seek a parley while I confer with Sir William.'

CHAPTER 27

Jared stood with Hugh on the walls as the party rode out in the unearthly quiet.

'Knew it would settle down. Both lots have too much to lose,' Hugh said.

'It'll cost a hill of ducats.'

'Which won't concern the likes of we, m' friend.'

They followed the party until it disappeared among the tents.

'So let's be back at work – or will a peace see us with nothing to do?'

Free from the threat of mangonel boulders the streets were thronged with people and traders.

Later that evening, however, with wailing and screaming, the news spread that the Sultan had bluntly demanded the keys of the city in an immediate surrender of Acre and its peoples as a condition of his gracious mercy. Failing which, the siege would be resumed until this last outpost of the Crusaders had been put to the sword.

In a frenzy of fear thousands went to the harbour with what they could carry and took ship, others milled about aimlessly in terror.

The merchants who had not fled earlier took counsel together; their decision, however, was to delay flight until the situation clarified. They had reinforcements, the city could never be starved out. They believed the Sultan's bluff would be called and he would strike camp and depart, as so many besiegers had done before.

And from the Grand Masters came valiant words that there would be no craven surrender. Those who had taken the cross would honour their vows, stand at the breach against the hordes and never yield.

CHAPTER 28

Jared tried to focus on his work but thoughts raced.

'Do you think . . . ?'

Hugh didn't answer, pounding his red-glowing piece as though it were offending him.

'I said—'

'You go if you want, I stay.'

'They'll come and murder us if we don't go,' Perkyn said miserably. 'There's too many out there!'

'They're all common soldiers, stoutheart, not a knight among 'em,' Jared said as breezily as he could. 'And we've the bravest knights in Christendom to defend us – they said so, didn't they?'

It didn't comfort Perkyn, who slunk away looking for the bellows boy.

Shortly after, Kettle stormed in. 'There's word the Saracens are making a grand assault if the walls go down. They wants five thousand crossbow bolts now, and won't stand for less. As if I can magic 'em out of nothing!'

Hugh looked him directly in the eyes then nodded. It seemed to calm the man.

'Where I'm to get the iron stock I've no idea, but for

you . . . Drop everything else and get started. Nobody to take rest before midnight, or . . . !'

Perkyn returned. It didn't seem the right thing to do to tell him what Kettle had said.

'Can't find the little devil. Looked everywhere and—'

'So you're back on the bellows, then. Get to it!' Hugh ordered.

Even against the clatter and banging in the forge and their distance from the walls they could hear it. A sullen continuous roar that carried from the north-east. Somewhere along their fortifications Acre was under frenzied assault. Its outcome would determine the fate of the city.

The three worked on, keeping their fears to themselves.

Later in the morning Kettle came by, assuring them that while a fierce battle was being waged about the Accursed Tower, a key stronghold, it was not in doubt – both Grand Masters were there in an epic encounter and heroes beyond counting had thrown the Saracens from the walls as they battered at the defences.

The entire perimeter of Acre was now coming under attack and the need for arrowheads and crossbow quarrels was becoming critical. There was no time to rest or eat – only a merciless round of hammering and firing, quenching and heating, muscles burning and fatigue blunting the aim of the blows.

In the early afternoon the background roar changed its note – now louder, an insistent clamour that pressed in on the senses.

It grew to a crescendo, individual cries and rumbles, baying trumpets and the massed uproar of thousands locked in combat, until a full-throated screech and howl of victory brought it all to a disordered chaos.

They paused in their work; what did it all mean?

Baldovino raced in, panting hard, 'The bastards have broken

through! They're in the city killing and looting. We been told to fall back on Templar's Castle – now!

'Leave everything! Go – go for your lives.'

'That's it – I'm away from here!' Hugh said, throwing down his hammer. 'To the boats just as quick as m' legs'll take me.'

'Not the castle?'

'No way am I staying in the same place as those murdering heathen. We can't do any more, I'm off – you coming?'

Jared hesitated, but only for a moment. The writing was on the wall for Acre.

'I'm coming. Me and Perkyn both. Where is the silly bastard?'

He looked around but the lad had disappeared.

'Leave him! We've got to make that boat.' Hugh snatched up his bag and left.

'Perkyn! Perkyn you thick-skulled lackwit! We're going, you hear me?'

There was no response and in despair Jared turned and hurried after Hugh. As they ran off down the narrow street he felt a twinge of guilt. Hadn't Perkyn placed himself as bondsman in his care? He cursed and slowed. The simpleton had hidden in terror at word of the Saracens flooding in – and he had a good idea where.

'I'm going back for the stupid wight,' he wheezed. 'Don't wait, we'll catch you.'

Against an increasing tide of fleeing humanity Jared fought his way back to the smithy. He went to the fuel bin where the wood and charcoal for the forge was stored and peered in. Crouched whimpering in the furthest corner was Perkyn, the whites of his eyes showing extremity of fear.

'There you are! Get out of it, you idiot! They'll be here soon and then—' Jared broke off, for he wasn't being heard.

Leave him? To be slaughtered by a blood-crazed Saracen? He couldn't do it.

He forced his way through the little flap door of the bin and crawled over to him. 'We've got to get to the boats – now!' he said as kindly but as urgently as he could.

Perkyn bit his knuckles and shook his head.

'If we don't . . .'

Jared yanked at a leg. It was instantly pulled back. He tried again, more insistently, but it only brought on broken cries.

Roughly, he forced the terrified eyes round to face him. 'Hear me – hear me well! I'm going now. If you don't come with me, you'll be all alone. All alone!'

Keeping his eyes fixed on him Jared backed out of the bin slowly. Perkyn watched and suddenly scrabbled after him.

Both of them emerged filthy with charcoal dust.

'Good lad. We'll be back on the boat—'

Very close a shriek was cut off with the despairing bubbling of death.

They froze.

Then came the sound of running feet and two warriors with pointed helmets and alien lapped armour burst into the smithy forecourt.

Their cruel eyes took in the scene, bloodstained swords out.

With a sob Perkyn dropped to a huddle.

One warrior gave a hoarse cry and rushed forward with his blade raised. Jared snatched up a long hammer and stood over his friend, swinging it wildly.

The other warrior shouted a command and the first came to a stop, his sword still out and circling menacingly.

He shouted again – this time unmistakeably at Jared.

With heart thumping Jared glared back.

Again – this time accompanied by angry gestures, he made a circular motion about the smithy forecourt and a stabbing back at him.

At first he didn't understand. Then he realised they were asking was this where he belonged, was he a blacksmith. And therefore worth sparing?

He nodded.

With a grunt of satisfaction there was a barked command and the other drew back.

Jared and Perkyn were now prisoners of the Saracens.

CHAPTER 29

The University of Oxford, AD 1268

'Thomas Aylward of Exeter. I'd take it good in you, were you to direct me to Friar Bacon's lodging place.'

The porter looked him up and down. A prosperous gentleman, and in keeping with the visitors the good friar had been receiving since attaining so much renown with the philosophicals.

'That's Brother Bacon yonder, walking by the river. Likes to do it in the afternoon, he does.'

Aylward went up to the dreamily pacing slight figure in Franciscan grey wearing a schoolman's cap and said respectfully, 'Brother Bacon, I believe? I hope I'm not intruding on your worthy thoughts.'

Bacon gave a start and stopped. 'You have business with me? I do not recollect . . .'

'Thomas Aylward, advocate of Exeter. We haven't met, but I have long been your disciple at a remove, an ardent admirer of your methods. Tell me, is your study of optics advanced at all on the question of reflection or emission?'

'It is, Master Aylward. In no small part due to the diligence and insight of the well-thinking Alhazen of Arabia, whose observing of rainbows and such shows conclusively that light proceeds inwards to the eye, not away, and in a straight line. My own recent trifling contribution with glass spheres only confirms his hypothesis. Are you, then, an experimenter?'

'Not at all, Brother,' Aylward said hastily. 'My interest is solely admiration, and passing by I bethought myself to express this directly.'

'Thank you. These are dark but exciting times and there are many jewels of God's creation awaiting discovery. For instance, in the study of alchemy you would hardly credit that . . . but it were better we sit at ease to discuss such marvels. Have you the time?'

They retired to the eccentric little study perched above the road and Bacon shared with him secrets of nature won from the darkness by men's minds not afraid to question the authority of the ancients, to wrestle with contradictions and allow their judgements to be dictated by evidence won from experience.

'Then what is your chief study at this time?' Alyward asked respectfully.

'A most disturbing conjecture, one that I can scarce believe myself had I not set against it all my powers of reasoning without a deliverance.'

'Pray what can this be?'

'By my study of the motions of the heavenly bodies and much calculation I have proved to my satisfaction that the equinoxes and solstices are incorrect – the length of a year has been in error since the time of the Roman dictator Julius Caesar!'

'This is . . . hard to credit.'

'You will be therefore much distressed to observe that if I am correct – and you must accept that I am – the entire Christian faith has been celebrating Easter on the wrong day!'

'A most lamentable situation.'

'His Holiness Pope Clement is much disturbed and has mandated that I should discourse to him on the relationship of philosophy and theology, a work in parts in which I am now engaged.'

'You have a solution?'

'I have, but I find I'm forgetting my manners. Do tell me, there are fine and excellent scholars at Exeter. Have you had fellowship with them recently? What news?'

'Brother, I confess I spend little time in Exeter. I am a jurist and latterly I've been intercessionary between the Venetians and Byzantium regarding trade in the Aegean.'

'A worthy calling, and in a fascinating part of the world. I'm a martyr to travel and envy those who reach far parts.'

'Then I may tell you that the court of Michael VIII Palaeologus is much diminished in splendour since the Crusader conquering and in subsequent times the Latin empire has been expelled; traditions are oriental and schismatic. Such trade as they can maintain is under grave threat – squeezed between the Hungarians and Mongols in the north and the Seljuq Turks in the south. There will be a reckoning before very long, is my conviction.'

'Yet it is a region fecund of ideas and philosophies.'

'Undoubtedly – which reminds me. In the bazaars where any bauble might be had for a pittance, I chanced upon a curious trifle that put me in mind of your good self. I thought to bring it to show you, a trivial thing indeed to set before your learning but it has its portion of curiosities.'

He reached into his jerkin and brought out a small, well-thumbed book.

'Of only a slight number of pages and on a peculiar subject that I confess I could not readily grasp its meaning. Here – it is the *Liber Ignium* – the *Book of Fires* by one Marcus Graecus.'

Bacon took it with interest. 'Ah – here we have a compiling of recipes of earth and fire for various purposes. Umm, this one for instance: "Take the juice of a double mallow, the white of an egg and fleawort seed together with lime, powder them and prepare with radish juice.' And what is achieved? Nothing less than to empower a man to walk in fire or carry a hot iron in his hand with impunity!'

He chuckled. 'Another – pigeon's dung, tartar and so on buried for fifteen days will provide you with a species of fire that can never be extinguished. Your gift is well taken, Master Aylward, in affording me a measure of amusement, but I fear holds little of value for a natural philosopher.'

Turning over more pages he picked another and said, 'Take this for example. Here it is saying—'

He stopped and to Aylward's dismay, turned pale and rigid.

His eyes followed the text, his lips moving silently and he looked up with an expression of horror and shock.

'Brother Bacon, what is it? Have I—?'

'Take it! It's the work of the Devil! It's what I feared all these years – and now to see . . .'

'Reverend Brother, if I've—'

'Take it and burn it! On your soul, do not seek to know what it contains – it is a profane and evil work that in the hands of the wicked will bring down upon this world such dire calamities as will darken the years for ever.'

'I'm truly sorry if I've distressed you, Brother Bacon. I had no idea—'

'Go! Leave me – I must this very minute acquaint His Holiness in Rome of this, with my most earnest and sincere warnings for the future.'

At Aylward's hesitation he added, 'I thank you for showing me, it is polite of you – but it contains dreadful things you cannot be expected to know of. Go now, if you please.'

He turned to depart, but Bacon took his arm and fixed him with a gaze of peculiar intensity. 'Do not fail to destroy it, or Christendom itself will rue it!'

CHAPTER 30

Tabriz, the Mongol Empire, AD 1299

The sun beat down. It was always hot in summer and Jared Bey, chief *silâhtar* to Sultan Ghazan of the Ilkhanate Mongols knew better than to be working at this hour in the afternoon. He sprawled in a hammock on the shady balcony of his whitewashed stone house, clear of the stench and noise of the street below, letting his eyes rest on the hazy immediacy of the mountains across the plain.

Softly his concubine Kadrİye laid a sherbet down on the little table and backed away, her hands respectfully together.

'*Teşekkür ederim*,' he murmured, grateful for its cool refreshment. She had always placed his own comforts before her own and he wondered what she really thought of her foreign master.

He'd done well and should be content with the chance of fortune that had seen him to this place. It was now eight years after the humiliation at Acre. The captives of value had been paraded in chains before the triumphant Khalil, made to bear the banners of the defeated Crusaders upside down in derision – and the heads of the less valued dangling from poles.

Later, away in the distance he saw the last knights and their treasure embark by treaty on Templar ships to sail away for ever.

He would never forgive their betrayal, for it would have been only Christian charity to bargain for the freedom of the Saracens' prisoners.

His own fate was efficiently determined: sold into slavery to the Mongols in the north for a goodly sum as a skilled foreign craftsman.

The early years had been hard, but his natural ability had brought respect and advancement – and preservation for Perkyn, who he'd claimed as his indispensable assistant. Together they'd fought for standing in an alien and merciless land. The small competences he had learnt in Acre had since progressed to valuable skills as an armourer, capable of producing weapons, armour and the peculiar battlefield devices favoured by the Mongols.

He was put in charge of the field armourers, a high position that brought with it a residence here in the capital and a crew of smiths and artificers. They were a motley band, men from all parts of the empire in outlandish dress and habit and were troublesome to rule.

Nevertheless it was a far more agreeable life than he'd ever experienced, much more than in England – but he was a slave and would never now know any other life. Occasionally his thoughts had turned to his son but he knew it was becoming increasingly unlikely he would see him again.

However, shortly he must leave these comforts for a time to join another campaign. Later in the evening cool, ox-trains would set out to the border bearing their equipment: tools, forges, charcoal, iron scrap, specialist anvils, heat treating oils, all the impedimenta of fire and iron made transportable.

It was trouble with the Seljuq Turks, a border disturbance normally settled with massed horsemen. It seemed that this was a more than usually stubborn display by the Seljuqs, probably a siege, given that he and other long-stay units had been sent for. He hoped not, for this would be his third, and the customary conclusion to a Mongol siege was mass slaughter with bodies piled outside the gates to rot while he tried to get on with his repairing.

It turned out to be as he'd feared: a small walled city whose name escaped him, in the foothills of the borderlands that had thought it could outlast the patience of a Mongol horde.

The outcome was inevitable but in the meantime it was life in an encampment on a dusty plain – tents, meagre rations, stinking field latrines and boredom.

His workplace was in the rear, well protected among the baggage train and stores, and he had little to fear except pilfering and their lack of care in the use of fires. His tent set up, he was free to rest from the long ride, leaving Perkyn to get the long, leather forge tent stocked and laid out. His *ustabaşı* could be relied on to get the men's quarters erected and ready for occupation.

As the days passed there was no movement in the situation that he could see. Mining was proving near impossible as there was bedrock just under the surface and open ground was making it hard to close in on the walls. The Mongol commander would need to think again if he was going to end the siege in weeks instead of months.

'What's this, then?' Perkyn asked, pausing counting nails. He nodded to a column of soldiers approaching in the distance, hauling a structure shrouded in cloth.

'Only one?' Jared retorted with contempt. It wasn't hard to make out that this was a mangonel, quite big – and there were no others.

The column passed through the camp. These men were different to any he'd seen before, slighter in build, more oriental but escorted by mounted Mongols with their characteristic short, recurved bows.

They moved on and he saw them take position squarely before the massive main gates of the city. He shook his head in disbelief – this had been the object of so many bloody attacks that had been beaten off – surely they didn't think that with this one engine they could do better? Dozens of even bigger ones had not made any difference at Acre.

He watched them set up camp around it but then lost interest.

CHAPTER 31

In the morning before he'd even finished his mutton dumplings there was a deputation led by the burly Köse Hilmi, quartermaster of the Mongol technicals.

'This here is Wang something or other,' he said, thumbing behind him to a blank-faced oriental in a peculiar tunic and pointed shoes. 'He's got a problem with his engine. Needs you to look at it.'

'Chu-li Wang, and I'd be grateful if you can help.' The voice was cultured, the Arabic scarcely accented but studiously neutral.

The request had no doubt been cleared at a high level for it to come from Hilmi personally.

The gaunt structure of the siege engine was uncovered for Jared. To his surprise it was not a mangonel but a tall structure with a beam, having a sling at one end and a ponderous counterweight the other. On each side was a man-sized treadmill.

It must be a trebuchet, he realised, a recent development that he'd not seen until now. More efficient, it needed many fewer men than the mangonel to arm and fire it – in fact there were only about a dozen of the odd-featured men standing about.

He approached it with care; it was of considerable size, reaching up twice the size of a house.

'This!' Wang said, going to the end of the beam by the sling and pointing underneath.

At first Jared couldn't see what the problem was – the beam was high in the air, presumably after firing and below it was some sort of iron device operated by a long lanyard.

Then he worked it out: it was a release mechanism for the engine, a trigger but different to those used in crossbows, for it would have to take immensely more powerful forces.

Below the beam was an eye with a free-swinging releasing link. Securely fixed to the base of the trebuchet was the iron device, a finger rotating about a bolt to engage the link. He noted how the finger was part of a sinuous design to keep a hold on the link until the last, when it would slip in sudden release.

But it had failed. The finger had worn and bent with use until it no longer held back, rendering the entire engine useless, unable to be cocked.

Probably a copy, and a poor one. They hadn't realised that wear under pressure of common wrought iron had to be countered by special treatments at the forge.

Jared straightened and allowed a look of regret to shadow his features. 'Ah. A difficult repair. I would like to help but . . .'

To his satisfaction it produced consternation.

'Respected *silâhtar*, the engine is crucial to our plans to end the siege. We beg you to consider how it might be brought back to service.'

Already he had in mind what he would do, but he was not going to let it seem too easy.

'Very well, Hilmi Bey, I'll try – but no promises!'

The big man eased. 'You shall be well rewarded.'

Taking the piece Jared headed back to his smithy, rapping out orders as he strode.

He got busy with chalk and line and quickly had his pattern. But who knew the quality of that iron – to be sure he'd make a new one from scratch.

'Get that fire going, you sluggards!'

He'd do this one himself, and in front of an admiring audience with a flourish of sparks and hammer blows he drew out the iron billet into shape, leaving a stronger web at the recurve of the finger and the lever.

It was vital to bring about a true case-hardening but the gear for this process had not been brought along. He'd have to improvise.

An iron tool chest was found and he sent out the idle spectators to bring him hooves, old leather and rock salt, which he packed around the finished object. Perkyn and two others obliged with urine and the box was sealed shut and consigned to the core of the fire.

It was now a matter of time – and that intuition a master smith had, to know precisely when to bring out the piece. The longer it remained, the deeper the hardening but there had to be a balance between the increasing brittleness and the resilience of the underlying iron to produce a tough but at the same time hard-wearing part.

'Enough!' he announced.

The box was broken open and as the piece cooled, the magical appearing on its surface of blue and purple colours, blotched with darker ones, told him that it was perfect.

At the sight of the trebuchet the city had woken up to the threat. Crossbow bolts and arrows hissed and thunked but the besiegers had angled palisades covered with felt in place and work could continue without hazard.

Jared fitted the trigger-piece and stood well back. There was no way of testing the workmanship short of actually firing the engine.

Shouts rang out in a tongue he didn't understand. Ropes were connected and reeved, and with a creaking rumble the treadmills started up and the beam was pulled down against the mass of the great counterweight until the link eye reached the trigger-piece.

The treadmills stopped while the finger was inserted and then were eased away.

Wang ordered everyone clear, went to the device and gingerly tapped it. It held.

He lifted the lanyard and stood out to the side. In a smooth pull he operated the trigger and with a mighty convulsion the engine swung its beam, the sling following, but there was nothing in it and the trebuchet settled back.

It had worked – there were smiles everywhere.

'Do not go, Jared Bey. Now I will show you something!' Wang said mysteriously.

The trebuchet was armed and there was activity around the sling, then Jared's attention was drawn to the front, to the looming gates in the massive walls.

He heard the sudden clatter and thump of the engine and was aware of a dark object sailing over and down, falling short of the walls.

And with a flash and almighty clap of thunder the morning was torn apart, a roiling cloud of dirty smoke drifting out the only evidence that the world had gone demented!

Jared jerked with shock, stunned by what had happened. Was it a lightning strike, called down by some wizard?

The trebuchet kicked again, and nearer the walls the same thing happened.

Nothing could have prepared him for the violence, the naked venom of the thing. In a life where only a heavenly thunder could produce anything like it in sound this was stupefying, touching deep primeval fears of the underworld and the Devil.

Jared became aware of a party of men grouping behind him but could only stare out at the dissipating smoke.

Another: this time it sailed over the walls to disappear beyond – and the flash and shattering roar could be clearly heard from within the city.

Suddenly the men jostled out past him, heading for the gates.

Jared couldn't make sense of what was going on but saw that they scuttled out completely unmolested. The battlements and towers that looked down on them were empty – the defenders had fled in panic.

The men did something with a frame and bundle against the gates, then ran back.

There was an even bigger crash of thunder and when the smoke cleared the gates were teetering in splintered ruins.

A bloodthirsty howl broke out along the siege lines. Warriors surged forward toward the breach, pouring into the city in an unstoppable tide. The slaughter began.

Numb by what he'd seen Jared turned away.

'Wh-what did you do?' was all he could think to ask Wang.

The man gave a superior smile. 'We sons of Han did discover the secret of *huo yao* many years ago. It is naught but this . . .'

In his palm was a pinch of ash-grey powder.

Gingerly Jared took some and smelt it. Beyond a metallic, sulphurous odour there was nothing remarkable about it.

'I don't understand,' he said.

'You are not expected to. Our philosophy would be needed and you foreigners are deficient in this.'

'Try me!'

'Then I have to tell you that this is a mixture of substances of opposite *yin* and *yang* properties. If fire is brought to them they are excited and try to escape the embraces of the other. If in a confined space, they must bring heaven's wrath down to enable them to break away.'

He pointed to a series of clay pots ranged ready by the trebuchet.

Jared shook his head in wonder and headed back to the smithy held in thrall.

Carousing was well under way; artificers like himself did not join in the sacking of the unfortunate city. As skilled men making it all possible, they were assured of a share of the loot and had only to wait for the bloodshed and destruction to conclude and a high-level division of spoils to be made.

But Jared had no taste for merriment while the brutal hacking was still going on and he wanted to think.

Picking his way over the debauchery he was confronted by a gaggle of his Persian forge-hands, glassy-eyed and swaying.

'The most high and wise *silâhtar* Jared Bey,' one of them said with an exaggerated Arab gesture of respect, 'who did restore the engine of the Cathayans to its dread purpose, we salute you!'

He held up an obviously looted chalice. 'Sire! We offer you due libation.'

Jared took it and sniffed suspiciously. It was not any kind of ale. Instead a rich wafting of rose-petal and honey rose up, no doubt pillaged from some rich merchant's pantry. He saw no reason to refuse it and took it off to his tent.

Kicking off his sandals he stretched out on his bed, the appalling crash and violence at the trebuchet still dominating his thoughts. He took a sip of the ambrosia – it was sweet and had an elusive herb-like scent that was very pleasant.

It didn't make sense: the strange powder he'd been shown couldn't possibly produce the effects he'd seen. Either the Cathayan was lying or it was part of a much more elaborate magic spell to call down thunder and lightning on demand.

Taking another pull of his drink he felt a rising elation. To be possessor of such power! To reach out and tumble to ruin his enemy and his works – nothing could stand before it!

A strange lassitude crept over him at the same time as his thoughts soared. He took another drink – the saints preserve him, but it was good.

Supposing he had the secret and invoked the spells to their maximum power: he would see rivers change their course, the sky fall . . . whole towns swept away in a glorious tide of chaos. A lurid and colourful image filled his mind of dogs and pigs whirling helplessly through the air, blown away by the forces he was raining down, god-like.

He blinked blearily. The bastards had put hashish in the drink, which explained their generosity and mirth, but he didn't care, for an even more compelling picture was forming.

With his fearful powers he was now wreaking a cruel revenge on those who had wronged him, and at the head of the line were the knights of Acre who had abandoned him to the Saracens. In a surge of glee he saw their ship shivered in pieces, the floundering armoured nobility sinking helpless into the depths.

Then slamming into his vision with stark clarity came Castle Ravenstock, every lineament in pitiless, loathsome detail.

In a fury of hatred he hurled his terrifying bolts of destruction at the walls, one after the other, until they began crumbling before their irresistible onslaught. More! The whole face of the grim fortification was now hidden in the flash and thunder of his assault and out of the smoke and ruin began tumbling the figures of lords and ladies, bailiffs and stewards, men-at-arms and horses until at last he was spent – and there was left only a smoking heap of stones!

Beyond, another castle loomed and he visited the same on it – and another, each in turn succumbing to ruination until he lay back, exhausted.

In a haze of euphoria, his senses dissolved and he slid into a deep sleep.

CHAPTER 32

Jared woke in a sweat, muzzy-headed.

As his mind cleared there was one thing that refused to leave – the vision of castles tumbling to ruin.

It could happen. He was certain there was nothing in Christendom like these powers, or why hadn't the Templars made use of them at Acre? In some way these beings from far Cathay had discovered how to create the dread devices that he had seen with his own eyes. And as a man of practical experience with fire and iron he felt instinctively that this was no mere magic spell.

Just supposing the possessor of such a secret appeared suddenly in the old country. In a very short time it would be taken up and unleashed. Castles everywhere would be brought down. And for each one the proud, arrogant and all-powerful occupants would be robbed of their impregnable sanctuary and be forced to the same level as all others, compelled to live by the same laws and to face their fellow man.

Was it all a foolish dream?

Here he was, a slave of the Mongols and in a land far away and after these long years vanishingly little hope of tasting freedom. Besides which, he didn't even possess the secret. But by all that was holy, if it ever did happen, what a stroke of vengeance!

This was madness: it was not given to such as he to do such deeds, that was the business of warlords and princes. Who was he to . . .

Like a bewitching enchantress the thought remained to beckon him on. He wouldn't need to be a Richard the Lionheart, just the instrument of justice, by his action a humble means to an end.

What was he talking about? Without the secret knowledge it was all nonsense!

Yet he was a man of skill with his hands, it shouldn't be too difficult to learn. The Cathayans would soon be moving on, their job done. Who knew if they'd ever meet again. He must seize the chance now and trust to fortune to see him eventually free – ransomed or whatever, it could come at any time or not at all but if it did, within him would be his deadly knowledge.

He had to see Wang now.

'So how did you like our little show?' the man said, sipping his usual hot drink with the small leaves swimming in it.

'Well enough, Wang. It was no spell you conjured – was it?'

'Not at all. Our philosophies are sufficient. All is managed by our *huo yao* powder.'

'*Hoh yow* – I see.'

Wang winced.

'Then where do you find this, um, powder?'

'That's no concern of yours, Jared Bey,' he replied smoothly. 'Let it remain as our little mystery.'

'By all means,' he replied lightly. He was not going to let it rest, in his pouch nestled his second line of attack.

'So. The city's fallen, you'll be on your way?'

'Very soon.'

'After we share the plunder.'

'Quite.'

'Then how would you like to take away double your share? Gold, incense, elephants' teeth – you'll have all the girls you ever want.'

'How?'

'Why, on a gamble, Wang.'

'On what?' he asked suspiciously.

'Oh, just the local favourite. Knucklebones.' It had been the work of minutes with a tiny red-hot wire to prepare a cavity for lead in one of the bones.

Wang inspected them closely. 'What stakes?'

'This is my third siege, I've plenty put by. As high as you like.'

Sometime later, Wang shook his head. 'The stars are not right, the gods have deserted me,' he muttered surlily, eyeing the neat pile of stones next to Jared.

'Bad luck, brother. That puts me ahead . . . let me see . . .' He made much of counting up his winnings, then paused as though struck by something.

'I tell you what. It would pain me if we parted bad friends. I'll give you a last chance: let's call it doubles on the next throw, my whole pot.'

'Against that?' Wang sneered. 'I've nothing left.'

'Yes you have! You're going to stake satisfying my curiosity about your *hoh yow*. Show me, or something.'

'No!'

'I said I wanted to be friends . . .'

'How do I know that you won't start setting up on your own?'

'Me? A blacksmith? Hah! No one is going to listen to me. No, Wang, all I want is my curiosity satisfied or all my life I'll think you used magic. And to make it sweeter, if you do teach me I'll forget what you owe me!'

It didn't take long to come to a decision.

'If they catch me telling you . . .' Wang said nervously, coming back with some containers, then pulled the door-flaps of the tent firmly closed.

'They won't. And naturally you're going to tell me true, and I'll want to see you make a right good show at the end from your conjuring, or . . .'

'You will. So this is what we must do. There are three elements.'

The charcoal was easy. Willow or hazelwood was open-pored, and the best.

Then sulphur. He'd seen it before being fumed in a house of plague, but *huo yao* needed it well purified.

The last was *hsiao*, a white crystal powder.

'Taste it.'

Gingerly Jared dipped in his tongue – an odd, sweetish sensation.

'You taste salt, it's bad.'

'What's it for?'

'I don't know everything! The ancients say it's the chief of the elements and must be included, so I do.'

'Well, where do you get it?'

'It's everywhere, but you cannot notice. I've three men whose duty is to look about in any quarter we stop and bring me back what they find. If you're so interested you can go with them.'

'I'm curious – I will.'

Wang shrugged and went on impatiently. 'We have just these

three ingredients. They have been purified. Now they must be mixed.'

He brought out a mortar and pestle and began work. Jared frowned. Was this going to be some sort of dabbling in alchemy?

Wang straightened and held out the pestle. 'See?'

It was the same ash-grey, finely ground powder he'd seen before but now he knew how it was prepared.

'Make it . . . speak, then.'

With a sly smile Wang produced a small bamboo tube, shook the substance carefully into it and tamped and sealed the openings. A wisp of cloth hung out of one end.

'Here.'

To Jared it looked and smelt like any man-made trifle, not in the slightest like a sleeping menace. Doubtfully he handed it back.

'And we awake it with fire. Stand back!'

He took it to the oil lamp and when the cloth caught, tossed it lightly at Jared's feet.

The livid flash and ear-splitting crack was petrifying at close quarters, the eddying smoke sulphurous and diabolical.

It also brought three of Wang's crew running.

'Showing the *kwei lo* that we do not need magic to perform our wonders. A suitable demonstration, is that not so, Jared Bey?'

'I do agree, it does perfectly satisfy,' he replied with a significant look.

Wang beamed.

CHAPTER 33

The Cathayans left – but he had their secret. It was thrilling, terrifying and overwhelming all at the same time, but he had it!

Charcoal and sulphur he knew, but the *hsiao* was another matter. For this, Wang's men had gone to an ancient camel stable and had located, then scraped away, the white frosting from under the powerfully stinking straw.

He didn't question their actions – if this was what had to be done, then so be it.

He'd watched carefully the purifying and mixing, for as a master of his craft he knew that much depended on the quality of a process. Patiently he observed and everything he'd seen was etched deep into his memory.

There was no reason to think he would be returning to the land of castles and nobles. It was much more likely that he would leave his remains in this far country – he didn't even know for sure what it was called, still less the direction to take to find his way back.

Home was now Tabriz, with the patient and loyal Kadrİye.

There was plenty to do in the aftermath of the siege. A mountain of damaged weapons and armour, a sizeable pile of captured material to assess for utility and two or three spared captives claiming skills. At least this would be attended to back in Tabriz.

The heat of summer eased gently into the cool of autumn and the red heights of the Eynali mountains became touched with white.

But then angry word came from Sultan Ghazan that as Hetoum, King of Cilicia had shown obstinate in the matter of respect, an immediate descent on his kingdom was to be mounted.

Jared groaned, for as far as he was vaguely aware Cilicia was away to the south-west, safely tucked behind a girdling of mountains. It would not be pleasant to return through the snows and bitter winds if the campaign went well, or worse, to stay encamped in field conditions indefinitely if there was any kind of resistance.

The expedition set off two weeks later, long columns of camels and men-at-arms preceded by the main force – the feared Mongol cavalry. In the rear was the baggage train and with it Jared and his detachment of assorted smiths and workers, forges and supplies.

They reached the foothills; Jared a-horse could only rein in while the clumsy ox-drawn carts made their way up the increasingly steep and ill-made roads into the mountains proper.

The expedition was moving fast – the Mongol commander was clearly of a mind to finish the job before the snows arrived and occupied himself sending ill-tempered messages back to the laggards.

For Jared's detachment it was quite impossible to progress any faster. With the weight of anvils, iron tools and forge equipment the straining oxen simply couldn't give more.

Two days into the mountains the commander's patience gave

out. The elements at the rear that could not keep up were separated, provided with a small escort and told to follow on the main force as it made for Bile and the Cilicians.

Four days later the red-faced escort captain was compelled to admit that they'd lost their way in the bitter winds and sleet. There was nothing for it but to make camp and endure while the escort was sent in different directions to find a route.

It was there that the enemy found them.

Unprepared, the remaining men of the escort fought the flood of triumphant horsemen bravely but were slaughtered to a man.

Once again a prisoner, Jared waited in despair for his fate.

He knew nothing of Cilicia and its people. As they were marched away, his neat and orderly blacksmithing impedimenta abandoned by the ignorant hill tribesmen, he could only think of Kadrİye and her warm devotion.

From now on he would have nothing to bargain with for status and respect – as a common slave his future would be bleak, unpleasant and short.

Sunk in misery he couldn't find it in him to answer Perkyn's increasingly anxious worries as they made their way over the passes, then, quite unexpectedly, to where the mountains fell away to the sea and a broad bay with a town nestling in a fold of the hills.

It smelt different – the usual dog and human stink but as well a cooking odour that reminded him of long-ago Acre.

They were herded into a colonnaded plaza of sorts, each street exit well guarded and in the centre a raised dais. Jared didn't need to be told a slave auction was about to take place.

The likelihood was that without a reason to keep them together, he and Perkyn would soon be parted. Instinctively he backed away to the furthest corner from the dais, where two colonnades met. Impassive guards watched as he squatted down in the dust and wretchedly waited, Perkyn off to one side.

Numbers of people were making their way along the colonnades, viewing the stock on offer. Jared obstinately sat with his back to them.

Their foreign babble meant nothing to him and with dull eyes he gazed unseeing into the distance. The hours passed.

CHAPTER 34

Cilicia, Armenia, AD 1301

'Rather a poor lot, don't you think?' came a voice from a little distance away, behind him.

It didn't register at first.

'Can't see any as I'd like to see touching my victuals, by m' lady,' another replied.

Jared leapt to his feet and spun about, staring, searching. Someone was speaking English!

And as if from a hashish dream he saw two Knights Hospitallers strolling together, mildly curious at his display.

In a frenzy of emotion he tried to call out to them – but it came out only as a croak, his native tongue buried under long years of Arabic and Turkish.

They moved on but he couldn't let them escape. He blundered after them, tripping over bodies and bringing curses and imprecations but he didn't care.

At last the words came. 'Help me!' he howled, nearly demented with hope.

The knights stopped and stared at him.

'Help meeee!' he shrieked, falling to his knees.

One came over. 'Who are you, fellow, that you make such a noise?'

'The Blessed Lady be praised!' Jared blurted, weeping with emotion. 'By God's sweet passion, hear me, I beg!'

'What is it?'

Gulping, he burst out, 'I'm Jared of Hurnwych, a pilgrim, taken at Acre by the infidels. Sold into slavery with the Mongols and now taken by . . . by . . .'

The knight gave a bemused smile. 'Good fellow, this is Armenian Cilicia.'

At Jared's wild incomprehension he added, 'A Christian kingdom and our allies. So there's been a mistake, they've no right to sell a Christian like you. I'll have a word with the slavemaster and have you released directly.'

He clapped Jared on the shoulder. 'And then, poor fellow, perhaps we can see about getting you home to England – this after a pilgrimage such as you'll remember.'

CHAPTER 35

Hurnwych, England, AD 1302

As if in a dream the last mile before Hurnwych opened up before them.

Jared walked easy in respect for Perkyn's hobble and had time to take it all in. They were dressed as pilgrims just as they had been when they'd departed but this was from the generosity of the Order who had cared for them as sheep restored to the fold. Alms clinked in their scrip, their sclaveins plain but robust. Their staffs were stout and their broad hats were adorned by the pewter palm badge of the Holy Land pilgrim.

They walked on. Jared was keyed up for an emotional tide of recognition but it didn't come. The gnarled oak at the bend he remembered, but it was strangely bereft of significance – it was just there. And the gentle rolling country in all its grace and beauty was if anything startling, so deeply green with rain-washed verdancy after the arid near-desert he'd known for years.

Villeins toiled in their strip fields, ignoring mere travellers, and a boy who drove a flock of geese only gave them a glance.

The manor house came into view: he saw a sad shabbiness. It was so much smaller than he recalled, far less grand and imperious.

And beyond, sitting massively on the hill was Castle Ravenstock.

Prepared for a surge of hatred and memory, instead he saw that washed by sunlight the bluff walls had somehow lost their menace. After the great Crusader fortresses he'd seen this was very much a lesser, mediocre pile and he was strangely moved; he'd changed more than he'd known.

Beside him Perkyn was quiet and apprehensive.

This was the Banbury road with pilgrims a not uncommon sight and they reached the bridge and the common without being stopped.

As they drew nearer, Jared's heart began beating painfully. Over to the left was the rude street of his birthplace and home, for which he had so long wistfully pined. It was not far – and then he stood before the place he had left so many years ago in grief and fury.

It was smaller and changed: was that another room added to the rear? The tavern was still there, and with a couple of early customers.

'Here we go, then, Perkyn.' He went to the door and gave a hail.

A woman unknown to him opened it and frowned. 'No use coming here for alms, brother. I has three bantlings and a sick husband to nurse!'

'Oh. Sorry to disturb you, sister.'

His home was now that of another.

Uncertain, he hesitated then made for the other side, to the smithy, which from the pungency of smoke and quenched metal was in full use.

At the open-fronted forge was the unmistakeable form of Osbert, inspecting the piece he had just worked. A young lad was at the bellows and another stood back – he knew neither.

Osbert wheeled round to see who had come. A moment's incredulity and he gave a hoarse cry. 'Jared! By the God that sits above and you're restored to us!'

He clasped Jared tightly to him and a sob escaped.

Himself overcome, Jared's eyes stung as he croaked a response.

'By all that's holy,' Osbert swore. 'And I'll not rest until I've heard your story!' Flushed with pleasure he threw over his shoulder, 'We're finished for the day, you two. Get the forge down and you'll find us in the tavern. Come, Jared – and you, Perkyn. We've a pile of things to talk about, I fancy!'

It was dreamlike – so much the same, so different.

In the tavern they sat on the comfortably dark-worn seats in the old way, but the serving maid was a stranger as were the two customers nearby who looked up curiously.

'Osbert. How goes my mother? There's a stranger in—'

'Sorry to tell you, lad, but she passed on.'

'She always knew you'd come back. Made us keep all your old things – they're still here.'

Jared blinked back tears but knew that for him the past was for ever out of reach.

The young boy he'd seen in the forge appeared at the door. 'Fire's out, tools away – can I go now?'

'No.' Osbert said with an odd catch in his throat. 'Come here, lad.'

The boy approached Jared uncertainly. Only twelve or so he held himself well, his dark hair the same as his own and with a pleasing countenance.

'As this is my apprentice and will desire to make your acquaintance. Younker, this is Master Jared.'

He paused for just a moment then added softly, 'And he is your father.'

Daw! Little David – could it be . . . ?

The lad stood staring, his eyes wide and hands working at the cap he held.

'I . . . I'm right pleased to see you, David,' Jared said in a low voice. 'How are you?'

Their child who he'd held in his arms and . . .

The youngster held back, unsure and guarded, saying nothing.

'Daw, I . . .'

Osbert intervened gently. 'You can go, lad. Tell 'em there'll be another two to sup tonight.'

When he'd left he added, 'A fine boy – does what he's told and quick with it.'

Touched by the encounter more than he could admit Jared took refuge in asking for news of the village.

There was not a lot to tell. A new lord of the manor, an earnest churchgoer who nevertheless ensured that his dues would be met in full and on time. The miller had slipped and lost a hand to the millstones. A clutch of marriages, births and deaths and the year that the harvest was all but lost to a great storm.

His house had been let to a family and the proceeds put away for David's future – as an apprentice blacksmith he was doing well, liking the craft and taking to its mysteries with a will.

'Jared?' Nolly, nervous and blinking, laid eyes on his old friend. He was careworn, with lines in his features, almost unrecognisable as the jack-me-lad he'd shared frolics with in those long ago summers.

'Hoy there, Nolly!' he replied, but the carefree banter of old died in his throat.

'I heard you was returned and . . . and . . .'

'Sit yourself down,' Osbert invited. 'And you're in time to hear of our Jared's adventures!'

Another ale arrived and with it Old Yarwell, seamed and aged, his knobbly stick trembling as he shuffled in. 'Just heard o' you back with us,' he wheezed. 'You'll have a tale to tell, I told m'self, so here I is to hear it. Get on with it, lad!'

Jared sat there, bemused. How was it possible to even begin, when not a one of those eagerly clustered around had even seen the sea, let alone the vastness of Persia. To describe a camel? A Mongol army on the move?

'Well, I . . .'

'You tell it, Master Jared,' Perkyn came in unexpectedly. 'I . . . I'm going to . . .'

Of course – he had his memories and friends, and after all, he'd only agreed to be a servant for the span of a pilgrimage.

'Away you go, Perkyn. Mind you come back soon and I want to thank you properly, you hear?'

His place was taken by Will Dunning, the miller's son who he'd thrown into the pond one May Day. Mature and balding he stood until bidden to sit, his eyes wide and respectful. Others began appearing behind him – word was spreading fast in the little village.

'So we set out . . . when was it, the seventeenth or was it the eighteenth year of our King Edward, bound for Woodstock and . . .'

It was easy going at first as he told of familiar landscapes and names, but when he tried to convey the fear and torment of a sea voyage it came out as either bland or fantastical. His growing audience, however, was greatly appreciative and listened for every word.

When he reached the point where the knights engaged him for Acre a short, burly man with an empty socket for one eye worked himself to the front. 'Know what you mean, young fellow. Was the same when I shipped on crusade with King Richard, the Lionheart we called 'im, fine soldier, very fine. Did I ever tell you how we—'

A chorus of cries cut him short and Jared remembered the veteran crusader archer Watkyn Sharpeye. He smiled inwardly. His own story went far beyond the tallest tales this man could ever tell.

Evening drew in before he'd even reached Tabriz and he was suddenly overcome by a tide of weariness and promised more for the next day.

'Osbert, if my house is—'

'Pay no mind to it. You'll be with us this night.'

'Kind of you, Osbert, but—'

'It's the way of it – Hurnwych'll set to and we'll have you a new house in a week.'

As it had always been done: if any of the tight-knit community needed to replace or build, all would lend a hand and the favour would be returned in due course. And for Jared it would meet a deeper need – he was unsure how he would face the memories alone.

'I'd be grateful, Osbert. Wouldn't want to turn out the tenants in the old place, o' course.'

'They'll be happy to hear that. One more thing: the smithy. Will you be . . . ?'

Jared smiled broadly, flexing his muscles. 'I start at once!'

'It's just that I've more work in hand I can jump over. Daw's a help but the forge-hand is nothing but a thick-skulled fool of a dirt tosser, all I could get.'

'Rest easy, Osbert. I'm sure Perkyn won't want to go back to the fields – he's steady enough, worked with me in Persia. He doesn't know a ploughshare from a coulter blade but can turn in a Saracen crossbow bolt in a twinkle, should you ask kindly!'

CHAPTER 36

The days passed. In the forge Jared made short work of the backlog and in the process came to know a little more of his son, but Daw kept his distance from the exotic man with the extravagant fables claiming to be his father.

Occasionally he and Perkyn would lark about and lapse into Turkish, to the exasperation of Osbert and the wonder of the boy, or turn a piece in the Arab fashion, curved and exotic, and perhaps go for outlandish compounds in quenching oils to bring up curious patterns on the bare metal.

Father Bertrand chanced by and was disappointed that he'd been unable to visit the Holy Sepulchre and speak of it to him for he'd never been there himself.

A little later a stiff-faced John Frauncey called, sent by the bailiff to beg him for a pair of ornamental barn hinges in the Moorish style. After only the minimum foolery and teasing of the self-important lackey Jared agreed and two days of diverting work later produced a fanciful set that had the whole village talking.

The house was built: the only available space rather closer to the woods than he cared for but it was good to settle in to his own dwelling. He offered a place in it to Perkyn – in return for what they'd shared but also he didn't want to be alone. Daw had decided he'd prefer for now to stay with his Uncle Osbert.

And merciful heavens, the nightmares had not returned. His mind sometimes briefly shied at fleeting reminders, but it had been years ago now and the hurt had faded into wistful remembrance.

Jared wanted to go forward with life but apart from Daw he had no family, no one to care for.

He missed Kadrİye. She would have been given his share of the plunder and be comfortably off. They'd never been close, the distance from concubine to master too great to bridge, but a woman to share a life with was surely fundamental to existence.

But here in Hurnwych there were none his age – gone thirty – who hadn't been married off years before. And it had to be faced, after what he'd seen, could he find contentment with a young and innocent village girl?

Perkyn was quiet, clearly affected by his experiences but insisted that he wanted nothing but peace and calm.

The towering vision that had seized Jared of tearing down castle walls with devil dust had now faded. Although the knowledge was within him the ambition seemed absurd and didn't fit with this land of peace and order, so different to the surging waves of slaughter and violence he'd known. All he wanted now was blessed normality, to take up the life he once had, to fit in to the rhythms of the seasons and the lives of everyday folk in Hurnwych.

The villagers treated him with respect and deference but this was not what he wanted. In the tavern and in conversation they would hold back in awe at what he might say and his opinion on things was final. Even Father Bertrand would anxiously look his way as if in fear of contradiction if a sermon happened to mention the Holy Land.

He had to accept it: he was not of their world any more. His ordeal and adventures had separated him from them, his knowledge of the world so infinitely greater, his perspectives not theirs.

At least he had his work. He took to adding Turkish flourishes to farm tools, a warlike gleam to a scythe blade, socketed three-edged arrowheads for an appreciative Watkyn.

It brought results but not what he expected. One afternoon a hard-faced stranger took a seat in the tavern and asked for him. It turned out to be the Ravenstock armourer.

After some guarded talk it became clear that he was much impressed with Jared's skills. The craft of armour and blades was greatly superior to pedestrian blacksmithing and Jared was putting out work with the mark of a first-class artificer. Not only that, after his experiences he could be expected to be up with the latest know-how and military fashions from out there in the wider world.

The man was concerned for his job!

If ever they heard about it, Jared would certainly be a catch for the castle. The irony was that he would spit on any offer to work up there. However, he agreed that for a useful fee he would take in work to be passed off as the armourer's own, which would bolster his position there with its quality and modern touch.

The smithy was prosperous and busy. There was now security and a future for Jared but he was restless.

Daw was still preferring his Uncle Osbert's company, possibly because they'd been so close for these years, or was it that the young lad was finding it hard to deal with a man so at odds with every other around him? Either way it was hurtful.

He would persevere, of course, for Daw was all he had in this world, but meanwhile there was one great need he had to satisfy.

He had to find himself again.

CHAPTER 37

It was so real, so appalling. Jared woke up breathless, heart hammering, staring into the blackness.

A desultory dream of stumbling over an endless night plain had suddenly tightened into a presence, a monstrous manifestation that had swelled yet remained unseen.

He had an awareness that something had passed into his consciousness – confronting, demanding, overpowering and insistent. With the hard question: why was he delaying? If he had a burden placed upon him why was he not doing his utmost to meet it? What was the hindrance?

He was powerless to resist the message that he'd been set firmly on a path that was leading to his destiny. A harsh but necessary act had put him on a course that had ultimately taken him to Persia and the deadly secret he had acquired. Predestined, he'd been plucked from slavery – made free in order to accomplish his purpose, which was no less than to take the wondrous and terrible powder and, for the good of mankind, go on to wreak a vengeful humbling of those who set themselves above all others in towers of stone.

He – Jared of Hurnwych – had been summoned to a higher mission.

Was this . . . God calling to him, or the Holy Ghost, or . . . ?

In the darkness he grappled with the revelation.

If God had spoken, who was he to resist the call? He'd been told in church of David and Samuel and others who'd heard the Lord speak – but nowhere was there any indication what it sounded like. And his was more a conviction rather than a command – but if it was not a divine charge, who or what else could it be?

He lay back in awe, letting it all sink in while Perkyn's gentle snores and the wafting reek of the village kept his hold on reality.

On the face of it the whole thing was ludicrous. Did he make an enormous pile of his powder and personally go forth and set this at the base of the walls of every castle in England? How long would it take – and would they let him?

This was foolish thinking. There had to be another way, one which had real prospects of success. But he, single-handed against the world?

There had been saints and others who had stood tall and achieved greatness but he was no hero. In any case, what could he do that—

Of course! A way that was so obvious: let them bring down their own walls!

Give powder to one and point out that it would be sure medicine against a rival. The advantage would be irresistible and very soon the others would demand the same. In only a short while there would not be a castle wall standing anywhere.

This was it.

He feverishly thought it through again. His role would only be to provide the means and stand aside while they hammered each other to a ruin.

It couldn't fail!

What was he waiting for?

He couldn't sleep.

Inside him was the secret of *huo yao*. It was secure and true, for all that he'd been told and seen was engraved on his heart. All he had to do was put it in motion.

There was the sulphur, the charcoal and the *hsiao* and the various pans and vessels, mortar and pestle. He'd have to get these from somewhere, but more importantly, a place to work that was private and not liable to interruption.

And somewhere to test the result that wouldn't have the villagers fleeing in terror at the cataclysm.

Then came a cool breath of caution. Here he was, working to bring about the ruination of castles – if Ravenstock ever got a whiff of what he was up to his fate would not be pleasant. Therefore all that he did must be hidden from men. None – not even his friends or family should know anything of what he was doing.

A hard thing but very necessary – and near impossible to carry out.

But as the light of day began stealing in he had the answer: the old priory, deep in the forest and shunned by all God-fearing men. Its rooms could serve as workshops; the deep cellars would muffle the violence of *huo yao*, and with the bones of D'Amory in helpless witness to what he was doing it could not be better.

In the cold dawn he wavered. His prospects were favourable and he could reasonably look forward to a respectable life in Hurnwych. To hazard all this with a demented notion to bring to ruin all the realm's castles was surely the act of a madman.

As Jared worked at the forge his thoughts chased each other

but there was no getting away from it: he'd been called, and uniquely able to make it happen, he could not turn his back on it.

That evening in his little house he began to plan.

CHAPTER 38

'Hey ho, the smith!' breezed the pedlar. 'And I heard you've need o' my wares?'

'Yes, Wagge Longface. I've been troubled by lice and fleas in this new house near the woods. I'll thank you for a half-peck of your finest brimstone.'

'So much? And it'll take long in the finding, God's truth on it.'

'Go to it, old man. Mark you, I pay well for the best.'

The charcoal was easy. Good willow cut from beside the River Dene and fed to the burner by Daw, all believing that this was yet another of his Moorish tricks, perhaps to achieve more fierce heat at the forge.

When it came, the sulphur was of reasonable quality, a thick-smelling dull-yellow grit but with inclusions. It would need purifying.

The hard part was going to be the *hsiao*. Where was he to find camel stables here? And when he had it, there was the preparation process – the cauldrons, barrels and pipes – these had to be gathered together without raising suspicion.

He needed an accomplice. One who not only understood what he was going to do but was of the utmost trustworthiness. Who knew fire techniques, handling hazardous objects and would in turn trust him.

Perkyn Slewfoot was the only one he could turn to.

Could he ask it of him? He'd taken his exile hard and now wanted nothing more than a peaceful existence. This was going to be secret, exciting and frightening – and dangerous.

Supper finished and the maidservant left.

'Perkyn, old friend,' Jared began in a serious tone. 'I have a matter of great consequence weighing on me. I wondered if you could help at all.'

'Me?'

'Yes, as you are the only one who might understand.'

'I-I'll try.'

'Thank you, Perkyn. I knew you'd like to help.'

'If it eases your burden I'd—'

'A dream was sent to me. A great and burning presence did place upon me a charge and duty that I must obey. Perkyn, I'm called to a purpose I cannot refuse.'

'C-called?'

'Yes. And I'm vexed to know how I can proceed.'

Jared had Perkyn's wide-eyed attention. 'It is my stern duty to humble those who dwell in high places and oppress the common folk.'

'D-dwell in . . . ?'

'Castles, Perkyn, castles.'

Perkyn gave a saintly smile. 'Ah. And you must humble them. I understand now.'

Jared suppressed his irritation. 'Yes. And I will do it!

'You remember the siege of . . . whatever the place was called, the last one before we were delivered?'

'Ah, yes.'

'And do you recall what broke the siege?'

'I do,' he said in a rush, 'such magic! Thunderbolts and lightning, I was sore afeared and hid.'

'Perkyn. It was not magic. It was the Cathayan's artifice. And I have their secret.'

'What are you saying?'

'I have it. And it will be the means to bring down the walls of every castle in the realm, that they must then live and bide with their people.'

'You . . . you're going to bring this magic against all the castles by yourself – and you want me to help you?' Perkyn gasped.

'No, no! Only to make up the *huo yao* for them to throw at each other. We stand aside while they're at it.'

Perkyn stumbled over the pronunciation.

'I don't know what it's called in English. A kind of dust, powder which burns with great violence. We have to make it from things – charcoal, brimstone and, er, *hsiao*.'

Rigid with apprehension, Perkyn could not speak.

'Will you help me, Perkyn? It'll be exciting work, much more than a forge-hand usually sees.'

'Um, I . . .'

'Wouldn't you like to take a tilt at those peacocks? They once had you at the end of a rope as I remember . . .'

'I'm frightened,' he said miserably. 'It was very loud and—'

'We're not using it, only making it. Let *them* hear it.'

'But . . .'

'I knew you'd help me! Stout fellow. Here's my hand on it, Perkyn.'

It took a round of metheglin to seal the pact but then Jared had the priceless boon of someone to talk to, however unworldly.

CHAPTER 39

Sworn to secrecy, it was time to set to. The first business was the purifying of the sulphur, and for that they needed to get out to the priory to set up a workshop of sorts, complete with apparatus. Iron pots and kettles, coarse cloth, dippers, tongs. Flint and steel, the mortar and pestle from the forge occasionally used to grind fine sand for quality moulds, a small table, chairs. And this was only the beginning.

There was only one way to get it out to the priory. At night, without telling Perkyn where they were going, Jared loaded him down and humping his own bag stealthily led him out.

The moonless, chilly night was as still as the grave. His little house closely backed on to the woods and it took only a matter of moments to slip in among the trees to the path that he'd previously located. He could hear Perkyn's teeth chattering and it wasn't just the cold.

Under their feet the brush crackled and snapped but Jared knew it would be muffled by the thick greenery.

'Wh-where are we g-going?' hissed Perkyn.

'A safe place,' Jared assured him. 'Dry and comfortable.'

In his impatience he stepped out faster, leaving Perkyn to

hobble behind as best he could. He was carried on a flood tide of exhilaration. It was going forward – he was actually going to make *huo yao* and change the world!

The clearing was dark and mysterious, the ruins rearing up black and threatening.

'No! You didn't tell me it was this!' Perkyn blurted, dropping his bundle. 'The plaguey nuns! Christ shield me, but the ghosts and—'

'Be still, simkin! They've all left long since, mark my word. Why do you think we're here? I came . . . before, I know it well and there's none of that kind any more!'

The cellar hatch opened with a long *scrrreak*. Jared went down the steps to the echoing space and lit a candle. Perkyn hesitantly came down.

'As I promised. Here we'll work our wonders.'

The table was set up and gear arranged along the walls.

The old kitchen had a hearth, suitably enclosed but open above to the night sky. Firewood in the middle of a forest was no problem and Jared soon had his sulphur heating slowly with an ungodly stench until it melted, at which he could scoop the impurities from the gently simmering dull-yellow froth.

Perkyn ladled it out over an old cloth filter and in the pot below a bright yellow began to spread. He was finding the pungency of brimstone in the confined space difficult to take, but Jared sharply reminded him that this was how physicians treated those with disease and therefore he must by now be the healthiest in Hurnwych.

The cycle continued until all the pedlar's sulphur had been transformed.

It was enough for one night.

They slipped back into the house, startled once by an owl. Jared was thrilled: they had started on the road that led to success! Perkyn said nothing and crept to bed.

In the smithy it was hard for Jared to concentrate. In a very short while he'd assembled two of the three ingredients, had created a secret workshop and brought together what he needed to produce the powder. It was not impossible that very soon *he* would be master of heaven's thunder!

There remained the last and most difficult: *hsiao*.

He blessed his resolve to go with the Cathayan's servants as they hunted it out. If they located *hsiao* in Persia, far from Cathay, then it must be found in other parts of the world – such as England. The principle would be the same, namely, that where death and decay, vile baseness and unspeakable ordure reigned, there the precious substance would be hidden.

That night, with Perkyn obediently behind carrying a small sack, Jared began work at the catacombs at the priory ruins.

'Wh-what are we looking for?' Perkyn asked pitifully as they explored each underground chamber. Jared hid a wry grin; the truthful answer – dead bodies – was not the answer Perkyn needed now.

Jared led him down a small stone-enshrouded entrance at the end of the chapel.

'Come on, we've work to do,' he said, putting flame to an oil lamp.

It lit up the space with a flickering yellow that brought as many moving shadows as it did light. And it revealed rows of neatly stacked bones and skulls that stretched away into the blackness in a thick and choking atmosphere of dust and decay.

'No!' wailed Perkyn, clutching the sack to him as if for protection. 'I can't!'

'Get here!'

The bones were not what Jared wanted but what was on the stone immediately under them, as he remembered from a Seljuq charnel house.

Perkyn whimpered behind him. Lowering the lamp Jared looked under the shelf and there it was. Against the wall, a line of white at a seam in the stonework, tiny icicles hanging down, just as he'd seen it before.

'Help me,' he muttered, and pulled at the bones, which suddenly clattered down in an unholy avalanche.

Perkyn gave a howl of fear and made for the entrance but Jared caught his tunic and yanked him back.

'Stay here and hold the sack,' he growled, and leant into the gap with his scraper. It came away easily and in his fist was the first of his harvest!

Gingerly he extended a tongue. It was rewarded with a sharp but sweet taste, no trace of salt at all. It was *hsiao* right enough.

'What's wrong now?' he asked in exasperation. Perkyn was bent over, retching hopelessly. 'A great help you're turning out to be!'

There were just two rows of bones each side and only one had any betraying white at all. At this rate it would take forever to gather it in the quantities he'd seen in Persia. It was going to be a long night.

By the time he'd forced all the tombs he could find, it was the cold hours before dawn and he had to return with barely two handfuls of crumbling white and a near-gibbering Perkyn.

* * *

'Where've you been?' Osbert grumbled as he entered the smithy later.

Jared tensed – but then realised that he was referring more to his late arrival than anything else.

'Oh, er, Perkyn is ailing, I thought to see him comfortable.'

Osbert gave his stooped body and red eyes a keen glance but said nothing more.

CHAPTER 40

To be so near was galling, he had to find another source. At midday Jared pleaded fatigue and snatched a nap, and lay thinking. The place that had yielded the most *hsiao* had been the camel stables. The nearest thing here was the manor stables. The droppings of camels were not that much different to those of horses – that's where he'd be sure to find it.

The caustic Master of the Horse, Harpe, would take instant suspicion if he asked to root around beneath his horses, so the only way was to go there unseen. He knew from a previous visit that the side gate to the quadrangle had a defective hinge, which the manor was too mean to send in for repair.

He left Perkyn to his frights, and once it was dark crossed quickly over the bridge to the stable and let himself in.

The first box was filled with the warm bulk of a horse, which whinnied softly at seeing him. Freezing, he listened carefully. Nothing.

There was no way he could risk a light but he was relying on the vivid white to show in the gloom. Even if he stuffed other material with it in his sack it could be extracted later.

He remembered it was usually layered under the straw, thin

sheets of white, clumping occasionally, and close to the floor. Experimentally he lifted up an interlocking mat of rank and odorous straw.

In the gloom he wasn't sure of what he saw, whether it was *hsiao* or common putrid rot. Should he taste it first or—

He felt a bump to the elbow. In a wash of relief he saw that it was a dog and shoved the animal away impatiently.

It was the wrong thing to do. Backing away it raised a din of witless barking, on and on.

Jared shot to his feet and ran out into the yard.

Opposite there was movement and shouts. He flung himself at the gate but the baulky hinge at first refused to give until with a manic heave he had it open. He fled for his life out and across the bridge, ducking down instantly into the passage between Nolly's house and the smithy, emerging the other side to dive into the familiar darkness and smells of his workplace where he lay next to the forge, heart pounding.

The puzzled shouting and barking died away and he breathed again. But then he made out a figure standing outside, the unmistakeable shape of a club in his hands.

'Come on out, you thieving bastard!' Osbert snarled, slapping the weapon into his palm.

'Jared – you!' he gasped, dropping the club. 'What in the name of Christ . . . ?'

Thinking quickly, he hung his head. 'The nightmares. They've returned.'

'Like you had before? You poor wight! I had no idea . . . I thought you and Perkyn was on the piss all night.'

'No, he's been with me, a-following as I wander in my torment. You see, after I get to sleep, these wild dreams come, of all the foul and dreadful things I suffered in my exile in the land of the Saracens. Locked in my nightmare I ramble abroad, not knowing where I am or what I'm doing. I do pray they leave me soon or . . .'

Osbert's eyes widened in understanding. 'Such an awful thing, and you on pilgrimage and all,' he murmured. 'If there's anything I can do – follow you about to give Perkyn a rest . . . ?'

'Oh, er, your charity does you honour, but Perkyn insists that as he served me in those evil places, so his duty is to me still. I crave only you keep this sadness to yourself and that this time of trial will soon pass.'

Lifting his head nobly he stepped out into the night. He'd have to be more careful while he looked elsewhere.

CHAPTER 41

In the morning Jared ambled slowly down the muddy street. At the end, Godswein's widow kept a fowl-coop, small but raised off the ground. It was set away from the houses on account of its stink. The throat-catching reek of their droppings promised much.

As dark settled they set off. It was essential Perkyn played his part for Jared had to squirm under the structure and pass out handfuls of old ordure that had fallen below.

Jared crept up quietly, talking softly to the sleeping fowls inside so as not to alarm them.

The coop was set up three hands' breadth on crude stilts and he found he was just able to wiggle in, choking and gagging on the thick ammoniac stench. Sudden scurrying erupted as rats scattered, some running over his body and past his face.

But he hadn't bargained on the pitch blackness beneath which made it impossible to make out even a trace of precious whiteness. Worse, it made him bang his head on a frame which shook the structure and started the poultry off in an indignant squawking.

Backing out as quickly as he could, he rose up – and while

Perkyn was nowhere to be seen, he soon made out a line of still figures that stood quietly watching him.

'I . . . I . . .'

'Don't trouble yourself, Jared, we understand.' It was the kindly voice of widow Godswein.

'But I didn't . . .' he began and tailed off.

'That's all right, m' honey, Osbert told us about your troubles, poor lamb. Is there anything . . . ?'

Frustration made him bad-tempered and he lashed out at Perkyn when he got back.

He recoiled piteously. 'M-master Jared,' he whimpered, 'I don't understand! What are we doing, that we're spending our nights picking over this old shit and—'

'Are you going to puzzle me with a load of questions, or help me when I need you?'

'I'm to help, but—'

'Good. Now let me think.'

There was the common pigsty over the river but this was in with the villeins who could not be expected to be sympathetic. But their ox-house, where they kept the draught animals, had been there for as long as any could remember and he'd promised a new bolt and fittings. Straw was thrown over the dung and in turn trampled down, and if *hsiao* could not be found there, where could it be?

Not only that, he could go in daylight and would be able to see what he was doing.

Perkyn's bag of tools held a sack inside and he had every intention of filling it before they returned.

Most of the villeins were out in the fields and an awed maid showed them the building, long and broad and gratifyingly thick-smelling. The beasts at their troughs looked up in interest at his entry.

'What? Still with oxen? I must have them out or how might I work, woman!' Jared demanded.

It was easy. Left on their own, it was minutes' work to lever up a lifetime or more of filth and there, in plain view, was a skein of white, in places thick enough to peel away. Within a short time they had the sack full.

At last! The only remaining task now was the wresting out of the *hsiao* and then they would have everything necessary for their awesome creation.

Carefully, Jared planned out what was still needed. Only a substantial cauldron, like that Cathayan three-footed bronze kind.

Where on God's earth could he find something like that?

It came to him quickly. The quenching tub next to the forge. Four feet of it, but of heavy beaten iron and intended for warm work.

And just as important, he must have washing lye. Lots of it. The washerwoman in the manor house was most obliging, giving over a generous pail of strong bleaching lye she swore by. The greyish-brown slop looked different to what he'd seen in Persia but later he dropped an egg in it, and saw with satisfaction that it floated jauntily, a sure sign of quality.

It was a struggle to heft it all through Wolfscote Forest to the priory.

'A fire, Perkyn. Good and hot.'

He looked at Jared wretchedly. 'You're going to . . . cook it?'

Jared sensed the edge of hysteria at his evidently moonstruck acts and softened. 'Rest your soul, Perkyn. Here I'm driving out the dross to leave the *hsiao* which hides in its midst.'

He dropped handfuls of their hard-won muck into the tub of boiling water and after an interval began ladling out the impurities. The rank effluvia was overpowering at first but he persevered, remembering how Wang's crew had to take it in turns.

Hour after hour Jared laboured on in the ghostly ruins. When the mixture was half-gone he decided to let it settle and left for home.

The next night the work continued until it had boiled quite away. Jared snatched the oil lamp and peered into the bottom of the tub – and there, dully glistening, was the miracle of the white crystals of *hsiao*!

His heartbeat quickened. The last step!

Taking the keg of lye Jared carefully poured it into the tub, watching it gushing in a hissing roil of eye-watering steam until it steadied. He topped up the mixture with water and with the crystals now dissolved the boiling started again. And again. He was determined to do it right, for Wang had said that *hsiao* was the chief of the elements.

After three nights he had it. A fair pile of pure-white crystals.

Hard work and sorely won. But he had it!

Jared allowed himself a night free, for the last stage was very short. Mixing the ingredients to make the live *huo yao*. And then . . .

CHAPTER 42

'Hurry, Perkyn. This night we shall be well rewarded for our pains.'

Jared laid out the elements neatly on the table.

Charcoal, small uniformly blackened twigs in a basket.

Sulphur, a startling pristine yellow in a basin.

The *hsiao*. Pure-white crystals that gleamed in the lamplight.

And then the mortar and pestle. Cleaned spotless, it had an iron bowl and bronze pestle, easily up to the job it faced now.

With Perkyn looking on nervously Jared started with the charcoal. Heaping it into the mortar he ground it down, feeling the gritty resistance gradually give as he worked.

The bowl was soon half-full of fine dust – with the same for the rest he would have plenty for the first trial. He set it aside and cleaned the bowl.

Then the sulphur. A careful crunch and twist, crunch and twist until it too was a fine-ground dust.

Finally the *hsiao*. He gave it everything he had until it fell through his fingers, a perfectly consistent waterfall of tiny glittering crystals.

'And this is our finish, Perkyn,' he announced gravely. 'Each of these will now be brought to embrace the other closely, but when they are roused by fire, they fly apart in a terrible rage.'

Jared emptied in some ground charcoal to the bowl and added the sulphur, grinding away until the yellow swirl had been subsumed into a grey-black. Then the *hsiao* was ground into the mixture and when the result was a uniform dull-grey coarse dust with the barest suggestion of a sheen he stopped work.

It was done.

It looked like *huo yao* – and a tentative sniff instantly brought it all back to him. This was it!

Jared didn't have bamboo but he'd made up some tubes from moulding clay of the same dimensions. He carefully poured the grey powder into one of them, sealed it with a twist of cloth and took it to the end of the cellar.

'Perkyn. I'm now about to release the demons. It will be loud and dreadful – do stop your ears if you don't want to be frightened.'

'No, not yet – I'm going outside!' he gulped and scrambled to get away.

So he would be the only witness. Jared shrugged, but there was no stopping now.

Setting the tube down on a shelf he took the lamp and taking a deep breath applied it to the cloth, then rapidly retreated.

He tensed for the shock.

The flame progressed merrily until it reached the end of the tube. It died momentarily – then there was only a feeble pop and show of flame and a suddenly mounting cloud of grey-white smoke.

Hardly believing what he'd seen he approached gingerly. The clay tube had split lengthways, revealing a blackish ash inside, but as a show of violence it was pitiful.

He'd followed everything scrupulously, and to be let down like this!

Jared paced up and down, barely noticing the rank stink that lay on the air. What could have gone wrong? He'd followed his mentally rehearsed instructions with meticulous attention and was certain that he'd missed nothing.

It just had to work – he'd try again with double the powder.

But this made no difference.

Was it the quality of the ingredients? With the possible exception of the *hsiao* they had been identical to Wang's.

Was it that the tube had not been bamboo? The principle was to stop the fire-maddened elements fleeing each other until they'd called on heaven's thunder to free them. This had been done.

Dispirited, Jared concluded it had to be the ingredients – and he'd have to start again from scratch.

He left the cellar heavily and saw Perkyn rise shamefacedly from behind a tombstone. They trudged home together.

CHAPTER 43

The next morning Osbert was in a foul temper. Not only had some rat-faced thief some nights ago taken off with their quenching tub – handed down from Jared's father's father – but now, their mortar and pestle had gone missing.

Jared muttered sympathies but his mind was elsewhere.

He'd try willow twigs from the opposite bank this time for a new batch of charcoal.

Wagge the pedlar was surprised to take another order for best sulphur but suggested he would be more than satisfied by a sack on its way to the leper hospital.

The *hsiao*? Jared gave it much careful thought. The wet, stinking material he'd been so careful to select didn't particularly look much like what the Cathayans had gathered, even if it yielded very similar crystals. The dry heat of that land had made it seem more dense, friable almost. And they'd always preferred scrapings of those white icicles from stone mausoleums and sepulchres. Was England's cool and misty climate not infusing sufficient fervency into the *hsiao*?

He'd no way of knowing. Better to go for the stone scrapings.

There hadn't been a good haul at the priory. The other place that suggested itself was the parish church and its ancient crypts, but Jared knew he'd not get away with ransacking that.

The manor pigeon-cote? This lord of the manor was not partial to pigeon pie and it had been empty these years. Stone-built with a domed roof it had all the makings of a prime source.

The door was not locked: empty, it had no attraction for thieves or other. Jared entered and looked up. The entire ceiling was gloriously white with encrusted *hsiao*, a princely haul!

An old ladder stood against the wall and with Perkyn holding it Jared clambered up.

The roof was out of reach but he transferred his feet to the multitude of pigeonholes in the wall and was soon up among the rank efflorescence that sprouted like flowers from all parts. Gleefully he plied his scraper and in no time had a bag weighty with good, reeking *hsiao*.

'That's enough for now,' he called down to Perkyn and descended.

They opened the door and to his horror saw the bulk of Harpe standing outside, impassive, holding back an eager mastiff on a leash.

'Er, Saint Michael's blessing upon you, this fine evening,' Jared managed.

'Master Blacksmith. And can I ask what you're doing here?'

'Oh. Um, looking.'

'For what?'

'F-for treasure.'

'Treasure? Give me that bag.'

Harpe glared inside, sniffing and frowning, then handed it back expressionless, distancing himself.

'Ah, and I hopes you feel better in the morning.'

CHAPTER 44

It was utterly frustrating. Even with fresh ingredients purified over three nights it was still a miserable pop and gouts of smoke, nothing that would frighten even a mouse.

He had used the best contents in his concoction he could find, and if they were not good enough there were no others he could lay hands on.

Unless he could find an explanation he was finished.

Was it simply that he'd been fooled? Had Wang misled him in some way? But he'd followed the process eagle-eyed from start to thunderous finale and was certain there'd been no foul play.

Jared was staring into his ale at the tavern three days later when he it came to him. The proud alewife took care with her brew to make it distinctive and lip-smacking. She added alecost and pennyroyal, other herbs, to make her gruit that which gave her particular ale a right true flavour and the proportions of which were always a jealously guarded secret.

Could it be . . . that his ingredients were sufficient in themselves but that they had to be mixed in due proportion?

It made sense – where nothing else did.

The first trial, an extra handful of sulphur, produced

results. An angry red and blue blaze but no concussion.

Another, less charcoal, and it was a fitful spitting.

Yet another, more *hsiao*, produced a sprightly flaring for some seconds but no violence.

It could go on for ever. No wonder the alewives could keep the secret of their brews. The combinations were endless.

He had three elements. If he went by tens, he could try one-tenth of the first and ten-tenths of the others. Then two-tenths of the first to ten-tenths of the others and so on, but even with his elementary arithmetic, didn't it come out to, er, ten times ten times ten – a thousand trials?

Any reasonable man would give up in the face of these odds.

But he would do it. However long it took, using a small wooden spoon as the standard measure and seeing it through to the very end.

There was little Perkyn could do so Jared attended to his combinations alone.

Some of these resulted in a bright flaring but most ended as a dull sputtering, all producing gouts of rank-smelling smoke.

At one point he nearly broke down when he realised that to be thorough he should, by rights, at the end of this cycle, brew a fresh batch of the first element and run through the entire cycle of combinations again. Which would mean that at this rate he would be an old man before he'd half-completed the interminable course.

Doggedly, night after night, as the weather grew colder and blustery rain made the trudge to the priory a misery, Jared persevered.

CHAPTER 45

One grey day a grim procession led by a flint-eyed man in black cassock and ecclesiastical ornamentation, flanked by two others who swung thuribles of incense, made their way to the smithy. They were followed by the shire reeve's men.

'We come for the person of Jared of Hurnwych,' intoned the flint-eyed man. 'In the Name of the Christ who is risen.'

Jared stepped forward.

'I am Edward of Lincoln, summoner to His Grace the Bishop of Coventry, here to enquire into matters of grave moment for which you will answer.'

From the bishop? Despite the heat of the forge Jared felt a chill that swiftly sliced through his tiredness.

'Reverend Father, what is it you want to know?'

Nearby Osbert stood uncertainly, his face troubled, with him a wide-eyed Daw with his outsize blacksmith's cap.

'This is not the rightful place to hear your words. You are herewith detained in the name of the Holy and Apostolic Church to render up such defence when called upon before a lawfully convened consistory court, for which this is my warrant.'

With all the dread authority of the Church he passed across

an impressive document in Latin, sealed with a ribbon. It meant nothing to Jared.

'Why . . . that is, what am I accused of?'

'Maleficium, of the foulest kind.'

'I . . . I don't know—'

The summoner nodded to the shire reeve's men and they took Jared in charge. The procession moved off, Jared's last despairing glance back taking in Daw's white face staring at him as he was held protectively by Osbert.

As they passed, folk emerged from their houses to gape silently at the spectacle.

He was not taken to the castle for it was an ecclesiastical court that had jurisdiction, but this brought with it a problem. The little village of Hurnwych, in which no crime worthy of more than the stocks on the village green had happened in living memory, now had to detain a prisoner of the Church of some notoriety. Castle Ravenstock's dungeons would not be appropriate until the guilty malefactor was handed over for punishment.

Jared found himself confined in the church steeple.

After some hours he was visited by a sharp-faced priest in black who introduced himself as the episcopal confessor. He told Jared that if he truly confessed to his misdeeds there would be a quick end to it, but if he persisted in denial the confession may well need to be extracted by more persuasive and painful methods. Better to save himself the torments and acknowledge his sins: who knew, in that case the court may be inclined to leniency in the sentence.

At Jared's plea of ignorance of his sin the priest frowned – he must know very well how he'd transgressed, for why else would he be accused of such evil? In any case, he was not in a condition to discuss any case before it was heard.

It wasn't until Father Bertrand came that it all became clear. The grey-haired cleric was clearly distressed and could not speak for some time, then raised his eyes and said softly, 'Jared, my son, are you possessed at all? Tell me true, for His Grace is inclined to be merciful, you as an innocent pilgrim having suffered so grievously in the Lord's Name.'

'Father – please! Tell me what sin I have done, I beg you.'

'Why, you are accused of sorcery and conjuring the Devil, a heresy of the vilest kind. I pray that this can not be so, but we are faced with no less than five staunch witnesses to your guilt.'

'I'm not possessed, Father! I can't know what they mean for—'

'I must tell you, my son, there is no more heinous sin under heaven. If you are found guilty then . . . it is my duty to tell you that as a consequence, immolation at the stake is the customary penalty.'

'I didn't . . . they're mistaken, I never—'

'The inquisition will visit in four days. Do you not feel that time would better be spent in prayer? Let us then begin . . .'

CHAPTER 46

'Jared of Hurnwych, blacksmith of this parish, come into the court!'

The manor Great Hall, which had seen so many banquets and bawdy entertainments, was now an echoing vastness. One end was set up as an episcopal inquisition with tables and a dais. The judge, a heavy-faced and sour individual in black with a winged scholar's cap, sat in the centre high chair. Others in severe robes attended on either side.

'Approach the judge in due obeisance,' ordered the proctor.

Jared quailed. This was not a court of law, it was a bishop's inquisition into an accusation and if this judge deemed it upheld and he guilty, he would be handed over to the civil authorities for punishment – with this charge, nothing less than the stake!

He moved forward and fell to one knee, his head bowed.

'Rise.'

The rest of the court was packed with village folk: curious, sorrowful, perplexed – everyone who knew him and was known by him. Would they be the ones to howl and dance as the flames put an end to his existence?

'My lord, this man stands accused of the most heinous diabolical practices, of a nature that is worthy of the extreme sanction.'

'Bring forth the chief accuser.'

There was a stir to one side and John Frauncey came forth. He gave a quick glance at Jared then refused to catch his eye.

Frauncey! The high-and-mighty bailiff's clerk, whose courting of Aldith he'd frustrated.

Was this mysterious and baffling charge an act of revenge by a deranged suitor? If it was, then it would be Frauncey who would suffer. Bearing false witness was both a churchly and civil felony, heavily punishable. But then Jared remembered that there were no less than five witnesses. If this was vengeance it was well planned.

'John Frauncey, give your evidence.'

Sworn on oath, he spoke with quiet venom. 'My lord, I accuse Jared of Hurnwych with falsehood, deceit – and sorcery.'

The judge waited for the ripple of shock to subside. 'Go on.'

'He did abuse the charity of the Holy Church by representing himself to be a pilgrim to the Holy Sepulchre. My lord, not only did he fail to make worship there, he had quite another object in mind.'

'And what was that?'

'To enter in on the lands of the Saracen and infidel, there to learn their black arts and heretical practices, which presently he does indulge privily here in Hurnwych.'

This time there was open disbelief and dismay that had the judge threatening to clear the court.

'Let the accusation be recorded. Master Frauncey, you have evidence?'

'I do, My Lord. Four more witnesses to his detestable conduct other than myself.'

Hardly believing his ears, Jared heard how his nightly visits to the old priory had aroused suspicion and perplexity, and this had reached Frauncey's ears. He'd taken four men and followed him and they'd been terrified and unnerved to see him conjure fire and brimstone deep in the haunted ruins, manifestly in an attempt to raise the Devil himself.

'If further evidence is required, it can be produced, My Lord.'

'Do so.'

'Since his arrest, his house has been searched, and with this result.'

Two clay jars and a series of small bags were offered up.

'And what is that?'

'The apparatus of sorcery, My Lord. Brimstone, which he acquired from a pedlar with a tale of pestilence in his house, but which is well known as necessary in the summoning of Satan, his master. Various other substances of strange and unknown purpose, and—'

'I see. Any further evidence?'

'There is, My Lord, particularly concerning his lunatic behaviour under diabolic influence among the pigsties and animal dung of this village . . .'

'We may hear of this later. Have you any further first-hand witnesses?'

'His servant Perkyn Slewfoot will have beholden these foul deeds and might be examined to advantage.'

'Let him be called.'

There was something both noble and pathetic about Perkyn when he was brought forward. No longer young and artless he was now stooped and worried and moved with a spiritless shuffle, bringing murmurs of sympathy from the villagers.

'What can you tell us about what took place at the priory?'

Clearly awed by his surroundings he lifted his head, glancing nervously at Jared as if for strength, but then drew himself up. He was now going to pay back the debt of life he owed his old master.

'It's not right, he going to worship the Devil. He never did and I never saw Satan ever!' he burst out bravely. 'On my life, I never!'

A murmur began among the villagers that the judge ignored, coming back immediately, 'Then what was he doing in a far place with those substances – a ruin that all do shun?'

Jared tensed. What would Perkyn answer?

'Come along!' the judge rapped testily. 'You were there with him, you must know what he was about.'

Perkyn looked despairingly at Jared.

'You are on oath and sworn to tell this court—'

'He was trying to make *huo yao*,' he blurted. 'Not calling the Devil at all!'

'What are you talking about, you villain?' spluttered the judge.

Cringing, Jared heard Perkyn continue.

'Why, that's a secret powder that he's going to use to tear down the walls of every castle in the kingdom!' he said proudly.

It was met with incredulous gasps and pitying laughter, but the judge glowered.

'Your loyalty does you credit but as a witness you are worthless. I believe I've heard enough and am minded to conclude the proceedings. Jared of Hurnwych, have you anything wherewith to rebut these accusations?'

He swallowed hard. What he said next would either cast him to the flames or . . .

'I do, My Lord.'

'Then let us hear it.'

'Only because of the respect in which I hold this court will my secret now be revealed.'

'If you are trifling with me it will go hard with you, that I can assure you!'

'Not at all, My Lord. I only crave understanding.'

'What is this secret, then?'

'I am toiling hard to devise works of fire that do surprise and entertain for holy day occasions and feasts. I work privily for fear my discoveries will be stolen by those who will set up in rivalry to me. The old ruins are convenient for another reason, My Lord. The stink of the *huo yao* is offensive to some and I would spare them.'

'Works of fire! You expect me to believe such nonsense? You'd better find another line of rebuttal, or this inquisition must draw its own conclusions!'

'Then you'll take an evidence, My Lord?' he asked innocently.

'Evidence? What evidence?'

'If I am so indulged, I can produce these works of fire for your enlightening, here in this very place before you all.'

The judge blinked, and sat back, baffled.

'And from the very materials that were taken from my house!'

He prayed he'd remembered right what he had on hand, or it could be a sorry and tragic spectacle.

'You will conjure works of fire as you call them, before me now?'

'My lord.'

'From the substances seized as evidence against you?'

'I will.'

A table was brought and space cleared around it. A plain pottery dish had also been asked for and with heart thumping Jared checked the jars. The lord be praised – here was a three-day-old trial with the five-part *hsiao*, last week's failed three-part sulphur and another that he hadn't trialled yet.

'This is my *huo yao*, My Lord.'

He passed up a scruple, which the judge sniffed suspiciously.

'This smells to me like nothing other than the Devil's own dust, I swear.'

'You will see it is not, My Lord.'

Taking the five-part *hsiao* powder he heaped it generously on the plate, an inert dull grey.

The hall held its collective breath in a deathly silence as he prepared the display.

'My lord, the *huo yao* sleeps now, but when touched by flame it does awaken in violence. I beg pardon for any dismay it might cause. Are you ready?'

'Yes, yes. Get on with it.'

A taper was brought and Jared paused, looking up significantly. 'Upon your command, My Lord.'

'Very well.'

He brought the flame slowly down to the tail of the ridge. It caught, and in an instant flared up blindingly, quickly replaced by a roiling pillar of smoke mounting to the ceiling, the sulphurous reek of the combustion drifting down on the stunned spectators.

A shocked silence was followed moments later by gasps of admiration and cries from all sides.

'Here is another.'

The three-part sulphur behaved as he knew it would, with a fizz and splutter of yellow and blue, bringing yet more applause.

'And finally . . .'

It was the untried batch, which he spread liberally across the blackened plate.

This time it went up in a satisfying *whoomf,* which had some falling to their knees, overcome.

The judge took a little time to recover then intoned, 'I rule that these accusations may be shown to have an alternate explanation and therefore cannot be sustained. Jared of Hurnwych is hereby discharged.'

CHAPTER 47

The days that followed were anything but jubiliant for Jared. The sympathy shown to him after he'd returned from pilgrimage had evaporated with the realisation that the nocturnal wanderings they'd charitably attributed to his disordered mind was merely cover for base experimenting in fairground magic. Some were curious, most disillusioned and others even hostile.

His play with *huo yao* at the trial had saved his skin, but he despised himself for turning his great vision into a magic trick to entertain. And it had just revealed the utter impossibility that he could go on with it, given that every eye was on him now, his months of labour only resulting in that paltry show.

The wisest thing was simply to give up. Wang had probably tricked him somehow, but what was that to him now. He had to lay to rest the quest that had driven him for so long and get on with life.

But he felt an emptiness; he was now approaching forty, no wife or family save Daw, who must now despise him . . . nothing to live for in fact.

Depression clamped down.

* * *

He was late at the smithy and a red-faced Osbert swore at his forge-hand and rounded on Daw before confronting him.

'Jared, we're going to have words!'

'Well?'

'I've got . . . we've got a right to know what you're about now. Have you finished with your devil's dust that you can give your forge the attention it sorely needs? Spit it out, now, we deserve an answer!'

It was the last thing Jared wanted, given the mood he was in, and he bit his lip without reply.

'Christ's bones, man!' Osbert exploded. 'All this time we're feeling sorry for you wandering abroad at night and you're footling about with your cursed fire playthings. Isn't it time to put it behind you and bear a hand here?'

Jared picked up the tongs and pulled a mattock tang from the fire, taking it to the anvil and welting it sullenly.

Osbert pulled him around roughly. 'That won't do, Jared! We've got a heap of work – see?' His anger was building, distorting his face. 'Unless you get rid of what's riding you, I'll . . .'

'You'll what?' Jared snarled. 'It's my life, I do what I please.'

'. . . I'll buy you out!'

It was said.

Astonished, Jared paused, peering at him in disbelief. 'You'd . . . buy the smithy, take it from me?'

Osbert's red but obstinate features were all the answer he needed.

Thoughts rushed in. It would leave him free and with money in his pocket, but to what end?

To leave the village.

The sudden realisation that this was what he wanted came as a fearful but wonderful self-discovery. He'd returned to his place of origin to find his friends changed, and with his son estranged he had no one close to share his life. As a man who had travelled and seen marvels uncounted he was being suffocated in Hurnwych.

This was his opportunity. To start again, take another course to who knew where . . . to chance it!

'I agree. It'll be your smithy and I'll get out.'

'Done!'

Suddenly there was a muffled sob and Daw scurried away.

'You'll take care of my boy?'

'He's my apprentice, Jared.'

'So . . .'

Osbert shuffled his feet together awkwardly. 'Where will you go?'

'To a big place, a town.'

He turned to his loyal companion on his earlier travels but before he could say anything Perkyn shuffled awkwardly. 'Master Jared. We've seen a lump of things together but I'm not a youngling any more. I don't like the big world, too much to worry on. I'm happy here with Master Osbert; the old village is where I want to lay down at my end. You do understand, Master Jared?'

He gave him a friendly pat on the shoulder. 'Be a good forge-hand for Osbert and you'll make me happy.'

It was going to be a complete and total break.

So be it.

CHAPTER 48

Coventry, AD 1307

It was a great city of ancient lineage and three cathedrals – and a stinking, noisy, jostling and exuberant new world that set Jared's pulse racing. Nothing could be better calculated to set him to rights. Here he could make something of his life – if he took the chance with both hands.

His horse shied from the grisly heads arrayed above the gatehouse with birds at work on the eyes. And his nose twitched at the reek of the black ditch he crossed over; half-naked children at play along it, old women searching among its rubbish.

To the left was a street leading to a packed market square. A flock of lambs was being driven towards it through the bustle. To the right a narrow passage opened to a street with a maze of stalls.

His destination was straight ahead into a complex of inns and taverns and he kneed the horse forward. The Cock and Hen took his fancy and he clopped into the courtyard, leaving his horse and pack animal with the stable boys.

After so many hours in the saddle he straightened painfully and made for the hall to find the landlord.

'A bed and bread – and a sup of ale will see me content.'

The beefy leather-aproned innkeeper gave him a brief glance, then grunted, 'B' horse?'

Assured that this was Jared's transport and therefore he could not be a penniless itinerant, the man named the price. 'A silver penny the bed, three ha'pence the meal and it'll be tuppence the horse. Servant?'

'Not yet come,' Jared said loftily.

It was no trivial amount but there was no choice – he had no desire to start his town life in one of the hostelries he remembered from his pilgrim days.

The hall was smoky and smelt of concentrated humanity and stale food, the trestle tables alive with travellers taking their pottage and quaffing ale.

Jared saw, however, that the strewn rushes were not unduly caked with mould and dung and even had traces of fleabane and hyssop to alleviate the stinks. It would do.

That night he lay awake, unused to town noises: the barking of dogs, snores of dozens of others, the grind of cartwheels and the carousing of late arrivals. How unlike the stillness of Hurnwych, where the soft hooting of an owl in Wolfscote Forest could easily be heard floating on the night air.

Above all was the daunting thought that he was now entirely alone in what lay ahead – had he done the right thing by cutting all ties with his past and heading out into the unknown?

He'd left his son stricken and tearful with Osbert but also with half the proceedings from the buy-out, and a vague promise to return one day to see how he was going. It had torn him to leave but he knew he wasn't the kind of father Daw needed.

Perkyn was grateful to continue as a forge-hand and the little house was now his.

For himself, he now had a well-filled purse of silver, but this was all he had to see him set up in his trade. And it was already beginning to drain.

He'd come to Coventry for one very good reason: a cousin of his, Geoffrey Barnwell, had been born in Hurnwych and left to seek his fortune in the city. He'd gone when Jared was a small child but his father had later spoken of his success as a maker of candlesticks. All he had to do was find him to get his advice and protection.

Given his varied experience in all kinds of blacksmithing there shouldn't be much difficulty finding a comfortable niche, but it was the outlay needed before he'd made a name that was the chanciest thing.

He set off early in the morning to find his relative, wearing his favourite russet tunic with a hood that hung down ending in a short liripipe, green hose and calf-length boots. His dark-brown felt hat with a saucy point had a twinkling sun motif brooch and he felt ready to face whatever the day would bring.

The innkeeper hadn't been much help, gruffly pointing out that there wouldn't be more than half a hundred candlestick makers in Coventry. He did add that if he cared to visit Bishopsgate he would find most of them there together and pointed out how to get there.

Jared stepped out down the road, past raucous market stalls and the fronts of craft shops, pushing through crowds, careful to guard against robbers and cutpurses, as he'd learnt the hard way in cities across the Levant.

Pie stalls, mercers, cobblers – it went on and on in a tumultuous din as he made his way along muddy streets, passages and alleys. It was over an hour before he'd found the candlestick makers and their characteristic billowing reek of tallow.

But there he was told that there was most definitely no Geoffrey Barnwell in their number.

This was a sad blow. Without anyone to speak for him his entry into the closed world of the skilled tradesman would be hard indeed.

CHAPTER 49

Jared couldn't let it rest. The man could have moved elsewhere, who knew – he had to find someone who could give him tidings of his kinsman.

It took the rest of the afternoon to come upon one who did. An old tally-clerk told him that Geoffrey had done well for himself and set up as a merchant, no longer to live among the noisome workings. Not only that, although it was many years ago, his books would show where he'd removed to.

At last!

With hope renewed Jared set out the next day. The merchants lived in the Chauntry, quite another quarter, and considerably better off. Their houses were of black post and beam and handsome stone infill, some with three or four angular storeys jutting out. The street was clean, the odours subdued. It was another existence.

As he paced along he became aware that he was no longer the well-dressed visitor but a stranger come to town. The fashion here was of bright colour, cote and doublet, and his practical country garb marked him out as an outsider.

The houses now were of quality and he rehearsed the words he would say when facing Barnwell, whom he'd not seen since he was a small boy.

Here it was: a four-storey house on the corner of the Whitefriars highway and Cheaping Lane, with a single high watchtower.

He rapped respectfully with the wrought-iron knocker, which he noted was of appreciable workmanship.

'Jared of Hurnwych to call upon Master Geoffrey Barnwell,' he told the smartly attired servant who answered.

'Who sent you?' he demanded suspiciously.

'I'm his kinsman,' retorted Jared, 'who desires to be remembered to him.'

He was allowed in, to stand irresolute in an ornamented anteroom that could well serve in a manor house. To one side was a door firmly closed and on the other a staircase leading up to the next floor. There was no question, he was out of his depth in these surroundings.

The servant told him to wait and left.

A short time later a lady appeared at the top of the stairs and looked sharply down at him.

'Why do you seek Master Barnwell, fellow?'

Strong-featured and imperious, she was a few years older than he.

'I'm Jared, his cousin of Hurnwych Green, and beg to be made known to him again,' he said stiffly. 'Um, my lady,' he added, feeling intimidated.

She considered him at length. 'You are your father's . . .'

'Yes, m' lady.'

'Come!' she commanded and turned away out of sight.

Feeling every bit a country bumpkin Jared obediently went up the steep stairs and emerged on to the second floor – the main hall.

A fire blazed on one side and the room was richly decorated with two portraits and embroidered hangings over the dark-stained walls, the centrepiece a long polished table.

Two imposing upright chairs were at the end of the room and she gracefully sat in one but indicated he should take the bench.

'How goes Hurnwych Green these days, Master Jared? Is the new cathedral yet built?'

'Cathedral?' he asked, confused. 'The village has no such.'

'Then what does it have?'

'Why, St Mary's with Father Bertrand. No cathedral, m' lady.'

Her appearance was more striking than beautiful, her blood-red surcoat in faultless taste.

'And the lord of the manor – I quite forget, who is it?'

'It was Sir Robert le Warde who lately died and—'

'Quite. So I'm to conclude that you do indeed come from Hurnwych.'

She considered for a moment, then said in a kinder tone, 'You've had a long journey – but I'm dismayed to tell you it has been in vain.'

'In vain?' he said, with a sinking feeling.

'Yes. My name is Rosamunde and I am . . . his widow.'

It hit him like a blow. It was so unfair: no protector, no one to speak for him or even to give advice in the face of the hostile town guilds. It was going to be a hard road ahead.

She saw him wilt and went on softly, 'Do believe I'm sorry you had to hear it from me. Did you know him well?'

'Only as a boy.'

The quicker he was out of here and looking for some sort of refuge and—

'Then it seems you came for some other purpose.'

There was no reason not to admit to his real intention, even if this high merchant lady would now look down on him.

'Yes, m' lady. I . . . I'm a blacksmith and look to setting up in Coventry and did hope that Master Geoffrey might speak for me.'

To his surprise she nodded slowly and said kindly, 'As is a noble craft and calling. You were right, Geoffrey would have done what he could, but I fear you will have much to do before the guild allows you to set up in trade. Are you accounted a master of your skill?'

'I'm in a fair way of knowing more than most, I'm told,' he replied defiantly.

'As a village blacksmith?' she chided gently.

He reddened and said curtly, 'My experiences are many and I do not forget any lessons I learn.'

She stood up and turned to him with a smile, her hands clasped together. 'I didn't mean to pry. But I'm forgetting myself. Do you take wine?'

He'd never had a chance to taste wine in his life but stoutly admitted that he did.

A servant was called and he found himself with a goblet of red wine and promoted to the second chair.

'I've a fancy there's more about you than it appears,' she said, curious. 'Have you lived in Hurnwych all your days?'

The wine was soft and produced a glow quite different to a hearty ale.

'Not all my years, m' lady.'

'I thought not. You have the look of a man of some seasoning. Have you ever travelled?'

The wine was going far to settle his discomfort at his surroundings.

'Far. To the land of the Mongols and Saracens.'

'By the Rood and this must be a tale worth hearing.' She noticed his glass and replenished it. 'Do tell me about it.'

Gratified by her interest he told briefly of how, his wife taken from him, he'd embarked on a pilgrimage, which had ended in his being sold into slavery: yet gaining much by his trial before finding freedom in Cilicia.

'No doubt life in the village is a mite humble after such,' she said with a shrewd look.

''Tis why I'm come to town, to seek my fortune,' he said shortly, and finished his glass. 'I do thank you for your kindness and must leave to find it.' He stood up and gave an awkward bow.

'Wait!' She rose and faced him. 'You came to see my husband. He cannot help you, but I can. It will be hard to find a situation in the city – at least I can offer lodgings while you do.'

Jared blushed at her generosity. 'I thank you, my lady.'

CHAPTER 50

It was a small but clean room next to the kitchen and out of the way. With its dresser and jug of water, a room better by far than he'd stayed in since Tabriz, he acknowledged with a twinge. He ate with the servants who seemed satisfied that he was some sort of distant relation and told him with relish just what he'd landed into.

The lady Rosamunde came from a good family and had married the fast-rising merchant Barnwell after he had made venture into wool and from there the cloth industry. She was quick and intelligent and rapidly made herself indispensable in his affairs.

When he'd been suddenly carried away of a fever three years ago she'd refused to be put aside, and as his widow, had grasped the reins as *femme sole*, in her own right. She had succeeded well, taking her cloth interests to the Continent, trading with the Hansa ports in English dunster broadcloth for Dutch and German linen and was now a respected and moneyed Coventry merchant.

No, she'd shown no interest in remarrying, even if in her position she could command attention from knights and aldermen both. And no, she had no issue and lived essentially alone in this mansion, running a tight and no-nonsense household.

How long could he expect to . . . ?

A brisk pace in finding a situation would, it seemed, be advisable.

He lost no time in setting out the next day for the Guildhall where he found the name and place of business of the Prime Warden of the Worshipful Company of Blacksmiths. This was not far and soon he was making himself known.

'Hurnwych Green? Never heard of it,' the corpulent official said over his ale, bought for him by Jared. 'Not as if it'll get you anywhere.'

He drained his pot and held it out significantly.

'All I want is a start, a pitch with a forge and—'

'Can't be done. We're a close crew here in Coventry, don't hold with outsiders rushing in and taking our bread. And how do we know you're even proper apprenticed? We'd be sad loons to let a shyster set up under our name!'

Jared burnt but this was not the time to argue. Guilds controlled the right to trade in a city, their word alone allowing a tradesman to set out his wares. In a way it was reasonable, for bad workmanship would bring the reputation of the whole city into question, and more importantly, direct jurisdiction ensured that none would dare undercut the going working rate for all.

'Then how do I get started?' he asked bitterly.

He'd noticed that the smithies were all set back from the market proper, feeding their products directly into the mass of shops and stalls. Here there'd be for a certainty a cosy arrangement in place that he could never get around without the right connections.

'Well now, and this is your problem. We can see you as a forge-hand straight off, even a journeyman if the company agrees on it, but setting up on your own, well, needs you to be a master blacksmith with a masterpiece accepted by us and such. Can't see that happening quick, can you?'

He knew what was going on and seethed. A fat bribe would devour his start-up money and leave him worse off than before.

Jared sat in dejection in his room, only a guttering rush light for company.

Start from the bottom and see it through? He was not young and most his age had settled down well before and this would take years. Yet he had to do something.

Not even a jobbing blacksmith was going to be possible – what else was?

His thoughts were interrupted by a page. 'Mistress wants to see you,' he piped.

Rosamunde was in her chair in the upper room and smiled to see him enter. 'May I know how the day went for you, Master Jared?'

He pulled himself together. 'Today, not so well m' lady,' he said off-handedly.

'Oh? I'm grieved to hear it.'

'The guilds. They won't have an outsider lay out for a smithy.'

'I feared as much.'

'That swag-bellied tosspot of a warden, he knew the others wouldn't take me on without they have his say,' he added bitterly.

She said nothing so he ended baldly, 'I'll not be able to set up a forge as I wanted, so must think again about coming to town.'

'You're a bright sort of man, I should think you'll soon find a way to better yourself here in Coventry. Meanwhile, do feel able to remain in your lodgings as you need to.'

'I thank you, m' lady,' he said sincerely.

'And as we're kin of a sort, Rosamunde would be pleasing to me.'

Her widening smile added a soft beauty to her appearance that startled him.

'As you desire, um, Rosamunde.'

'If you are at liberty tonight, I would take it kindly should you sup with me, Jared.'

'Yes, of course.'

'I'd like to know more of you, your travels and adventures. And to be truthful, it would be pleasant to have company that isn't concerned with trade and books of account.'

He came at the appointed hour to see the table set for two.

She entered at the same time, her wimple removed, her auburn hair fetchingly plaited and doubled over her ears.

'Wine? I think you'd like this Rhenish, new landed.' It was a pale wine, quite unlike the previous and no less appealing.

She put the jug down and looked at him with a clear interest. 'Now do tell me. To be a slave of the Moors, what must you have suffered?'

Under the influence of the wine and her insistence he opened up. Instead of the bare facts of before he went into details he knew would intrigue – the foods, exotic clothing, veiled faces, singular religious rituals.

As the dishes were brought he told of the hard desert landscapes, walled cities, the ruthless efficiency and merciless behaviour in battle of the Mongols. He spoke too of the beauty and remoteness of Tabriz; rose-petal salve after bathing, a pomegranate sherbet in the heat of the day, the savour of roast goat and herbs, but tactfully leaving out any mention of Kadrİye.

She was entranced, listening dreamily as with more wine

he grew bolder, weaving a spell of the oriental world that she would never know.

The dishes were cleared away but Rosamunde showed no signs of wanting him to leave. Instead she said, 'You've been to lands far beyond those seen by the common pilgrim and now you've come back to England. Are you not unsettled, restless with your lot? Mayhap this is what drove you out of Hurnwych.'

He smiled sadly. 'It did, I do confess it.'

'And I think there's more to it than that,' she said shrewdly, eyeing him. 'There's something that's inside you, driving you on. I can tell, I know much of men from my daily affairs.'

It stopped him short. She would not have achieved so as a merchant without a very astute and perceptive mastery of human nature. She must have seen something of what his vision had done to his soul, the wrenching abandoning of it and—

'Rosamunde – how would you feel if you knew you were the only one with a secret, a wonderful and scaresome secret that could shake the world but you can't do anything with it?'

She looked at him steadily. 'If you have such a one, you have only two choices. You live with it inside you for ever or . . . you share it with someone who may be able to understand.'

To share the vision! To share the burden of knowing, of helplessness.

Jared regarded her for a long moment then decided. 'I will tell you. While with the Mongols on a siege I witnessed such a sight, such a miracle . . .'

It all came out. Everything – the demoniac flash and thunder that brought down the gates and ruin and slaughter to the city. The extraction from Wang of the secret and its burning on his memory. His deliverance into freedom and return to Hurnwych, then his futile attempts to bring it into existence here in England.

'If I can make this *huo yao,* then with it I can tear down every castle wall in the kingdom! All those vain and arrogant lords and ladies will then be made to live among the people they would rule!'

At first he quailed, realising too late that she herself was a proud lady, but then in time remembered that as a merchant whose success was of her own making she might very well sympathise.

'This *huo yao*, is . . . ?'

'The Cathayan name for it.' He thought for a moment, then recalled the trial and the inquisitor's term for the powder. It would serve for now. 'You may call it devil's dust.'

'Then with your devil's dust you will achieve this?' This was no mocking, only a serious enquiry.

'Its force is terrible and unlimited and nothing may stand against it. If indeed I could bring it to life then it will be so, but . . .'

She shook her head slowly in wonder. 'If any other told me a tale as yours I would make scorn of them, but you have no reason to gull me and I must accept what you say.'

'You don't despise my quest?'

'No, Jared, I do not. It does you honour, but if you were successful I believe it would have a wider purpose.'

'But I'm not!'

'Are you sure?'

'I've tried everything and—'

'There may be something. Some years ago our family lawyer died and left his library to my husband. As I must, I read all his volumes to discover anything of value to commerce, and I do well remember one small book with a note in it that this very work frightened no less than the great and worthy Friar Roger Bacon. I was interested and studied it, a curious work brought back from your part of the world, but in the end to me it seemed a fraud, full of superstition. But there was a section on fire that gives a recipe for a thunder weapon. Do you think—?'

'Do you still have it?'

'Yes, I'm sure of it.'

'Please . . . can I see it – now?'

His intensity took her aback but she agreed and left. In a short while she returned with a small and frayed book.

'Here.'

Jared took it and devoured it with his eyes, but he could make out nothing of its small, dense script. Thanks to his father he was familiar with the English of accounts and orders but this was like nothing he'd come across before.

'It's in Latin,' she prompted. 'Shall I read it to you?'

He handed it back defensively.

'It's by a Marcus Graecus – Mark the Greek, who I've never heard of. A collection of recipes concerning fire,' she murmured, flicking over the pages. 'Some are difficult to construe, I don't know the Moorish names. Others are . . . well, nonsense, ridiculous. Do you want me to go on?'

'You said thunder weapons?'

'I'm trying to remember. They were . . . ah, here we are. It's mixed up with the recipe for flying fire. It says, "Take a pound of living sulphur, two pounds of willow charcoal and six pounds of saltpetre. Grind very finely then mix together. For making thunder, place in a stout case bound with iron wire, for the force thereof is very great."'

The world stood still. In his bones he knew this was the *huo yao* he'd been unable to create – except for one thing.

'This salt peter. Does it say anything about—'

'Yes, *salis petrosi* it certainly says. Common saltpetre.'

'C-common?'

'Of course! We use it in cooking to preserve meats for the winter, but then you're not to know this, being a man,' she teased.

'Have you – could we find some?' he stammered.

'Really? Cook has gone home by now, but I'll see if there is any in her larder.'

She returned with a small handful of something wrapped in a cloth. 'This is our saltpetre.'

He opened it up on the table and stared at it.

Crystals, white but flecked.

He dipped a wet finger in, and almost afraid to hope, tasted it.

The quite unmistakeable sweet tingle of *hsiao*!

His thoughts roared. The three ingredients the same, it had to be the formulary for devil's dust but the proportions were wildly different to what he'd been painfully working through. The *hsiao* – that is to say the saltpetre – six times that of sulphur? He'd started by equal measures for all, but this was far more skewed, and if it was the real thing it could well explain his failure!

He sat down suddenly. Wang had demonstrated the *huo yao* before his eyes, knowing that the highest secret was in the proportions, which he'd gone on to cleverly conceal.

Raising his eyes he saw her looking at him in concern. He gave a twisted smile and said with feeling, 'I can't rest until I've tried this. If it's true, then . . .'

'Then we'd better see if it is,' she said flatly. 'There's no use dreaming until you have something in your hands.'

'We?' he asked softly.

'You're going to need somewhere to work and another place to try it out. Now let me see . . . yes. I have a storeroom, which I could get cleared and then let it be known that you're experimenting with a new dyeing method, which is not to be revealed to my rivals. This has happened before, it will be accepted. You may work there in peace. The other – where to try it out – is more of a question.'

She thought deeply, then smiled. 'Yes – perfect. Not so far from here the road leaves the river because it comes over a high precipice in a waterfall and it must go around. The waterfall is at the end of a small ravine that no one visits because it ends at the cliff itself. Should your thunder work, then the sound will be well enclosed and people will think it a distant cloudburst.'

'Rosamunde – why are you doing this?'

'Because . . . I think you are a man who deserves something from me . . . for my husband's sake. And besides, I believe you in what you say and if you succeed, I wish it that I was the one who made the way smooth for you.'

CHAPTER 51

Jared set up his workshop quickly. The charcoal was easy and the sulphur could be readily refined as he'd done before. The saltpetre, however, would need much more purifying before it could be used and for the amount he needed was ruinously expensive. Rosamunde had made no comment, letting him get on with it.

This was his last and only chance and he was not going to take shortcuts. The alchemist's sulphur looked pure but he was going to make sure, and soon the throat-catching reek of sulphur fumes filled the air and eddied up into the opening to the outside. He wasn't concerned, for here in the city there were far worse stinks, such as those from tanning.

He did the pulverising with the utmost care, twice the time the Cathayans took. And he would complete it just like them – clay pots and cloth fuses.

He found three empty herb pots in the kitchen and prepared for the big trial in rising excitement.

Saddling up a palfrey from the stable, he followed Rosamunde's directions and arrived at the spot where the road diverged from the river. There, he found a barely noticeable path, which he rode along until continuing on horseback became impractical. Tying his mount to a tree he walked on and soon met the edge of the river – not a large one but issuing out from a dark ravine over a tumble of smoothed boulders.

The only way ahead was to jump from rock to rock but it enabled him to enter the dank coolness, past the steep face of the scarp and into the ravine. It was more a narrowing cleft, but of surprising length and took a good ten minutes to reach the dull roar of the waterfall.

He looked about and saw nothing but sheer heights to the edge of the woodland above.

As Rosamunde had said, it was perfect.

There was no reason to delay – he had to know if he had the secret in his grasp at last.

'I'm ready to give trial to the devil's dust. Would you like to come?' he asked Rosamunde the next morning.

It seemed, however, that she was not available so Jared readied for the trial on his own.

Each of the ingredients carefully packed in separate bags.

Flint and steel, the mortar and pestle and the three pots.

He rode slowly toward the diverging path, stopped and dismounted as if adjusting the beast's girth. With nobody in sight he continued along the path to the same place as before and he left his mount, the bridle looped over a branch.

He made his way into the ravine. On one side near the waterfall he found what he was looking for – a flat rock untouched by mist from the cascade.

Taking a last look around, Jared addressed himself to the task. Using a spoon as a standard measure he carefully added the ingredients to the mortar in the proportions given. After industriously grinding the mixture to a suitable fineness the result looked exactly the same as before: a grey, anonymous powder.

He half-filled one of the pots and wound in the cloth. For a moment he held it in his hands; very soon he would know.

Collecting his things he took them to a safe distance and putting the flint and steel to work he quickly had a taper candle alight.

Heart hammering, he took it across the rocks to the waiting pot and extended the flame. The cloth caught.

He wheeled away, scrambling over the boulders as fast as he could.

Behind him a colossal thunderclap erupted, its sound magnified by the funnelling ravine; a frightful, glorious blast!

He felt its hot wind and turned to see grey-white smoke towering up in a triumphant plume, the pitter-patter of fragments falling all about him – and then an echoing silence.

In that moment he knew his life was going to change beyond recognition.

CHAPTER 52

'Then what is your result?' Rosamunde asked sweetly, putting down her slate of accounts.

He took a deep breath. 'I have to tell you . . . that this day I called down heaven's thunder for my own.'

She stared at him. 'You mean that . . . ?'

'Yes! I have the secret and nothing will stop me now!'

There was shock on her face, disbelief.

'Did you not think I could do it?' he said exultantly.

'To be honest with you, Jared, I thought it all a strange fancy you brought back from your ordeal that needed purging, and . . .' She trailed off.

He leant back, a satisfied smile playing. 'The folk in those castles will never—'

Suddenly she turned to face him. 'Leave that for the moment – this needs a deal of working out,' she said sharply, now as hard as any close-fisted merchant.

He frowned. 'The castles – this is why—'

'So you're going to walk up to them, and with your thunderbolts tear down their walls? Every castle in the land?' she said cuttingly. 'Why? Will they let you? What will you do when they send out their knights to cut you to pieces?'

'I, er . . .'

'Well, tell me – how will you do it? What did the Mongols do, for instance?'

'A party of brave men rushed up and stacked pots against the city walls with a tail of fire to set them off.'

She gave a hard look. 'Do I need to go on? If you haven't noticed, all castles in our part of Christendom have a wide moat and drawbridge before any of your gates. Must they then jump to place their pots?'

There was no answering this.

'Let me be plain. You now have the secret of fire and thunder. That's well done and clever of you. But worthless! No one's going to pay hard coin for a trifle.'

'Coin?' he said, hurt. 'This is not—'

'Jared. The world out there is harder in a way that with all your trials you've never had to go up against. It's a world where things are decided by the power that comes with wealth. Now let's put aside the nonsense that you're going to tear down castle walls yourself. You told me before you'll get others to do it for you. They won't do it unless you make it attractive to them to do so. For that you have to find some way of turning your devil's dust into something they can see and desire, that will enable them to break down walls. Then they'll pay you good money to secure it and at the same time do your job for you. This is the way of the world – do you understand me?'

He nodded dumbly. Here was a practicality grounded in an experience of a kind he was a stranger to, but which made so much sense.

'And I'll be honest with you. I decided to bear with your

imaginings because you're a good man, and I . . . like you. A terrible destroyer of castles made from meat preservative, leper medicine and wood charcoal – your common alchemist can come up with a far better tale, as they do. I was going to indulge you as a kindness to a kinsman, and then make my farewell as you left to whatever fortune would bring you in this life. Now it seems you've succeeded in that very thing – and I have to think hard about it.'

It was another side of Rosamunde: calculating, forceful, level-headed. He'd never known one as clear-thinking, let alone a woman. He was drawn to her strength.

'This is what I'll do. You have one month. If in that time you can bring to me an idea of how you'll turn your *huo yao* into something practical, I'll fund it.'

'Can I ask why?'

'If you achieve this, it will be a great matter and I want to profit from it.'

'We'll join together,' Jared enthused.

'We'll have a relationship. A business affair, if that is your meaning,' she said firmly. 'Your part is clear and your month starts in the morn.'

CHAPTER 53

In the days that followed Jared paced about his room, hammering at the problem until his head ached. Several times he rode into the countryside for peace and solitude. He had caught what Rosamunde was saying: that offering the *huo yao* on its own would get no interest. What was needed was a ready means of using it, a saleable thing of sorts.

But what? The clay pots were impractical in England. The only thing he could think of was to put them into a mangonel and throw it at the walls. But this would not do the job – stones lofted high came back down at a sharp angle then glanced off. This method would end with the pots shattered.

It was a conundrum. Any device to throw the pots would not work. There had to be an answer.

And it came to him in a completely unexpected way.

Outside in the street, children were playing noisily in bursts of glee at some devilment. He crossed to the window to shout down at them, and from his viewpoint saw that one lad was hiding behind a horse. He was wielding a powpe, a small toy that he was using to shoot peas at his unsuspecting friends.

Jared opened his mouth to bellow at the children but in a

sudden flash of insight he saw something that left him speechless.

The powpe was simply the stem of some plant with the pith removed, leaving a smooth tube. A pea was inserted at one end and with a mighty puff at the other it was sent on its way.

If instead of a boy's huffing it was the *huo yao* doing the work, then judging from the violence he'd seen in the ravine, the pea would rush out as if all the demons of hell were after it.

He thought feverishly. This was more than possible – and if the whole thing were scaled up, instead of a tiny pea, a great rock like those of the mangonel could be used. And these like the pea would hit the walls straight and direct in a smashing strike that no castle could withstand!

At the awesome vision he had to sit and calm himself.

The device should contain all the power of the *huo yao*, letting it exit just one way – by forcing out the 'pea' from one end only. So was that all? A tube closed off at one end? It would have to be strong, very strong – made of iron, in fact.

He'd start small, a 'pea' the size of a grape perhaps, just to test the principle. This would define the size of the instrument. About a foot or two long and a bore no greater than an inch.

Fill the thing with devil's dust, drop in a grape-sized object, point it towards the foe and set it off.

But his blacksmith's craft told him that making it wouldn't be quite so straightforward. In his experience there were plenty of articles in the form of a tube, such as the socket on a scythe blade to take the wooden haft or a halberd's affixing to the spear shaft, but all of these were short and shaped at the horn of an anvil. Nowhere was there a need outside lead plumbing for a continuous length of pipe.

In the absence of a parallel-sided mandrel for interior shaping there was no other recourse than hand beating: a rectangular iron plate, heated at the edge then upset back on itself until it had been rolled into a pipe. Then forge-welded along the seam with one end crimped off.

In his mind's eye he saw his iron tube and filled it with devil's dust, dropping perhaps a child's marble on top. Then he'd only need to . . .

How was he going to get at the devil's dust to set it off?

A long thread burning from the open end? It couldn't get past the 'pea', for the devil's dust was by definition sealed off from the outside world.

He bunched his fists in frustration but the solution soon came.

If he needed to get at the *huo yao*, he'd have to make a discreet passageway to it – spike a hole to where it lay inside, and let the fire rouse it to action.

For the rest of the day he tested the idea in his mind, tracing through the stages one by one, and could see no gaps in his reasoning. Yet if he went on with an expensive smithy job and he'd overlooked something it would be the end for him – Rosamunde would lose faith in his abilities and call a halt.

Jared was confident of the ironwork but would the *huo yao* behave as he'd predicted or under forced restraint would it just lie there sullenly? He had to find out before going any further.

He'd make the thing cheaply out of fired clay and wound around with iron wire, as Marcus the Greek had said.

CHAPTER 54

Jared slapped potter's clay around a wooden former, with a straw inserted into it at the closed end as his fire passage, and then fired it in the kiln. Attaching stout wire around the base end, he had his devil's dust peashooter.

He made three, the bore of one equal to an acorn, the other two the size of an onion. There was no crimping possible so it would be set on end, shooting up in the air with the base sitting immovably on a rock.

He packed his contrivances carefully and headed out for the ravine.

It was grey, threatening rain, but he was going to try if heaven itself was against him.

At the flat rock he took out the smaller of the three but on sudden impulse made it the larger one. It seemed so odd sitting there, defiantly upright and looking about as lethal as a flower vase, but it was about to deliver him an answer.

For the first trial he decided to use the minimum devil's dust just to see if it worked, and then increase it by stages. One spoon's worth, carefully poured down into the dark void and tamped down with a stick. An onion, dropped in over it. A twisted cloth in the fire-passage.

It was ready!

Jared got the taper going and brought it to the cloth – it caught and he hastily scrambled across the rocks, braced ready for the cataclysm.

Nothing.

The makeshift contraption just stood there in the distance, a wisp of smoke lazily dispersing.

What had gone wrong? If it was true that the *huo yao* didn't like being confined, his entire—

But then there was a livid flash and roiling smoke. Its sound echoed to and fro before fading and seconds later, and almost as an afterthought, the onion plummeted back from the sky and smashed to pieces on a nearby rock.

Shaken, Jared came to the heady realisation that it had actually worked! A wave of exultation washed over him as he went back to examine the split and blackened vessel. And such a small bit of *huo yao* for so much ferocity!

CHAPTER 55

'So let me understand you,' Rosamunde said carefully. 'You've shot an onion in the air from a jar and this is what you want to tell me?'

'It's the last matter to prove before I make the first . . . um, powpe. You see, I've proved that if fire is brought to the devil's dust in its prison, it gets so enraged it rushes to secure an escape – which it only finds at one end – by pushing on what confines it at such a force that it flies out faster than a bird on the wing.'

'And this is the use you've found for your devil's dust?'

'I'll now make an iron powpe that shoots a pebble, just to show you it will work, fired straight out at a target like in archery. Then a mighty powpe that can hurl boulders. You can't tell me but that any great lord will pay much to possess the means of bringing his neighbour's castle to ruin!'

'Ah. This is more promising. You'll tell me now that to make an iron one, you'll require a fully stocked smithy with all its tools and things.'

'Well, to work on such a piece I'd need much . . .' He trailed off at her expression.

'Until there's something to show, we'll make do with my usual workaday blacksmith – under your eye, naturally.'

It was agreed. He would produce his work and this time she would be witness to its powers. Should it turn out as he promised, then she would take a view as to serious investigation.

John Gosse was stolid and reliable as a smith, but was loudly stubborn that things would only be done his way.

'What's it to be, then?' he demanded, leaning forward truculently.

'A special.'

'Well, a special what?'

A long and wearying two days later Jared took delivery of his powpe.

Awkward and heavy, crude and disfigured on the outside by hammer marks, it was nevertheless what he'd asked for.

The trials now would be in deadly earnest.

There were still some details to be resolved, however.

The first of these was the hole for the fire-passage. If it was too big, the devil's dust would find it a more convenient exit, but too small and he wouldn't be able to stuff in his cloth.

Another was the 'pea'. He'd assumed a pebble would be what was wanted but there were very few he could find that fitted well. He didn't want them to jam inside so the only option was to make some clay balls of the right size.

He set up by the waterfall. The target was a white sheet with a large diagonal cross and he laid things out on a flat rock thirty yards away.

The iron was cold and dinged alarmingly on the stone as he set it down on the little legs he'd attached at the front and back.

A single spoon of *huo yao* to start with, then the clay ball.

Finally the wispy cloth twisted hard to get it into the fire-passage, and he was ready.

He juggled the powpe tube until it pointed at the target, and got his taper going.

The cloth started flaming quickly and he retreated and waited.

Long minutes of absolute stillness passed.

Jared waited until it became clear that nothing was going to happen.

Gingerly he went up to it and saw the reason why: the fire had gone out when it reached the constriction of the hole. It was obvious when he thought about it: unless there was space for the flame to go inside it would be smothered.

The trial was a failure.

There had to be another way of getting fire to the devil's dust!

In the darkness of the early hours his half-awake mind gave him the answer. If he couldn't get to the devil's dust, bring it out to meet him! Make a continuous path of *huo yao* from the inside to the outside of the hole and set it off in one.

Almost immediately he saw a snag. He'd be on top of the thing when it let go. Could he survive the noise and violence?

Perhaps modifying the outside of the hole with a small cup-shape indentation would expose enough devil's dust to touch off with the taper?

He set up as before and hung the target. One spoon of *huo yao*, then the clay ball followed by a small shake into the hole until grey powder spilt out into the daylight.

With his heart in his mouth he got the taper going. It was tied to the end of a pole, and at a distance from the powpe Jared swung it around and hovered it near the fire-passage. In his nervousness it swayed about and then maddeningly stubbed out against the powpe.

He had to get closer.

Holding the pole halfway helped and he saw the tiny flame

of the taper descend slowly to the waiting grey blotch.

Not knowing what to expect he flinched as the flame lowered.

His mind barely registered what happened next: an alarming fizz of white smoke for a split-second then a savage crack that left his ears ringing. The powpe reared up and was flung backwards with such fury that it barely missed him, ending on its side.

Recovering, Jared looked at the target. It was innocently hanging in the breeze without a mark.

He sat down to think it through. For now he would reduce the amount of *huo yao* and take the powpe nearer to the target to be sure of a hit – and he'd most surely have to tame the kick of the beast.

He set up, the powpe now held down by slabs of rock. This time: half a spoonful of *huo yao* and the clay ball.

Warily lowering the taper, he set it off with another ringing crack but he was ready for that, and the improvised restraints did their duty.

Maddeningly the target still floated serenely when it should have been holed. Where could the ball have gone, to miss so decisively?

It must be the clay, unable to stand the raging *huo yao* and turned to dust.

He had with him the only two pebbles he'd found. Would these fly true?

The *huo yao*, the pebble. A careful lining up of the iron powpe. And then the flame.

There was an obedient crash of sound – and incredibly, almost instantly, the target folded in like a warrior taking a death blow!

Jared gave a long shuddering sigh.

CHAPTER 56

Rosamunde had promised to witness his success and she kept her word.

They rode slowly together out to the ravine and she waited patiently while he set up. He now had good pebbles and a rough baulk of wood to take the place of the rock-slabs in steadying the piece.

'Stand away from the powpe,' he ordered sternly.

She meekly obeyed.

The flame came down slowly as he called out, 'Now!'

The brutal crack came as a shock, sending her to her knees but she rose slowly with a look of wonder and admiration at the far-off target, hit fair and squarely.

'I-I did not think . . .'

'Another one?'

'No, no', she answered faintly. 'That was quite enough for me, thank you.'

The ride back was in silence and when they stabled the horses she pleaded a headache and retired.

At supper she was quiet and withdrawn, then said softly, 'Jared, we must talk.'

The room was cleared.

'Are you . . . do you know what it is that you've done?'

He chuckled. 'Made an iron powpe?'

'I beg you'll be serious, Jared. And do swear to me that you will speak not a word of any of this to a soul.'

'I promise,' he replied, affected by her intensity, but couldn't resist adding, 'Do you not think I've found a use, then, for my devil's dust?'

'Yes, Jared, I do. Now, I said that if you made it happen I'd help you.'

'Join me as a partner.'

'Make common commercial cause with you.'

'I'm not sure I completely understand you, Rosamunde.'

'That is to say that the house of Barnwell is willing to invest a sum of money in your apparatus with a view to bringing it to market.'

'Ah.'

'On certain conditions.'

'Oh?'

'That the object of the investing is the producing of a machine or similar with a fixed purpose that may be constructed and sold for a profit. No wild schemes of turning castle walls to ruin or some such.'

He bristled but had to accept. If Mammon was the only path to the higher, then so be it.

'Secondly, that you are the master who will create the machine while the House of Barnwell takes charge of the mercantile.'

'Yes, I agree.'

'Which is to mean that each will be guided by the other.'

'Of course.'

'And lastly – that we agree on a proper name for your device. If it's to be offered up to princes and nobles I hardly think "powpe" will excite.'

'Then . . . we call it a "fire-tube", don't you think?'

'That is not what I had in mind.'

'A "thunder-stick", then?'

'No.'

He frowned in exasperation. 'Well, you tell me – what's the most frightening thing you know?'

She thought for a moment. 'It was something in my childhood, so dreadful I can still remember her.'

'Her?'

'I had a nurse from Norway. She took wicked joy in telling us of their awful history. Especially a war-maid married to Eric Bloodaxe, a sorcerer who bewitched men by loud shouts and became known as "mother of kings" after slaying Thorfinn Skull-Splitter. She must have been hideous to behold on the field of battle, I believe.'

'Like our powpe will be to the foe. What was her name?'

'Gunnhild Gormsdóttir.'

'A bit long for most. We shorten it to . . . Gunn. Not a powpe, a Gunn.'

'Hmm. I like that.'

'How would we spell it?'

'I would say, g-u-n-n-e. So then we can call your *huo yao* gunne-dust.'

'Or gunne-powder, as saying this is not dust to be swept from the house.'

'Done!'

They laughed together then sobered in awe of the occasion.

'I rather think we must now toast our future.'

She called for a page and when the wine arrived, deep, rich and red, they raised their goblets.

'To Master Jared's magnificent and terrible creation – his gunne!'

'And to the two of us who are going to bring it into the world,' he said.

She hesitated, her expression unreadable.

Then she impulsively leant across and kissed him lightly on the cheek. 'I'll right willingly drink to that,' she said softly, her eyes fixed on him.

Unsure and confused, Jared took refuge in his wine.

The moment passed.

Rosamunde cleared her throat. 'There are still matters to settle.' She was the hard-eyed merchant investor again.

'The market. Who will most desire our . . . gunnes? England is calm after the Scottish treaty, we are not at war with France.'

With none to buy the devices there would be no profit – no profit and the whole thing must fail.

'Then . . . ?'

'I have my agent reporting to me shortly. He comes from a country that wars with itself without ceasing, one that glories in one town's striving over another and who would greedily seize the chance to snatch unfair advantage over the other.'

'Which can this be?'

'Well, I rather fancy you will very shortly be on your way to Italy.'

CHAPTER 57

The English Channel, AD 1309

With a ponderous curtsey the well-laden cog acknowledged the open sea, its big sail slapping imperiously as it worked to claw to windward.

Standing at the rail on the raised deck aft, Jared watched the little port of Hythe fall astern, its details merging in the haze to an anonymous blur.

The familiar stinks and fresh salt air aboard a sea vessel had by now asserted themselves but this was a very different experience to the one before, for he was not a hapless pilgrim in the bowels of the ship – he was a respectable factor of the House of Barnwell and had accommodation to suit. His attire proved it to the world, especially his new half-circle scarlet cloak.

Jared suppressed a sigh; he was on his way to a destiny that was inconceivable in Hurnwych, outward bound to Italy to seek his fortune in the most fantastical way.

It had been quick – as soon as the agent had agreed with Rosamunde that the best prospects were to be found in Italy, plans had been drawn up, costed and an understanding finalised.

She had spoken to him incisively, telling him his days as a blacksmith were over and now he was to conduct himself as a respected member of the House, to remember his manners always and to regard the augmenting of revenue and frugality in expenses as the highest calling. Her agent would take care of his commercial affairs and it were well to take his advice to heart, for Italy was a much different place to England.

At their parting she'd wished him well of his venture and had pressed on him a lavishly set gold ring, a large amethyst surrounded with emeralds. As he contemplated what it might mean she had coolly explained that it was insurance should he be stranded without funds in some foreign quarter. It seemed an extravagant gesture to wear it, so it was now under his tunic on a string around his neck.

Jared took a last look round and went to the cabin under the afterdeck to join the agent.

Messer Domenico Sforza was writing at the little table. The candle guttered at the sea draughts that made their way past the embroidered hangings that offered a degree of warmth and gentility.

He was a neat individual with a permanently grave expression of unassailable dignity and looked up as Jared entered, laying down the pen.

'I do trust these quarters are to your liking,' he said in his impeccable English. The cabin was to be shared, but only between themselves.

'How long will it be?' Jared asked diffidently, unsure how to relate to the agent, who was in every respect so unlike himself.

'To Genoa? With good winds, no more than six weeks, God willing. Wine?'

There was a jug on the side table and he poured two glasses. 'The time will pass – we have much to do.

'Signor Jared, I have firm instructions from Mistress Barnwell that you're to imbibe as many of the Italian civilities as we have time for, in order that you're able to maintain a countenance in high places. For this you must be aware of many things, our history and culture, manners and delights. It will be my honour to be your teacher.

'And she did suggest that as you are as yet unacquainted with the more delicate aspects of the station of gentleman, it might profit you to—'

'I'm happy as I am,' he retorted. 'I'll never wear a false front!'

Sforza sighed. 'Signor, we all wear a front, false or no, in whatever situation we find ourselves. It is the way of the world and in my country it is nothing less than essential. Why? We shall discuss this later.'

'As we're speaking plain, Messer Sforza, it would satisfy me to know just what interest you have yourself in this venture.'

'Speaking plain is never a good plan in Italy, but I let it pass. I am a trusted agent for the House and have been for some years. In this venture I shall be choosing and making the first approach to those who will be offered your . . . er, gunne. For this service I shall be satisfied with a due proportion of the outcome. By this you will understand that it is in my interest to ensure you have all the funding and assistance necessary to achieve your objective.'

'I see.'

'Which is why I fear that all our expense and effort will be in vain were you to fail to impress. You are a striking figure of a man and will attract much curiosity, which we may turn to our advantage, therefore I beg you will be patient in this.'

Jared's education began that evening.

Sforza was a gracious host and gentle teacher and on the

understanding that it was accepted that there did not necessarily have to be a good reason for any or all of the arts of politeness, gradually these were acquired.

By the craggy Cornwall coast Jared was performing the ornate Roman bow as a work of art, the removing of his hat and the odd, almost mincing gait of a noble court.

He was stumbling over common phrases in Italian as Ushant appeared out of the rain squalls and as they passed the wine ports of France some of the traps and snares of polite discourse were revealed; by Lisbon he was ready for the larger picture.

Italy, he learnt, was far from being a country under one king and nobles owing fealty, with laws that all must obey and a single language. Left with the Pope in Rome without an army and a Holy Roman Emperor with a large one but far away over the Alps in Germany, the people had learnt to rule and defend themselves in the form of walled-town communes.

Each independent and proud, there was a constant rivalry between them, often erupting into open warfare without any strong central power at hand to mediate.

There were the magnificent city-states in the north – Florence, Mantua, Milan, Pisa, but only a backward relic of the Vikings and Moors in the south. Rome stood alone but was powerless beside the vanity and puissance of princes, save for churchly influence and increasingly scorned threats of excommunication.

And these with their traditions of individualism were a ferment of creative enterprise and cruel arrogance, swelling with wealth from the trade that came from Italy's central position between east and west.

They had changed, too. From town communes that ruled themselves through public-elected councils they'd been usurped by single rich and powerful families seizing the reins of power and living as princes. The burning desire of their head, the *signore*, for show and display of their wealth had provided colour and splendour but all lived in a deadly tangle of intrigue and rivalry.

'It is my judgement that we will get the fairest hearing at the court of Guido Malatesta, Conte d'Arezzo,' Sforza announced as they dined on sole with basil and pine nuts in the warm Mediterranean evening after an afternoon exploring the touchier aspects of honour as it concerned the family.

'How so?'

'Arezzo is Tuscan, prosperous above many others and the *signore* is ambitious to be a prince. In this he has been humiliated by the larger Perugia, which has lately bested him in a contest at arms and he would give much to be revenged.'

'You know this *signore*?'

'I have been of use to him in matters pertaining to Venetian loans – he will hear me.' He pulled his cloak tighter around him in an unconscious gesture.

'The city is aligned to the Ghibelline cause, which is to say it favours the Holy Roman Emperor above that of His Holiness in Rome. Perugia is Guelph – they cleave therefore to the papacy. It will, I believe, be sufficient excuse to keep them at each other's throats for a considerable while yet.'

Despite the warm night Jared felt a chill of foreboding – but then did not his venture require such a state of affairs?

CHAPTER 58

Genoa, Italy

Set against a buttress of mountain ranges this was a fine place to set foot in Italy.

While Sforza attended to matters with his broker and deputy, Jared strolled about the ancient city, marvelling at the spacious piazzas set about with great buildings in weathered dusky red, the crowds flooding the open areas in swarms of noise and colour. It was so much more exciting and alive than English market towns with their stolid calm.

He was taken to a tailor and his sober northern garments were replaced by velvet and brocade, more fitting an Italian merchant. There was no time to lose, however, and their baggage was quickly transferred to a local craft for the voyage south, to Pisa.

An even more imposing and monumental city, it was the main port of Tuscany and in the River Arno it had a sovereign highway inland to Florence and Arezzo.

After a cramped boat trip of several days they arrived at their destination. The town was set on a steep hill above the plains of the river.

They took a carriage through a tall ornamented gateway and progressing up steep streets passed several-storeyed houses of stone, imposing towers with flaring crenellations, markets of striking variety – and on all sides energetic and florid Italians in an exuberant hubbub.

They were to stay with a merchant acquaintance of Sforza's, the better to hear the gossip. Jared caught little of what was being said and tried not to be overawed by the urbane sophistication of his surroundings.

'Here we will lodge until we have had audience with the *signore*. If we are successful be assured I will include in my arrangement your accommodating in some comfort.'

The acquaintance was not to be troubled with knowledge of what they were about and Jared's precious gunne and supplies remained locked in a chest.

In two days Sforza announced with satisfaction, 'I have gained audience three days hence. If it goes well you should stand ready to display your wares to best advantage.'

'To make demonstration?'

'Just so. Is there anything that you require to . . . ?'

Jared had done all he could before they left. The gunne was strengthened with iron bands around it and he had considered the question of the 'pea' carefully. Clay balls were useless and pebbles of the right dimensions hard to find, but he'd come up with an easier way: making a mould of the ball that would best fit the bore and filling it with molten lead. With this its accuracy was also noticeably better. And he had prepared the constituents of the gunne-powder separately, sealed in jars, and these would be mixed together when the time came.

CHAPTER 59

Arezzo, Italy

'You will leave all to me.' Sforza was uncharacteristically short with him as they waited in an outer room of the *Palazzo del Podestà*, the palace of the *signoria*, and home of the tyrant Conte di Arezzo, Guido Malatesta. 'Any question His Grace raises concerning costs or revenue you will not answer under any circumstances. Do you understand?'

Jared nodded but was uneasy. Sforza was obviously perturbed. The sight of so many armed men in gaudy costume standing watching them, easily outnumbering the servants, didn't help. The palace was grand and richly appointed, plainly meant to intimidate.

'Do remember, I beg, all I told you of the dignities and civilities of this court. You are a foreigner but will not be forgiven slights.'

An official strode through the doors and barked something at Sforza, who stretched his mouth to a smile and bowed.

'Come. We are bid.'

They followed along a colonnade, across a manicured garden and into much grander surroundings. Then it was down a corridor lined with banners and portraits to a massive door flanked with ceremonial guards.

'This is the *signore* now,' Sforza said tightly. 'Do not forget it.'

The doors were flung wide and they entered.

Sforza fell to one knee with head bowed and Jared followed his lead.

'Come forward, Sforza, you villain,' a lazy voice commanded in Italian. 'You've something for me, I've heard.'

'Highness, I most certainly have,' Sforza replied with an oily confidence, rising and moving forward to stand before the dais, on which in a grossly ornamented chair, sat the most terrifying man Jared had ever seen. An iron jaw, deeply incised lines in his face and with dark eyes filled with menace he radiated lethal power.

'Then who is this you've dragged before me?' Malatesta cast a disinterested glance at Jared, who bowed as low as he could.

He bit into a pomegranate, tearing the skin and spitting the result to one side.

'Sire, he is the reason I sought audience,' Sforza said importantly. 'A gentleman alchemist but recently returned from studies in the land of the Saracens.'

'Oh?' The gaze was unnerving.

'I met him quite by chance in England, Your Excellency, while he was engaged in the most remarkable and dramatic of experiments.'

'What is that to me, Sforza?'

'As soon as I perceived its nature, I immediately realised that it would have the most lively application in your service were you to be insulted again by the vile Perugian Guelphs, and I naturally hurried here as quickly as possible and . . . here we are, sire.'

Malatesta stopped eating and leant forward, alert and dangerous.

'Tell!'

'Your Highness, Messer Jared is able to conjure heaven's thunder and lightning at his command. Not only that, but in the same act he may invisibly reach out in the blink of an eye to strike dead any he chooses.'

'You should know better than to bring tales of such dog-vomit to me, Sforza! If you—'

'Sire. With my own eyes I saw his powers and do vouch upon my honour for its truth.'

The deadly eyes swivelled to Jared again, speculative, rapacious.

Not understanding a word, Jared gave a weak smile.

'What is it you're offering, you rogue?'

'My friend here is able to create an apparatus that will allow any man to do likewise. A number of these, operated by your very own soldiers and set in the face of the Perugian mercenaries, will clear the field with terror and death and leave you master of the battlefield.'

'Your words are those of a pedlar, Sforza,' Malatesta said dismissively. 'And I won't have it! You'll next be asking me for a sack of florins for this foreigner to fritter away on his magic with nothing at all at the end of it, isn't that so?'

'Sire!' Sforza said in a shocked tone. 'I have a reputation that I hold dear. If you so desire, I shall ask Messer Jared if he will be so good as to demonstrate his powers before you, that there can be no doubt.'

A flicker of surprise was quickly followed by a crisp, 'Do so.'

With a studied dignity he turned to Jared and spoke in English. 'He asks for a demonstration. Look confident and smile as you give words of assent, if you please.'

Sforza bowed to Malatesta. 'Messer Jared agrees to your request.'

'Here and now!'

'Oh, sire, that would not be a good idea. The sulphurous exhalations would spoil your priceless tapestries. Can we not . . . ?'

'Tomorrow. At the Villa d'Arezzo. Do not fail me, Sforza, or you will rue it!'

CHAPTER 60

The next day they arrived with the chest at the countryside villa.

'All I can say is that if you do not succeed, it will go hard with us,' Sforza said in a low voice.

'It will,' Jared answered, a serene confidence from somewhere bearing him on.

They were welcomed by a double file of halberdiers who flanked them and the servants sent to carry the chest, and marched off towards a spacious courtyard.

'They ask us to prepare the demonstration and the *signore* will then be summoned.'

A quick glance around showed a suitable open distance ending in a stone wall.

The chest was unlocked, curious eyes following every move.

The gunne was new-painted in smart black, the wood block on which it lay well varnished, an impressive display.

On a portable table Jared got to work with the mortar and pestle and produced enough gunne-powder for several performances.

An oil lamp was lit and the tapers laid by. The target they'd cunningly brought along was a flag bearing the griffin of Perugia on red, which was hung on a frame before the wall.

Finally the gunne was made ready with a modicum of powder and an orb of lead.

'Messer Jared states he is ready to manifest his powers.'

Malatesta appeared at the doorway and descended the steps to the sun-scorched dusty arena. An elaborately carved chair was placed close to the gunne.

'I don't think it a wise idea to have him so close,' Jared muttered to Sforza.

'He wants a good view, I believe.'

It suddenly came to him that Sforza had never been at a trial. 'You've not heard the gunne speak, have you?'

'Well, no.'

'Set him up halfway between the gunne and target, then.'

Dozens of spectators craned to see the spectacle and faces appeared at the windows of the villa. An expectant hush fell.

'At your command, Your Highness,' Sforza invited.

A grim-faced Malatesta acknowledged and raised a hand, then chopped it down.

Jared lowered the taper – and with a hideous bang the gunne gave tongue and flame, briefly enshrouding him in smoke.

The effect was all that could be wished for.

A wave of fright and hysteria gripped the spectators; some, including Sforza, fell to their knees, others ran, still more stood transfixed.

Sforza picked himself up, mortified, while the acrid smoke drifted down on those who stood their ground. They hesitated until they caught the dry brimstone reek and they too broke and ran.

The *signore* still sat but his face was pale and he gripped the armrests with both hands, staring at the smoke-wreathed gunne.

A sudden cry sounded. Someone had gone to the target and was holding it up; there was an ugly tear, not far from its centre.

All eyes turned to Malatesta.

'Another!' he demanded hoarsely.

Those who remained fell back as Jared readied the gunne.

The hand fell and the spiteful fury crashed out once again producing another rent in the cloth.

This time there was such a hubbub with men crowding about to see the magic apparatus that Jared felt it expedient to begin packing it away.

An irritated bellow came from the *signore* and the men fell back.

An official hurried over towards Jared with a message.

Sforza tensed, swallowing hard. 'Um, the *signore* is demanding a final trial. Messer Jared – if we do it we'll be able to name our own price.'

His nervousness and inability to meet Jared's eyes sent a shaft of unease through him.

'I can do it, never fear.'

'He wishes . . . that is to say, he will be providing his own target this time.'

'Very well.'

'Simply to prove the effectiveness of your gunne.'

'Yes. No difficulty. Why do you—'

'The new target will be a condemned criminal, to suffer death by your gunne.'

'No!' Jared gasped. 'Never! I just . . . can't do it!' He recoiled, appalled.

Sforza rounded on him, gripping his tunic savagely with both hands. 'Listen to me, you fool!' he grated in a low voice. 'This is our big opportunity! Not just with this tyrant, but all – they'll each and every one pant after it when they hear what that gunne can do!'

'B-but it's not—'

'Imbecile! Then think on this: you walk away now and you're a dead man. Malatesta dare not let you go while his enemies can seize you for themselves!'

Jared stood petrified.

'And, dare I say it, what did you conceive your gunne was for, if not this?'

A group appeared from a small doorway at the opposite side of the courtyard, one man was in chains, shuffling and blinking in the bright sunshine.

Excited chatter fell away as the man was led to where the remains of the Perugian flag were being taken down.

He was turned to face the gunne, not understanding, waiting meekly in his fetters.

All eyes turned on Jared. In that moment he knew that there could be no backing down.

This was the logical outcome and he should have seen it. Theoretical talk of working to scale a gunne up to a point where it could bloodlessly bring ruin to a castle's walls must inevitably give way to its immediate application as a war weapon.

In a wash of desolation he turned back to the gunne.

He concentrated fiercely, forcing his racing thoughts to focus on what had to be done. Powder and lead. And then line it up on the target, not more than fifty feet away – a living, breathing human.

'Take no mind of that scum,' Sforza said harshly. 'A criminal only and we've saved the hangman a job.'

It steadied Jared. Not that the man was a felon but that as an alternative to choking his life away at the end of a rope for up to fifteen minutes, this would be merciful and swift.

Or would it? The skewered victims of an archer often suffered in agony for hours. Would a pill of lead be quicker?

'Highness?' called Sforza.

The *signore* looked their way briefly, his expression implacable.

He raised his hand in a fist, his gaze now fixed on the victim who still stood uncertainly, apprehensive at the many faces turned towards him.

Malatesta's fist slashed down and with a trembling hand Jared applied the flame.

There was a harsh crash of the gunne, smoke writhing, then the man doubled over and fell. Shrieking and threshing on the ground, his bowels torn and bloody, he flopped helplessly about.

Jared wrenched from the sight and vomited helplessly beside the gunne, missing Malatesta's cruel smile and slow nodding of satisfaction, the spreading cries of delighted horror, the soldier sent to finish it all.

The demonstration was over.

CHAPTER 61

'And I do declare it a famous success,' Sforza purred, topping up Jared's wine, which he'd hardly touched. 'I'm bidden with all urgency to attend on the *signore* on the morrow with a view to discussing terms. I can tell you, these will not be made easy for him.'

'You're happy with it all, then,' Jared muttered, still shaken.

'Why so dolorous? I can see how this will lead to a bright future for the House, can't you? Provided we take suitable precautions.'

'Oh?'

'You will want to keep your trade secrets safe. Should others learn of the processes we lose our monopoly and our usefulness.'

'Yes, I see.'

'And therefore any who join with us, work for us, we do not in any circumstances trust. At all times they are under our eye and suspicion. And as well, after today's events, from this time forward there will be spies, assassins and those with honeyed words all about, which you should guard against the whole while.'

'Anything else you'd recommend?' Jared asked caustically. 'Perhaps a daily escort?'

'That will not be necessary at this time,' Sforza came back smoothly. 'But there are two things more – the first, I'd advise a poignard to be carried about you at all times.' He lifted his tunic to reveal the gleaming hilt of his own.

'And the second?'

'Learn the Italian fluently. If not tomorrow, then by the next day. It may save your life.'

The buoyant mood that he'd had at their progress had evaporated and he went on in a sombre voice, 'You have seen enough to know that it is the most favourable to us of any situation. Kindly do your part and I'll do mine.'

The next day Sforza was his old self again, urbane, considerate and dignified. 'We have an agreement.'

'May I know of it?' Jared asked.

'For the provision of not less than fifty gunnes of a power capable of slaying a man at a hundred paces we receive, well, a considerable sum on the Frescobaldi Bianchi of Florence in gold florins. Together with an advance of one quarter of the sum, and a handsome provision for your subsistence and workshop expenses.'

'Ah. The workshop. I thought that—'

'An entire smithy and its workers has been taken in hand and turned over to you to conduct matters to your satisfaction, its materials and running costs to the account of the *signore*.'

'Where will I live?'

'A town house and servants close by the palazzo will be assigned to you for the duration of the works. And to allay your anxieties further, I've been able to make an arrangement that satisfies more than one condition.'

'Oh?'

'The *signore* has specified that at the same time as the gunnes are being made, a body of men be taught their operation.'

A look remarkably like that of smugness briefly appeared. 'And for these I know where I can go.

'First you must understand that it is the practice in Italy, including Arezzo, to forswear maintaining an army. It's expensive and needs quartering between wars. Instead, prosperous cities hire in their soldiers who can be dismissed at the peace. These mercenary bands are then unemployed, roaming and pillaging unless bought off. They call themselves free companies and we find some mainly German, others Gascon, still others from Navarre.

'To our advantage there are several English free companies and I suggest that a middling-level band be approached with an offer to train as gunne-people with us. They stand to win constant employment for little danger and will have a war skill that will soon be most lucrative. This is to the one side. To the other is that the captain of the band will interpret for you in the workshop and elsewhere until you have the Italian, but more to your liking will be that he and his band will be your protectors and allies. And dare I say it, a friend to you in a strange place.'

'But are you not my friend?'

'Our friendship is of the highest value to me,' Sforza replied loftily. 'But alas, my duty to the House of Barnwell calls me away to my customary responsibilities. After we have settled here I must be on my way. For financial and other matters I have appointed a trusted merchant to act for me – and for yourself, of course.'

He gave a broad smile. 'Shall we now inspect your lodgings? Should they not be to your satisfaction . . .'

CHAPTER 62

To Jared it was princely: a substantial three-storey house with an upper balcony fronting on to a sloping paved street that efficiently carried away the filth of urban living. The lower storey for his work, the middle for his entertaining and the upper for repose.

His staff stood in a line before him. A page, two servants and a cook, together with a housekeeper.

'Messer Jared,' Sforza said, hiding a glimmer of a smile, 'this is Giannina di Ferrara. She will see to your comfort and rule the house.'

The striking dark-haired young girl stepped out from the line, dressed in a simple gown and apron.

'It is my honour to serve you, *chiarissimo* Jared,' she said, her eyes downcast prettily.

'You speak English?' he asked, delighted.

Sforza looked pleased with himself. 'With much diligence I looked to find you one with your tongue. She comes from a half-English family of Emilia-Romagna. You will be safe in her hands, I believe.'

'These quarters will do, I find,' Jared said quickly, adding awkwardly, 'It's much to my taste.'

The girl looked up and there was no mistaking the dancing light in her eyes.

'Then we should find your baggage. Tonight we will be dining with the *signore*, a great privilege and distinction.'

CHAPTER 63

It was a warm evening and Jared was grateful for the cool passage of air as they rode together into the countryside, a detachment of men-at-arms jingling behind. Sforza said nothing, his eyes on the winding, dusty road as they passed by well-tended olive groves in the soft violet light.

The villa was set in a fold of hills looking down over a broad plain, a sprawl of buildings in soft browns, slender towers, an enormous square ornamental pond – as unlike an English grey-grim castle as anything that Jared could have imagined.

They were met and their dusty riding cloaks removed before being conducted to the gathering assembly in the gardens above the pond. Flaming braziers banished the gloom at either end, adding their ruddy glare to the portable candelabras and picking out the richness of the garments of the guests.

At the centre of an animated group was the *signore* in dark-blue robes embroidered with gold and silver. Next to him bearing a haughty expression was a lady wearing rich garments and an ornate pearl collar and necklace.

He broke off his conversation with an extravagantly attired

young man when he saw them approach and Sforza lost no time in paying his obeisance.

The cruel face eased and words of welcome were bestowed. The contessa awarded them an inclination of the head and they made their escape into the crush.

'That was Cosima,' Sforza muttered. 'She bore him six sons and won't let any forget. Butter her up well with all the recognition and honours of rank and you'll get by.'

'Ah! Sforza, you cunning old toad. I was looking for you.' A suave and affable figure in impossibly tight hose took him by the arm and steered him away, leaving Jared to stand foolishly with a fixed smile as the throng surged about him.

Several young ladies came up, eyeing his decidedly un-magnificent attire and giggling, making fun of him until Sforza returned to shoo them away.

The pure sound of trumpets in harmony came from the left. 'We enter for dinner,' Sforza announced. 'Stay by me!'

The scene in the hall was breathtaking. The high table dominated with lavish crystal and silver table furniture on a white cloth strewn with flowers. Gold-threaded tapestries hung behind on the wall. At each end lesser tables were set at right angles to form an enclosing 'U' shape. Discreetly on both sides were lengthy sideboards groaning with dishes of food.

Malatesta stood at the centre of the high table nodding and murmuring pleasantly as the guests filed in to the sweet sounds from the musicians' loft above. Struck dumb with awe, Jared followed Sforza.

They were to take places of honour to the right of the *signore* and he found himself between Sforza and an unsmiling churchman of some kind.

In front of him was laid a silver spoon and a carved wooden plate with a trencher of bread atop, and to his right was a flagon of wine. He gave a weak smile at the cleric, who stared at him then looked away in contempt.

Never in his life had he felt so inadequate, especially with the occasional curious glances from the some hundred guests at the lesser tables.

The trumpets sounded again and the *signore* held up both his hands until the babble had died. Then he glanced significantly at the prelate who proceeded to say grace in imperious tones.

The hubbub began again as finger bowls were brought around and out of sight a sprightly melody was picked out on lute and shawm. Sforza leant over and filled Jared's goblet, exquisitely crafted of translucent swirled green glass.

'Serve the bishop, then,' he hissed.

Clumsily Jared manipulated his flagon around and said in English, 'M' lord, some wine?'

He received only a venomous look and a hand placed over the glass.

Sforza sensed his discomfort and said loudly, 'The bishop resents our presence at high-table. He's a prig and a Guelph.'

It took Jared a moment to catch on that it had been said in English and thus not a soul in the room apart from themselves was in a position to understand.

On impulse he leant forward with a smile and bowed his head obsequiously to the man, who sniffed as if he was accepting an apology, then turned pointedly to the guest on his other side.

'Who else do we have here?' Jared asked Sforza.

'The usual. That's the captain of the *podestà* over there in green – Umberto di Campaldino – with his odious wife Beatrice.'

Jared took in a bluff figure in bottle-green and gold with a plumed cap set exactly square and an acid-faced woman who stared at him without shame.

'Glories in the old days when the commune republics ruled and chivalry was properly valued,' Sforza added.

'And over there—'

He was interrupted by the arrival of the highlight of the first course, borne proudly in by servants in tabards emblazoned with the arms of Malatesta – a prancing black horse on pure white.

It was a noble dish. Baked sturgeon picked out with a convoluted design in garlic and a red sauce. This evidently meant something, for the room burst into applause at its appearance.

'You were telling me . . . ?' Jared prompted.

'Ah, yes. On the right, the handsome young blade in red and black. That's Corso Ezzelino. A thrusting, unruly fellow who has unlimited ambitions and—'

Across the distance of tables the young man had seen their interest and flashed a broad smile directly at Jared, raising his glass in salute.

Taken by surprise, he could only lift his own in reply but the moment had passed and Ezzelino was talking with animation to the lady by his side.

The fish was wreathed with the subtle scent of a herb Jared couldn't place and on a level of delicacy that left his memory of the muddy flesh of Dene River trout fading to embarrassment.

Sforza raised his goblet and whispered, 'And mark well the ill-faced wretch at the end of the table on the left.'

Jared saw a dark-featured man whose eyes flicked everywhere but shrank from conversation.

'This is Giacomo Capuletti, and he's the *capitano del popolo*, the representative of the people, that is to say the merchants and guilds. He and Umberto hate each other but he can do nothing against a captain of the *podestà,* which is where the true power lies.'

More dishes followed seemingly without limit: four kinds of soup: a 'flying pie' – when the lid was removed live birds flew out; an imitation porcupine made of slivered almonds.

Out of sight the trumpets pealed as a procession approached, led by a tall, resplendent figure in extremely long pointed shoes. Beaming with pride he acknowledged the rising acclaim as the main object of interest came into view. It was an entire roast stag, still in its skin and arranged as if in sleep in the forest undergrowth. Behind it was an endless line of other splendid dishes: a peacock in full display, partridge, heron, wild duck and cormorant.

The man performed an elegant obeisance before the *signore* and flourishing a long knife and prongs in the air descended on the stag and began carving. The first succulent pieces went to Malatesta and his lady and then faultlessly by place of honour, long beautifully finished slices laid swiftly but delicately in a fan-like pattern. After the high table was served he swept down in a bow as his performance was vigorously applauded. Lesser beings attended on the lower tables.

Music burst forth and two clowns bounced in. They mimed and contorted, pranced grotesquely and sang duets in a falsetto. Sforza grimaced. 'The buffoons – I never had a taste for their art.'

Jared wanted to know more about the guests and asked,

'The smooth-looking one over there, in blue. Is he . . . ?'

'Ruggieri Villani. A sly creature who's related to the Lady Cosima and thereby tolerated. There's talk that he and Perugia are no strangers. I should not show yourself too attentive to him before Malatesta's spies.'

'And the lady?' A strikingly beautiful woman was by Villani's side, in perfect control and barely touching her dish.

'Lucia. His wife – do not underestimate her, I beg. Her family is powerful and she has no scruple about making use of her connections.'

The evening wore on; the buffoons were replaced by dancers and then a troubadour singing softly of sweet sorrows. By turns elated and overawed, Jared's head was swimming with impressions.

He tried to make sense of it. 'Why are we here? I mean . . .' he asked Sforza.

'You do not question fortune. It is sufficient that the *signore* has taken notice of us – but in this he has his reasons. To encourage us in his cause? Possibly, but more than that, to show the world that we are his creatures. And that at the moment we are securely within his favour and therefore unassailable.'

'Are we?'

Sforza laid down his knife purposefully. 'Do listen to what I say, Messer Jared, for I shall soon be gone from you.

'Each of those here hides a lust for something desired – a woman, power, the throne of the *signoria* itself. Each therefore ceaselessly plots and connives, and knows the other does likewise. You and I are not part of this, therefore we guard our tongue and keep to ourselves. Never meddle in some others' quarrel. There is only one we serve – the *signore,* and this we display on every occasion we can. Insofar as we please him we are safe. You understand?'

'If I'm left alone to my work, nothing will please me more,' Jared replied with deep sincerity.

Towels and perfumed water were brought around to a sprightly accompaniment on the fife and shawm. The *signore* rose – the whole room did likewise and they progressed out to the pond with its glittering gold reflections, to talk and render their thanks for the magnificence of the banquet.

CHAPTER 64

Sforza was impatient to be away and their inspection of the smithy was cursory. It was sizeable and well-equipped with no less than five forges, each attended by a blacksmith and three.

The *capo* of the smithy was introduced simply as Alonzo, a hulking bear of a man who stood impassive and unblinking in his well-used leather apron with his brawny arms folded as he heard the arrangements.

'I've told him you don't speak Italian yet, but there will be someone to translate. That will be your mercenary friend, who I expect very shortly.'

There was no point in staying any longer without an interpreter and Jared went back to his house to wait for Sforza's call.

'A white wine, Giannina,' he dared to the waiting housekeeper.

'Oh – a trebbiano or a vermintino?' she suggested anxiously.

'Um, one you like yourself, we must talk together.'

The balcony had discreet curtains that could be lowered and they sat at a small table in the rising warmth of the morning. She looked at him in something like awe, waiting for him to speak.

'Giannina, I'm only a simple man,' Jared began awkwardly. 'Here to do a job, and I find so much strange in your country and . . . and

I'd take it kindly if you'd set me straight on anything I do that's not right. You know, like a friend!' he finished with a blush.

'Anything, Messer Jared?'

'Is what I said.'

'Then the first!' she giggled. 'If a friend, you will call me Nina – not in front of servants, o' course.'

'So I will be Jared,' he replied, taken by her bubbling spirit.

She grew serious. 'You are receive by the *signore*. You are important man, all Arezzo talks of your magic. You be careful – I must take care for you also, or I be in high trouble.'

'I'll be careful, Nina. Now tell me – how does my house work?'

She looked incredulous then broke into laughter. 'Which way you want it! You tell me, it will done.'

It was quickly settled. Shaking her head at his simple tastes it was agreed that a single manservant would be more than enough, the cook, laundry maid and two others on call only, quite sufficient for his needs.

The middle floor he would have little use for as he had no plans for entertaining; his upper room would be his retreat. There, a capacious bed sat squarely to one side with corded veils hanging down; the thickness of the mattress was astonishing. A broad writing desk was on the other side and a dressing table was already arrayed with pots and shaving implements.

With a room area larger than an entire house in Hurnwych he would not lack for comfort.

CHAPTER 65

A messenger came from Sforza. The gunne crew had arrived and were ready to see Jared.

He met them in the smithy courtyard. Twelve hard-faced men, fully armed and in faded and threadbare surcoats under which the dull gleam of mail armour showed. Beyond, the smithy hands stood apprehensively.

'Ah, this is Master Edward Peppin, of the Black Company.' Sforza smoothly introduced a lank-haired individual with lined and cynical features who sprang forward with cat-like grace.

'At y' service, Master.' The tone was oily, the eyes hooded and appraising.

'Ah. Then you wish to be a gunne . . . person.'

'We do that.' The feral intensity that lay behind the gaze was unnerving. These were men of a stamp that he'd never come up against, their easy menace and bold look telling of a life he could only guess at.

'Well, this will come later, Master Peppin. We must first make the gunnes, mustn't we!' His words rang hollow even to himself. And one thing was certain: the wolfish predator in front of him was not about to be his closest friend and confidant.

'Oh, one matter,' he mentioned as casually as he could. 'I don't have the Italian and need to tell the smithy crew what to do. You'll do this for me, will you?'

The lips curled in contempt. 'No. I'm not paid to be anybody's pageboy.'

The eyes challenged him. Jared burnt with embarrassment and resentment. With these he was expected to change the world?

'Well, and we must find some other,' Sforza breezed. 'Messer Peppin will have other duties, of course. So as I understand it, there will be no requirement for these gentlemen to be here until—'

'I want six quartered here at all times for watch duty,' Jared snapped in a sudden temper. 'And Peppin to advise where he is at any time. Right?'

'We're not here to be poxy sentinels!' growled one of the others. 'Find another—'

'You're here to be gunners!' Jared retorted. 'I'm in charge and Peppin is my second. If you don't like taking orders then you've lost your chance to be one. Stay – or go?'

This time Peppin was the one to yield, which he did with exaggerated deference. 'Very well, the *capitano* of gunners. And what are your orders, then?'

CHAPTER 66

There was now a pressing imperative to get to some level of skill with the language but at the same time Jared realised that he had to get the smiths to work without delay.

He decided that Nina must teach him Italian. But he could not expect her to translate for him at the smithy in those conditions. Might she know another English speaker, he wondered forlornly.

'Of course! My pleasure to be teacher to *Il Pregiato* Jared! You will work hard to be my learner and—'

'Thank you, but until I have had your lessons I need one to tell my words to the forge men. Do you know . . . ?'

'Yes! When should he start?'

Taken aback at the prompt response he heard that in her family was a young lad, Cesarino, who would be delighted at the chance to be in such exciting company.

It was starting but there was so much to plan.

Without delay he must set out to scale up the gunne from puny grape-sized gunne-balls to wall-shattering boulders. These would presumably consume scaled-up amounts of gunne-powder. If it was a few ounces for the smaller then at a hundred times the weight it must be many pounds of powder for the larger.

Production should start immediately.

What he was about could not be concealed. The building of the gunnes would be known and any getting hold of one could build it for themselves. But without the gunne-powder they were useless lumps of iron. He would therefore separate out the processes for making the powder so no single person would know all, and if necessary play the same trick that Wang had: keep the proportions secret.

Training? This could not be started until the gunne was perfected and then it would take some thought to devise a fixed sequence of actions that would make it safe for rough and illiterate soldiers to handle the lethal powder and avoid the mule kick of the gunne.

What else was there?

CHAPTER 67

Evening turned into night and he'd sent the manservant, Beppe, to bed before he turned in himself but thoughts kept coming as he lay in the dark trying to find sleep.

He became vaguely aware there was a light outside his door and then a soft knock.

'Who is it?'

'I, Nina. You wish a caudle, help you sleep?'

He levered himself up. 'That's kind of you.'

She came in with a cup on a small tray, dressed in a linen chemise.

The candlelight caught her long hair in myriad tiny lights and softly illuminated her face.

Jared was uncomfortably aware of her female presence. 'But you didn't have to stay up yourself, Nina.'

She gave Jared a look of great tenderness as she put the tray down. 'I say I will take care for you.'

The chemise fell to the floor and she stood naked for a long moment then eased into his bed.

It seemed the most natural thing in the world.

'And tomorrow we learn words?' she said innocently when their passion was spent.

CHAPTER 68

If gunne-powder was to be his secret its production and testing needed to be well guarded. The *signore*'s office was obliging, understanding immediately Jared's pleading for privacy and a farm was swiftly emptied of its inhabitants and stock. He had his base. It solved as well the simmering resentment at the smithy – this would be safeguarded by the gunners themselves who would live there and had an interest in keeping it secure.

At the smithy Cesarino, bright as a button and quick-witted, soon made himself popular, filling in boring interludes with acrobatics and singing. The head smith Alonzo presented him with his own leather apron and Jared solemnly gave him an official gunner's cap complete with little bell.

The big smith was no fool. He inspected Jared's gunne and shrewdly pointed out where he could increase strength by ribbing the bands but Jared had no intention of staying with the design. They would be working on much bigger articles before long.

The days passed agreeably, his Italian improving swiftly, for with a common technical basis for communication it didn't take long to add the verbs and adjectives. And under Nina's patient and enthusiastic teaching his competence grew even more.

Jared realised that the smithy would not be where difficulties might arise. It would be the farm, the *presidio* as Peppin would have it. He would have to trust that his orders were carried out to the letter. And these would test the credibility of the most hardened veteran.

Alonzo would help him to source charcoal and sulphur but the saltpetre was another matter. How was he to get the scrapings of tombs and stables in quantity? Cooking saltpetre was available but in quantities far too small and impure, so another way had to be found.

Jared decided to simply let it be known that for reasons that need not be entered into, a sum in hard cash would be paid for any folk who presented an acceptable quantity. Human ingenuity would then seek it out.

There were barns and pigsties in the *presidio* ready to serve as preparation rooms. Each would have its own process: the boiling reduction of sulphur, the messier refining of the saltpetre, the grinding and packing. And an outhouse of his own where the final mixing would be done. He listed down the workers he'd need. There would be no second chance.

His *presidio* hands were wary and unsure but they were put to work straight away, cleaning and preparing.

It was happening!

The iron arrived from Pisa and he and Alonzo inspected it closely. Its quality was reasonable with mercifully few whorls and slag inclusions, which would have to be painfully beaten out.

Time to get to work.

The forge was raised from cherry-red to a violet-flamed roar and the plate brought to working temperature. Alonzo took the lead but Jared snatched an apron and acted as his partner at the anvil, quickly falling in with the harsh rhythm of strikes as the edge was worked round.

They exchanged positions and Jared's now ruddy face grinned at the ruination of his clothes.

They rested at noon, and joined by Cesarino, sat down to a bite of food.

'You're good – for a foreigner,' grunted Alonzo, throwing a keen look at Jared. He cut a piece off a long dried sausage, and laid out bread and cheese.

'What's this called?' he asked through a mouthful of a chunk of the deliciously flavoured meat.

'Finocchiona,' piped up Cesarino. 'Alonzo say is why he so strong!'

To Jared this was good, plain and tasty fare, much to be preferred to feasting.

'Why you come to Arezzo doing this work?' The *capo* blacksmith was quick, smarter than he looked.

'It's the best place to make money with these gunnes.'

'You go with the *signore*, you take care – evil men there,' Alonzo said, tapping his nose knowingly.

Jared warmed to the big man and wondered just how much he knew about what went on at the palazzo.

CHAPTER 69

The newer, bigger gunne was taking shape over days of hard work. This would shoot a 'pea' as big as a hen's egg and could probably batter its way through the gates of a small town. Reluctantly, Jared left it to Alonzo while he checked on the gunne-powder.

Fine-ground charcoal was piling up nicely and the sulphur – freely gathered from volcanoes in the south – was of gratifying purity.

But the saltpetre was another matter. It seemed that the townsfolk weren't prepared to make the journey out to the farm, doubting that anyone would pay good coin for such. There was only one answer to that: he would set up a collecting shop in Arezzo itself.

At the smithy progress was good. He and Alonzo completed the heroic task of bringing the thick plate together and fire-welding the seam, but Jared had his concerns about its strength and they worked on making bands in imitation of wine barrels.

The big man often jovially sparred with Jared in low Italian and they laughed as they worked.

One evening Alonzo put down his hammer and wiped his hands. 'I'm supposing you're too dandified to sup with a *maniscalco*,' he grumbled. 'Wife's curious, wants to set eyes on you for some reason. I'll catch it if you don't come.'

The plump, beady-eyed woman was overjoyed to see Jared, throwing her arms around and kissing him with a torrent of Tuscan vernacular.

It was an uproarious time, wide-eyed bambinos brought to meet the strange Englishman, helpless mirth at his attempts at Italian jokes and respectful attention when after the wine he sang some of the old English folk songs he'd learnt at his mother's knee.

Alonzo was much taken with his guest and regaled him with tales and mysteries of old Arezzo, once bringing out a treasured ancient blood-red stone with baffling characters deeply incised on it. He went on to tell of how before the rise of powerful families the communes had taken care of them, and things had been less fearful.

Jared knew then that here was the friend he could call on if matters took a dark turn.

CHAPTER 70

'Alonzo say you have to come,' Cesarino announced importantly.

Jared emerged from the outbuilding to see his friend, battered cap in hand, respectfully stood before a richly dressed young man. Closer to, he could see that this was Corso Ezzolino. This was the ambitious young noble pointed out to him at the feast.

'*Buongiorno*, Messer Jared,' Ezzolino said with a flourish. 'I did not wish to disturb your work, but curiosity does so drive me.'

'*Saluti*,' Jared replied, carefully avoiding the question of whether he was in fact being disturbed. 'What can I do for you?'

'I'd be much obliged if you'd tell me more of your fine invention. You must be very proud!'

Alonzo slipped away.

'It's not yet finished, *signore*.'

'I understand. I'm much interested in its capabilities. How far away can it strike down a man? Is it—?'

'The gunne I am working on is not intended to slay men, but castles.' He hadn't intended to talk about it but pride drove him on. 'I'm bringing it up to a size that will shoot a ball as big as that from a mangonel but instead of hurling it high in the sky, it will direct it straight against the wall with a violence nothing can resist.'

'I see.' Ezzolino said, stroking his chin. 'And the force that throws it I've heard is naught but farmyard dung. I find this hard to believe, Messer Jared.'

'It's more complicated than that. Perhaps one day I can tell you more. When I'm not so busy,' he added pointedly.

'Oh, yes. Well, I can see great things for such an engine and you can count me as one of your admirers. If there's anything that I can do to assist you . . . ?'

'Thank you, *signore*, but nothing at the moment.'

Alonzo was subdued. 'He gave me coin to see you. I couldn't stop him anyway, but why was he so anxious to say hello? I mislike his interest.'

Jared merely grunted. There was much more to concern him: the testing of the larger gunne. He was only a month or so into his work but Malatesta would want to see results very soon.

The saltpetre was at last being produced at the *presidio*. Insisting on a triple-boiling condensate the result was promising, white crystals with not a trace of salt in them.

He collected his implements and in his gunne-powder outhouse set to grinding and mixing.

The testing place was in a cleared area with a hill conveniently behind to take the 'pea'.

The trial was important but straightforward, merely a stepping up of what had been successful before, so Jared didn't send away the spectators who came to watch: Peppin and the gunners, the saltpetre workers, guards, women from the kitchen.

The first thing was to see if range was effected by the heavier ball.

A scaled-up amount of gunne-powder would probably translate

to a much louder sound; better he shooed the spectators back before carefully readying the gunne.

He set the target up at the same distance; if it did maintain range he could always move it further out.

The taper lowered to the small grey pile at the fire-passage—

There was a deafening detonation and a sheet of flame washed over his face. The blast sent him staggering back to fall to all fours.

Stupefied Jared tried to make sense of it through his ringing head and pain of the burns on his face – mercifully he'd had his eyes closed in a flinch when the gunne had let go.

The gunne was in a ruined state, split open, the iron contemptuously peeled apart and thrown clear of its block.

Ignoring the screams of alarm from the spectators Jared crawled nearer. There was no doubt of it: for reasons he couldn't even guess at, the raging force of the gunne-powder had multiplied much faster than the increase of bore size and even the thickest iron plate couldn't take it.

Peppin arrived, hanging back fearfully. 'What's this, your gunne torn asunder? Why did it—?'

'I made a mistake,' Jared replied, trying to make light of the event so as not to panic the gunners. 'Too much gunne-powder. Pay no mind to it, Master Peppin. The gunne you'll be using will be well tested, never fear.'

But this was a big setback. He'd carefully worked it out, knowing the weight of the original 'pea' and the gunne-powder it required, to a straight increase of powder in proportion to the new weight of ball.

In the next days, with goose-grease on his burns and burnt eyebrows he tried to reason the best way forward and resolved to try again but in smaller steps.

Another gunne was made with still more reinforcing. This time he'd start with the same measure of gunne-powder for this large ball as for the smaller.

The results were as expected, dismal. Then, by small steps, the powder charge was increased and as Jared hoped, the ball flew with increasing venom and range.

But after another increase of powder charge the gunne split again, with smoke issuing ominously from a long fissure.

It hit him like a blow. He was only a little over a third into the stepped increases and the whole idea of scaling up from a pea-shooter to a castle-wrecking monster was now looking increasingly like a dream.

He'd used the hardest and toughest material known to him – wrought iron – and even this had not been enough to contain the ferocity of the gunne-powder as it swelled against the greater-sized ball, even if only a hen's egg in size. If he was ever to move to a point where he was dealing with, for instance, head-sized balls, he would need a gunne with iron far thicker than any that could be worked at the anvil.

He nearly wept. There was no solution. The thickest forged iron was not enough – it must be a peashooter or nothing.

What would Malatesta say – or more to the point Rosamunde, who had trusted him and laid out her own coin at his word?

CHAPTER 71

The irritable Malatesta was in fact puzzled why he was wasting time on such foolishness when he'd asked for fifty man-slayers. Just when would these be ready?

Jared kept the harsh discovery of the problem of the thickness of the iron to himself and told the concerned Alonzo that he'd been told to step up production of a smaller kind. The capo gave him a curious look and Jared suspected that he'd come to the same conclusion but was saying nothing.

However the man-slayers would bring in revenue and pay back Rosamunde. He would get on with the project.

But it was not a matter simply of making dozens of his original gunne. It was far too heavy and awkward. If this was to be a military weapon, it had to be rugged and transportable.

The wooden block would have to go. But how could he manage the kick without it? And at the same time protect the gunner from the gout of flame from the fire-passage? He'd noticed that the fiery breath of the powder quickly heated the iron to uncomfortable levels.

Eventually Jared came up with an answer: to secure the iron to a projecting tiller of wood that butted into the ground. The weight would then be taken by a yoke rest. The gunner was relieved of the weight and removed from the fire-passage but that brought the problem of how to bring the taper to the powder. Was a candle the right way to go?

A good blacksmithing solution suggested itself: iron wire, heated red in a brazier; long, and with a crook in the end to safely lower on to the powder.

And regrettably, a 'pea' no bigger than a grape.

With testing, he would soon be in a position to bring out the first real weapons.

CHAPTER 72

Nina set down her sewing. 'You've never talked about your home, back in England, Jared. Will you be returning there after you've finished your gunnes?'

'Who knows what the future will bring, *mia cara*,' he said.

'A man must have a place to call home, my sweet.'

Jared could see where the conversation was leading; he'd never really given it much thought but now was not the time to—

'*Che cavolo*,' he swore. 'That Beppe – where's my caudle, the lazy rascal!'

As if in answer there was a muffled crash from below. They looked at each other and laughed.

'He's taken in drink, dropped the whole lot and must start again.'

Nina smiled. 'I'll get another for you.'

In less than a minute a piercing scream from below shattered the stillness of the night. Heart thumping Jared hurtled down the narrow staircase. Nina was pressed back against the wall staring at the body of Beppe, lying in the remains of a caudle.

There was no blood. Had he fallen in a drunken stupor?

The eyes were open, fixed and staring. There was clearly no life in him.

'Is he . . . is he . . . ?'

'Yes,' Jared said, his mind in a furious whirl. It could only be poison – and in the caudle meant for him that Beppe had tasted to his cost.

But there could be another interpretation: that it had been arranged to show that he himself had poisoned the loyal servant to hide his lustful access to Giannina.

Nina wept, her hands to her mouth in horror.

At this hour they were alone in the house and whoever had done this thing might well be lurking about, preparing to move on them.

'Go to our room and lock the door,' Jared said, trying not to look at the corpse.

Nina ran upstairs with a sob.

Jared had to face the fact that someone out in the night was trying to eliminate him. Who? He needed time to think – but first he must get help.

What friends could he call on? Not Alonzo, he would never involve his friend in something like this. He needed someone with power, influence.

Like . . . like Corso Ezzolino, who'd more or less pledged his assistance.

He went to Nina, frightened and trembling in the bedplace. 'I'm going to have to leave you alone for a little while. I go to seek help from Corso Ezzolino. Stay here and don't move.'

There was no other way. She nodded tearfully, and buckling on his poignard Jared went out into the night.

It was cold and dark. Sudden scuttling movements were rats disturbed in their nightly scavenging – but this meant that there was no one else about.

Jared ran as quietly as he could to the corner and looked up the street. There were one or two lights abroad but the rest was impenetrable night. At least what was dark for him would be the same for any following after him.

He tried to recall where he'd been told the Ezzolino *casa maestosa* was located and remembered a tower that dominated the square. That was surely up this sharp incline and to the right. He broke into a lope and made the square and saw the outline of the tower with a torch ablaze and a sentry standing beneath.

Now he was faced with the task of not only rousing the young noble out of whatever bed he was in but getting some kind of help whose nature he hadn't even considered.

The sentry looked bored and sleepy. 'I have urgent tidings for *il Conte*,' Jared said importantly. 'He's to be woken and told immediately.'

The man frowned, then leant back on the high wooden door and tapped it. Voices sounded querulously inside and a face poked out.

'Who are you?'

'Messer Jared of the *signoria*!'

It brought results but not what he was expecting. He was pinioned, rushed inside and thrust rudely into the gatehouse. The door was slammed in his face.

'We'll let *il Conte* know, *inglese barbaro*!'

Ezzolino came quickly, pulling his nightgown around him, alert and dangerous.

'Messer Jared! What is it – tell quickly!'

The saints be praised – he'd taken it the right way. 'Can we talk privily?'

It didn't take long to put across the essence of what had

happened and Ezzolino's features hardened. 'There's a plot to kill you, to stop your gunnes, and I've a notion who's behind it. For now you're in grave danger.'

He shouted orders and armed men turned out to assemble in the inner courtyard. 'Go with these back to your house, my friend, they're under orders to guard you well. I'll be with you presently.'

In a short time his house was surrounded and sealed off. Nina was still hiding in the upper rooms but safe and Jared breathed a sigh of relief.

Ezzolino arrived soon after with a torchlit procession of soldiers, in armour and with an extravagantly plumed helmet as though he was about to go to war.

He strode in and seeing the body, crisply ordered it to be taken away.

'Should we not—'

'The signore is not to be troubled with this, it is a not uncommon event.'

'But—'

'If Malatesta hears of this attempt on your life you will lose this house. He will seize you and place you under lock and key with none to have access. Is this what you want?'

Jared could only shake his head.

'Then allow me to take charge of your safety. From this hour there will be posted in this lower floor ten soldiers. I will send a food and drink taster and your cook is replaced by one of mine.'

'I thank you, but do you think all this will be necessary?'

'For the creator of the means to take sweet revenge on the Perugians – nothing is too much.'

'You said you knew who'd plotted this.'

'I should rather say the many who would do this. Think on it. What you are doing threatens a number of people. One: that old warhorse Umberto di Campaldino. Does he want to see a noble knight brought down invisibly from a distance by a despicable peasant? No, better to put a stop to it before it takes root.

'Another: your sly Giacomo Capuletti, leader of the *popolo*. He sees Malatesta with powers that cannot be contested. He no longer has to curry favour with the *popolo* for he need not fear them with his magic weapons. It will be absolute tyranny. Kill you and this will not happen.

'And then these: Arezzo is seething with Perugian spies. They know or will soon find out what will shortly face them. What riches and rewards will fall in the hands of any who remove you, by whatever means!'

Jared sank to a chair in despair. For all his success with the *huo yao* he was now a hunted man and but for Ezzolino would probably now be lying in a ditch somewhere. It was a situation of his own making and he was trapped within it.

Alonzo said nothing but his face was troubled. They worked rapidly and within the week had a useable sample of the new gunne.

The yoke rest acted as a pivot from which the gunne could be aimed simply by bringing around the tiller butt, with the added advantage that greater range was possible – with no pretence at accuracy at all, hits could be obtained at considerably more than the hundred paces required.

Tired but content Jared gave the orders that began the making of the fifty gunnes.

CHAPTER 73

The next morning Jared and Nina were woken suddenly not by a cock crow or the usual city noises but by what felt like a subterranean rumble, a succession of bumping that could have been a giant awakening from slumber under the earth and about to burst forth.

Petrified he lay rigid as he heard other sounds. Faint screams, shouts – the roar of a great crowd.

Then Nina laughed with relief. 'Of course – today is the festival of Ciambragina! We celebrate young lovers everywhere, enjoy ourselves. Let's go, Jared and forget our trouble!'

They dressed quickly. 'To the square! There'll be acrobats, parades, dancing – how wonderful!'

She had been despondent of late, clearly under the spell of death that had nearly claimed him and it was touching to see the child-like glee in her face.

'Hurry – this way!'

Nina knew a short cut through an alley. As they ran panting breathlessly along past tight-packed flat-roofed houses, the sound of big drums and discordant music became louder and Nina's excitement grew.

'Nearly there!' she said, as they arrived at a long narrow passage.

Jared turned into it first and without warning the heavens fell on him. A crushing weight knocked him to the ground near senseless, leaving him sprawled and bewildered and instinctively trying to throw it off.

It twitched in a spasm once and he realised then that the weight was a human body, and that it did not move.

He rolled to one side and it slithered from him. He stood up shakily – and saw Nina standing rigid over him. In her hand was a bloodied stiletto.

'He tried to kill you,' she whispered.

A long dagger was still clutched in the corpse's hand. The man had dropped on him from a flat roof and but for her quick thinking he would now be lying dead in his place.

Shaking with reaction he tried to smile. 'Where did you get that knife, *cara* Nina?'

'I know they will not stop, I carry it always. Go back – we must run!'

He was safe in his house, even more so in the *presidio*, and he could have an escort any time he chose but the killers were closing in. With a crossbow shot, an assassin's blade, a betrayal – who knew when it would be?

CHAPTER 74

Ezzolino was enraged when he heard of the attack. 'Messer Jared,' he breathed slowly. 'This is the foolishness of a child! You jeopardise not just yourself but the future of Arezzo.'

He paced up and down, then rapped, 'From this time forward there will be three armed men by your side each time you leave this house. You stay with these only, you understand me?'

'Yes.'

'Good.' He stopped pacing and turned to face him. 'I believe we must take further precautions.'

'Oh?'

'Yes. If you should be struck down then there will be no one to produce our gunnes.'

'Alonzo the blacksmith knows how to make them.'

'But none has the secret of your gunne-powder. For safety's sake we should know of it.'

Thinking quickly he answered, 'I do regret that my contract with the Signore Malatesta does not allow me to disclose it to any one else.'

'Then this is a very worrying matter. We must find a solution.'

Jared said nothing.

'I know! You shall tell it only to myself. The *signore* would understand why and it's a prudent move. After all, what use is this to me unless you're dead and we need it? For the sake of Arezzo I ask that this be done.'

'I understand your concern, but I've already taken steps to preserve Arezzo's interests, that at the same time does not violate my contract.'

'May I know these?'

'The secret and process of creating gunne-powder is written down, in full, in a document that lies now in concealment. In the event of my death it will be handed without delay to the *signore*. Does this not satisfy your unease?'

It was a lie, but who could prove it?

'A good plan,' said Ezzolino with an effort. 'But why do you not leave it with me for safekeeping? My *casa maestosa* is proof against an army!'

'It is safe.'

There could be no reply to that.

CHAPTER 75

'Come near then, you brave *condottieri*,' Jared threw at Peppin and his crew of gunners mustered for their first lesson.

It was to be just a simple introduction to principles but the hard men held back in suspicion and apprehension.

'This is a gunne,' Jared said after they'd been chivvied forward. 'You see it has an iron tube like a peashooter. This staff is to hold it with, resting on this yoke. To use it in war all we do is put two things in the gunne tube. First the devil dust, what we call gunne-powder, which will sleep there for now. Then the "pea" – here's one.' He tossed a grape-sized lead to one of the gunners, who promptly dropped it in fear. This brought muted cackles.

'To make it . . . er, throw the "pea" we must wake the gunne-powder in the tube. It will get very angry and force the "pea" to flee away from it as fast as it may. How do we do this? There's a hole that leads from the outside to the sleeping powder. On this we sprinkle some extra and add fire, which will set off all the gunne-powder.'

There was incredulity on some of the faces, expressions of sullen disbelief on others.

'We'll call this "firing the gunne" for now.'

Out of the corner of his eye Jared saw a figure approaching. It was Ezzolino.

Jared caught his eye briefly, then went on. 'You'll now learn about gunne-powder. Cesarino, one packet to every man.'

The lad darted out with a screw of paper for each. Inside was just a pinch of the magic powder.

'Smell – taste! It's quite harmless. Only fire will rouse it.'

There were puzzled looks and outright distrust. Ezzolino, standing close by, was following every word, his forehead furrowed in concentration.

'Messer Peppin. Your packet if you please.'

Jared emptied it into a dish, heaping the little pile together.

'What will happen when I give fire to this?' he asked mildly. 'Shall we see?'

He went to the brazier and lifting out a firing wire advanced on the little grey pile. The company scattered in consternation.

His gentle lowering of the wire resulted in a cheerful flare and then ashes.

'Our gunne-powder is amiable when free, but barbarous when confined, as in our gunne.

'Now we will make our gunne speak!'

A target was hung on the frame, a crudely sketched figure.

'I will ready the first gunne, you will follow after.'

In slow, deliberate moves Jared charged the gun, added the ball of lead and rested.

He pointed to one of the gunners. 'You – yes, you. Your packet?'

It was handed over and with the gunne in line with the target he smothered the fire-passage with its contents.

'Are you ready, brave warriors?'

He brought the wire down and the gunne viciously cracked out with a gratifying amount of smoke.

'A hit!' cried the distant target-man, dancing about.

'And that is all,' Jared said, stepping back.

'We do it again, this time by numbers. Number one: clean out . . .'

After the second shot he had them chanting out the sequence for an imaginary firing.

'A volunteer. Thank you, Captain Peppin!'

Blank-faced, the mercenary gunner stepped forward.

'One shot at the target, if you please.' There would be no scoring for accuracy as there would be in an archery contest – simply hitting the big sheet would be enough.

Slowly and carefully, Peppin prepared the gun, his packet shaken over the firing-passage the last thing before he aimed.

It was only when Jared handed him the red-hot wire that he showed any emotion – a trembling of his hand as it lowered to the lethal grey dust.

The gunne cracked out happily and the target was duly struck.

Struggling to retain his severe expression he returned to the ranks.

Next would be the five corporals.

Under a dozen watchful eyes the procedure went smoothly, but on a battlefield a simple fumble, which could so easily happen, could end in grisly calamity.

By the end of the day Jared was happy that the Gunners Band of the Black Company knew how their weapons worked – but there was much to learn yet before he could turn them over as a trained military asset.

When he got back to the house he decided that the next day he'd test them individually, watching for carelessness, blunders. Then solid drill until they knew it backwards.

Gunne-powder making was more of a worry. As usual it was the saltpetre, a large proportion of which he'd had to send back for further refining. He had enough for now but if there was a serious need . . .

Nina entered the room and put her arm around his shoulders. 'Jared, *il mio amore*. You work so hard. It's not fair!'

'I can do it another way?'

She sat on his lap and stroked his hair. 'You don't have to waste your life like this, you know.'

'Nina. What are you saying, you silly cabbage.'

'You'll get angry at me,' she pouted.

'No I won't!'

'Promise?'

'I promise. Now tell me how I don't have do this any more.'

'I worry of you. I ask my friend. She tells me something which is very good, you can stop – leave and go away and no more scared of you killed any more.'

'Oh? What did she say, then?'

Nina got to her feet and smoothed her gown. 'I think you be interested. So – I ask her here to speak at you.'

'What!'

She opened the door. 'Lucia, here is Messer Jared.'

In stepped a remarkably beautiful woman in an exquisite silk gown. For a moment Jared tried to remember where he'd seen her and then recalled the banquet – she was the wife of Villani, and related to the *signore*.

'*La mia signora*,' he managed.

'*Il Pregiato* Jared,' she replied with a graceful bow. Her features were perfectly composed, almost emotionless.

'You will speak with me?'

'Yes. You will be killed in a very short while. I am sure of that.' The voice was cool and controlled and carried a certainty that chilled him.

'You are a stranger and stand no chance against those whose life is spent here. Do you realise this?'

'What else can I do?'

'You can do something that not only preserves your life but gives you the means to leave here for ever and live like a prince.'

Jared was beginning to suspect where this was going.

'I'm here to offer you the sum of two thousand gold ducats for your secrets.'

This translated to something like the income of Hurnwych Manor for some years.

'Hear her!' Nina pleaded, clutching his arm. 'We can go this night, *mio caro*!'

'You will buy my gunnes – and the secret of gunne-powder? What will become of Arezzo?'

'Is not a problem. I will continue your good work when you leave, there will be no difference.'

Then he recalled something Sforza had said that made it all clear. He'd play Lucia along a little.

'Three thousand.'

She bit her lip, then nodded. 'Very well. But it must be written down, that it can be tested as the complete knowledge.'

'I don't believe you,' Jared said simply.

'What did you say?' she said sharply.

'What lady commands wealth of her own? Is this your husband speaking to me, or . . . ?'

'You do not need to know!'

'Oh, but I do. How can I be sure that such a sum is available to you, a woman?'

'I have powerful friends. They will provide it this night if I ask it of them.'

'Perugian friends.'

'Does it matter to you?' she flared. 'Three thousand ducats in gold is a prince's ransom. Do you want it in your hands or no?'

'Ah. Very tempting. I'll think about it.'

'You—'

'I shall consider your offer, *la mia signora*. Goodnight.'

After she'd left Nina rounded on him. 'You fool! Why didn't you—?'

'Giannina. Why did you do this?'

She burst into tears then threw herself into his arms.

Tearing herself away she looked at Jared with great tenderness. 'I so scared you be killed. And maybe me, too.'

Jared's heart went out to her. She had feelings for him and he for her, but unspoken was the fact that when he had finished his gunnes he would go back to England alone.

He hoped he would be able to give her some security for her future when he left.

But that aside, he now knew one important thing: the Perugians did not want him dead; their only concern was the secret.

CHAPTER 76

'Why do we have to prance around like some poxy king's soldier?' snarled one of the line of mercenaries trudging along with their gunnes on their backs. 'We're the Gunner's Band, we are!'

'Tell your thick-skulled crew,' Jared said heavily to Peppin, 'that there's a pile more to being a useful gunner than setting off a gunne. Tell 'em . . . well, say that.'

It was not going to plan, for it was becoming clear to him and probably Peppin that there were many more things to think about in actually using gunners in combat than he'd initially assumed. Were they part of the attack or defences? Anti-cavalry or simple man-slayers? How did the leader of an army communicate his orders to them? He was no military man but he'd seen more than his fair share of battles and these were only the first questions that needed answering.

Peppin was of little use, shrugging and laconic. Jared was starting to have his suspicions about him. What if Peppin was playing another game, waiting until the first clash with gunnes swept the field and then it would be he, leader of the only Gunner's Band, who would be getting the fat bids. That only he himself had the secret of gunne-powder would then be of little use – all arrangements would be with the band and he'd be forced to deal with them only.

Sourly he gave the next order, to stop and deploy. It had to be done right or the gunnes in the field would be nothing but useless ornaments.

Besides bringing the weapon to face the enemy by order, from the supply cart had to be carried the braziers, one to every four of them, and then the wires ready-heated. Also a quantity of lead balls to be placed next to each and finally, the gunne-powder delivered by hand from the wagon.

Who knew what the conditions of battle would do to his plans.

Already he'd found that there were grave disadvantages to gunnes on the battlefield.

Firstly, they were unwieldy, unable to be sent at a moment's notice to distant parts of a battlefield. Secondly, they were expensive – not the gunnes but the labour-intensive gunne-powder that was taking such a distressingly long time to make. Thirdly, their rate of fire was far less than an archer and even slower than a crossbow. Lastly, their lightning and thunder would inevitably panic not only the foe but their own warhorses assembling to meet the enemy.

He kept all this to himself and concentrated on the instruction of the gunners. In only a little while these dozen would be the serjeants of four gunnes each, with all responsibility for teaching and drilling them. At the rate they were going, he was probably going to hand over an undisciplined rabble to Malatesta.

In a dark mood Jared returned to his house.

To his surprise, his room upstairs was untidy, the bedclothes sketchily thrown down and the side table a jumble. He went to the next room and saw a similar state. This was not like Nina, who couldn't bear things out of their place, let alone disordered.

Had she left him in a rage over his refusal to deal with Lucia? With a sinking heart he went down the stairs.

He heard voices outside and Nina and the cook came in carrying food baskets. Both looked up at him in surprise.

'I . . . er, was wondering what we'll be having tonight,' he muttered feebly.

Nina headed up the stairs past him to the upper floors. A moment later she cried out from the top of the staircase. 'What you do, *diavolo* – why you do this to me?'

Suddenly Jared realised there was a simple explanation for the untidiness. There had been a hurried rummage by someone for a hidden document that didn't exist.

And what that implied was chilling. His friend and protector, Ezzolino, was not all he seemed.

Alonzo had never trusted the young, thrusting noble for his ambitions and he had been right. Ezzolino had witnessed what the gunnes could do and seen that if he had them for himself he could stand astride Arezzo. They would be vital to his plans, which was why he'd gone out of his way to protect Jared while they were in development. Now they were close to being handed over – not to him but to the tyrant Malatesta, who would then hold them all in subjection.

This was now acutely dangerous: Ezzolino had been unable to lay his hands on the gunne-powder secret and therefore the only way left of frustrating the *signore* would be to eliminate Jared.

Even now he would be receiving the news of the fruitless search and in all probability was on his way to a confrontation.

Jared forced his mind to an icy control. Did he flee into the streets into the arms of the assassins, now completely unprotected or—?

Shouted orders sounded from outside; time had run out.

Footsteps thudded up the staircase and Ezzolino burst into the room. Three armed men took up position outside. With a sob Nina fled downstairs.

Jared stood before Ezzolino, heart in his mouth.

'You know why I've come,' he said impatiently, slapping his gloves down and pacing to and fro. 'I'll not be denied it, this you will understand.'

Gone was the amiable and courteous Corso – this man had a murderous expression and spoke with a harsh venom.

'Give it to me now!'

The one thing Jared clung to was the knowledge that he would live for as long as the secret held.

'The document does not exist,' he said as calmly as he could. 'I lied. All the knowledge is held in my head.'

'Then it's so simple,' Ezzolino sneered. 'You'll write it down before me now.'

'No.'

In a single savage movement a blade was unsheathed, the glittering point stopping at Jared's throat. 'Now! Or I promise you, your end will be unpleasant.'

'And you will lose your secret!'

'I may lose the secret but so will Malatesta. No one then has a power over the other!'

His bluff was called. If he didn't give up the mystery he would leave this earth in agony – if he did he would be dispatched as a complication later.

Jared's mind raced as the noise of some kind of disturbance in the street below intruded into the scene.

'See what that's about!' Ezzolino threw at the door, then in silky tones hissed, 'While Messer Jared begins his writing.'

A corporal of the guard came up. 'Sire, it's the *capitano di podestà*. He claims we're mounting a private army within the city walls contrary to the law and demands we disperse.'

'Tell him I'm here to guard the person of Messer Jared, valued above all men by the *signore*.'

'He knows that, Highness, and declares he will act in that duty himself.'

Ezzolino eased in something like satisfaction. 'So the matter is settled.'

Jared said nothing, not understanding.

Ezzolino gave a cruel smirk. 'Don't you realise? No, I can see you don't. Your assassins – these were not from Capuletti, the miserable *popolo*, nor from Perugia, who desire your secrets, not your death. So that leaves one only. Umberto di Campaldino: who is the *capitano di podestà* we find waiting patiently below. I have no need to sully my hands with your blood – when he sees my men withdraw, Umberto will be free to have the undoubted satisfaction of ridding this world of you and your gunnes. Farewell, then, little man!'

Jared bit back a retort as he left. Had everyone who he'd accounted his friends been shown to be false? This was now the end for him.

But there was one last, small hope. One who he could count on, could trust his life to – but who had no authority, weight of rank or men-at-arms to command.

He found Nina below, pale-faced and trembling.

'*Mia cara*. I beg you on my life to flee away from here. You'll pass through the guards, they'll not stop a kitchen maid. Go to Alonzo the blacksmith and tell him what's happening here. He'll know what to do.'

CHAPTER 77

The hammers swung in skilled synchrony, orange sparks shooting out sideways as the plate edge was turned. Jared snatched a glance at the burly form of Alonzo, his face creased in concentration and yet again his heart went out to the simple and honest craftsman. It had been his master stroke that had saved him, the only thing that could have succeeded – he'd gone straight to the *signore*.

Malatesta had not wasted a moment. At the head of an overwhelming force from the *palazzo* he'd marched by torchlight to the rescue, surrounding the house with his men and bursting in on a gloating Umberto. What happened next was not generally known but it was given out later that on hearing of a plot against Messer Jared, it had been first the *capitano di podestà* and then he himself who had rushed to the rescue.

Regrettably, in the confusion the noble Umberto di Campaldino, bravely tackling the assassins, had inadvertently fallen to his death from the roof.

But as a consequence of the threat to the life of the talented Master of Gunnes, he was now confined to a room at the palazzo, under guard at all times.

A *signoria* messenger arrived, standing uncertainly before the cacophonous scene of fire and metal.

The hammering ceased and Jared was informed that the *signore* wanted to know when this last batch of eight gunnes would be completed.

Wearily, he allowed that these would be complete before the end of the week but other matters needed settling before he could think to possess a corps of gunners.

Fifty gunnes, fifty firing wires, gunne-powder boxes, cleaning swabs, spares for all. Then the seventy men supplied to be common gunners under his twelve. Not much better than farmhands they were stolid, slow and frightened. If these were to function without flinching in the heat and terror of battle they would need better training than they were getting from Peppin's crew, who swaggered and bullied their way about in everything they did.

In store was now enough of the gunne-powder elements to make up just three firings for each. Three volleys! When archers carried a dozen or more arrows – it was as well that no war was being talked about.

He made a reluctant farewell to Alonzo and returned to the *presidio*. The sheer physical satisfaction to be gained at the forge was a treat he rarely allowed himself these days; there was so much to do. And Nina had fled back to her family and he missed her.

At the *presidio* he was confronted with the sight of his half-trained gunners capering about in extravagantly coloured costumes. A preening Peppin told him that Malatesta wanted all his elite Gunner's Band to be attired as he specified – over a plain mail corselet a surcoat of flaming orange and red to mark them out before all as the most fearsome warriors in the field.

Shaking his head in despair Jared saw how the flaring fabric in any kind of a breeze could wrap over the gunner and even obscure the crucial firing-passage. Now was not the time to argue, however, and he went back to his accounts.

CHAPTER 78

On the next day everything changed.

A herald clad in a tabard with the griffin of Perugia appeared at the main city gates.

Trumpets sounded and he proceeded to loudly declaim from a document. Jared's Italian was much improved but he had to ask Alonzo to translate its ornate delivery.

'Not so good, *il mio compagno*,' he said with a tight expression. 'It's come to the notice of the vicar general of Rome, who's really the Bishop of Perugia, that unclean and unholy practices are being encouraged, namely the diabolic conjuring of heavenly powers. It's demanded that the person of you, m' friend, be detained for examination.'

'Do you think Malatesta will hand me over?' he asked in a low voice.

'O' course not! This is the Guelphs making their move. They weary of getting their hands on your secret and think to strike before your gunnes are ready. Their spies will tell them this, for they stand to be defeated by your terror weapon unless they do something.'

'Then what will happen?'

'War, of course. If they don't have it now, your gunnes will increase in number and ferocity and they stand to cravenly bow to Arezzo.'

The pennons fluttered bravely in the breeze, the fitful sun picking out the sharp glitter of blades, the workmanlike steel shimmer of armour and above all the glorious blazon of colour: knightly riders atop destriers with their courtly graces and ornamented helmets, ranks of soldiers in white and red quartered tunics bearing the rearing black horse of Arezzo, and in the centre – the extravagant opulence of the *signore*'s own Gunner's Band.

Directly in front of them was the commanding figure of Malatesta, in a black velvet robe mounted on a jet-black steed and with an expression of single-minded ferocity.

After emerging from the city gates the column took the road southward, stepping it out in order to reach the low San Zeno pass before the Perugian horde, still out of sight.

It was going to be the old story – the ancient chivalry of Perugia advancing from the south and the two meeting on the wide flood plain of the Chiana. This time there was going to be a quite different outcome and the Arezzo line of march buzzed with the expectation of how great a humiliation it would be for their foe.

Jared had not been required to be among them but this was the first time he would see his gunnes speak in anger so he needed to be there. He rode a mild-mannered rouncey and while wearing the required colours of the band he carried no arms, nor did he wear a formidable coxcomb helmet and streamer like Peppin.

As they proceeded in a noisy column he was struck by the theatrical unreality of it all. His experience of battle was by no means meagre, he'd seen some of the worst.

Mongol savagery leaving hills of dead in a whirlwind of destruction and the brutal head-on clash of two great armies but in every case the array on the battlefield was utilitarian, hard and bleak, the chief colour that of blood and bright steel.

Here there were acrobats whirling flags, a din of music and much prinking and posturing from both knight and foot-soldier. In Jared's eyes this was not war, it was a cavalcade!

After two or three miles they were through the pass and the plain lay before them, the puissance of Perugia still not yet in sight.

He was not a tactician but Jared saw that to deploy in the open with an inferior force vulnerable to charge by knights or encirclement and slaughter would not be a wise move. And if Malatesta placed overmuch faith in the Gunners Band . . .

They were not yet descended to the plain when a halt was ordered and Jared thankfully saw Malatesta stand tall in the saddle and crisply direct his army to take position. They were going to stay here and await the Perugian attack from prepared positions.

On the flanks of the hills on either side, forward companies of crossbowmen assembled. In the centre was the main army, but standing in the forefront with Malatesta was the Gunners Band at his command.

Any attack was thus constrained to the front. If the enemy advanced, the crossbowmen would take them in the flank. If they came on further the gunnes would finish them.

So his gunners were to be kept for last resort until they'd proved themselves.

Their position was sound, placed directly ahead of the massed soldiers. Archers were ready to move out on either wing against any threatening attack on the knights who were milling impatiently ahead and poised to throw themselves on the fleeing Perugians.

They set up with a forward positioning on either side, of two companies of eight gunnes. Behind these were the remainder, spread across the front in eight sets of four gunnes with two spares, each with its line of supply to the support carts carrying the powder and spares. It was as much as Jared could do, and now it was up to Peppin to take charge and see it through.

The sun rose and warmed the air. Insects busied themselves and the occasional cries of birds were heard above the continuous murmur of an army in waiting.

The previous evening Jared had written a letter to Rosamunde, a dutiful reciting of recent events as they affected her commercial interests, but omitting his own perils and adventures. It was a respectable achievement; to have completed a full fifty gunnes in just months, now delivered and payment due. As well he'd been able to renegotiate terms to include training and support services, an important source of revenue for the future in his estimation.

It had been a painful exercise for one unused to the quill, in fact it had been his first letter to anyone. He was unsure how to word the bit about what it was like to be on the eve of battle and again how best to close the letter.

But it had gone off and now he had other things on his mind.

CHAPTER 79

Mid morning there was a ripple of excitement and scattered shouts – a dust cloud over to the south was watched with much interest: the Perugian advance.

In the next two hours it grew until at a five-mile distance it stopped and began to spread out. There was going to be an encounter and conditions were perfect.

Peppin fell back to be with Jared, shading his eyes as he scanned the horde.

'Ha! They've hired Germans. That's Otto's lot, there in the middle. A fair set of hackers, in close. I see they're setting 'em in the centre to take what our gunnes are going to do to them. He won't like that, not one bit!' he snorted gleefully.

'There's not so many knights,' Jared observed.

'True, but they've laid out big on grunters, all of 'em with pikes and spikes. We'll be working hard this day, I'll wager.'

'Yes, but do remember what I said about discipline. We'll be in much trouble if they forget their—'

'They're good lads, them. Stand their ground whatever. You leave 'em to me and make sure we're well supplied with what we want.'

Jared moved to stand by the carts.

Trumpeters sounded clear and compelling. In turns heralds crossed to deliver each side's demands and titled commanders rode out to arrogantly exchange taunts.

They galloped back to their lines and battle was joined.

A tremendous shout and thunder of drums rose up on both sides but Malatesta held cool, rapping orders to his knights and bringing up more archers while the tumult died away.

The two armies faced each other for long minutes. Then with a roar the Perugian knights hurled themselves forward directly towards Malatesta, who watched them dispassionately, making no move whatsoever.

His crossbowmen advanced from the flanks and shot a hail of bolts into the thundering mass. It told – in an instant several horses cartwheeled, they and their riders trampled by those following, others racing sideways were met with a rain of arrows. They slowed, wheeling, gyrating and baffled, then galloped back.

Jared shook his head at the sheer ineptness. This was useless flamboyance and had achieved nothing – but behind those the main mass was on the move, in disciplined lines with gonfalons aloft and banners streaming in a baleful flood of hatred.

Arezzo chivalry rode out to meet them, splitting in two to drive in on their flank and in a pandemonium of noise foot soldiers moved forward to envelop their front.

Fairly soon the rising dust made it impossible for Jared to see much of what was happening. The mass of soldiers that had passed him on either side were now locked in combat out there and neither their crossbowmen nor their archers could affect the outcome while they were mixed inextricably.

Malatesta on his black but now dust-smeared horse remained still and watchful.

He'd sent in the bulk of his army, together with French and Swiss mercenaries and allies from Siena but had kept back two divisions of his best, which stood impatiently on either side.

The din was indescribable, shrieks and brutish howls sounding above the continuous clash of steel on steel, terror-stricken screams of horses and the unceasing dull roar of war.

The hours wore on with no slackening of the onslaught. The Gunners Band had long since stopped their taunts and fist-waving and now waited apprehensively. When the dust cleared would they see a fleeing enemy – or a mass of bloodied and vengeful warriors making for them?

A lull descended but Malatesta was not easy, peering ahead impatiently into the swirling haze. Then, ominously, their own men were running and stumbling out, more and more until a stream of retreating soldiers were making for the safety of their own lines.

'Stand to, the gunnes!' Malatesta threw over his shoulder.

The two reserve divisions drew up in defensive lines at an angle either side of the gunnes, the mouth of the pass ensuring that the enemy must be funnelled towards them.

This was the finality of all he'd done, the moment of truth for Jared and his gunnes and he gulped at the realisation.

The enemy came out of the smother of dust tramping forward in a terrible host, heart-freezing in its intent.

In the increasing clarity Jared focused his gaze on the two forward placements of four gunnes readying, the gunners easily seen in their extravagant colours testing their yoke rest and moving the tiller butt to approximate a better sight line.

Peppin swaggered up to them and stood legs astride watching the oncoming array.

He held up his hand.

The enemy slowed visibly, heads turning in the first rank in rising fear. Among them serjeants and veterans were urging them on but there was now palpable terror. It would not take much to break the advance.

Peppin's arm slashed down. In an irregular salvo not one but eight gunnes cracked out – livid flashes of lightning in grey-white smoke, invisibly reaching out to take the lives of their victims.

The appalled mass wavered and hesitated and when the smoke with its stench of sulphur and the Devil reached them they broke.

A storm of cheers erupted in the Arezzo lines. Peppin arrogantly strutted his acknowledgement.

But it was premature: the crush of men moving forward did not allow these to retreat – the main body still came on, relentlessly, filling the pass from side to side in a disorderly flood that was growing nearer every moment.

Peppin saw the danger and got the second eight opening fire but with the same result: terror, alarm and men dropping but all unable to flee.

With a stab of fear Jared realised what was happening. The gunnes were doing their work but the conditions of a battlefield did not allow their potent magic of Devil-sent thunder and death randomly meted out to create the easy rout that had been expected.

And then the worst happened.

In a panic, the rest of the gunners opened up until there was a frenzy of firing that grew quickly to a storm but then slackened to nothing.

Instead of disciplined volleys timed to allow reloading of the weapons while others continued, they were now caught with empty gunnes. The terrified enemy, driven helplessly from behind soon sensed the situation and surged forward in a howling fury.

The gunners turned and fled – but the Perugian commander who had without much doubt cynically set up the whole thing had foreseen this, and around both wings of the horde came a torrent of caparisoned horsemen thundering past to head them off.

There was no sign of Malatesta. His best divisions in reserve had seen the trap and threw down their weapons while those who could were making for the hills.

The oncoming mass divided and continued past to complete the encirclement.

It was a catastrophic defeat for Arezzo.

The Perugians surrounding them roared and shouted, flourishing their weapons – but something was holding them back from a final massacre.

Then Jared saw a tall, white-haired figure in gold and scarlet over his armour, his helmet removed, directing his men. They were going into the prisoners and separating out the gunners, easily recognisable in their colours and assembling them next to the carts together with their gunnes and equipment.

'By every saint in the book and I thought we were done!' Peppin breathed. 'Now comes the hard bit, as you'll leave to me.'

'Hard part? What do you mean?'

'Why, negotiating our price to go over to him, o' course! Not so easy, as we hadn't a chance to show good in this fight and Braccio is a wily old wolf.'

'Who?'

'Il Visconte Braccio da Baglioni, Signore of Perugia. Him with the white hair.'

There was no more time to talk for they were in turn separated and brought across.

Only when it was reported that there were no more gunners did Braccio deign to notice them, riding forward and regarding them with supercilious disdain. The Perugian army was kept back in a wide circle around them, watching resentfully and fingering their weapons.

'Who is your captain?'

'I'm Peppin, Master o' Gunnes, Excellency.' Peppin grovelled.

'And your serjeants?'

'These, Highness. This is—'

'I don't need to know their names.' The Black Company men were brought up for his inspection. Smoothly, a soldier slipped into place behind each one.

'And that one?' he said, pointing to Jared. 'Why is he unarmed?'

'Oh, that's Messer Jared as—'

'Ah! I've heard of him,' he said, raising an eyebrow.

Then his face turned to stone.

'Kneel!'

Obediently they prostrated before him.

There was a moment's pause and a breathless hush spread.

Braccio didn't waste words. With a vicious gesture across his throat he gave his order and watched its execution with a cruel smile.

One by one the kneeling men's hair was seized, jerked back and a knife stabbed into their throats and sawn across, and in a violent gush of blood and mortal gurgling they were let fall.

A spreading howl of triumph that went on and on seized the Perugians. Jared's bowels froze as his fate approached.

His hair was yanked back and—

'Hold! Spare me that one.'

The soldier released him and sheathed his knife, leaving Jared weak and trembling.

The rest was quickly completed. A dozen corpses lay untidily on the ground.

'The block!' growled Braccio.

A well-used butcher's chopping table was produced.

Eyes dull with horror, Jared watched as each of the remaining gunners, not much more than ignorant villeins, was brought to the block and with a single crunching blow from a cleaver their right hands were severed to join the obscene pile beneath.

The bleeding victims were pointed in the direction of Arezzo and kicked stumbling away to cackles of pitiless laughter.

A crackling of fire sounded behind him – Braccio's men were setting light to the carts and dancing ecstatically around them. When the flames reached gunne-powder there was a powerful *whooomf* and they scattered in terror.

Braccio gestured at the mound of gunnes. 'Throw those cursed things in the river!'

Jared fought down his emotions. Now there was nothing left of his great dream but smoking wreckage and stiffening bodies.

CHAPTER 80

Perugia, Italy, AD 1312

The dungeon was dimly lit through a grating above. It stank of human waste and rancid straw, and its dark stone walls ran with condensation. It was nothing, however, compared to the misery Jared felt in his heart at the laying waste of his vision. As far as both sides were concerned gunnes had been comprehensively shown to be a failure. Now they no longer existed in the world of men and with his execution so would pass their secrets.

Sforza would hear of his fate and would relay to Rosamunde that as a commercial venture, gunnes had no future. It had all ended.

Two days later a ladder was let down and Jared was taken out of the dungeon, blinking in the unbearable sunlight. He was escorted to a small but richly appointed room. Braccio sat at a desk, his fingers arched, his eyes giving nothing away.

Jared was flung to a kneeling position and two guards stood to attention at the door.

Braccio indicated Jared was to stand. 'I'm commanded by My Lord Bishop Pandolfo to yield you up for a public burning. No more than you deserve, of course, with your Satanic devices.'

So it was to be the stake. Life suddenly became very precious.

'But before I do, you'll tell me what you expected to achieve with those . . .'

'Gunnes,' Jared said with as much dignity as he could.

'Gunnes, then. You conjured a story that Malatesta swallowed and now he rues the day he heard you. Those things are entertaining, what with their noise and smoke, but compared to any half-competent bowman they're a joke!'

He ruminated for a moment, lips pursed. 'One thing makes me pause. If you were in the common run of tricksters you'd not stand with the fools that trusted you. You did, so we must accept that you believe in the absurdity yourself. Can this be true?'

Jared burnt at the unfairness of it all and determined to have his say before it was all ended for him.

'It was not my choice! Malatesta forced me to—'

'Oh, dear. I was hoping for something a little more . . . creative.'

'Listen to me!' Jared barked.

Braccio's head snapped up in surprise, then the eyes narrowed. 'Go on.'

'These gunnes. Are new-devised by me to one true purpose – to bring to ruin the walls of castles and cities. None other! Malatesta saw a small gunne for trial and he it was who decided a man-slayer in hand was better than a wall-breaker in the future!'

'These are nothing but toys, and you are telling me—'

'What can be shown as a baby will grow to a man. Should this gunne be multiplied in size many times, you will have a monster weapon to fire giant stones as big as a man – nothing built of man can endure!'

'I see . . . so you're saying to me, given a chance you can create a castle-smasher yourself.'

'The gunne itself stands as my creation.'

'Umm. And the possessor of such might then challenge the haughtiest in the land. I like it.'

He looked up as if for inspiration, then seemed to decide.

'The good bishop believes that your extermination will wipe the stain of your diabolic weapons from the face of the earth. He's probably right, but I believe there are higher purposes to be served before that happens. Such as putting an end for all time to the Ghibelline heresy! This is devoutly to be wished for and must take precedence.'

He looked at Jared keenly. 'I can save you from the stake and set you up in great comfort, while you make me a wall-breaker. Does this interest you . . . ?'

There was no alternative. A change of masters, but infinitely preferable to the flames.

'Very well. But to my rules, which you will be bound to without recourse. Shall we say that, first, it will be let out that unhappily you did not survive my dungeons to be tormented at the stake. Feelings run high against you in Perugia, therefore you will be kept out of sight and under another name to do your work, in all secrecy in my country villa where you will be guarded night and day. You shall be provided with a workshop and all materials you desire, but mark well, you are there to provide me with a wall-smasher, never these playthings.'

CHAPTER 81

Jared gave a grim smile at the irony. He had managed to save his life, acquired lodgings even more splendid than before and all he had to do was achieve what he'd been placed on this earth to do – fulfil his vision.

And yet he now knew it was impossible. His gunnes would split and burst well before they could throw stones even as big as an orange. He could never do it. Even the best wrought iron was not enough. So it had to be faced: he was on a futile quest and would inevitably be found out.

His quarters were very comfortable and he was waited upon like a lord – but he was a prisoner. He ate and slept alone. Guards marched behind and ahead of him as he crossed the quadrangle to the stables converted to a workshop.

And everyone waited upon his word on how to begin on the Great Gunne.

There was no escaping it. Braccio insisted on weekly reports taken down by a confidential clerk. At first Jared got by with the plea that this was the theoretical design stage and nothing could be physically shown but that began to pall and he resorted to spouting technical nonsense. After that he had the bright idea of letting off blasts of gunne-powder at irregular intervals, a satisfying noise that would be sure to reach the ears of the *signore*.

But it couldn't go on. He lay awake at night trying to work around the problem to no avail.

He was trapped.

One morning he was sent for.

'Messer Jared. I was simply wondering how your work is progressing?' purred Braccio.

Instantly wary, Jared mumbled a reassuring reply.

'That is good. Now I want you to do something for me. Are you able to leave your work at this time? I desire you will accompany me down to meet somebody.'

Out in the quadrangle a short and undistinguished individual whose brown tunic was too large and whose hose hung limply from skimpy legs stood beside a large cloth-covered object. When he saw Braccio he bowed low and fell to his knee.

'Ah. You're ready. My friend, this is Bartolomeo Farnese, who has ventured all the way from Padua to show me his pride and joy.'

Farnese tried to smile but was clearly overcome.

Braccio turned to Jared, 'You will be interested in what he has for me, and I'd be most grateful for your judgement upon it.'

'Um, of course.'

'What he has here is . . . a gunne. Although he does not call it that. And this gunne he assures me can assail castles and city walls by means of a secret powder. Would you like to see it?'

For Jared it was a shock of appalling force – like a thunderbolt from a clear sky. It couldn't be!

Farnese clumsily removed the cloth – and there, neatly placed in a scooped-out baulk of wood was a gleaming object. Bronze, polished to perfection, a gunne certainly, but in the shape of a flower vase on its side, bulbous at one end and flared at the other. And at about five feet long, bigger by far than any he'd made himself.

'Ah, yes,' Jared heard himself saying faintly.

Conscious of Braccio's keen gaze, he made inspection.

One thing hammered in on him. It was not wrought, it was cast! And with a beautifully clean bore the size of a hen's egg with walls many times thicker than his own. At the other end, where his gunne was painfully crimped, the casting allowed a fat termination complete with a neat fire-passage, even furnished with a dish-shaped recess for the gunne-powder.

'A bronze gunne,' he muttered flatly.

'You like it?' Farnese burbled in relief. 'It took me more than five months to—'

'Are we to see it fire?' Jared directed the question to Braccio, in a wash of chagrin unable to speak to Farnese.

'Well?'

'Yes, Excellency, certainly.'

Farnese busied himself with his apparatus, which Jared couldn't tear his eyes from. Much of it was similar to his own but one thing was so bizarre that it took his breath away. At this point where Jared would be placing a lead ball into his gunne Farnese had opened a long chest, within which lay a dozen arrows. They were much bigger than those any archer would recognise, bulky and with leather padding at two places. Farnese selected one and eased it into the bore until it met the powder, a foot or so of the barbed end protruding.

'You're going to . . . that?' Jared gasped.

'The fire-arrow, I call it,' Farnese said proudly, patting the shaft.

'With this I can send the flames of hell into an enemy city and none can withstand it. And—'

'Where's your target?' Jared bit off.

'Target? Oh, no. You've no need to aim! Simply fill the air with my fire-arrows and—'

'Shall we see it, then?'

The device was levered around to face a wall.

'Carry on, Highness?' the man fawned.

'Do.'

Drawing Braccio well clear Jared watched as Farnese readied the gunne – but there was no brazier, he had some kind of cord that glowed at the end. He blew on it then held it in a stick to the fire-passage and the gunne fired.

There was a gouting of yellow flame and through vast quantities of light-brown smoke Jared watched the arrow trailing fire as it sailed down and shattered on the wall in flaming fragments. But Jared had noted something vital: the sound was weak, pitiful even against his own.

'Thank you, Messer Farnese,' he said. 'We'll call upon you when we need to.'

Turning to Braccio, Jared gave a confident smile. 'I don't think we need go further with this, *Signore*. The man is demented if he thinks that a true wall-smasher. Arrows – ha! And so heavy a gunne to carry on the battlefield, it's really not worth trifling with.'

'You think so? The gunne is very handsome compared to yours.'

'Ah, yes. That's the point – everyone knows that bronze is softer than steel, but prettier. Which would you rather it be – in a military sense, that is?'

'I see. Very well, you may carry on with your own work.'

While the crestfallen Farnese packed away his things Jared

asked innocently, 'Er, who is the man – a local fellow?'

'No, a bell-founder of Padua. How goes your gunne?' Braccio added meaningfully.

'Ah, yes, Highness. I must get back to work, some difficult testing to do.'

In his quarters Jared flopped on the bed, staring sightlessly at the ceiling, his thoughts running wild.

The most burning was the realisation that he was no longer alone in the quest. But then wasn't it to be expected that somewhere out there, one with a similar experience to his own, would return to Europe with the secret? It had been chance and accident that had made him witness to the Cathayan *huo yao*, how could he have thought that no one else might not have followed the same path? It had been years now and . . .

He tried to order his thoughts.

So there were others who knew the secret, could produce gunnes. That meant he could no longer trade on the fact that he was the only one who possessed the knowledge. Even as he laboured on in a fruitless mission to produce a wall-smashing gunne there were now others who were his rivals, and probably some with better ideas.

A cast gunne was a stroke of genius. Where his iron gunne was limited by what a blacksmith could physically achieve at the anvil, casting meant that thickness was no longer a limitation – if the gunne needed stouter walls to take a bigger charge, then you simply increased the thickness until it could. Never mind that bronze was softer, just make it thicker to compensate.

A gunne the size of a horse could reasonably be expected to fire a ball the size of a man's head. Larger still . . . and for a surety he had his boulder-throwing monster!

Frantic with impatience and frustration Jared realised that here was a leap forward that made everything and anything possible – it was all within reach!

Farnese must have got the idea from somewhere and as a bell-founder had naturally thought of casting a gunne, as he himself had naturally turned to blacksmithing. Farnese, however, had been let down by his poor gunne-powder, which had not shown the weapon to advantage.

But *his gunne* with Jared's powder . . .

And there must be others at work along different paths . . .

There were now two very good reasons why he had to make his escape.

The first was that he was not going to be able to give Braccio what he wanted and he would be quickly discarded or worse. The other was that he had to put himself in the middle of whatever was happening – or die in the attempt.

CHAPTER 82

Padua, Italy

It had been easier than Jared had dared hope, thanks to Rosamunde. She had given him a ring when they'd parted on the understanding that it could be used if he found himself without funds in a foreign land. He'd worn it out of sight on a string around his neck and had almost forgotten its existence but it had raised a remarkable sum – after the bribes it had left enough to get him to Padua. As a fleeing Arezzo citizen he was quite safe in the Ghibelline stronghold.

Finding Farnese was straightforward, he being one of the only two bell-founders in the city. Jared left an anonymous message asking to meet him in a public wine shop.

The man arrived, looking nervous and tense. Jared went up to him. 'Messer Farnese? So good of you to come.'

There was a flash of recognition. 'You're a Guelph of Perugia! Sent by—'

'No, no, er, Bartolomeo. Only in temporary employ of the *signore*,' Jared said with a friendly smile. 'I'm English, as you must know, and have no interest in these rivalries.'

'Then why do you—?'

'I was passing through Padua, and thought to tell you why you had a hard time at Perugia. You see, the *signore* has recently triumphed over Arezzo, who rashly employed gunnes which were . . . er, ineffective and therefore not of value in his eyes.'

'Gunnes? An odd word to call them. I name them *cannones*, as being hollow tubes. *Cannula* – Latin of course . . .' He trailed off at Jared's look.

'Tell me, where did you get the idea for these . . . *cannones*?'

'It was not my idea, but my friend Marco of Florence. He's new returned from Constantinople and—'

'How interesting!' Jared enthused. 'I'd like to meet him. I've some small experience with, um, *cannone*-powder, which I'm sure he'd like to hear.'

'Well . . . he's very shy, he's worried some may take against his work. But I'll ask him.'

It was working out. Soon he'd be with others who'd ventured down his path. But what then? Were they rivals or fellow discoverers, or were they all dreamers and visionaries of some lost cause?

Marco turned out to be a mousey young man who could not stop fiddling. During supper at Farnese's modest house he warmed to Jared and told of what he knew: a trading voyage in the Black Sea; Sinope on the southern shores – the Seljuq Turks arrayed against the Trebizond empire; pillars of flame and smoke traced to projectors hurling objects against the city; the secret of *huo yao,* however, not granted him. Then he was shown writings by the great English scholar Roger Bacon and found enlightenment.

Jared poured more wine for Marco and asked mildly, 'Your powder is weak, lacking spirit. What is your mixture?'

Unbelievably it seemed the good friar had laid down five parts each of sulphur and charcoal but only seven of saltpetre. Did the scholar really not know his gunne-powder . . . or was he trying to distract and decoy to prevent its spread?

Jared knew he was at a crossroads. Should he join Farnese or Marco or walk away and leave them to it, but take their idea of the *cannone* and go on to make his own, superior, weapon?

But these two were hopeful dreamers, compared to his experiences, callow and unworldly. They'd been open with him, why not with others – the secret would soon be known far and wide and all would be the loser.

There was another way, he realised, one which could well prove both secure and profitable to them all – a guild. To be effective it must extend beyond a single city, perhaps over lands and seas. Like the guild of blacksmiths it would preserve trade secrets, regulate prices, act as a fraternity of equals and have the strength of many.

Jared's brow furled deeply in concentration. Yes, this was what must be done. Here and now!

At his serious expression Marco and Farnese looked at him in concern but a broad smile soon surfaced.

'My friends! I think I should tell you the real reason I'm here.'

The first thing was to establish credentials.

While Marco had been a casual observer he himself had actually been in battle alongside the mysterious Cathayans and had learnt the secret at source. He could demonstrate to them a gunne-powder many times the power, and would in due course.

He was skilled at the military arts having worked with the knights at Acre and with the Mongols and knew both. He could therefore talk with military lords on their own terms.

Therefore he was one to be trusted when he said the time was ripe to bring the art of gunnes to fruition.

It was like talking to children to explain that if they gave away their secrets, would not their rivals steal their bread? And if inferior craftwork, however well intentioned, was what was seen by those who would take up their handiwork, this would rebound on each and all.

Much better that they keep together in the same way all artisans did, in a proper guild with rules and protection covering them all.

The two sat open-mouthed then gave their vigorous agreement.

'There will be much to decide on,' Jared cautioned. 'And we must swear to keep it and our work privily from the world for now.'

CHAPTER 83

They met again, this time with another, Streuvel of Münster. Brought in by Farnese, he was a quiet, respectful man who'd shown an interest in what he'd been doing.

With all feeling confident to talk, the ideas came. It was exhilarating.

A chest was to be kept, not merely for those fallen on hard times but so that if a new idea came from a member there would be funds available to try it for the benefit of all. Communications and meetings would be between all chapters of the guild such that successful discoveries and inventions could be passed on. And flowing from that, a system of the sharing of profit if one member assisted another to fulfil a big order.

It was taking shape, and they met again the next night.

This time it was the guild itself – to be a clandestine fellowship of the mysteries of fire and iron, with all proper oaths and ceremonies, feast days and signs.

And to be known provisionally as 'The Guild of Master Gunners' with a prime warden wearing a chain of office at a central lodge in a city, to be elected.

On the third night the main point of discussion was whether a list of names and terms be drawn up to bring into line everybody's notion of what their fire-breathing devices were to be known as, the parts thereof and what to call their operators.

The quiet Streuvel held up his hand to be heard. 'It is a fine thing, it must be declared,' he said in his broken Italian. 'But I ask, where is the money at the back of this? A guild asks a hall at least, I'm thinking.'

Jared was vaguely aware that if this was to be a main regulating and organising centre it would need to have clerks and officers to run it and no doubt there would be other expenses. Until there was some sort of revenue flowing they simply could not have it. But without it they couldn't make the guild work.

It was a reality that he had to deal with and his spirits fell. It was not enough to have these soaring dreams – a good sound practical head better than his was needed to bring it all down to earth and devise ways and means to make it work.

He flinched at the thought of approaching Rosamunde. She had lost an unimaginable sum by trusting him and he couldn't go back to her with another foolhardy scheme.

A rush of warmth came as he remembered her standing cool and poised as he left, wishing him well of his venture. Did she mean anything more when she gave him the ring? No, of course not. She was a great lady. Jared dismissed the notion – but the warmth remained.

What wouldn't he give to have her here, next to him, now . . . She would know what to do. He felt the wish sharpen to a need – a strong desire to see her, to have her by his side, hand in hand as they faced things together and . . . and . . .

He coldly buried the thought. This was no time for fantasy. He was now next to penniless and needed to make something of his life. He was over forty now, and his blacksmith's strength would not last indefinitely.

Therefore he had to make the guild happen.

And like a betraying temptress his mind led him directly back to Rosamunde. She was the only hope of raising an investment, and he trusted her in whatever arrangement or conditions she might demand – if in fact she still believed in him. There was no other course left than to put his fate in her hands.

CHAPTER 84

Coventry, England, AD 1318

The cold, windswept rain of the city was as unlike the sunny uplands of Italy as it was possible to find. The streets, so much the same, so subtly different, the careless filth of the lower quarters, the English placidity of the more spacious merchant quarter, the folk scurrying heads down in the rain cursing in his native tongue – and then at the corner of Whitefriars the storeyed house he'd turned to after leaving Hurnwych so long ago.

With a lurch of the heart Jared rattled the door-knocker. A servant he didn't know asked his business.

'To see Mistress Barnwell upon an affair of funds.'

Jared waited apprehensively, dripping water on the floor, wondering what he'd do if Rosamunde refused to see him.

A door opened – not the one at the top of the stairs but at the compting room to his left and he was caught off guard.

It was Rosamunde. She looked at him as if he was a ghost. Jared took off his rain-sodden cap and held it but before he could say anything she gave a muffled cry and ran up the stairs weeping.

The servant looked at him in astonishment.

Hesitating for a moment, Jared went up the well-known staircase and found her by the fire, her face averted.

'I'm returned, mistress. To tell you—'

'I'd heard you were dead,' she said in a high, strained voice.

'Dead? Oh, well no, as you see I'm not—'

She turned about abruptly, the sparkle of tears staining her face, her expression unreadable. Then she flew to him and threw her arms about his neck and sobbed – just once, her womanly essence enveloping him before she pulled away and drew herself up to face him. 'I'm . . . I'm happy to see you alive, Master Jared, that you must believe.'

Shaken by her display of emotion he said carefully, 'Thank you, mistress. I thought you'd not wish to see me after . . .'

'Yes, you cost me dear.' Once more cool and practical, she smoothed her gown. 'And I shall desire a report of it from you at supper but in the meantime we must find you dry raiment.'

The food was satisfyingly English and he fell to, for he hadn't been able to afford the comforts of travel.

Rosamunde was reserved but attentive.

'I'm so sorry you lost your money,' Jared said awkwardly.

'Don't be,' she said flatly.

'I thank you—'

'A merchant hazards his pelf according to his judgement, upon the principle "If nothing is ventured, nothing may be gained." Therefore it is entirely at my own determination whether it be considered a regret or a commercial loss.'

'Do you say, then, that it is a regret or . . . ?' he dared.

'My judgement stands. Given all you have told me, I was not wrong in the investing. Things turned out against me – us. That is all.'

It was now or never. 'Rosamunde. If you had the chance once more but under different circumstances, would you invest again?'

'Every opportunity is taken on its own qualities,' she answered coolly. 'I thus cannot answer that.'

He hesitated; not at what he must say next, but the realisation that setting aside the cold tenacity of her business imperatives, she had a beauty – an aura, a nobility, that he'd never seen in a woman before and it was affecting him as a man.

'Well . . . um, could I ask your advice in a matter of investing?'

She quickly had it out of him – the vision, the reality, the risks.

'And you are expecting me to chance my fortune in a trade guild of four persons that stands against the world as it is?'

'Not as if it were like that,' he said uncomfortably. 'Your advice and direction would be gratefully followed, I'm sure.'

'Yes. Well, I shall think on this.'

'You will consider a small investment?'

'You shall have my answer only when I'm ready. Shall we take more wine and talk further?'

The servants cleared the table as they sat each side of the fire. Rosamunde asked many questions – his life, his opinions and tastes. Her clear-eyed gaze was one of appraisal and evaluation. Jared had expected to talk more about the guild and this was unnerving.

The questions tailed off and she looked away.

A servant came to refresh their goblets but was dismissed for the night.

Rosamunde said nothing until he'd left and closed the door, then looked at Jared and said simply, 'I have decided.'

'What did you decide, mistress?'

'I'm a good judge of character and a better judge of men. I'm resolved that I will invest.'

In a gust of relief Jared blurted, 'I won't let you down, mistress! I'll—'

'With only one, but strict condition.'

'Anything!'

'You may not like it, Master Jared.'

'I shall,' he replied stoutly.

'If you agree it, then my entire fortune is yours.'

'Your . . . ?'

'You must marry me.'

He stared at her in shock, thinking he'd misheard. 'I thought you said . . .'

'If this is not to your liking you will tell me now.'

'I-I—'

She held out a hand, which he had the wit to kneel and kiss.

'So it is not altogether distasteful to you?'

He shook his head in helpless wonder. 'Mistress—that is, Rosamunde. If you're jesting I find it not worthy of you, but if true then . . .'

'May I take that as signifying agreement?'

He pulled himself together. 'You've taught me much. And one thing is to search out the reasons for an offer of trade – what, then, are yours? I'm a simple blacksmith of no family and you . . .'

'The chief reason? I will tell you truly. It is that I no longer want to go to a cold bed. The next? As I told you before, I'm a judge of men and by your actions you show yourself as a true man, tempered by trials that would daunt a lesser. And if truth must be revealed, your calling has shaped you as a man as strong and comely as any woman might desire. If I'm to be wed, let it be one like you, Jared!'

Tears prickled: she reached for him and they kissed. Softly and tenderly.

CHAPTER 85

'Really, Edward, you're making complications,' Rosamunde said crossly to the lawyer. 'I know the law as well as you. I may choose whomever I will to wed and the world must watch.'

'It is the House of Barnwell that is my concern,' he went on carefully. 'As it pertains to the conveying of all goods and chattels to the new husband, which must include your mercantile interests, I'm obliged to remind you.'

'If that is all that ails you, Edward, let me put your mind at rest. Master Jared has interests of his own and desires I might continue in my merchantry as before. If any funds are touched they are accounted for in the usual way and there is no question that there will be any disturbance in the standing of the House.'

'I see you are determined on this union.'

'I am.'

'Then I can only wish you well of it,' he said, with a barely concealed expression of reproach.

'Sir, your manner is distasteful to me,' she flared. 'You're a servant of the House and I am its mistress!

'For all your laws and deeds you cannot see that which is so plain to any merchant of wit and acumen. That is, the fortune of a House is one thing, and the getting of it another. If you fear that Master Jared will rule and ruin, know that between tradesfolk it is one's word that wins the dealing, not the price. Neither he nor any will make trade save I give my word on it.'

Later, as she and Jared ate together she mentioned the conversation and added, 'Our marrying is one thing – the other is to bring you to the notice of the men of power and substance. Then you must act the man of acuity and sagacity – but on your own. For this you will need to take in our ways in full measure.'

'Sweeting, I am your pupil and will learn at your knee.'

It was hard to grasp even now that his days at a forge were over for good. It was not brawn and skill that would realise his vision but quick wit and precise judgement and Rosamunde would be his teacher. He was determined on it, for he was going to venture out into a harsh world armed only with his wits to justify her trust.

The shape of the future was becoming clearer. He would go back with all the powers and resources of a merchant investor, sustained by the intricate web of agents and factors of the House of Barnwell, and set about making the guild grow.

And one thing was vital to his standing and success: a second, one who he could not only confide in but trust in the hardest situations.

He knew one he could turn to. Daw. He'd be in his twenties now and in the strained times he'd known him had proved bright and steady.

Jared spent a long time pondering the wording of a letter, ending up with a simple desire to see him and enclosing travelling expenses. His son had known him as a returned pilgrim touched by his experiences and indulging in deranged pursuits. Would he want to come to his father – or be repelled?

Within the week Daw was shyly standing at the door of the Barnwell home with his bundle, looking up in wonder at the richly dressed burgher who was his father.

'Daw! Bless you for coming, my son.' With a manly hug and a squeezed tear Jared drew him indoors.

'Father – w-what's this that you're so . . . ?'

He'd grown taller. A direct gaze, upright and strong, a son to be proud of.

'A long tale, Daw. As will wait. This is my home now and I want you to meet . . . my wife, your stepmother.'

Rosamunde came forward with a smile and extended a hand.

Jared tenderly touched her shoulder. 'Do forgive us, my dear, we've much to talk on.'

She left them to the two chairs by the fireside.

'Daw . . . I . . .' Where even to begin?

'A long time ago, when you were but a kitling a . . . bad thing happened.' It was not going well – this was a grown man, he could take it.

'Your mother . . .' He couldn't go on.

'Yes, Father. She drowned one night in the weir. I know this.'

'No!' he blurted hoarsely. 'Never so! Aldith was torn from me by those half-faced hell-spawn in Ravenstock Castle and done to death by . . . by . . .'

Daw went pale. 'She was taken and—'

'Yes, yes, *yes!*'

It was cruel, heartless – but the truth had passed into his son's soul.

Daw's shoulders began shaking, he looked helplessly this way and that – but no tears came . . .

'I told you this because I want you to understand me,' Jared whispered.

The eyes looked up at him, pits of misery.

'I can tell you from the heart, dear Daw, that revenge is useless, empty, because nothing is changed by it.'

At the intensity of his words the young man choked, 'You . . . D'Amory?'

Jared's head fell. 'Yes, son.'

Daw sat rigid, silently weeping.

'I told you revenge is empty because it changes nothing. This is true. So I went on pilgrimage to find release but instead found quite another thing.'

He waited patiently for Daw to compose himself then went on, 'I ask this of you. What must you feel, if gifted to you and you alone, was a great power, one that can and will change things for all of time?'

At the incomprehension he eased into a bleak smile. 'I'm speaking of the power to tear down castles into ruin and helplessness. That throws lords and ladies, every one, down to the level of the common folk, never more to tyrannise and oppress from their mighty fortress on high!'

'Father. This is wild talk! I do understand your—'

'Daw. I was given that power and you shall soon see this in all its terror and beauty. I came upon it when enslaved by the Mongols who had the secret, and have never forgotten how to summon it to my bidding. Now I've succeeded, here in England. In my own hands I have the means to bring down castles and cities – and I mean to do it! My son, this is not revenge but justice!' he breathed.

The wide-eyed youth sat rigid, speechless.

Jared sat back and went on in quite another tone, 'All this you will find hard to believe. But if I tell you that a guild is being formed for just this purpose and that Mistress Rosamunde, wise and astute, is hazarding her fortune to support it, can you find it in you to accept that it is both real and true?'

'Father, I hear what you're saying but cannot conceive what you mean.'

For the next hour Jared told him all, his voice breaking at times in emotion. He spoke of gunnes and *huo yao*, sulphur and saltpetre, iron and bronze. Of the months in Hurnwych grubbing about in chicken coops and tombs seeking answers and finding none at the cost of his wits and reputation. The chance discovery in Coventry of the method of proportions, and then success.

'Now you know of it. The whole of it. And what lies ahead – a chance for putting right the world such as none has had before! Daw, what I'm asking is that you're there by my side when it's achieved. To be the one who I trust and confide in, whoever's against us. Will you do it?'

CHAPTER 86

Ghent, Flanders, AD 1320

'I welcome you all, each and every one,' Jared said warmly, looking about the table. 'Some have travelled far, and I honour you for it.'

Here were Marco of Florence, Bartolomeo Farnese of Padua, Streuvel of Münster – and they had come to Ghent to found a guild that each believed would change their fortunes and their lives.

The room was not large but was well appointed – it was the meeting hall of the House of Barnwell in this great trading capital, well chosen for its proximity both to the rich lands of northern Europe and the rising Hansa ports of the Holy Roman Empire.

And above him was the prime symbol of the guild: a giant blue lightning bolt from the heavens stabbing down to demolish a red castle, the whole surmounted by an angel with a trumpet.

'I first desire to introduce the lady Barnwell – who is my wife,' Jared said proudly. On his elevation to the ranks of the merchantry he'd taken the name of his cousin as his in addition to his village name and was now known to all as Master Jared Barnwell of Coventry.

'My lady.' There were wary acknowledgements as they recognised the one who was making it all possible.

She addressed them respectfully. 'Good gentlemen, I bid you

welcome also but know that it will be my husband who will lead your meeting. My position here is honorary and that of advisor only. I wish that you will conduct your affairs in whatsoever manner you see fit.'

There was the tiniest pause and then she said firmly, 'Knowing that should the structure and soundness of your guild be found wanting, the House of Barnwell would find it difficult to increase the scale of its funding.'

He and Rosamunde had worked hard together, drawing up a plan of action and he now presented it as a working outline under five main headings.

The purpose of the guild:

In large, to gather strength from working together instead of separately. To regulate the quality of workmanship and services. To offer mutual support where needed. To share ideas and resources to the benefit of all.

Its conduct:

No single authority, but as independent enterprises each in its area, attracting interest and commerce to its own self, calling on others if large orders lay in peril of being unfulfilled. To provide gunnes, powder and, if requested, trained men.

The structure:

A Grand Hall to co-ordinate, and others located in convenient lands and trading cities in constant communication.

Organisation:

Each hall to govern its own but all on the same basis.

At the top, the order of Master, one holding to himself all the mysteries of the guild, the secret of gunne-powder, the knowledge of gunne-making, the constantly renewed wisdom regularly exchanged with other Masters.

Under them, the order of Yeoman Gunner, he who knew as an adept the craft and skills of the gunne and who could take charge of a hired troop of gunnes. And below him the Gunner whose prowess it was in the firing and serving.

Only a Master could bestow the degree of Yeoman Gunner to deserving initiates and only they to bring forward Gunners.

Probity and fidelity to the guild:

All guild members to be sworn in loyalty to it and their brethren. To swear never to divulge its secrets and mysteries. To unfailingly come to the aid of brothers in distress. To be bound by the decisions of the Grand Hall in matters of dispute or conduct.

'And the whole to be named and styled – "The Worshipful Company of Saint Barbara",' Jared concluded.

'Why so?' Farnese wanted to know. 'Why not "The Guild of Master Gunners"?'

Rosamunde smiled sweetly. 'You know that you will have many adversaries, those who would see you as threatening and evil. It were better to trade under such a name, keeping your business discreet always and making your approach quiet and confiding.'

'Saint Barbara?'

'A lady who was cruelly martyred and took revenge on her wrongdoers with a heaven-sent thunderbolt.'

There were additional matters to consider: the searching out and inducting of new members, the establishing of a feast day, the design of a secret emblem and other such.

However, as evening was drawing in, general agreement had been reached in the meeting and Jared Barnwell of Coventry was elected as first Grand Master and the chain of office was laid upon him.

Led by his lady he entered a darkened chamber, a lone candle throwing into relief a richly worked reliquary on a small table.

'Kneel, sire.'

He did so, and laid both hands on the casket.

'You will make oath on a saint's bones. Repeat after me . . .'

It was the swearing, and at its end the dread words, 'And if I transgress my sworn oath in any kind may Saint Barbara visit on me the same fate by her hands . . .'

One by one the others were led in to take the oath. At the last Jared saw a shadow at the door.

'Father. I would be sworn . . .'

CHAPTER 87

'Farewell, Grand Master,' Farnese said slowly. 'You have taught us well.'

To Jared's embarrassment he insisted on kneeling and kissing his ring.

'Go forth, Brother Bartolomeo, and may good fortune always attend you.'

The members of the guild had spent much time together working out how they might best proceed. Jared had imparted his discovery of the true proportions of gunne-powder and Farnese had taken them all to a bell foundry and pointed out the limitations of bronze casting as well as its opportunities. Others had contributed their knowledge and experience and now they were ready to go out into the world.

Streuvel recruited three Hollanders who had been venturing with what they called 'fire-lances' and were astonished and gratified to now be part of a greater brethren. They were quickly followed by two from Cividale sent by Marco, young men of enterprise who had heard of the mystifying thunder devices fielded by Arezzo and had guessed their nature.

They were heady times for Jared. For every man that was

emerging to join them there must be many more – and it was only the beginning!

At the same time he had to make a start on his own business. There was a prospective interest that suggested itself in Ghent – the Great Portal and miles of walls that needed defending – and what better than the fearsome roar of gunnes to keep attackers at bay? It was a rich city that could well afford such and would be a good thing for the guild to point to.

It needed much planning.

With casting he had more freedom in designing the gunne but there were practical limits. He needed to find a bell-founder to make them and secure a place of testing.

He decided to start with the size of 'pea' and the measure of the gunne would then suggest itself. If it were an 'orange' that would imply a size of near six feet long on the basis of the *cannones* he'd seen.

Fortunately there were six bell foundries in Ghent.

Finding a testing place proved troublesome until he hit on the idea of taking an island in the miles-wide Scheldt estuary. This was directly connected to Ghent by the Leie River, which allowed merchant shipping to enter the city itself and what better highway to move the gunnes?

Low-lying, marshy and uninhabited it didn't even have a name. It was perfect for the job and Jared set up a workshop and began, leaving Daw in the city with Rosamunde handling correspondence.

With Farnese's requirements listed down he was able to give the Stoverij bell foundry a workmanlike parchment of a device and the bell-metal ratio of copper to tin more for strength in place of musical tone.

It was a curious order for the foundry but the promise of further work ensured discretion and speed.

Working up sufficient quantities of gunne-powder was next. He had the charcoal and knew now where the best sulphur was to be had but saltpetre?

Rosamunde's business network gave the answer: there was a small but reliable trade in preservative saltpetre already in existence deriving from the rich deposits along the Syrian camel caravan routes. It would need building up, and when the material arrived a further purification and refining would be required. But now at last he had a secure source.

CHAPTER 88

'Daw. It's time you were blooded. Our island is ready – you shall hear the gunnes speak!'

It was gratifying to see his son overcome his fears to revel in the fearsome thunder of the beasts as he saw with his own eyes what his father was achieving.

Jared's cast design was performing well with a hen's egg 'pea' and a five-foot length. The further scaling up could wait – he had a saleable device and needed to attend to the revenue.

But if no other city had gunnes why should Ghent be singled out? And what were they anyway?

Only a field demonstration began to change minds among the worthies of the council. The crash of three gunnes firing together, the sulphurous smoke and the demolishing of a ruined hut concentrated minds. Jared knew that the independence of their city from the French forces of Robert of Artois had been bought at great cost in lives only several years previously and with the fear that they could return at any time, what better than to provide an unpleasant and unexpected welcome?

It resulted in an order for gunnes for the city walls – but the miserly burghers stopped at four, claiming that they wanted to see them in action in battle before any more were considered. No amount of arguing could get them to see that if the French attacked just four were not going to save them.

Still, it was income.

What was needed was a clash at arms where before all the world gunnes would save the day – but how could they, in such small numbers that were being placed?

Over the months Jared heard the same story from other halls. Disbelief, reluctance to commit, cautious orders.

At the first anniversary of the guild there was much promise but little pay-off reported and at the round-table meeting it was conceded that there had to be one particular big step forward before gunnes could take their rightful place in war.

Unless the clumsy gunnes could be brought to where they were needed quickly they could never play a crucial part. And in the event that a retreat was ordered, the pieces had to be specifically defended or abandoned to the enemy. There was no easy answer and Jared wrestled with the problem.

Rosamunde was not dismayed and stood by Jared, keeping the Barnwell main commercial interests safe.

Jared's mind kept straying back to the same alluring prize: if a true wall-smasher finally made the light of day, warfare would be changed for ever.

As he travelled about on the business of the guild the thought stayed with him. It was not out of reach – he could see the path forward but it was going to be a long and expensive journey.

The snows of winter had only recently retreated when a visitor called.

The man introduced himself with a sweeping bow. 'Peter

van Vullaere of Bruges. Do I find myself addressing the Grand Master, perchance?'

A jovial, confident fellow but with an air of shrewd worldliness, he was dressed in a considerably superior manner to most of the members of the guild.

'You do. Jared Barnwell of Coventry.'

'Then I dare to say we have business together. I've a friend in Bruges, thought I'd be interested in a curiosity. A gunne – a devilish contrivance that attracted me greatly. I've a mind to go further with it.'

'In the commercial line?'

'Indeed. Yet I observe that this gunne has a fatal flaw – it is too heavy and lumpish for its purpose. Master Jared, I have an idea that's set fair to answer this, but I've not the mechanicals to make it. *Mijnheer* Streuvel urges me to seek your guidance. Do you . . . ?'

Instantly alert, Jared answered evenly, 'I'm sure we can assist. Tell me, this idea of yours to—'

'Yes, well, shall we to details? You have the craft, I have the idea. How do you think we might proceed?'

'The Worshipful Company of St Barbara desires nothing greater than that the gunne does take its just position as king of the battlefield. You have our every aid and encouragement . . . but I'm thinking it were better from within the fellowship of our guild.'

Jared detailed the advantages: mutual exchange of wisdom and ideas to accelerate development, collective support and above all the preservation of the mysteries to maintain quality and pricing.

He had van Vullaere's undivided attention.

'Should you desire to enter upon the guild then there's commercial advantage aplenty.' He went on to detail the value of the guild in providing gunne foundry services, the hire of ready-trained gunners and, if needed, an extra supply of gunne-powder.

There was a definite quickening of interest but Jared judged it better not to show too eager and left it to Rosamunde to lay out the details.

She came back well satisfied. Peter was known to her through reputation, a well-respected wine merchant who quite saw the merit of standing together to develop the market. He was willing to abide by the precepts and statutes of the guild and stood ready to be initiated. What was more, he had an immediate compelling prospect that in due course he would divulge.

Peter's idea turned out to be simple enough but had impressive possibilities.

It seemed the armies of the Low Countries used a fiendish device to make up for their lack of numbers. It consisted of a wide platform with wheels to the side and with an upright shield in the front with ports for archers.

Its employment was for one cruel purpose. Fixed immovably along the broad front of the vehicle was every kind of blade, from spear to halberd, pike to spontoon, protruding in a lethal hedge of steel. At the rear of the device was a trailing pole, and in the shelter of the shield soldiers would lift and launch the vehicle forward and ram it bodily at speed into the crowded ranks of the enemy, skewering a dozen or more at a time, before drawing it back for another mass killing.

Peter's plan was to mount a gunne behind the shield where it would be protected but more to the point, the wheeled platform would give full and instant mobility for rapid deploying.

'Brother, your idea is masterly!' Jared told him. 'I've a mind to assist you myself. What's the name of this engine at all?'

'Name? Oh, most soldiers would call it a ribaudequin.'

One was acquired and in the privacy of the island workshop Jared inspected it carefully. There was no doubt that it could be done – the gunne block would be made fast to the platform and the gunners need not fear arrow or bolt while they plied their weapon when wheeled close to the foe.

Yet there was a disadvantage. A single gunne with its slow rate of fire was not going to terrify the enemy indefinitely. What was needed were several that could be deployed alternately, keeping up a dismayingly unpredictable succession of firings.

More gunnes? This would make for a heavy, unwieldy apparatus taking away its chief advantage.

'Make 'em smaller?' Peter suggested doubtfully.

It was one way, and would have the advantage of increasing the firepower and therefore terror value. What if it were taken to extremes, say a gunne with a 'pea' the size of a grape or less? It would be much smaller, lighter and more could be mounted. This was a battlefield weapon!

The design of the gunne suggested itself: one not a long way from his first attempts, but taking advantage of bronze casting. From one mould would be made dozens of identical weapons, pointing to a mounting of anything up to four or six on one ribaudequin. Several of these would make for almost a continual fire and it would be a fearless opponent who could withstand this for hours – and the mercenary armies he'd seen were far from this.

CHAPTER 89

The first piece arrived from the foundry and was tested.

Used to the slam of sound from a full-sized gunne the harsh cracks of the smaller were disappointing to Jared's ears. The lead ball carried for several hundred yards but had lost its force over a hundred, but this was not the point: a movable focus of terror was what was being provided.

Assembling more pieces had shown serious problems, however.

When they were side by side it was found out of the question to load one while the other was firing. This was overcome by mounting all six gunnes in a frame and treating them as one – loading separately then firing together, in a single hideous volley of death.

The other complication was that because loading was from the mouth of the gunne, the gunners exposed themselves while readying. The answer to this was a hinged shield placed a pace or two in front, dropped only when the gunnes fired.

By trial and error it was found that not just six but as many as a round dozen gunnes clamped together could be serviced in one ribaudequin. With trivial improvements this was what they were going with!

'You mentioned a prospect?' Jared asked Peter as they prepared the accounting for their making.

'Robert, Count of Nevers.'

He looked for a start of recognition but seeing none, sniffed and added, 'As you English know nothing of what's happening outside your precious island, he we call "The Lion of Flanders", for we must lay our independence as Flemings at his feet. Tireless to defend us against the French, who desire nothing better than to possess our lands for its wealth and trading position, he'd lust after any means to add teeth to our army.'

It was but a day's barge journey for a demonstration ribaudequin to round the coast to Zeebrugge, the Hansa trading port for Bruges. In a few days more they were outside the frowning red-brick towers of the residence of Count Robert.

'This is what you're showing me, for all your noise?' The heavy-faced and unsmiling nobleman said, circling the ribaudequin with a sceptical leer, an ungainly low wagon with twelve pipes laid side by side and not much else.

'I beg you may allow us to show you its spite,' Peter said with a bow.

He signalled to the waiting assistants who raced away to stretch a line between two posts. A score of cattle hides, still bloody from the shambles, were quickly hung up.

'These are the enemy, sire, who dare to oppose you,' Peter explained, drawing the count away from the ribaudequin, 'For which they will pay dearly – upon your order.'

Robert looked at the ribaudequin and then grunted, 'So? Do what you must.'

Peter raised his hand. Six men, newly trained, grasped the trail pole and rapidly wheeled it into place, taking position behind it. The yeoman gunner snatched a hot wire from the brazier and leaping up behind the gunnes, waited for the signal.

The hand dropped. In a single movement to the connected powder train he touched them off as one.

It was cataclysmic – the synchronised crash of a dozen gunnes through lightning flash and smoke, an appalling shock that stunned the senses.

And when eyes turned to the hides there was no more doubt. Over half of them now bore gaping rents and tears, silent witness to the beast's ferocity.

CHAPTER 90

Diksmuide, the Netherlands, AD 1321

The long line of Flemish soldiers wound ahead on the ruler-flat land, the dour figure of Count Robert riding in the van, his coat-of-arms of sable lion rampant on a yellow shield visible to all. Their destination was Diksmuide, where Baron Courcy had brazenly led his Burgundians in an ambitious attempt against the heartland of Flanders.

There were six ribaudequins in his train with their support carts, the gunners marching alongside. And with them were Peter van Vullaere and Jared Barnwell, riding together.

The French were waiting for them: a spreading line in the distance; the pennon-topped tents of their camp just visible behind them; standards, colours and the jagged glitter of weapons in the forefront.

Jared was by now a fair judge of military affairs and saw that while it would be a clash of some thousands it would by no means be on the scale of some he'd seen.

The Flemings were nearly all foot soldiers, a mix of stolid Hollanders and German mercenaries with few knights or men-at-arms a-horse. The enemy seemed to be composed similarly and their massing promised an evenly matched pitched battle of the bloodiest sort.

The Lion of Flanders and his men marched forward with determination and spirit. Count Robert was an astute warrior and had prevailed again and again against some of the best the French had thrown at him.

A mile clear he halted. The French were the invaders, they could come to him.

One close-packed horde ranged against another. Pikes, swords, war-hammers, maces, daggers. There was little point in manoeuvring in the din of battle and all would be decided by deadly hackery, man on man until one or the other broke or made a heroic last stand.

Robert's position was risky. Spread thin, five separate blocks of pikemen faced out, each heading a larger force of foot soldiers. The front facing the enemy, therefore, was broader than they but at the same time invited the French to punch through their centre – but was that what Robert wanted? Allow the enemy to pierce the line and then enfold them from the flanks?

The gunners were summoned and all became clear.

With a massed beating of drums and a bloodthirsty roar the French began their advance but there would be no concentrating to a central thrust – the baron was going for a crude bludgeoning frontal attack.

The Lion of Flanders did not flinch, patiently waiting for the host to draw near, his plans well laid.

Then he struck. From the rear and between the blocks to the front poured every archer he possessed. And with the bowmen were the gunners, wheeling their engines of war to where they would play their part, at an angle to the enemy flanks.

The archers loosed off three volleys and the enemy advance halted to face the hail. The bowmen retired and the ribaudequins were brought forward.

Both sides seemed to hold their breath at this audacity – until the gunnes spoke.

Diabolical lightning and thunder were called down and invisible death struck deep into the French ranks. In terror they turned to flee but were held to a crush by those behind.

The archers returned to the slaughter followed by a second ribaudequin to each side.

It was merciless. Not only was there maiming and killing by plunging arrows and unseen death-dealing missiles, but as dread and panic seized them, instinctively the soldiers fell back and the crowded ranks were wedged into a tight, immovable press. It grew worse, the rear not seeing what was happening, shoving forward and making the inner a living hell of heaving, desperate bodies, helpless, suffocating, dying.

Exactly what Count Robert had intended.

The third ribaudequin came up and delivered yet another savage onslaught into the struggling mass. Now there was blind panic as the outer ranks turned in to escape the appalling punishment and one which they could not fight against: the end could not be far off.

As if in grieving for the misery and slaughter taking place on the earth beneath, the grey heavens wept – a gentle, sad light rain. It sharpened the colours of steel and heraldry and thinned the runnels of blood in a forlorn endeavour at cleansing away the brutality of man.

And it nearly ended the battle.

Recharged, the first ribaudequin was propelled to the fore and the yeoman gunner raised his red-hot wire and fired the weapon.

One gunne alone cracked out viciously – the others varied from a fizzing pop and gouts of evil-smelling smoke to a tired sparking or nothing at all.

The ribaudequin was rapidly withdrawn and Jared hurried over to see what had happened.

It was the powder; even the smallest hint of damp it seemed killed its ardour. This was calamitous: and if gunnes must retire at the first sprinkling on the field of battle . . .

Jared felt all eyes on him as he tried to think.

The gunnes must be sheltered while they were charged ready, but as soon as they were exposed to fire they would be silenced by the rain.

Meanwhile the drawn-back ribaudequin had to be readied. Gunnes half-fired had to be cleaned of their coarse fouling – and worse, the unfired ones awkwardly emptied of their contents.

It was deadly work and at the third gunne the inevitable happened – a sudden flash and smoke and the gunner was looking in dazed shock at the stump of his right hand.

A second ribaudequin was brought up. This time there was no firing at all.

A messenger from the count rode up, demanding to know why the gunnes were not serving out death at this critical stage of the battle. Distracted, Jared mumbled something about a temporary resting but it was clear they were in deep trouble.

All six ribaudequins were now silent and the enemy had taken notice of this, regrouping and facing the dread engines, plainly of a mind to wreak a terrible vengeance.

The rain shower petered out, leaving the ground wet and slippery but this came too late: it had done its worst. All powder was now suspect, for every barrel in the supply carts had been opened to feed the gunnes. It was nothing less than a complete routing.

Distant shouts turned into an impetuous clamour. The French were on the move again.

A weak sun began to appear – did they stand or flee?

Unlike at Arezzo, these gunnes could be moved and Jared had every man available clapping on to the trail poles and heaving the sorry contrivances, slipping and sliding back through the blocks of Flemish soldiers who jeered and cursed them – and past a furious Lion of Flanders.

The archers were sent out to delay the inevitable, the bowmen hooting and mocking as they passed.

Every barrel of powder was ruined but there was a chance. In one of the supply carts Jared had had the foresight to put aside sealed pots containing the elements that would be mixed together to yield more gunne-powder should the battle have spilt over into the next day.

He worked like a madman at the mortar and pestle. All it needed was enough to charge say, three gunnes apiece on each ribaudequin.

The first was made ready and launched at a trot through the ranks again and positioned.

At the sight of it the enemy's forward impetus slowed and quietened.

The ribaudequin remained silent. And by degrees the advance turned into an uneasy milling – then the gunnes cracked out viciously, finding an easy mark in the tight-packed host. Another was hastened up on the other flank and the punishment resumed.

It couldn't last.

Baron Courcy sent in his knights against the gunnes. In a massed thunder of hooves they burst out around the trapped mass in a heroic martial display, lunging straight for the gunnes.

Jared knew it would be nothing less than butchery at the exposed ribaudequins but he had one last card to play.

Every one of them, full-charged or no, was turned to face their galloping nemesis and touched off together.

As he'd dared hope the flash and blast of the gunnes was too much for the horses. They swerved and skidded to a halt, rearing up in fright. Their riders were sent crashing to the ground and the animals fled in terror.

It was more or less a stalemate.

Then, as if by common consent, the two opponents drew back slowly, leaving the field to no man.

Peter was well satisfied with his ribaudequins and from his own pocket rewarded the gunners, but Count Robert was less enthusiastic. True, the gunnes had done their work: the trapping of men in a lethal crushing, but in his view the cost of it all was exorbitant and much the same would have been achieved by outlaying on more common archers.

He pointed to the scattered bodies – a hundred or more, but coming at such a price . . . It could only be concluded that the main work would as before have to be done in a traditional brutal hand-to-hand melee. As to the shock value of the gunnes firing, in due course soldiers would overcome their fear as they had for every other ghastly battlefield horror.

Still, the count allowed, the gunnes had shown promise.

Jared had his own concerns. In addition to their problems in wet weather, if moved forward to fire, their exposure to counter-attack was a serious flaw, as was the relatively low number of casualties they could inflict. There was no denying that to this point they were unlikely to change the way battles were fought.

This only strengthened his conviction that the future of gunnes was not on the field of battle but in the developing of castle levellers, which in one world-shaking move would turn everything on its head.

CHAPTER 91

First things first: a bronze gunne of the size of any he'd seen was expensive enough but he was going for one very much bigger and that would take a great deal of money.

Rosamunde heard him out. 'It is a risk, this I know – but the prize is great. And if any are to seize it, this must be you, dear Jared. Make your plans.'

'My heart, I shall not cease to bless you!'

Jared lost no time in contacting Farnese.

'Bartolomeo, so good of you to come,' he warmly greeted the man who had shown him the way to break through the limitations of iron forging.

'I've a mind to construct a gunne bigger than any, as will turn a castle's walls to ruin. Do you desire to help me?'

'I do, Grand Master, and that right willingly.'

The challenges, however, were great.

Farnese's earlier *cannone* had been adapted to fire a hen's-egg-sized ball but had been the size of a small pig and many times heavier and he'd put it aside while involved with the ribaudequins. If this new gunne was to throw a 'pea' the span of, say, a turnip then it would have to be not twice but many times the size.

The cost in bronze would be fearful. Just the tin, rare and only found in far places, to blend with eight times its weight in pure copper to give a total probably several times that of a man, was going to amount to a grave sum. Added to this were the expenses of the foundry, which even with Farnese's guidance would have to find considerable outlay for non-standard tools and workshop gear.

The bell-founders, who had done well out of Peter van Vullaere's ribaudequin gunne casting, were hesitant: this would be the biggest job they'd ever done.

Jared saw their problem. Bell moulds of various shapes and sizes lined the walls of the dusty foundry, none of which was larger than a boy. And everything was established and fitted for the making of bells – inner and outer moulds, mantles and so forth all for the same purpose. To set up for a single special was going to take some persuading.

However, the prospect of a future leading position in the craft of gunne-making decided it – even to the extent of paying half of the costs of a new melting furnace, made necessary by the much greater volume of metal needed. A single pour was critical to ensure a sound casting and this required multiplying the capacity by several times.

Heady with excitement, Jared tried to maintain a serious composure when the gunne was ready to be brought into existence.

The furnace was roaring at full capacity with three sweating men on the bellows. Jared looked down into the casting pit. There was nothing much to see; the gunne mould was set vertically in the ground and the filling orifice was offset to the central bore mould with sand and dust piled around.

'Stand back for your life!' roared the master bell-founder, pointing to the base of the furnace. A foundry hand worked free a tiny door and suddenly a luminous orange-white glow began streaming out and into brick-lined channels that led to the casting pit, pouring into the mould with a passing blast of heat.

It died away to a trickle and then stopped.

Jared waited expectantly. Did fresh-cast bronze gleam forth its newness?

But nothing happened. The workmen left, and the master folded his arms and looked at him with heavy patience.

'Is that all?' Jared said.

'We go now,' Farnese told him, pulling at his arm. 'They can't touch it, it'll take a week or over to cool.'

When the gunne finally emerged it glimmered with a fine sand-rough red-bronze finish and looked as deadly as Jared had hoped. Yet it proved a brute to handle and even with the waterway close by it took all of two days to get it aboard the barge for the island.

Jared approached the testing cautiously. This was passing into the unknown and nothing could be taken for granted.

The size of bore meant that lead balls were not practical; he'd had to find a mason and have spheres of stone laboriously chiselled to the right diameter.

The gunne was mounted on massive timber blocks, sinking them slowly into the soggy ground under its ponderous weight.

Conveniently, at one end of the island was a long deserted monk's retreat, a substantial structure of stone that could stand in for a castle's walls.

A proving shot would be fired first.

Suspecting the effect of the much heavier charge of powder and shot, Jared wound cloth over his ears and sent all his attendants away.

Hesitating only for a moment he touched it off.

The gunne bellowed its rage, rearing off the blocks and toppling down, a great volume of smoke taking minutes to clear. It had been a rounder, deeper sound but on a giant scale, the blast briefly enclosing him and sucking the air from his lungs.

Ears still ringing he went to see the effect.

To his immense satisfaction he saw that he was right – at a flat and direct trajectory the force of the missile was completely expended on the upright wall.

Here the ancient moss-covered grey stones had taken the full force of his turnip-sized 'pea' and a jagged wound with tumbled stone was the result. While a stone ball might be a clumsy thing in itself, he saw that on impact with the wall it had shattered into countless shards. These were wickedly sharp and would shred defenders unfortunate enough to be on the battlements when a ball hit nearby.

It was true that a castle's walls were immensely thicker but he could now show what even a small ball could do when fired from a gunne – what could not be achieved with a great ball?

On the way back his mind bounded with ideas and he was unprepared for the grave and solemn mood about the House of Barnwell.

Rosamunde took him aside. She heard him out then said quietly, 'There is a great matter that has come to pass that bears on your endeavours.'

Jared was chilled at what he heard, not so much that a serious difficulty of some kind had arisen but that she'd used the word 'your' and not 'our' in its connection.

'You must know of it this day and be guided by your conscience.'

Her gaze was direct and grave, with none of the intimacy that had matured between them.

'Then tell me of it, my sweetling,' he said as lightly as he could manage.

It could hardly have been worse. The action at Diksmuide had brought consequences that were catastrophic. The French King had been indignant at the humiliation of Baron de Courcy and had intrigued at Avignon with the Pope, a Frenchman.

In due course a thundering papal denunciation was issued. The Devil-driven evil of gunnes was to be entirely cast out of Christian lands. Any who at the peril of their soul conjured with powder and shot or who employed them as weapons of war faced the wrath of the Church and excommunication – as from this moment they all suffered the same condemnation as sorcerers and magicians.

'We're confounded, Rosamunde. No one will talk to us, take up our gunnes at that risk!'

'I asked you to be guided by your conscience, Jared. Tell me truly if you will be bound by this proclaiming or no.'

'My conscience is clear. I know that gunnes are not the work of the Devil, and so His Holiness must have been given false counsel. I can tell you I will not be so bound.'

She touched his arm. 'That is what I wanted to hear, my dear husband. That you're still staunch in your vision.'

She had given him liberty of conscience and then rejoiced at his decision – she shared his vision!

'Ah, yes. But if we can't go any further without—'

'We go on,' she said flatly. 'With changes. The guild continues, but keeps out of the sight of man. A secret company, but everywhere, closing together for our own surviving in the face of persecution.'

'There are so many who would see us cast into Hell for the menace we show to their ways. How can we—?'

'Not so difficult. The Holy Father in all his wisdom has granted us a boon for which we should be duly grateful.'

Jared blinked in perplexity. 'Boon?'

'Yes. The papal bull has gone out into all the world and any that have not heard of the gunne have now, and are curious at why it is so strongly condemned. They will discover its potency and will desire to have this for themselves.'

'At the cost of their excommunication?'

'Dear Jared, there is still much for you to learn of the ways of commerce. Where there is a desire that can be met, there is a market for the enterprising. This is our opportunity – we offer them a form of owning and possessing that does not offend the scrupulous wording of the bull. Shall we say, for example, that their gunnes remain our property, even though stored within their grounds. Should they be required for a rightful defence against another with gunnes then our agreement shows that we promptly provide powder, ball and gunners as needful.'

'Ha! And who can say in this world that they'll never be assailed by another with gunnes? They'll be under necessity to take precautions . . . but who will speak with us under such penalty?'

'They will. Provided it is done privily, as they can deny it later.'

'Beloved, you are wise and beautiful and I lay my heart before you.'

With the ghost of a smile she went on briskly. 'The ribaudequin is one thing,' she said. 'We need another. Pray, how is your wall-smasher proceeding?'

CHAPTER 92

After the exhilaration of success and the satisfaction of having been proved right, reality set in.

The gunne worked – a larger, monster-sized wall-smasher would bring down the stoutest defences, that much was now proved, and Jared could hold it to his heart that he had succeeded in his vision.

Yet the final step, to set it before a real castle and bring about his world-changing upheaval was throwing up awkward challenges.

He believed Rosamunde when she said that those who wanted gunnes would find a way around the papal bull, this was the least of his worries. In his feverish rush to bring his castle-slayer to life he'd ignored everything except the mechanical.

The most serious of these concerns was cost.

The amount necessary to see his wall-smasher cast had been staggering. To throw a ball the same size as ones shot from a mangonel would need a gunne say, three or four times the size – tons weight of bronze, a frightful expense. And this for only the one!

And to fire one of such gigantic dimensions would take a formidable powder charge, one to be measured in pounds. The final price of devil dust had made Rosamunde frown and in such quantities would be a shocking cost in working the gunne. But then what was this, set against the value of a surrendered castle?

Then a final problem began to loom, one that was truly dismaying and one that he should have seen from the first.

Swelling the size of the gunne was all very well, but its weight increased with it. At something like the bulk of a horse it would be nearly impossible to move; no wagon could take its weight, and even on sledges with oxen it would grind along infinitely slowly over tracks and hillsides and likely be heavily mired in any soft ground. To bring a gunne of this kind to the site of a siege would take far too long.

In despair he remembered the many sieges that he'd seen; the first thing attackers did after isolating their objective was to start offensive operations against it. The alternative was to starve them out, and the burden of maintaining an army in idleness for months on end was dire. A siege gunne should be capable of being brought up quickly to begin its work or it was worthless, and plainly this was not the case with his design.

This was unanswerable and a cruel blow. Having triumphantly established that his vision was attainable, now to have it snatched away . . .

Jared held his head in his hands but a tiny voice within tried to console him – the leap forward to this point from his early fumblings had come out of the blue – who was to say that another twist of man's inventing was not around the corner that would see it overcome?

CHAPTER 93

'So you're telling me you can't go any further with your gunne?'

Rosamunde was looking at him with an infinite sadness, which he knew was not simply sympathy, and he tensed.

'It's too heavy. Until I can find a way to reduce its weight . . .' It sounded weak, even to himself.

She got up slowly without catching his eye and moved over to the fire, staring into it for long moments.

Jared went to stand beside her, reaching for her, playfully tugging her close. 'What's troubling you? Tell me, my best beloved,' he asked softly.

At first she would not answer, then pulled away and returned to the table where she'd been working with the accounts.

She looked up at him. 'Jared. There's something you should know. I'd my hopes that your gunne would save it.'

'Save it?'

'The guild. I was praying your wall-breaker would be something that all the world would shout for, that would set us on the road to profit and security but . . .'

'You're saying you can't go on with the investment.'

'It's not your fault.' Her eyes were filling, causing a numbness within him.

'Your gunnes are growing better all the time, you've achieved a miracle – but if we haven't a market, then there's no money coming in and . . . and . . .'

'My sweetling,' he said gently, stroking her hair, 'Know that you've done more for me than I ever hoped, and you must never chide yourself. It's myself who—'

'I'm hearing the same thing from everybody. No one knows what a gunne is and doesn't want to spend good coin to see. And when you sum the expenses you can understand this. The best price I can let gunne-powder go for is not less than thirty-five silver pence the pound. When they know a first-class archer can be bought for just three pennies the day it makes no sense to talk florins and ducats for a novelty.

'Dear one, the Ghent traders are smelling difficulties and my credit with them is weakening. I cannot help it – the funding of the guild must cease and all my efforts go into restoring our substance. You do understand, don't you?'

She had kept her worries over the endless drain on the Barnwell fortune from him so he might devote his mind to bringing his wall-smashing gunne into the world.

The Guild of St Barbara. Now it was to be abandoned to its own resources, and in the face of the market difficulties these would be slender.

Jared thought frantically. 'There's one thing we haven't tried,' he said as brightly as he could.

'Oh?'

'England. Go there, where gunnes and devil dust are not known, the market untried.'

'And?'

'Sweet love, haven't you heard? England is gone to war with

France. This second King Edward is no warrior like his father and I've a notion would hear any who would give him an advantage.'

'Jared, the kingdom is in upset, the people and barons do resent his rule. It is not the England you will remember.'

'Even so, I crave to go and try. We have the ribaudequin and a workable larger gunne – they're sure to impress!'

'And where would I find the funds for this, pray?'

'Melt down my wall-smasher for the metal.'

'You're determined on this, aren't you, my love.'

'Yes.' He could not give up his hopes and dreams without one last try.

'Then you shall go to England.'

CHAPTER 94

Coventry, England, AD 1325

Rosamunde had agreed they would to return to Coventry together. 'It will not be easy,' she murmured. 'Even to get audience at this time of strife and discord will be a hard thing.'

'But we will surely try.'

'Yes, however word from our agent is that the King is distracted, sore set to raise an army for this French war and, dare I say it, the Queen Isabella does not aid him in this, spending as she does. We provide the royal court with damask and fine stuff so we should not complain, but to persuade him to part with any part of his treasure at this time will be a toilsome matter.'

'Must I . . . do you say I will speak to His Majesty directly, that is to say myself?' This realisation was a terrifying prospect.

'Who else, beloved?' she answered briskly, then softened. 'You will fare very well, I know it. Hold always to your heart that it is written in the Book of Proverbs: "Seest thou a man diligent in his business: he shall stand before kings".'

Jared nodded gravely.

'And remember that when in parliament or council he wears a kingly face but even a prince must talk with those who supply him with what he desires. Never fear, I will instruct you on how to conduct yourself.'

The politeness and graces were one thing – no one would trouble themselves about a mere merchant's airs – it was the deadly maze of rivalries, jealousies and hidden allegiances that he was hearing about that were his greatest despair.

Surrounding the King at court were his favourites but so also were those plotting against him. Many would say the chief of which was his wife and queen – Isabella herself. On the one hand were the powerful and loathed Despensers, and on the other, most of the rest of the realm who were infuriated by the King's incompetence and indecisive ways, the careless indulging of his followers. It was a poisonous and treacherous court Jared was headed into.

He had brought with him two ribaudequins and a pair of his *cannones* with an apple-sized bore, the largest that could be said to be movable. With these he had to convince the King of England to take up gunnes as a military weapon.

Jared set out, Daw by his side. Not to Westminster Palace, for King Edward travelled the land taking his court with him, and at this time was at Wallingford Castle, to the south of Banbury.

It took slow days on horseback, following behind the creaking wagon as it crossed heath and meadowland, hillsides and streams but for Jared it was not lost time, as he was with his son. On the roadway, at supper in a tavern and before the fire with an ale, they talked together on subjects that time had not allowed before.

Daw's respect for Jared was boundless: a man who'd risen from a village freeman to talking with kings, one who'd seen foreign lands and marvellous sights but had returned to follow through a vision that was going to change the world.

And Jared saw in Daw someone who was level-headed, quiet

but resolute and who had mastered the gunnery arts through to his own level of understanding. As he faced his greatest trial it would be with the best possible companion.

In Wallingford they stayed at the Lamb, hard by the Corn Exchange; its stabling allowed them to keep their wagon safe.

The Barnwell agent, William Rawlin, met them there. 'There is nothing I can do that will set you before King Edward,' he said flatly. 'He trusts no one. Saving Mistress Barnwell's instructions, I only deal with the Queen's household, and that with worriments that would try a saint.'

'I think this may help me.' Jared handed over a letter of introduction and Rawlin studied it closely.

'Good, very good. It will probably get you as far as John Bury, the King's treasurer, but no further. I'd advise you to have a very good story for him, the vulture.'

It took a shameful amount in bribes but three days later he was brought to the chamber of the treasurer.

'Jared Barnwell. I've not heard of you that I should pay my respects?' Bury was a dry, shrewd individual in almost scholarly plain black, who didn't rise to greet him.

'My lord, I am new returned from the Low Countries and—'

'You will state your business with me, and pray be brief, I have little time.'

'Sire. I come for concern at the tidings of war with France.'

'And you're offering scutage or knight-service,' he said sarcastically. 'Or . . . ?'

'On my travels, My Lord, I came upon a new weapon, a terrifying man-slayer that may be placed on the killing field to do its work at a distance from the enemy, that no man need raise spear nor sword but let it ply its trade.'

'As does our archery, our mangonels, our crossbows . . .'

'Sire, this does its business invisibly, striking any, and with thunder and lightning at its command it can—'

'And for a trifle in the way of a fee you'll allow our Liege Lord to take it up in some wight.'

Jared felt the prick of desperation.

'My Lord, your caution is understandable. Therefore I have brought several of these gunnes with me to display and make manifest their powers. These are the very devices lately causing fear and despair in several battles in Italy and Brabant where they—'

'Odd. I've not heard of any "gunne" nor yet a calamitous battle from either kingdom.'

'If you witnessed these dread engines at the first hand, My Lord, you may judge for yourself their powers.'

'Yes, well, Master Barnwell, you have heard there is a war afoot. I'm sorely pressed. Do leave your name with the clerk and if we do find need for a . . . er, gunne, then be assured you will be the first to be summoned.'

'My dearling, there's nothing more you – or we can do,' Rosamunde said gently, resting her head on his shoulder. 'The world's not yet ready for your gunnes.'

Tears not far off, Jared turned away.

'After I'm concluded here in Coventry we'll go back to Ghent, and there I'll have time to turn you into a fine merchant prince whom all will respect and obey.'

'The guild?' he said huskily.

'It will have to take care of itself, my love. We have our lives to lead together.'

She looked at him fondly, teasing his hair. 'Have you seen

yourself in a mirror these days? I spy silver and grey in your locks, as you might in mine if I should let nature take its course.'

He kissed her lightly. 'As always you're in the right of it, dear Rosamunde. I've no right to question my fortune in this life and will do as you bid.'

'Bless you, Jared,' she said, her countenance unreadable. 'Besides, have you not heard? The French war is near over. The Queen and young Prince Edward have gone to France to parlay a treaty. They have no need of gunnes now.'

CHAPTER 95

As winter was drawing in shocking news reached England.

In a love affair with the exiled Marcher warlord Roger Mortimer, Queen Isabella had refused to return to England with the kingdom's prince and heir and was in open defiance of the King, her husband.

Worse was to come. Many of those who detested the King, and his powerful allies the Despensers, crossed over to Paris and joined them there.

It plunged the country into despair for there was every possibility that this was the opening move in a civil war. Memories of the terrible suffering of two centuries before when Stephen and Matilda had contended for the crown returned to prey on their fears.

Trade and commerce were thrown into turmoil – would the King invade France to seize back his queen and prince? Or was it to be Mortimer and his paramour landing in England to rally the country to his side to rid the King of his false counsellors?

Coventry seethed with rumours as the crisis deepened. Trade credit evaporated as risks increased.

If the King sailed with his army to France, England would be laid open to a counter landing by Mortimer. The northern lords could rise under his banner and a full-scale war would then lay waste to middle England as it had done before.

And if Mortimer landed with an army, every earl and baron in the land must choose sides, and who knew how the Earl of Warwick might act?

'Do we flee to Ghent?' Jared asked Rosamunde with concern. 'In war there's no place for gentlefolk.'

'I think not. Should there be battles and the city is plundered it's my bounden duty to do what I can to safeguard the House of Barnwell.'

'As I must too, sweetling.' In a twist of dark irony it crossed his mind that it would have been a good plan to use gunnes to fortify the house – if he had any.

Matters came to a head. Smuggling secret letters of readiness into the country, Mortimer betrothed the young prince and heir to Philippa of Hainault. His price for the alliance – a fleet of over a hundred ships. It was the invasion of England.

Their worst fears had come true: it was now in the open. This was a struggle to the finish between the forces of the usurper Mortimer and King Edward of England.

The invasion fleet put Mortimer ashore in Suffolk.

This was now the point of no return and in the clamping bitterness of winter it would be seen whether he would be welcomed, or fall before the avenging might of the King in his realm.

Heralds and messengers thundered along the flat roads and rumours flew.

It was becoming clear that the end could not be long coming –

the King had summoned the barons for the biggest army ever seen, some fifty thousand men to set against the almost insulting fifteen hundred of Mortimer's band.

Sighs of relief went up, but they were premature.

In a fierce show of defiance, the King's own uncle, the Earl of Norfolk, sent a thousand men to Mortimer's aid. It was a signal: waiting lords and knights thronged eastwards to join, swelling the array hourly. More and more flocked in until a mighty concourse was on the march, the Queen at its head with a future king at her side.

King Edward was now on the defensive.

Where were his men?

They were holding back, shying from their duty to defend country and King. Many did turn out but crossed to join the great host advancing on London.

In panic the King fled the capital as it rose up around him in chaos and riot.

Heading for the west to escape the pursuing host he entered the soft Cotswold countryside. It was there that he heard the worst. Henry of Lancaster, his cousin and paramount lord, had declared for Mortimer.

Abandoning the few men left to him, Edward made for the wilds of the Welsh hills, but in revenge for his brother's execution Henry turned on him and closing in on the fleeing monarch, captured him, together with the hated Despenser.

In triumph the King of England was taken to the great fastness of Kenilworth Castle where he was imprisoned.

It was over – but the kingdom held its breath. Who now ruled – King Edward or Lord Mortimer?

The canny Mortimer had an answer. Since the King had fled

beyond England without appointing a regent he would rectify the situation. He and Isabella would stand by the young Prince Edward, the King's fourteen-year-old son and heir, the new regent.

No one doubted for a moment who would be his protectors and advisers.

While the country seethed in excitement and fear at the fast-moving events, Isabella and Mortimer were on shaky ground. They had the reins of power but the King was back in England and a regent was no longer required.

The answer was obvious – but Isabella forbade any talk of murder.

Mortimer found another way. The King would give up the throne in favour of his son.

The people acclaimed it, and the barons took it as a guarantee that Mortimer was not reaching for the crown himself. Parliament assembled and shouted their approval.

The young Prince Edward was brought out to meet his people and formally offered his place on the throne of the King of England. But he refused it.

In the fevered times that followed turbulent crowds seethed through the streets of London and disorder spread through the countryside.

Again Mortimer found an answer. Going to the King he presented him with a stark choice. Either he resigned the crown to his son or that prince would be disinherited and the throne would pass to another.

In a climactic scene in Kenilworth Castle, the weeping King Edward the Second of England signed instruments of abdication.

Edward the son could now no longer refuse or the realm would be left without rule, and the boy prince took the crown as King Edward III.

Throughout the land there was relief and celebrations – the kingdom had a king and the whole business was over with but little bloodshed.

Naturally, there were executions and banishment but both the common people and the nobility craved order and peace and life resumed its old ways.

And while the past king lived out his days in a dank castle cell, and the new monarch began his rule shut off from the world under Mortimer's protection, Jared Barnwell of Coventry studied the ways of merchantry and the fine-cloth trade.

For Rosamunde's sake he applied himself, earning his place in the Guildhall, standing by her as the threads of business were picked up again and revenue began to flow.

As winter receded, the French peace allowed the continental trade to recover. Jared learnt more of foreign commerce, the practices of the great Florentine banking houses and the delicacies of form and courtesy in a merchant's world.

But he grieved for his lost gunnes, now a memory only.

Out of love for Rosamunde he had hidden his feelings, his only concession to what had been: the working of a miniature gunne, just six inches long but perfect in every way. Polished bronze, it was mounted on a handsome rosewood block and in full working order could even be made to fire a 'pea'.

Now it was on display in Barnwell Hall as a curio.

CHAPTER 96

As spring turned to summer on the northern border of England there were rumbles of discontent then outright fury. The aged Robert the Bruce, impatient in his desiring of independence for Scotland and in spite of peace treaties in existence since Bannockburn, had unleashed his kerns and gallowglasses once again to raid and plunder.

Jared heard rumours in the streets but initially didn't give it much thought; he was busy with the House of Barnwell and missing Rosamunde, who was in Italy settling some business matters.

The gossip among the merchants of Coventry was that the young king was incensed at this affront to his rule and yearned to punish the invaders as his grandfather, Edward 'Hammer of the Scots' had done. Sceptical voices wondered whether, in fact, this was Mortimer speaking, but later talk had it that in any event, an army was to be gathered that would put a stop once and for all to the harrying.

It would mean more taxes, tolls and levies and not too much in it for a merchant of fine stuffs even if there was little to fear of trade being affected.

But *what if . . .* ? Jared tried to thrust the thought away.

Rosamunde had trusted him to oversee affairs in her absence – what would she think? And given that he'd tried it before, did he have any right to . . . ?

He couldn't sleep that night, overwhelmed by whirling thoughts. Gunnes were not being placed because they were too costly for even a noble lord to field. But *what if* an entire nation did take them on under their king? Receiver of taxes, dispenser of treasure, if any had the means to, it was a country's sovereign, anxious to keep ahead of others and keen to display his might in the most conspicuous way.

Why not go to the young King and provide him with gunnes to take on his Scots war? It was an exciting fantasy, but after his experience with the court of the previous Edward, Jared knew it would take much even to reach one of his high officials. And he had nothing on hand to demonstrate in this gunne-less land.

In the cold light of day it was an undeniably foolish and impertinent notion – but his mind would not let it go.

The next morning Jared woke with a way to see it through. The more he pondered the overnight revelation the more certain he was that it would work, and he set about sketching out a plan. Simple, straightforward and costing little.

He knew one thing: he would have to go through with it or regret it for the rest of his life.

Rosamunde was still in Italy; he could neither ask her advice nor beg for money. He felt a twinge that he was not able to discuss this with her.

But as a principal of the House of Barnwell he had access to discretionary funds. And time was precious. He had to move fast.

* * *

Jared took great pains having a gift for King Edward alluringly wrapped in dark-blue satin and silver-threaded ribbon.

Discreet enquiry told him that the court was at present at Wallingford Castle, where he'd attended the year before last and not far away.

How should he dress? He had now a respectable wardrobe and could hold his own with any minor courtier. Yes, the new blue cote-hardie would be appropriate.

Next morning, with two servants, he took horse for the royal court.

He knew precisely what he was going to do: take rooms at the Lamb as before, then locate the under-steward of the Wardrobe, who for a certain consideration would see to it that the cofferer would place Jared's gift safely in the muniments chamber with the other offerings.

And then, sat anxiously by the fire, Jared awaited developments. If his outlay to the royal servants was in vain . . .

He'd give it three days, and if in that time . . .

CHAPTER 97

Wallingford Castle, England

The summons came the next afternoon.

Heart thudding, he followed the pursuivant into the royal apartments.

'Jared Barnwell of Coventry, Sire.'

He fell to one knee, head bent.

'Hail to you, honest burgher.' It was a youth's voice but held a sharp ring of authority.

Jared raised his eyes. Edward III, by the grace of God, King of England, Lord of Ireland, Duke of Aquitaine, and Count of Ponthieu and Montreuil was a handsome fourteen-year-old boy, with long fair hair and startling blue eyes. Attired in ermine and velvet he looked every inch a prince.

'Is this your work, Master Barnwell?' Edward went on, his childlike curiosity barely concealed.

It was Jared's miniature gunne, polished to perfection and nestling innocently on its rosewood block.

'Entirely, My Liege,' he answered, overawed at the splendour of the surroundings and so improbably finding himself addressing his King.

'Then I confess I cannot penetrate your riddle. Pray tell us its meaning.'

He picked up the square of parchment and asked Jared to read it.

Lay me down and charge me up
and at your bidding I will shout;
Yet spurn me not, O Majestie
for wonders yet your eyes may see!

His stratagem had been simple but effective. What boy could fail to be taken by such an attractive and mysterious object accompanied by a cryptic verse, its creator named beneath and conveniently to hand?

'Sire, by this we talk of the gunne, a wonderful engine indeed.' Jared looked about the apartment: a modest hall, its stone walls hung in tapestries, the furniture massive and stern. He spied what he needed – in the corner was a suit of armour on a stand.

'It asks that we charge it first.' He took the gunne to a table, carefully removing a crystal goblet. With a flourish he produced a vial from his purse and shook out some of the grey powder into his hand and showed it to the fascinated youth.

He upended the vial in the gunne's mouth. Then he produced a dried pea and displaying it like a magician used a wooden dowel to tamp the charge.

A little powder at the touch-hole and a quick glance to confirm the aim and he stood back.

'As it is written, the gunne will speak, but only at Your Majesty's express command.'

Jared took up a candle.

'We should tell it to . . . ?'

'It dare not disobey a sovereign's command, Sire.'

'Speak, then, O gunne!' the King responded with boyish glee.

Jared lowered the candle. With a spiteful crack the gunne gave forth, and through the flash and writhing smoke came a satisfying ping as the pea found its mark.

The young King fell back in awe, his arm protectively flung up, his eyes wide.

'By God's bones but what magic is this?' he spluttered.

Three men burst into the room, their swords drawn. Looking nervously this way and that, on seeing Jared they flung towards him.

'Stay!' commanded Edward and turned to Jared, 'Tell us true, what is this instrument?'

The wreathing smoke disappeared slowly but the sulphurous reek remained.

'It is a gunne, Sire. That is to say a toy only, not to be set beside those many times the size to be found on the field of battle.'

'A weapon!'

'Sire. You will see how even this contemptible device has made mark on your armour, for which I beg to be excused.' There was indeed an impression on the breastplate and below it the shattered remains of the pea.

'Seen on the battlefield?' The awe was rapidly being replaced with a crisp interrogatory.

'Only recently, and in Italy and the Low Countries, Sire.'

'How did it fare?'

'It sowed terror and death equally, My Liege.'

He paused significantly and added, 'I believed it my duty to bring these engines before Your Majesty should he desire to be possessed of their force in the Scots war to come.'

'That you can supply?'

Jared bowed wordlessly and held his breath.

Edward went to the gunne and stroked its gleaming bronze

thoughtfully. 'Good Master Jared, we're minded to consider them . . . but there are difficulties.'

'Sire?'

'While we lead our army, our Lord Mortimer does play the larger part in their supply. We have our own reasons to desire their keeping in my charge.'

Jared could find no response for this.

'And the other?' Edward gave a smile that was cynical beyond his years. 'That we've only seen a toy, never a gunne of war. How are we to be assured that such even exist, put aside the question that you can cause their provision as well. Have you any for our inspection? No? Then this is a pretty matter as we must think on.'

He turned about and paced the room. As he did so Jared couldn't help noticing his physique – even in youth, tall and muscular, quick and with the confidence of the well favoured. This was a warrior king.

Edward stopped and folded his arms. 'Yes. We have an answer to both. In the one, Lord Mortimer is not to be troubled in their acquiring, for the offices of our own Privy Wardrobe will provide both funds and housing for such as we receive. For the other – you stand ready to deliver these gunnes into our hands?'

'In a short while, Your Majesty.' Jared smothered the alarm that flooded in – where was he going to get hold of any gunnes at all?

'Very well. We offer you a bargain – we move to York this sennight to muster our army. Should you appear with your gunnes and they prove valiant against the foe we shall pay from our Wardrobe what is meet and proper into your hand that same day. Is this pleasing to you, Master Jared?'

'My Liege Lord,' he said quickly, dropping to his knee and taking the extended hand to kiss it.

'Then we shall see you before the Scottish array?'

'You will, Sire.'

CHAPTER 98

Against all the odds he'd done it! The King of England himself! And which was the more gratifying – the order for gunnes, or the knowledge that he'd acquitted himself well in what must be the most terrifying situation he'd ever been in?

But now the reckoning.

It was a hard bargain. At no risk to himself Edward had secured the services of gunnes in the upcoming campaign. Jared had hoped that there would be a payment to begin with but this was not to be. At his own cost he had to find gunnes and haul them to the field of battle together with their powder, shot and presumably gunners.

Then it would be chance alone that determined whether they would be in any position to influence the course of the fight enough to persuade the young King that these were contrivances worth investing in.

But the prize was worth any pains in the securing, and he would strain every fibre to see it through.

There was nowhere near the time to find a bell foundry and cast the gunnes, and in any case his discretionary funds didn't extend to that kind of expenditure. He was left in the intensely frustrating position of winning a princely order but not being able to move on it.

But there was the guild! He knew that it was slow going for them in Christian Europe but there had been some placements; there must be a small number of gunnes still in existence. He'd throw himself on their mercy.

Jared couldn't leave himself but he trusted Daw to go to Ghent and see what was possible. He'd need to journey quickly, for who knew how long it would take for Edward to muster his host.

In a bare two weeks Jared had a hasty message from Ghent that Farnese and Streuvel between them could get together a number of gunnes, which would be available for immediate shipping. In view of time pressures Daw had taken up their offer and they were on their way to the port of Sandwich.

The note had not gone into details and Jared was left in suspense as to what kind of pledge Daw had given that had them respond so promptly.

A later message arrived from Sandwich and desired that he come to take charge of his shipment of gunnes.

'By St Christopher and you've done right handsomely, son!'

Daw had persuasively argued that the value to the guild of a kingly deploying under Jared's direction was worth the risk of the deferring of full payment until after they'd been seen in action.

There were six of the three-inch bore bronze *cannone* and the parts for two ribaudequins, not enough to make a difference in a major engagement but more than adequate to show their worth.

Daw had also brought with him a substantial amount of the elements of gunne-powder in sealed pottery jars ready for mixing and three gunners who had volunteered to travel with him.

It was going to happen!

Exultation rapidly turned to sober calculation. York was two or three hundred miles north: how to transport the dead weight of six gunnes all that way fast enough that they wouldn't miss the war?

By sea? Too risky. If the wind blew from the wrong direction or a storm should batter a heavy-laden ship all would be lost. He couldn't take the chance – it would have to be by land, by wagon.

But there were problems with this. It would take a huge effort to heave the gunnes on to the wagon and with all the weight up high it would be unstable, ready to roll over as they followed an arduous hillside.

The answer came to Jared with a recollection from his childhood of the way the big anvil was delivered to the smithy.

Three of the gunnes were laid out in a line. A wagon was brought up to straddle the pieces. The wheels were removed leaving the body to lie directly over the gunnes. Stout straps were passed around and levering the body up to take its wheels again left the gunnes securely beneath, the weight low and the wagon free to take the gunne-powder elements as well.

Oxen would be too slow. Therefore it would have to be hauled by horses.

Almost forgetting, Jared made a last-minute arrangement with the local masons for the final item, dozens of ball-shaped stones of the right size, to be sent after them.

Before they set off he sent Daw ahead to York to inform the King that his gunnes were on their way, and what to expect.

They creaked slowly out of town on the London Road. Two wagons, two packhorses and a dozen riders, the gunners in the guise of an escort.

As dusk drew in they raised Canterbury – only a dozen miles and hundreds to go! They had to do better.

Next day they were on the road at first light, heading for Rochester, a score or so miles further on. The highway, Watling Street, which was an old Roman road, was level and well made and progress was good – better when Jared had the idea of using their individual mounts to take turns on the wagon hauling.

Skirting London to the south they crossed the Thames at Richmond.

Ermine Street was their road north – another Roman road to take them direct to their destination, York.

Jared was consumed by anxiety. Whatever else, they had to reach the King before he had a chance to settle with the Scots.

His fortitude was increasingly tried: twice they were mired in a slough requiring all the horses to be roped together to heave the wagon free but with a shattered axle taking precious hours to find and fit anew.

In all, four wheels gave way at varying places, each instance taking precious time to find a wheelwright and smith.

And as they proceeded into the northlands the road grew worse, its direct route all too attractive to the freight and packhorse traffic on its way to London.

Before Lincoln the weather turned against them. Rain – driving downpours with a flat, hard wind that brought misery with the cold and wet, a black humour lifting it slightly when the Italian gunners began cursing at the heathen country, unaware that Jared knew their tongue.

Pray God they were in time!

CHAPTER 99

York, England, AD 1327

Daw made economical progress, riding at a brisk walk, knowing his father would be following, but left far behind him.

His entry into the ancient city was wet and windswept but there was no mistaking where he should go. A continuous stream of carts and porters were leaving over the Ouse Bridge towards what could only be the royal host.

His horse stepped delicately through the puddled mud of the holed trackway and when Hob Moor outside the city came into view he could see a vast encampment in apparent disorder but at its centre a large number of tall tents, topped with pennons that hung wet and limp.

Soldiers beyond counting stood by in stolid endurance, others sheltered where they could. Everywhere cooking fires sputtered sending thin columns of smoke to spread and hang in the damp air, the woody odour blending with a dank stench of latrines and horse droppings.

Closer, the reek of wet leather and canvas added to the effluvium, together with the occasional wafting scent of burnt meat.

The tents were grouped together, perhaps a hundred or so but of course the thousands of common soldiery were not granted such extravagance of living. There were two tents considerably larger than the others, on one the blue and yellow stripes of Lord Mortimer's arms and on the other, the three gold lions on red that was King Edward's royal arms.

Daw's heart beat faster. This was no less than the King of England, but if his father had braved it, so would he.

To reach the King was no easy thing. After satisfying various officials Daw was allowed to wait in the rain as visitor after visitor was dealt with. Finally, he was given to understand that the King would shortly see him.

Then he was summoned.

Falling to his knee as he had been taught by his father, Daw was brusquely told to be upstanding by the handsome youth at a table.

Several clerks hovered to one side. 'State your business,' snapped one.

'David of Hurnwych. My Liege Lord, Jared Barnwell of Coventry, my father, bids me tell you that he is even now on his way with your gunnes. In number they are—'

'That is well, but we are much wearied. We shall be content should you apprise our seneschal armourer of them in every detail as will allow him to make proper dispensation.'

Edward rubbed his eyes with fatigue and seemed to remember something. 'Have you spoken to our Lord Mortimer, perchance?'

'I have not, Sire. If you desire me to—'

'No. For now their arriving is to be kept discreet. From all. You understand us?'

'It shall be so, Majesty.'

CHAPTER 100

Hugh Godefroy was not welcoming.

'You're saying as His Maj has paid for these gunne engines himself? Don't see anything on m' books. And m' Lord Mortimer not being told? Don't like it. Not at all, I don't.'

He glared at Daw as if he was the bringer of hideous complications into his life.

'Not exactly paid . . . yet. He wants to see them in action first.'

'Action? You tell me how I'm meant to provide for your gunnes when I haven't had a smell o' one in m' life!'

'Be easy, Master Armourer, all is well,' Daw soothed. 'Jared Barnwell brings all requisites with him and his gunnes – including the gunners to serve them. All we have to do is hear King Edward and obey his wishes in their employing.'

'We? We? Who are you then, as thinks to take the field with us? Hey?'

There was no earthly chance that he was going to miss the spectacle of his father's gunnes in battle and Godefroy would be the one to furnish a way.

He gave a bleak smile. 'Very well, I'll take my leave. I can see you know gunnes well enough to please the King in his contest with the Scots. You have a supply of devil's dust to hand? A stonemason would be a worthy addition to your numbers, I believe. And as to spares, does your blacksmith know enough to—'

'Hold, Master Daw – you can't leave me on m' own with them gunnes. Why don't you stay along with us, keep me company, like? Those as are present at a battle gets their chop o' the plunder, like.'

'Well . . .'

'We has a tent, mess at the common pot an' all, ale on me?'

The rain eased and stopped.

The vast encampment slowly livened but at the same time rumours circulated that the great summoning had all been in vain. In the face of such a formidable host the Scottish raiders had disappeared, probably to prudently withdraw back across the borders having done their worst. It looked likely therefore that this mighty army must soon be dissolved.

'Won't please His Maj, not at all!' rumbled Godefroy.

'Why not? It'll save him a mountain of coin,' Daw said. The sheer impossibility of trying to figure the cost of just feeding his thousands two meals every day was out of normal comprehension.

'Ah! See, Edward wants he should win in a bloodsome fight, show he's a man and can get out from under Lord Mortimer. But Mortimer ain't keen on a Scottish war, he wants to get back where he is with Isabella, a-spending his treasure as hard as he can.'

Daw gave a weak acknowledgement. Would his father finally arrive in York to find everyone had gone home?

CHAPTER 101

En route to Durham, England

A galloping messenger brought news. Far from disappearing over the border, the Scots army, accounted some twenty thousand strong and under the fierce Black Douglas, had struck south far into the desolate moors and fells of the centre of England, even beyond Newcastle and Carlisle, and was now laying waste to the remote villages and poor farmland there.

There was no question now of disbanding – the threat had to be met.

Camp was struck in two days and the long winding cavalcade of an army on the march with its baggage train stretching for miles began heading north.

'Why the north?' Daw asked from the comfort of the rear of a cart.

Godefroy prided himself that he knew everything going on behind the drawn flaps of the noble tents. 'This is because there's been an argument, Mortimer agin Edward.' He paused for effect. 'Our fair King thinks to stretch north at a pace and hook in, cutting off the Scottish line of retreat. Should bring about a right mauling fight. Seems a good idea, but Mortimer's finding every reason under God's heavens why not.'

‘So . . . ?’

‘We’re marching to Durham. Level to where the Scots must be, and I dare to say we’ll have our answer there.’

It took over a week before the louring outline of the castle emerged from the mists after a slow sixty-mile march.

A sprawling encampment of tents, and numberless men, wet and sullen for being forbidden the sweets of the city, grew outside the walls.

‘They’s at it again,’ sniffed Godefroy, poking at the fire. ‘Never heard such high words. Give you this, our Edward’s a good ’un. Lets Mortimer know his place even if he won’t move on it.’

There was no joy in the camp for it was clear the Scots were far from fools. In their lunge south they had seen to it that every foot soldier was equipped as a hobelar, mounted on a horse for movement and dismounting for battle. It gave them princely manoeuvrability, striking and away well before the lumbering mass of the usual kind of army could come up with them.

Where they were now was a complete mystery.

Outriders had been sent into the lonely uplands. Some had returned with nothing to show for their flogging through moorland and mountain in wretched weather, others had come back with reports of smoking ruins, evidence of a Scottish visitation recently past, and still more were never heard of again.

The Black Douglas was playing it well. The English host was bigger and had better weapons – but would it be sent into the rugged heath and moors, where its speed would be cut still further in hopeless pursuit of a more agile quarry? If it was, then it would be a merry chase that he could not lose, and if on the other hand there were no move against him, then he would be free to descend out of the hills on any one of the substantial towns in the lowlands.

The next move lay with the English.

Edward did not flinch in his duty. His army would throw themselves across the path of the retreating Scots and bring them to battle when they emerged from the uplands.

He set the army on a forced march to the valley of the Tyne, the river that had cut a passage through the highlands, and across which the Scots had passed on their path of ruination south.

The pitiless weather beat at the army as it stumbled over fells and marsh-ridden glens. And when they approached the crossing point they were ordered to don full armour and stand to.

For days they ate and slept in battle array, the merciless rain swelling the river and turning life into an idle misery.

And still the Scots failed to appear.

CHAPTER 102

North Weardale, England

'He's got to make a conclusion,' Godefroy muttered one grey daybreak. He and Daw were sitting together under a cart, sheltered from the rain but not from the runnels of water coming down the slope.

'Scottish, they's not human. Lives on cattle they takes, boils 'em in their own skins then throws in oatmeal they carries in a bag and hangs it all from their saddles. No baggage, provisions, they lives for war. Never happier as when hewing away at some poor Englishman with them sodding great two-handed swords.'

He was interrupted by the thin fanfare of trumpets somewhere towards where the dripping tents of the commanders stood.

The call to action! Stung by their helplessness the English commanders had resolved to give up waiting for the Scottish to come to them – now they were going to plunge directly into the highland fastness and find them, whatever it took.

For the first time in the encampment there were signs of heart and spirit. But the ferocious sally into the steep hills would be at a cost. To even up the odds Edward's army was going to advance without a baggage train – no impedimenta, no provisions other than what each man could carry with him. Everything would be sent back to Durham to avoid tying down the fast-moving columns.

From the Tyne in the north to the Wear in the south was a bare twenty-five miles – but this was over a bone-wearying succession of hills and crags with always the prospect of Black Douglas and his wild Scots over the next rise. Therefore, when the army moved off it was in a battle formation of three divisions: the tramping foot soldiers in the centre and men a-horse out on both flanks.

Halfway along their march they reached the Derwent river and then the tiny hamlet of Blanchland with its bluff, four-square priory, now just a burnt ruin.

Angry, tired and hungry the soldiers heard how the Scots had been through days before, stripping it of food and plunder. And now they could be anywhere at all – ahead of them lying in wait, or on their way back to Scotland behind them.

Mortimer sulked, Edward stormed at the fate that was leading them ever further into ruin and starvation – then without warning he caused the trumpets to sound the assembly.

His young voice cracked with emotion as he proclaimed, 'Any man here before me who dares ride in search of the Scots and can tell me where they are to be discovered, he I will honour with a knighthood that very hour – and one hundred pounds a year for the term of his life!'

Fifteen esquires took horse to try their fortune.

Four days later, after a harrowing wait, one Thomas de Rokeby galloped into the bedraggled camp and threw himself at the feet of his King. He had news of the Scots.

'I put you upon oath to tell me. How certain are you of your intelligence?' King Edward demanded with a terrible intensity.

It was humiliation – of a kind. Rokeby had not only seen the

Scots but he'd been captured by them. Fearing the worst of fates as a spy he'd been brought before Black Douglas who questioned him closely. When he admitted what drove his quest the great warrior had bellowed with laughter and bid him go on his way to claim his honour – and swore to remain where he was to meet the English King.

The Scottish battalions were waiting near Stanhope on the banks of the Wear river, no more than eight miles further down the mossy dale of the meandering Rookhope Burn.

CHAPTER 103

On the road to York

The flat country after Lincoln was kind to them, the straight highway taking them past the Wash and on towards York. They had been creaking northward for several weeks now and Jared felt relief that the end was in sight.

At the same time tension grew in his bowels. If Edward's army had achieved a victory and driven the Scots back, for a certainty it would be disbanded. And if that was the case his time of trial would have been in vain and he would have to return the gunnes and face both Rosamunde and the guild.

After they'd made sighting of the square rising towers of York Minster Jared looked about in vain for the royal camp with its thousands.

Where were they? The most reliable information came from a merchant who told him that Edward and his host had left suddenly for Durham for reasons not clear, taking most of the city's whores with them.

It was heartbreaking: another seventy miles of hauling with the promise of rougher going as they entered the northern uplands.

* * *

And at Durham came the worst of news: the entire army had set off into the inner wilds and nothing had been heard of them since.

Was there any point in going on? In country that was near trackless, rough and steep, vainly searching for a moving army while at risk of being found by the Scots?

Surely this was the end of the venture – he had let down King Edward and would never get another hearing.

But the next morning a long column of wagons and pack animals was spotted winding towards the city. It was not the army but bafflingly only its supply train.

Had there been a disastrous defeat?

It turned out that Edward had abandoned his baggage in a bid to find the Scots by striking south directly down the middle ground from the Tyne to the Wear.

If Jared wanted to find him, he'd only need follow the Wear river trackway westwards and intercept him. It flowed through Durham and was a known highway into the remote heartland. Just a dozen or so miles would put him well into the highlands and at the point of intersection.

It was a tempting thought, for even if a battle had been concluded the King would see that he'd kept faith and suffered much in bringing the gunnes, and might well grant him his expenses.

CHAPTER 104

Weardale, west of Stanhope

The steep sides of the Rookhope Burn valley fell away as the busy stream hurried on to meet the larger Wear crossing. With pennons aloft and trumpets sounding the English host advanced over the last mile – and unbelievably there ahead was what they had longed for all those weary miles: the Scots! The Black Douglas had kept his word.

All along the higher ground in front they stood silently in lines, watching, waiting.

Immediately before the English and away to the left was a near quarter-mile of low meadow, pasture, crops. A consummate battleground.

But – between the two armies the turbulent River Wear rushed and seethed. It was shallow but rocks and boulders concealed in it would make a crossing slow and risky and within easy reach of the arrows of the Scots on the heights above the river plain.

Once again The Black Douglas had outmanoeuvred the English. In his unassailable position high on the steeper far bank he could control any crossing and if the English moved up or down the river he could parallel anything they did.

Edward drew up his army on the flatland and rode along the ranks calling encouragement to his men, ignoring the insulting whoops and scornful cries from across the river. Then he faced them about and under a dozen of the flag of St George he stepped them slowly forward to the edge of the river.

'What's this?' Daw asked incredulously.

'He's wanting to bait the Scots to break ranks and come within range of his archers,' Godefroy muttered. 'They'm no fools, they'll never do it.'

He was right. Frustrated, impotent, the English achieved nothing.

As the afternoon wore on, idleness turned to rage and Daw received a royal summons.

King Edward did not waste words. 'Where are my gunnes?' he demanded.

'Sire, I beg to say I cannot tell you. The army has moved far and fast but I know in my heart that my father will not break faith with Your Majesty, and must be coming up with us as swiftly as he may.'

The young man turned away but not before Daw glimpsed the sudden glitter of tears of frustration.

'Then we must turn to other means. They may be Scots, but cannot be dead to the devoirs of chivalry – send forth for my herald!'

The man came, his surcoat and tabard emblazoned with the royal lions of England, his trumpet's hanging banner edged with gold.

'Go to the Scottish lord and declare to him these my words – that I should this hour withdraw my host to allow his army to cross the river and make array against me. Then we shall in fair equality try the fortune of our standards.'

Daw watched as the man made his way to a convenient rock mid-river and raised his trumpet in a strident peal – once, twice, three times.

From the lines of Scots above a single figure detached itself and came forward to stand arrogantly on a jutting crag.

Daw couldn't hear what was being hailed above the rush of waters but whatever the reply, it received wild acclamation from the throng above him.

The herald returned with a stiff dignity. 'Sire, Sir James Douglas does give reply in this manner. "I did enter England to annoy its King. Why then should I please him now?" he did say.'

Later that night horns bayed among the fires that ringed the hills opposite. More and more sounded in a barbaric clamour that was joined with a horde of unearthly hoots and wails that resounded up and down like the gates of hell itself.

The English camp stood to, hastily pulling on their chain mail hauberks and full armour, and readied for the assault.

For the rest of the dark night and into the grey of day they lay to arms, enduring the acute discomfort and misery of lying in the open in wet and bone-cold steel, their weapons to hand, endlessly waiting. As the wan light spread, the Scottish came down to jeer at how their trickery had worked.

It was bitter to take, the hopeless stalemate.

At the wretched slop that passed for a meal Godefroy relished a tale of how Mortimer had stormed into Edward's tent and demanded they disengage that day and return to York. The young King had retorted with spirit that upon his sacred honour he would never be seen to take flight before the Scottish. His banner would without question remain at this place until the affair was resolved.

Mortimer had taken it with the utmost bad grace but this could plainly be put down to the fact that Isabella had travelled to York and was waiting impatiently for him there.

The day continued wearily on.

Another miserable night beckoned. The rain had stopped but the ground was muddied and foul. Godefroy and Daw were lucky: they had one of the few carts and could sleep clear of the dross; nearby were the equally small number of tents – those of the King and Lord Mortimer atop a slight rising of the ground.

Darkness drew in, the Scots lines easily marked out by fires. Mercifully there was no repeating of the blasting horns and tumult and Daw drew his cloak about him and drifted to sleep, lulled by the rush of river waters.

Sometime in the early hours he awoke. There was something wrong: he lay rigid, but heard nothing beyond the restless snoring of the men about him and the desolate night calling of some creature.

Then he had it. A subliminal drumming. Eyes staring into the dimness he strained to make sense of it – and in a sudden rush of comprehension he knew it to be horses, many, the sound getting louder and louder until suddenly they were upon them, slashing, impaling, killing. Harsh cries rang out: 'A Douglas! A Douglas!'

The camp woke in confusion but the Scots had chosen well. Crossing the river well upstream they'd stealthily moved on the English and in a wild night charge had gone straight for the heart of the camp. Flaming torches held aloft threw light on a hellish scene. Hurtling black shapes swinging weapons that glittered terribly, shrieks from sleeping men mercilessly hewn down – it was a nightmare beyond grasping.

Several riders converged and thundered together for the tents of the nobles and whirled their blades, severing ropes and bringing them down in kicking folds. The riders circled briefly, plunging lances brutally into the humped figures desperately trying to escape.

From his hiding place under the cart Daw saw the King's tent suddenly surrounded, the ropes cut – and a huge figure on the closest horse roaring to the others to hold back, gyrating in impatience. 'Come out, the Sass'nach King!' he bellowed in fury, brandishing his great sword. 'Black Douglas wants ye!'

A figure struggled out shakily, raising both hands in a despairing gesture to the implacable Scot. It was the chaplain pleading for the life of the King.

'Be damned to ye!' Douglas snarled in rage and swung his sword, smashing the man's skull.

There were now shouts and running figures – the English camp was waking from its nightmare and was about to turn on the intruders.

In a final flurry of screams and curses the horsemen rode furiously back out into the night.

As the ravaged camp took stock and the dead and wounded were dragged away there was a last insult: the exulting cries and howls of the Scots across the river as they welcomed back their war party.

The King emerged next morning, his eyes red and his face strained. Daw's heart went out to him – in truth only a youth used to a life of the highest richness and security, but that night he'd seen for the first time the hideous cruelty, butchery and terror of war in which he himself had been nearly slain.

Refusing all food Edward let it be known that he would never upon the honour he held dear be known as a King of England who had slunk away before a barbarous Scottish war band. In full view of the capering clansmen above he strode about, offering words of comfort and cheer to the men he was leading, acknowledging their pain and hardship and vowing a terrible vengeance one day.

And still the stalemate held.

CHAPTER 105

On the Weardale trackway

Jared continued west into the interior, around hillsides and past endless barren ridges on either side. Always with the turbid Wear to the left.

There was no sign that an army had passed this way but that was to be expected if Edward was coming from the north.

If the Scots suddenly appeared Jared had no plans other than to flee for his life over the hill crests. In the event they captured the gunnes they wouldn't know what they were or what to do with them.

The dull grind onward continued.

They reached the village of Stanhope. It was completely deserted. Uneasily, Jared told a pair of the gunners to ride ahead and see what they could find.

They were soon back with thrilling news: not three miles ahead two great armies faced each other across the Wear. But the cataclysmic battle had not started – by the good God that sat above, he was in time!

They progressed around a slight bend. On the steep far side of the river were the Scots, looking down on a broad, flat meadow where King Edward was camped with his army.

A shaft of sun suddenly pierced the clouds and made bright patterns in among the opposing hosts.

He noted that the Scots were out of harm's way from the English, who in turn could not make a safe crossing of the swollen river under a hostile bank.

Jared and his little party were met by outlying sentinels who summoned an escort. As they entered the camp they were roundly cursed by starving soldiers who'd hoped for provisions.

King Edward hurried over. 'Our gunnes of war, Master Barnwell?'

'Indeed, Sire. In these wagons lie six of them ready to do their duty by their sovereign.'

The covering of one was thrown back and the King peered below the cart in perplexity.

'As we must take the greatest care of your dread engines, Your Majesty.'

Edward made a wide gesture at the throng opposite. 'If you can this day punish that hell-spawn yonder, know that I shall be well pleased.'

'Sire, they shall be, but I beg leave to say that to preserve my gunne-powder through its long travels I make delay in its making until the last. It will take longer to do this than we have hours left in this day.'

Edward's disappointment was barely disguised. 'Do what you must, then, Master Barnwell – and do acquaint me when it is you are ready to act.'

Daw hurried over, tired and strained but overjoyed to see his father.

They embraced, but Jared admonished, 'This is the hour we've been praying for. We must not waste it.'

He set Daw and a gunner to work with the mortar and pestle

while he called over the yeoman gunner and they surveyed the ground together.

The six gunnes they'd brought were only intended to show what could be done in a pitched battle in combination with general forces, and unless one side or the other crossed the river there was not going to be the opportunity.

Jared felt deep frustration. To have come so far . . .

But what if . . . It was dangerous, he'd never done it before and it might have no direct result but his idea had an advantage that greatly appealed.

They could begin their punishment in as little as three hours – by firing at night.

But there was a major drawback: how could he charge gunnes in the dark?

The weather was clearing, there would be a quarter moon.

It was a chance.

Looking across at the Scots he measured distances by eye. Their lines were drawn up carefully out of bowshot but Jared knew his gunnes. They could carry well over half a mile and while at this distance they'd be far from accurate this was not needed for what he had in mind.

'So we'll give 'em a fright they'll never forget!' he told the yeoman gunner. 'Help me lay these as will do the most good.'

With many idle hands to assist, the gunnes were brought to the water's edge. Sighting by eye they were wedged in position, their snouts raised to sweep the opposite slopes.

The Scots looked down, curious, uncomprehending.

The last of the daylight faded, as much gunne-powder was prepared as could be – and with all gunnes charged, they were ready.

Jared waited until the fullness of night was upon them. The braziers were started, the iron wires heated. It was an unearthly sight, the dull gleam of the sleeping bronze beasts catching the fitful silver of an overcast moon, the Scots as usual in a caterwaul on the slopes, and in the quiet camp of the English, a few low voices.

Jared sent word to Edward, who strode down to the gunnes.

'At night?'

'Sire. I do advise to step back from these gunnes and it would be wise to take all horses to the rear.'

Then, without ceremony he and the gunners took their red-hot wires from the brazier and went to work.

The night was instantly split by hideous flashes and ear-splitting detonations of appalling noise, magnified by the stillness and dark, reeking smoke drifting on the air, echoing claps of thunder rolling down from the hills.

There were howls of terror and panic in the English camp – soldiers able to face an attack by a ferocious enemy ran for their lives, horses reared and whinnied in fright in a tumult of shouting and confusion.

For a moment Jared found himself picturing the effect on the Scottish side – it must be a hellish scene. Not only the world gone mad, split asunder by unknown magic forces, but far into their ranks invisible death had reached out, leaving dead and maimed, others untouched. Who could know the next to be taken by Edward's sorcery?

Pushing aside these thoughts he knelt by a gunne and looked into its black mouth. He could make out the red dots of still burning material – there would be no premature firings while they could see to clean the bore. While commotion and uproar rose and fell around him he rehearsed the motions and was satisfied that with two serving the gunne and extreme care against spilling powder it could be recharged, even if it took much longer than usual.

One by one the gunnes thundered their defiance once again. Their ear-splitting roar and flash continued on and on into the early hours until all gunne-powder was exhausted. Then Jared laid down his implements, stumbled to the cart and fell into deep slumber.

'Father! Wake, please – the day is breaking!'

Daw's anxious voice cut through his sleep and he levered himself up. 'We has to start on more gunne-powder,' he slurred, gathering his wits.

'Look – Father, see . . . ?'

Jared forced his eyes open.

Every man in the English camp was silently staring across to the Scottish lines. No one moved in the still dim, hazy first light.

The hills were bare.

Edward broke the silence. 'Send out riders. I will know where the Scots have hid,' he commanded.

Five horses splashed through the Wear and climbed the opposite bank, then cantered off in different directions.

First one, then the others returned. 'My Liege – the Scots are fled!'

'How do you know this?'

'Sire, they've left bodies, plunder – their very meat is still in the pots a-cooking. There's not a Scot as far as a man can see!'

The English camp broke into thunderous cheering, their misery and starvation now, incredibly, at an end.

'Master Jared of Barnwell, come near.'

'My Liege?'

'You shall receive all that was promised and be paid well for this night's work.'

'I thank Your Grace.'

'There is one thing further.'

'Sire?'

'I bid you kneel before me.'

'Rise, Sir Jared Barnwell of Coventry.'

Ears ringing in disbelief he stood nobly before his King, Daw at his side.

'And now, I trow, we shall take drink together and make talk – we're this day minded to contrive a trusty band of men who will, henceforth, attend on the King's Gunnes.'

AUTHOR'S NOTE

If ever there was a turning point in history it was King Edward III's encounter with the Scots at Stanhope in 1327. From that point on, guns and artillery transformed from being a fearsome novelty to a battlefield necessity, taken up by the state which could afford to deploy them in numbers. Edward moved quickly to create a formal establishment of ordnance in the Tower of London, and within five years the King's Gunnes were pounding at the walls of Berwick. And even before the century was out giant wall-smashers – bombards – were firing stone balls weighing as much as two men. A final perspective is gained by noting that only a single century separates Crécy – the first great battle won by the longbow – and the English being driven from France, giving up the glorious gains of Crécy, Poitiers and Agincourt. This was achieved by guns; the French had learnt their lesson well and their superior artillery quickly reduced English castles across their nation, at one time at the rate of five a month. By then no more medieval castles would ever be built. It is of course an irony that Edward, the greatest knightly figure of the age, would in this way be the very one to set in motion the destruction of his world of jousts and chivalry.

I owe a debt of gratitude to the many people who have contributed in one way or another to the writing of this book. Space precludes naming them all but they have my deep thanks. I am particularly appreciative of the assistance given by Graeme Rimer FSA, Curator Emeritus, Royal Amouries; Stuart Ivorson, the Royal Armouries Librarian; and Liz Bregazzi, County Archivist, Durham.

This is my second book with Allison & Busby and as with the first it's been a pleasure working with Publishing Director Susie Dunlop and her team. And last, but certainly not least, my heartfelt thanks to my agent Carole Blake, who sadly passed away before this edition came to print, and my wife and literary partner, Kathy.

GLOSSARY

ague	a fever
amercement	penalty imposed by royal authority above that of a statutory fine
Beelzebub	alternative name for the Devil
boon-work	unpaid service to a lord, theoretically voluntary
buttery	service room for provisions and liquor
byre	a cowshed
Cathay	ancient term for China proper
caudle	sweet and thickened alcoholic drink
chain	ten chains to the furlong
cofferer	principal officer in royal household in charge of the counting house and other
cog	a common type of one-masted cargo ship, semi-decked to carry up to 200 tons
costrel	portable liquor flask used by field labourers

cote-hardie	Medieval tunic, buttoned
demesne	all land owned by a landlord for his own use
dibber	sharpened stick to make holes for planting seeds
Franciscans	mendicant friars of the order of St Francis of Assisi
franklin	alternative name for freeman
frankpledge	the compulsory sharing of responsibility by those connected by kinship or fealty to a lord
freeman	one not tied to the land as a serf
furlong	eight furlongs to the mile
gallowglass	heavily armoured elite Gaelic mercenaries
Gog and Magog	Satan's barbarian helpers in the final battle with Christ and the saints
gonfalon	heraldic flag suspended from a pole and crossbar
gonfanier	knight bearing the standard of the Order
Greek fire	a flame-thrower weapon thought to be based on naptha
groat	coin worth four pence
Hazard	popular two-dice betting game mentioned in Chaucer
jongleur	minstrel for the common folk

kern	Gaelic soldier known for marauding
kirtle	simple long tunic, with sleeves
Knights Hospitallers	Order of the Knights of Saint John of Jerusalem founded to provide care for poor or sick pilgrims to the Holy Land
Laws of the Forest	enacted to ensure the integrity of the chase in royal forests
liripipe	the long tail of a cloak or cap
maleficium	sorcery with evil intent
mandrel	blacksmith tool to aid in bending
mummers	folk players of an allegorical nature of good and evil
muniment	secure room for storing title deeds and rich objects
Nestorians	Christian sect with a differing view of the divine and human nature of Christ
ox-goad	for guiding and spurring oxen at the plough
pannage	the right to release pigs in a forest to forage
peck	dry measure equal to a quarter of a bushel
Peter Peregrinus	early pre-scientist of Paris known for work on magnetism
pottage	a thick stew involving all vegetables and meat to hand

Prester John	legendary Christian king said to be located in the middle of the heathen eastern lands
reeve	manager of a manor overseeing the peasants
rood screen	ornate partition between the chancel and nave of a church
scutage	fee payable in lieu of military service
share and coulter	ploughshare turns over the earth after the coulter has broken it
silâhtar	armourer
simkin	simple person
thurible	censer in which incense is burnt in a religious setting
tithe barn	where farm produce in payment of tithes was stored
trebuchet	artillery catapult using counterweights
ustabaşı	foreman
verderer	an official administering Forest Law
villein	a serf owing service on the land to his local lord
younker	youth below the age of 18
Yuletide	Christmas (from the Nordic 'jul')

ALSO IN THE MOMENTS OF HISTORY SERIES

THE SILK TREE

Rome 549 AD. Forced to flee the city, merchant Nicander and legionary Marius escape to a new life in Constantinople. Determined to make their fortune, they plot a number of outrageous money-making schemes, until they chance upon their greatest idea yet.

Armed with an audacious plan to steal precious silk seeds from the faraway land of Seres, Nicander and Marius must embark upon a terrifying and treacherous journey across unknown realms. But first they must deceive the powerful ruler Justinian and the rest of his formidable Byzantine Empire in order to begin their voyage into the unknown.

In an adventurous tale of mischief and deception, Nicander and Marius face danger of the highest order, where nothing in the land of the Roman Empire is quite what it seems.